"BUSINESS COMES FIRST WITH YOU, DOESN'T IT?"

Alex's tone was sharp. "You *have* grown up, Joanna."

His sarcasm was uncalled for. Joanna's eyes flashed in a warning her brothers wouldn't have ignored but Alex had probably forgotten. "Oh, you noticed, did you?"

Amusement lit his handsome features as his mood changed with quicksilver swiftness. "Yeah, I noticed." His gaze rested on her curves before caressing her long, tanned legs with a visual touch that was so tangible she trembled.

Defiantly she kept her eyes on his face, but a sensual heat trickled through her veins. No one had ever before aroused her with just a look.

"Joanna . . ." Alex moved closer.

She stood before him, tense with anticipation. The years receded, and she was young again, a child-woman enthralled by a boy who was almost a man. When he lowered his head, she let out a pent-up breath. The waiting was over. . . .

ABOUT THE AUTHOR

Tina Vasilos lives in British Columbia but has visited Greece many times with her husband and teenage son. Intrigued by the proud, spirited Greek people and their role in history, she decided to set her first Superromance there. *Echoes on the Wind* is a stirring, evocative tale that contains universal themes of love and trust. Tina is currently working on her next romance.

Tina Vasilos

ECHOES ON THE WIND

Harlequin Books

TORONTO • NEW YORK • LONDON
AMSTERDAM • PARIS • SYDNEY • HAMBURG
STOCKHOLM • ATHENS • TOKYO • MILAN

FORTY YEARS OF
Romance

Published April 1989

First printing February 1989

ISBN 0-373-70351-1

Printed in U.S.A.

This book is dedicated with love
to John, my husband,
and to the memory of Jenny,
a lady who could never grow old.

CHAPTER ONE

"WHY DO YOU HAVE TO GO NOW?" Tony threw his lanky frame onto a chair, his brow creasing in a frown that sat uneasily on his handsome face. "And to this benighted place in Greece. Mikrohori. Where's that?"

"South of Volos, in central Greece." Joanna Paradisis moved briskly across her office to the filing cabinet. She was a slender woman whose walk showed an athletic grace that belied the formality of her suit and high-heeled pumps.

Tony shook his head, his dark hair falling into boyish disarray. "But it's been a year since you inherited your godmother's house," he persisted. "What's a week or two more? We could go together when I have my holidays."

"I want to go on my own. I told you weeks ago that I needed a break, but I just couldn't fit it in."

The harsh metallic scrape of the drawer opening nearly drowned out her words as she continued speaking. "Besides, I have to look over that hotel in Volos that's for sale. Since the house is near there, it seems like a good time to take my vacation." Rifling through the neatly labeled files, she muttered beneath her breath when the desired folder failed to materialize.

"But your appointment isn't for another two weeks. And you don't even know if this house is habitable. If you take me along with you, I could get rid of the spiders and other beasties that may be living there."

Joanna slammed the drawer shut and pulled out the one below it, the quick smile she gave Tony failing to erase the tension from her face. "I can get rid of my own creepy-crawlies, Tony. If there are any. The place isn't a hovel, by any means. It was modernized the year before Katerina died. And the lawyer's letter assured me it's in perfect order."

She frowned as she bent over the next drawer. Tony cared about her. She couldn't blame him for wondering at the timing and length of her vacation. She'd never taken more than a week or ten days at a stretch before.

But, aside from her business appointment, she wanted to look up Alex Gregory. Although fifteen years had passed since Alex had lived next door to her family's house in Vancouver, the sense of unfinished business with him had become stronger in the past year, especially as Tony's attempts to deepen their relationship had become more frequent. She'd been in love with Alex once, puppy love perhaps, but she'd never forgotten him.

Alex now had his own law practice in Volos. It was likely that he was the present guardian of the house, since her late godmother was his aunt.

"Even if the place is a palace," Tony said, "what are you going to do on your own for two weeks? You'll be bored out of your skull."

Her smile returned, this time revealing genuine humor. "No, I won't. The house is in an authentic Greek village with a marvelous beach. Staying there will give me a chance to get acquainted with the area. It's supposed to be beautiful, spectacular scenery, but hardly developed for tourism at all. I'll be able to swim, catch up on reading, get a suntan.''

Tony looked skeptical. "You relaxing, Joanna? I'll believe it when I see it. You've never slowed down in your life. One or two days in that village, and you won't know what to do with yourself. Besides, what about the promotion? You'll want to be here when your father announces it.''

"I don't think he's in much of a hurry. He'll wait until I get back.'' The drawer banged as she closed it. Only half-aware of Tony's appreciative eyes on her as she bent to the bottom one, she muttered, "Now where has that girl put the file? Drat her anyway. She's never here when I need her.''

Tony leaned back in the chair, linking his hands behind his head. "Labor laws state that a secretary is entitled to a lunch hour even when her boss doesn't take one.'' When she made no reply, he went on. "You want to know what I think, Jo? Your father, with all due respect to him, is pulling some kind of power play by considering the two of us for the same promotion. Isn't he afraid one of us will resent the other?''

"Who knows what goes on in his devious mind? Maybe he thinks it'll bring us closer together, no matter what the outcome. The winner consoling the loser.'' She straightened, waving a tan folder above her head. "At last. It was right at the back of the drawer.''

"The *Z*'s usually are,'' Tony said dryly, getting up and taking the file from her hand. "Thanks, Jo. I knew I could count on you. Everyone counts on you, Joanna. You deserve to be our newest vice president.''

A little frown etched a crease above her short, straight nose. "If I get the promotion, won't people say it's because my father's the boss?'' She knew Socrates didn't give favors to anyone, least of all her, but she was aware that the office grapevine carried occasional grumbles of nepotism. Not true, of course. Socrates Paradisis, founder and owner of Paradise Hotels—which he had by sheer grit and perseverance made into an international corporation—rewarded only hard work. Promotions came by merit alone.

Joanna had joined the family business right after graduation from university. Although some of her colleagues might assume that she had gained her present executive position solely through Socrates's influence, those closest to her knew otherwise.

Joanna worked hard. Fortunately, despite the long hours she put in, she found the work exciting, enjoying the travel, the challenge of finding locations and developing new hotels and resorts in the various sun spots of the world.

At least she had until the past year. Nothing out of the ordinary had happened, but she had become conscious of restlessness, asking herself if this was what she wanted to do for the rest of her life. Challenge had indeed become the key word; enjoyment seemed harder and harder to maintain.

Tony threw one arm around her shoulders, his palm rubbing the soft wool of her lemon-yellow suit. ''Nobody would dare say anything, Jo. We all know you work longer hours and get more done than anyone in the company. I'll bet your father's already decided on you.''

''But what about you, Tony?''

''Hey, you know me better than that, Jo. I'd be happy for you. There'll be another opportunity for me. You've worked for the company longer than I have. You deserve to get it."

Pushing the drawer shut with one leather-shod toe, Joanna propped her elbow on the top of the cabinet. She combed her fingers through her thick brown hair, making a ruffled disorder of the bangs that covered her forehead.

"But he's more likely to give it to you." The smile she gave Tony was touched with irony. "You have the advantage in this. You know that."

Tony shrugged. "Yeah, he's a bit of a chauvinist, but he's never let personal feelings affect business decisions." His face became serious and his arm tightened around her. "You're not going to like what I have to say, Joanna...."

"Then don't say it," she teased, running a playful finger down his smoothly shaven cheek.

"Your father—" Tony went on as if she hadn't spoken, although he gave her a fleeting grin. "Your father would like us to get married."

Joanna pulled away, her movements abrupt as she folded her arms across her chest. "My father, dear man that he is, should know by now that I'm an adult. He can't dictate who I marry."

"No, he can't," Tony agreed. "But would it be such a bad idea? We get along well."

Joanna perched on the edge of her desk, her expressive face showing an odd mixture of amusement and severity. "Tony, we're friends. We've had some good times. Let's not spoil it."

Tony's brows rose. "Spoil it, Jo? Don't you think that friendship is the best grounds for marriage? Not rosy, romantic dreams that fall flat after the honeymoon."

Joanna fought an urge to smile. Tony had been known to send her two-dozen pink roses for no other reason than that the sun was shining. Of the two of them, he was the one who did charming, crazy, romantic things, while she was the realist.

"Marriage has also been known to ruin friendships," she said lightly, determined to keep their conversation from straying into treacherous emotional waters. She liked Tony, but she was not in love with him. She suspected his feelings for her might run deeper than he let on. "Would you want to risk that?"

He paused on his way to the door, giving her a meditative look. "Maybe I would, Joanna. If the outcome was worth it." Turning, he walked out of the office.

Joanna sank down into the chair Tony had just vacated. Wearily she rested her head against the padded upholstery. Pinching the bridge of her nose between her thumb and forefinger, she willed away the incipient headache.

Oh, Tony, what am I going to do with you? she thought. In her way, she did love him, but with the same unstinting affection she felt for her brothers. He was sincere, kind, a good-natured man who genuinely liked women, and who had the utmost respect for their achievements. And for Joanna's in particular. As for the promotion—he was sincere in wishing it for her.

But did she want it? Once it would have represented the ultimate accomplishment. Now she often felt ambivalent toward her career. Yes, she wanted the promotion, but not as wholeheartedly as she would have even a year ago. At the same time, she didn't want Tony to be hurt. Setting the two of them up for the same promotion had not been one of Socrates's more diplomatic moves. Maybe it *was* a ploy to bring the two of them closer together.

Almost from the day Tony had joined Paradise Hotels, Socrates had made no secret of the fact that he considered Tony the perfect match for Joanna.

Involuntarily she smiled. Socrates might once have thought no boy was good enough for his only daughter, but now that she was twenty-nine and a long way past girlhood, he really wanted her to marry. But she felt her personal life was her own. It didn't matter to her what Socrates thought of the men she knew. He approved of Tony, though, often assigning them joint projects to work on, in a not so subtle attempt at matchmaking. And Joanna knew she could do much worse than to marry Tony.

Except that she wasn't in love with him, nor did she feel ready for marriage. Somewhere in the hidden corners of her mind lingered dreams of an ardent love, a love such as she'd had for Alex. Was that kind of passion to be found only in adolescent fantasy, not in the world of adult realities?

She had to see Alex again to find out. Fifteen years was a long time to nurture a memory.

The phone on the desk emitted a well-mannered chirp but for the first time in her life she ignored it. Tony was mistaken about her enjoyment of the long hours, she thought. Too often in the past year she'd been running on adrenaline, a situation that left her feeling debilitated by the end of the day. She'd managed to hide it but knew she couldn't for much longer. She needed time away from the pressure of work.

Getting up from the chair, she walked to the window, looking out over the Vancouver skyline. The double glass insulated her from the sounds of traffic congestion on the streets below but didn't shut out the panoramic view that had often allowed her to regain peace of mind during a hectic day.

The north shore mountains, still snow covered in June, thrust their jagged silver peaks into the cloudless sky as always, but today their steadfast serenity failed to touch her. Her thoughts remained troubled as she pressed her forehead against the cool glass. Why did life have to be so complicated? Her career had blossomed; many of her ambitions had already been realized. But at what cost? It was a question she'd once asked herself only in the darkness of the night. Now it surfaced to haunt her days as well.

The phone began ringing again, and she cast it a glare that had no effect on its insistent summons. Turning back to the window, she smiled as two crows, their flight as erratic as bits of charred paper, fluttered past on the other side of the glass. She could almost hear their quarrelsome squawks.

A float plane taking off from the placid waters of Burrard Inlet crossed her vision in an orange streak. She clasped her elbows in her palms. Soon she too would be in a plane, a larger one, yes, but on a journey that might be called an odyssey into the past.

"Ahem!"

Joanna turned slowly, her brows knitting with annoyance at the interruption. The frown quickly turned into a smile as her father, looking distinguished in a light gray suit, stepped into the room.

"Didn't you hear the phone ringing?" he asked, giving her an indulgent smile that had more than a trace of mischief in it. "I suppose you were busy with Tony."

"Tony left some time ago, Dad. I was just think-ing." She kissed his cheek, pulling a humorous little face as she stepped back. "Prickly. I don't know how Mother stands it."

Socrates laughed as he took a seat. His heavy, fast-growing beard had been a joke between them since Joanna was practically a baby. "Mountains are pretty today," he commented, his gaze going past Joanna to the window.

"Yes, they are." Sitting down, she folded her hands on the desk before her and waited expectantly. Soc-rates wouldn't have come to her office just to pass the time of day. But he never came directly to the point, especially when it was important. Disarming his vic-tims through a laid-back charm was his policy.

"What did Tony want?" He kept his eyes on the view.

Joanna pretended to read a letter she had picked up from the In basket, taking her time about answering. "He wanted a file."

Socrates's dark gaze swung back to her. Although Joanna kept her eyes down, she was aware of his keen scrutiny. "Nothing else?"

He was so predictable. Hiding her amusement, she looked at him, her blue eyes wide and innocent. "What else could he want?"

"You to make up your mind," Socrates answered bluntly. "This business of going on holiday alone to some village in Greece that's barely a dot on the map... It's time you stopped dangling Tony on a string. He'd make an excellent husband."

Now we get to the real business, Joanna thought, trying to control her anger. "When and if I decide to marry, I will find my own husband.'' The words came out with deceptive mildness.

Socrates regarded her intently for a moment. ''Tony's in love with you, you know.''

Joanna kept her expression carefully bland. Although she suspected it, she hadn't realized anyone else could see the depth of Tony's feelings. ''Now, Papa,'' she said, reverting to her childhood name for him. ''We're just friends.''

He crossed one leg over the other, adjusting the crease in his immaculate trousers. ''Tony's not *just* friends. I've got eyes. But if you don't give him some encouragement, you'll lose him.''

''How can I lose him when I don't have him?'' Joanna busied herself with the next item from the In basket, hoping he'd take the hint.

''He loves you, but he's not going to wait forever.'' This last was said in a dark voice, portending doom. Joanna swallowed a laugh. Socrates reveled in the theatrical. ''And you're not getting any younger. Time you settled down and had some babies.''

''When I'm ready,'' Joanna said calmly, drawing on the experience of nearly three decades of dealing with her father's autocratic tendencies.

Socrates shifted in the chair, fussing with the knot in his red-and-gray-striped tie. ''Tony's ready now. Why, just the other day he was complaining about the way you've been keeping him at arm's length. And this business of rushing off to Greece, to Mikrohori, of all places.''

''I have business in Volos,'' she reminded him. ''And it's time I looked at Katerina's house and decided what to do with it.''

"Tony said something about your looking Alex up while you're in Volos?"

Joanna jerked her head up. She'd mentioned Alex a couple of times to Tony, even admitting to the crush she'd had on him when they'd discussed teenage escapades. Tony also knew that Alex lived in Volos, but Joanna hadn't discussed that aspect of her plans. Obviously he'd reached some rather astute conclusions on his own. "I may need legal counsel when I deal with the hotel manager there," she said in a neutral tone. "Alex is the logical choice."

Socrates scowled with a disapproval she hadn't seen him use toward her since she was about twelve. "There are other lawyers in Greece, Joanna. I know how it is between you and Alex—"

"How it *was*, past tense," Joanna interrupted crisply. "A lot of years have gone by since then."

"He hurt you, Joanna, leaving like that and then never writing."

"He wrote." But even as she said the words, a twinge of remembered pain stabbed her heart.

"Sure," Socrates said. "To your brothers, and to us as a family at Christmas, but never to you personally."

"You don't know that." Pride forced her to make the protest.

"Yes, I do. I saw the hurt in your eyes every time. There wasn't a single personal note for you."

Joanna shuffled the sheets of paper on her desk. "I've gotten over that. It would be rude for me to go to Volos and not look Alex up."

"As long as you remember it's business." Socrates stood up, buttoning his suit jacket across his still-flat stomach. "Joanna, if you want some advice—don't give me that long-suffering look—forget Alex. I know how it is with kids but it was puppy love, and over a long time ago. Tony's real and here. You can't bring back the past.''

Joanna met the fierceness of his gaze, her heart swelling at the realization of how much he loved her, how he would have died rather than see her hurt. But he had to know he couldn't protect her forever. Ever since she'd left her teens she'd had to assert her independence, and she'd generally succeeded by employing diplomacy and a knowledge of how Socrates thought. His interference had never diminished her love for him. Neither did his machinations now, but she wished he'd leave Tony out of them.

As for Alex, well, that was something she had to settle on her own.

"Dad, I do love you." She smiled as his expression softened. "But I am an adult," she continued firmly. "I have to live my own life, make my own mistakes."

"And this may be the biggest one." Socrates turned toward the door. "If you don't make up your mind about Tony soon . . .''

"Wait," Joanna called after him. "What was it you wanted?''

But he was gone, and she concluded that he'd gotten what he wanted, or at least said his piece. She sighed. Never mind. They'd had these little altercations before. One of the most serious had happened on the day Joanna had moved out of the family home into her own apartment. The storms always passed, leaving the bond between them stronger than ever. Socrates would come around.

BY THE FOLLOWING AFTERNOON Socrates had apparently forgotten their argument. He drove Joanna to the airport, respecting her silence as they entered the terminal. He knew she didn't particularly like to fly although it was a necessary part of her job. Every trip brought on an apprehension she tried to hide. It disappeared only when the plane was safely airborne.

In fact, the discomforts of flying were far from Joanna's mind, driven out by a vague guilt. She'd been unable to reach Tony to say goodbye. Her rather cavalier dismissal of his concerns yesterday had come back to bother her later in the day. She had gone to the office this morning with the intention of making it up to him only to find that he'd flown to San Francisco to take care of an emergency in the Paradise Hotel there. He'd left her a note wishing her good luck, but the impersonal tone of the words had left her dissatisfied.

At the departure gate Socrates hugged her tightly, conveying his love even though their conversation in the car had been confined to last-minute advice on how she should handle the possible purchase of the hotel in Volos. "Remember what I told you, Joanna."

"I know, Dad," Joanna assured him patiently. "It's not the first such negotiation I've handled."

"But this Mihalis Samaras is a Greek. They're very canny."

Joanna's eyes twinkled. Canny Greeks, she thought. With a father like Socrates, she knew all about that. "Yes, Dad, I'll be careful they don't put anything over on me. If I can't make a deal with Samaras, I'll demand to see the owner, the mystery man who keeps such a low profile. You didn't happen to find out his name, did you?''

Although Joanna had set up the appointment with Samaras, Socrates was the one who had originally told her the hotel was for sale, a piece of news he'd garnered through one or another of his friends. Networking was very much alive in the large Greek community in Vancouver. Few business opportunities were announced; business transactions often depended on following up a hot rumor.

''No, I haven't.'' Socrates shook his head. ''I've been asking around but so far, nothing.''

''Oh, well, it probably doesn't matter,'' Joanna said philosophically. She would have liked to have had more concrete information on the deal, but it wasn't critical. In the past, she'd gone into negotiations with even less. ''Samaras assured me he has full authority.''

''I'm sure you'll handle it, Joanna.'' Socrates enfolded her in an embrace that seemed more fervent than usual. She hugged him in return, her heart warming at his words, at the confidence he showed in her, which he rarely vocalized.

''I'll give you a call after the meeting,'' she promised, letting him go. ''Give Mother my love and tell her I'm sorry I didn't get a chance to speak to her this morning.''

''She's always at those charity things lately,'' Socrates grumbled. A standard grumble, Joanna knew. He was proud of Mary's success in fund-raising.

''You'll see her this evening, Dad.''

''Sure, I will.'' He gave her another quick hug. ''Have a good holiday, Joanna. And good luck with Samaras.'' He paused, then added, ''Be careful.''

With Samaras? Or with Alex? Joanna shook her head as she passed through the gate. Socrates worried too much.

REACHING MIKROHORI on the east coast of the Pelion peninsula in central Greece, proved to be more complicated than Joanna had anticipated. After a long, exhausting flight to Athens, she had to endure a tedious five hour bus trip to Volos, where she spent the night. She was aware that Alex's office wasn't far from her hotel, but she was too hot and tired to seriously consider dropping in. She wanted to be looking and feeling her very best when she met him again.

Early the next morning, discovering that buses to the village ran only once a day and made frequent stops, she struck a deal with a taxi driver to drive her there. Two hours in a noisy Mercedes along a twisting road that sometimes followed the coast and sometimes delved inland over hills covered with olive trees brought her to the village.

The house, she saw when she reached it, was in excellent condition, exactly as the lawyer's letter had described it. And considerably more substantial. She'd expected a cottage of perhaps four rooms. Instead she found a two-story structure solidly built of the gray local stone, sitting in a well-tended garden filled with flowers.

The key she'd possessed for over a year fitted smoothly into the lock, another indication that the house was being cared for by somebody. Alex? Or someone hired by him? She knew he owned most of the land that surrounded the place. He probably still used the house, which had served as a summer retreat for various members of his family in the past.

She shivered despite the oppressive heat. What was he like now? When they met, would she even know him?

The heavy wooden door swung open soundlessly, letting her into a ceramic tiled hall that was blessedly cool. Setting down her dusty suitcase, she exhaled slowly. It was perfect, a haven from the heat, a shelter from the pressure that had become a way of life for her. She could hardly wait to settle in and take a swim in the turquoise sea she'd glimpsed from the taxi.

Pushing the door closed, she lifted her arms above her head and, kicking off her sandals, executed an ecstatic little dance around the hall. She paused in the middle of a graceful movement, wriggling her toes against the cold tiles, and laughed aloud as she saw the damp footprints her hot, dusty feet had left behind.

Dust and sand seeped into everything, she'd noticed, although the spacious hall around her appeared immaculate. Her white cotton dress, crisply pressed when she'd put it on that morning, hung limp and wilted. Worst of all, she'd picked up a smudge on the skirt that looked suspiciously like engine oil, probably impossible to remove.

She glanced up the stairs, then at the doors opening off the hall. Where was the bathroom? She needed a shower.

She stooped to pick up the suitcase she'd set just inside the door, grimacing at the grittiness of sand against her palm. Dropping the handle, she pulled a tissue from her pocket to wipe her hands.

A muffled noise somewhere in the house jerked her to attention. She froze, listening intently, but when she heard nothing further she shook her head. Fancies, that was all. An old house like this was bound to give a few arthritic creaks as its timbers settled.

Using the ragged bit of tissue, she wiped the handle of the suitcase, then straightened, glancing around for a waste basket. A large framed print of a typical Greek cottage caught her eye. The brilliant clashing colors of a red door set in an ocher wall against a Prussian-blue backdrop of sea seemed to personify the charming exuberance of the Greek spirit. She would be happy here. She would be able to regain her perspective on her life. Lifting her arms above her head, she made another little pirouette around the hall, laughing in delight as a sunbeam slanted through the window high on the wall and set dust motes dancing.

A shadow crossed the sunbeam. She paused, hands slowly falling to her sides. The fine hairs on her nape prickling, she looked up.

And met a pair of black eyes that looked as startled as she felt.

For a moment, the hall spun around her as she fought to bring her emotions under control.

"Alex?" she said tentatively. "Alex Gregory?"

"Joanna?"

She would have known his voice anywhere. It had changed, become deeper, but he still had that hint of an indefinable accent that was the result of his having lived in a number of different countries.

For the space of ten heartbeats they stared at each other. Then Alex smiled faintly. "Joanna, welcome home."

A strange greeting, but she supposed it was partly correct. This was her house. She had a right to think of it as home. She gathered her tattered composure, willing her heart to stop pounding. "You scared me. I didn't expect to find anyone here."

His mouth curved, his smile broadening. "I often sail my boat down from Volos for a weekend, so I usually stay here. I didn't think you'd mind. How are you, Joanna? I see you've finally decided to visit the land of your ancestors."

She tilted her head to look squarely at him, wondering if she'd imagined a hint of sarcasm in his low voice. "I've been to Greece before."

"Flying over for a weekend to cut the ribbon of a new hotel hardly counts. How long are you staying?"

"Two weeks. Maybe a bit longer."

She couldn't take her gaze off him, the tissue crushed to shreds in her damp hand, forgotten. He leaned negligently on the stair rail, black eyes narrowed as he stared back at her.

He had changed over the years.

He was lean and muscular, but no longer skinny. His shoulders, filled out and broadened with maturity, were bronze and bare under the black tank top he wore tucked into off-white jeans so snug they outlined the masculine contours of him.

His face had altered most, the angular boy's features molded into a hard, handsome maturity. His eyes, black as moonless midnight, moved restlessly over her, and in them she saw cynicism, as if he'd lost the dreams he'd confided to her so long ago. Only around his mouth lingered traces of the sensitivity she knew he was capable of.

"Come on," he said, coming the rest of the way down and picking up her suitcase. "I'll show you around."

He stepped aside to let her go ahead up the stairs. She could hear the amusement in his voice as he murmured, "I so enjoyed that little dance you did just now. Proves you still know how to play."

The irony of the statement struck Joanna. In her mind the opposite was true. She looked down at her wrinkled dress, the black stain, seeing herself through his eyes. Her face felt hot; no doubt it was shiny and flushed. Alex must think her the urchin she'd so often resembled in her teens, with tangled hair and untidy clothes, she thought in dismay. Yes, she'd wanted to see him, but on her own terms.

"You haven't seen me in fifteen years, Alex," she said as he joined her at the top of the stairs. "I've changed."

He turned toward her, reaching out to run a fingertip along the faint lines that bracketed her mouth, lightly tracing the tiny furrow above her nose. His touch was cool, conveying a tenderness that was at odds with the dark intensity of his eyes. "Yes, you have changed, Joanna. You look stressed out. I recognize that look because it's how I was before I came to Volos."

Stressed out. Burned out. What was the difference? If he could see it, it only confirmed what she suspected.

Burnout. The word nagged her, like a dull toothache, but its implications had lost much of their power to frighten her. The question of whether she was allowing pride and ambition rather than personal choice to dictate her life and her career had become too important.

She followed him down the hall. He showed her several bedrooms, neatly arranged but obviously unused. Near the end of the hall he directed her into what must have been the master bedroom when the house had been occupied by his aunt. The room was large, with wide windows that gave a panoramic view of the pebbled beach, the sea and the village along its edge.

She looked around, noting the casual pine furniture, the wide bed covered by a light blanket. The ceilings were high, the open windows with their billowing lace curtains bringing the freshness of the sea into the room. She took a deep breath of the salt-scented breeze, already feeling more relaxed. Here she could rest, knit up her frayed inner resources and decide her future, even map out a new one if necessary. She'd always dreamed of buying a small country inn and running it on her own. Out here, away from corporate pressures, it didn't seem so impractical after all.

Her gaze fell on the masculine toiletries that lay on the mirrored, old-fashioned vanity, and serenity fled. Alex's things. With a start she realized this was where he was staying.

"You can have this room," he said, "since it's now your house."

"But—but it's yours," she stammered, her face flushing anew.

The muscles under the bronzed skin flexed as he lifted one shoulder. "I was leaving, anyway."

"Leaving?"

"Yes. The weekend's over. It's Monday and I've got to get back to my office. You'll have the house all to yourself."

As he spoke, he scooped the shaving gear and hairbrush into a small canvas bag, slinging the strap over his shoulder. "There're two closets. One is empty. You can use it." From a corner he took a duffel bag, stuffing a heap of wrinkled sheets into it. "I've put fresh sheets on the bed. I'll bring these back next time I come."

"But you didn't even know I was coming," she pointed out, puzzled.

"No, but I always leave the place tidy since it's not really mine anymore."

A chill crept into her stomach, a peculiar sense of apprehension, as if she'd forgotten something vital. Before she could analyze the feeling, or respond to Alex's apparently offhand remark, he spoke again.

"You weren't at the funeral."

Funeral? For a moment she floundered in confusion. Then comprehension dawned, followed swiftly by guilt. His aunt. Her godmother.

But her tone was determinedly steady. "No, I was trying to straighten out some trouble at one of our hotels in the Caribbean. I knew Katerina was in the hospital, but she seemed to be recovering. Then she had that second stroke and it was all over."

He gazed at her, his mouth a thin line below his perfect, straight nose. "You should have been there."

She'd told herself that a thousand times, racked with remorse when she'd returned to Vancouver to find the woman she'd looked on as a grandmother, not only gone but two days in her grave. "I couldn't," she said, hating the defensiveness in her voice. Excuses trembled on her lips, but she bit them back. They were valid, she knew, but Alex wouldn't see it that way. She hadn't, either. It was guilt that had kept her from claiming her inheritance before this.

"Really, Joanna?" he said, a cynical smile curling his lips.

Shouldering the duffel bag, he brushed past her and headed for the stairs. A moment later she heard the solid thud of the front door. The sound echoed in her heart with a painful finality.

CHAPTER TWO

AT ODD MOMENTS during the next several days Alex found himself thinking about Joanna. It had been rude of him to leave her like that, piling guilt on top of the pressures that obviously rode her. Half a dozen times he'd had an urge to contact her, to apologize, but speaking to her wasn't a simple matter since the house in the village had no telephone.

As the week went on his guilt subsided. However, he realized he was thinking about her more than ever, daydreaming, an activity that was unusual for him and, while pleasant, was not conducive to productivity.

His first sight of her, arms raised, long bare legs flashing under the skirt of her dress, stayed with him. If it hadn't been for that glimpse of the free-spirited child she'd been, he would barely have recognized her.

Swiveling his chair, he stared out at the sweltering streets. Volos was in the grip of a heat wave. The traffic honked irritably, stalled in the narrow canyons between modern buildings. His office was air-conditioned, but the overtaxed machinery reduced the temperature only to tolerable. His shirt clung damply to his back. He wished he was out on the open sea, where the wind could cool his body and clear his mind.

Joanna had grown up. Somehow though, her maturity had come as a surprise to Alex. That was preposterous. She couldn't remain fourteen forever.

He sighed, his face pensive. The four years he'd lived with his Aunt Katerina in Vancouver, next door to Joanna's boisterous family, had been virtually the only tranquil interlude of his youth. He'd been friends with her four older brothers, but it was Joanna who had seen beyond the rebellious facade to the lonely boy who lived inside him. Despite her youth, she had healed his wounds, helped him to regain his battered self-esteem. She had been there during a crucial juncture in his life. The memory of her sensitivity, her love, had remained with him always.

A beep from the intercom on his desk distracted him from his thoughts. He stabbed the button with one finger. "Yes?"

"Mihalis Samaras would like to speak to you."

"Fine. Put him through." Bringing the phone to his ear, Alex tilted his chair back to a precarious angle and swung his feet up onto the desk. On one level he welcomed the interruption. Trying to relive the past was an exercise in futility. Dreams left behind were gone forever, better forgotten.

"Yes, Mihalis, what's up?"

For several minutes his friend and business associate discussed policy and problems with him. Then the conversation took on a personal note, not that Mihalis could have known it was personal when he broached the subject. "I understand that the representative from Paradise Hotels is the owner's daughter."

"Yes, I know," Alex said.

"I didn't get the connection until I saw the letter confirming her appointment," Mihalis went on. "I hope she's not some flake who got her job only because of her father."

Joanna a flake? Definitely not. "No, I'm sure she's quite capable," Alex told Mihalis. "You see, I once knew her."

"You did?"

"Yeah, when we were kids," Alex said, conscious of a faint regret. "But it was a long time ago."

"Oh." Alex could hear the curiosity in Mihalis's voice but he didn't elaborate. "Does that mean you're going to get involved in the negotiations?"

Alex thought for a moment. Joanna couldn't know of his connection to the hotel. How would she react if she knew he was the owner? Would it put more stress on her?

"I'm not sure," he said slowly. "For the moment we'll keep to the original arrangement. You're in charge, as you've always been."

He had barely hung up the phone when his secretary buzzed to tell him she was going for lunch. "Go ahead," he said absently, his thoughts on Joanna and her appointment.

The hotel Mihalis managed for him represented only a minor part of Alex's various business interests. His law practice kept him occupied so he left the day-to-day operation of most of his ventures to other people.

He'd decided some months ago to sell the hotel, but only if certain conditions were met. When Mihalis had put the word out, Alex had been pleased to hear that Paradise Hotels, with their reputation for honesty and integrity, had shown an interest. The probability of

Joanna coming over as their representative hadn't crossed his mind.

Or had it? Maybe he had subconsciously wanted to meet her again on his own turf.

He shook his head, frowning. That was ridiculous. If he'd wanted to see Joanna, he could have flown to Vancouver any time.

His frown deepened. Joanna's appointment wasn't for nearly two weeks. Why had she come so early? To see the house she'd inherited, as she'd indicated? She'd ignored it for a year; she could have come a day or two in advance, looked the place over and decided what to do with it. The logical course of action would be for her to sell it to him, since he owned most of the adjacent land, and had seen to the upkeep of the house.

The phone rang again. He picked it up, wondering who was calling when most people were heading out of their offices for the siesta break.

"Jenny, how are you?" he exclaimed when he heard her voice. "You're just the person I wanted to talk to."

Jenny lived in Mikrohori. Brash, outspoken, the frequent object of village gossip, she was probably his dearest friend in all the world. In his early childhood when his Greek father had been alive, they had spent most summers in Mikrohori at his aunt's house—he and his father at any rate. His memories of his mother during that time were hazy. She'd come and gone a great deal.

Jenny had been the friend he took scrapes and hurts to, his confidante when life became impossibly chaotic. Sometimes it seemed to him that Jenny and his Aunt Katerina, and later Joanna, had been the only anchors in a life that had taken him all over Europe and North America by the time he was ten.

"Did you know that Joanna Paradisis is here?" the old lady asked in an acerbic tone. "And she's going to be trouble. Mark my words."

"Is she?" Alex kept his tone neutral while his mind still gnawed the question: why *had* Joanna come so soon?

"Yes," Jenny informed him indignantly. Although Joanna had spent the first couple of days sunbathing and swimming, she was now making the rounds of the village, taking notes on possible tourist attractions—not that Mikrohori had many of those. And she had interviewed the local innkeeper on the state of his business.

"I know Joanna is an executive at Paradise Hotels," Jenny added, "but we don't need one of their fancy resorts here."

"Now, Jenny," Alex teased, "think of how much more lively the village would be."

"I don't want lively. I want to live out my days in peace. Why, the next thing you know they'll be opening a noisy disco, all thumps and shrieks like banshees."

She went on like this until Alex was wincing at the thought of her phone bill. Finally he told her he had to go. "But I'll look into it," he promised. "You can be sure of that."

"When are you coming?" Jenny asked with blunt familiarity.

Alex hedged. "Soon. I have a few things to clear up."

"Well, when you do, bring her to meet me."

"You mean you haven't spoken to her?" Alex's brows flew up. "Come on, Jenny. You're losing your touch."

"I've had a summer cold," Jenny told him. She brushed off his sympathetic noises. "I haven't been out for a few days. Yes, *pedhi mou,* I'm fine now. Just bring her to see me." She hung up, taking it for granted that he would jump to her command.

He would, too, Alex thought as he got up and paced to the window. The harbor was quiet, blue water shimmering under a merciless sun, but for once he was oblivious to the view.

Joanna.

He turned back to his desk, applying himself to the work at hand. Suddenly it was urgent that he see her again, that he find out what she was up to.

He sailed down from Volos that evening, anchoring in a sheltered cove just north of the village and spending the night on his boat. At dawn he walked along the pebbled beach. A luminous pink sky arched over his head, making him feel as if he were inside a seashell. On his right the Gulf of Volos stretched, iridescent and calm, to the invisible horizon. He breathed deeply, inhaling the fresh scent of the water and the myriad perfumes of a June morning alive with blossoms.

Receiving no reply to his knock at the door of Katerina's house, he continued on to the semiprivate section of beach nearby.

Joanna had been swimming. Aware that she might resent his intrusion, he kept on walking toward her anyway. She rose from the water, sending gilt-edged ripples fanning outward over the mirror-flat surface. The wet black latex of her tank suit molded the supple lines of her body, and enhanced the light tan she had acquired. She raised her hands, slicking back her wet hair and lifting her face to the rising sun. When her lips parted in a radiant smile, the sheer beauty of her stole his breath away.

She appeared more rested. The faint lines around her mouth and above her nose had almost disappeared. Although her face no longer had the guileless purity of youth, it had lost the driven look that had disturbed him on Monday.

Her head jerked toward him and her smile vanished. For a moment her eyes, as deeply blue as the Aegean on a perfect sailing day, widened in alarm. Then, as she recognized him against the sun's glare, a look of wariness crept into those eyes. He knew she was remembering his abrupt exit from the house.

Despite his knowledge that her presence here might not be as innocuous as it seemed, he didn't want animosity between them. Not after what they'd been to each other. "Joanna, I'm sorry for what I said the other day. I had no right to judge you."

She hesitated, weighing his sincerity before deciding in his favor. "Okay, Alex. Can we be friends?"

He took the hand she extended, feeling the chill of the sea in her fingers. "Sure." Yielding to impulse, he pulled her against him for a brief hug, pressing his lips lightly to her forehead.

His hand lay on her back, half on the sleek spandex of her swimsuit, half on the cool silk of her skin. He couldn't let go as her scent, seawater mixed with a faint flower perfume, embraced him, awakening long-buried memories.

Joanna.

Joanna, the love of his youth. One touch and he was seventeen again, holding her for the first time and not even realizing how brief their time together would be.

She made a sound and he released her, suddenly aware of how tightly his hands gripped her waist. Her expression as she looked at him was quizzical but no longer wary. "It's been a long time, hasn't it, Alex?"

His eyes stung with unaccustomed emotion. He passed his hand over his face, coughing slightly to clear his throat. "Yes, a long time."

A little breeze quickened off the water, making her shiver. Stooping, she picked up the towel that lay on the beach, at the same time pushing her feet into a pair of rubber thongs. She wrapped the towel around her body as Alex reached out and smoothed back a wet strand of hair which had caught on her cheek. "It's chilly. You need to change out of your wet suit."

Laughing, she lifted her hands to wring most of the water out of her hair. "It won't be chilly for long." She scanned the sky. The rosiness of dawn was already fading. "That's some heat wave you've been having here. I've never seen weather like it."

SO ALEX HAD COME BACK, Joanna thought as they walked up the path to the house. Somehow, after the other day she hadn't expected to see him again, certainly not so soon.

But he had come. He had apologized. And hugged her. The hug had only lasted a couple of seconds, but she had felt the heavy thud of his heartbeat, the warmth of his touch.

She glanced at him as they reached the garden gate. What was their relationship going to be? Was the past really dead, or merely lying dormant waiting for them to revive it?

The gate latch was stubborn, and Alex stepped forward to help her with it. Although the air was cool on her wet skin, a sheen of perspiration glistened in the fine black hairs on his arm as he raised it to the latch. To Joanna, he smelled tangy, male, and before she could control it, her stomach executed a slow somersault. She raised her gaze to his lips. He turned his head as he pushed open the gate, his breath fanning across her face, as intimate as a kiss. All he had to do was bend slightly and his mouth would be on hers, in a greeting that would have been entirely appropriate.

A moment ago, but not now.

She willed herself to move back. He was a stranger now; she couldn't be feeling this, remembering....

Alex seemed unaware of the dark currents that eddied around them. Closing the gate, he walked beside her up the path. "So, Joanna, how have you been?"

She smiled, forcing out the memory of other times. "Fine, Alex. It's quiet here. I'm having a good rest."

"No, I meant with work, your career."

"That's fine, too. I've got a lot of responsibility."

He paused to pluck a red rose misted with dew from a bush next to the path, twirling the stem between his fingers. "You're the only one who went into the family business, aren't you?"

He must have known this but she sensed he was attempting to bridge the awkward gap between the past and present. "Yes, and although Dad says he's all for women in business, I can't help thinking that he wishes at least one of the boys had also joined the company. Still, he seems pleased with my work."

The smile that touched Alex's lips was faint and somehow ironic. "So you're a success."

She was puzzled by his odd tone but let it pass. "Yes, I guess you might say that."

They entered the cool dimness of the hall, and again she shivered. "Just make yourself at home, Alex. I'll be back as soon as I shower and change."

Alex watched her go toward the back of the house, his gaze appreciative as he noted the lightness in her step. The rich perfume of the rose he held drifted to his nostrils, teasing him. In an instant he was back in the garden behind her house, the fifteen years they'd been apart fading in his memory. All at once he understood why he'd felt that surge of emotion earlier. She reminded him of that time, when they had both been young, in love with life and each other.

Did she remember, too, even though he'd never written or contacted her? *Had* she loved him, in the boy-girl sense, at fourteen? Although he'd been only seventeen himself, he'd been deeply in love with her. To him her innocence had been like this rose, pure, untainted. When she'd looked at him with those sea-blue eyes and he'd seen the adoration she had neither the guile nor the desire to conceal, he'd wanted to love her forever.

There was little evidence of the young Joanna in the woman who wore strength and self-possession like a suit of armor, whose competence he suspected was often intimidating. Immersed in her career, she probably hadn't given him more than a passing thought in years.

Again Alex wondered—what had brought her to Mikrohori? Solitude, perhaps, but he was willing to bet his beloved sailboat against an empty clamshell that it was not her primary objective.

CLUTCHING A THIN COTTON ROBE around herself, Joanna emerged from the bathroom. There was no sign of Alex in the front hall. Grateful for a breathing space, she scurried up the stairs to her room. She quickly changed into shorts and a roomy shirt, which would keep her cool when the sun scorched the earth at midday. The sensuality that seemed to be part of the air one breathed in Greece had already cast its spell over her. Although unstructured clothing worn over bare skin had felt at first like an almost sinful indulgence, now she wondered how she'd ever go back to being "dressed."

Despite the heat wave, she loved the promise of endless summer in each blue-and-gold day. She could understand why Katerina, with her house in Vancouver and her prominent position in Greek community affairs there during her lifetime, had never given up this place.

She found Alex in the kitchen, standing at the old-fashioned gas stove on which she cooked her meals. Bacon sputtered and snapped in the pan, its savory aroma mingling with that of freshly brewed coffee.

Bacon? "I didn't have any bacon," she exclaimed, realizing the inanity of the comment as soon as it left her mouth.

He turned and gave her a faint smile. "I brought it with me, dropped it off by the back door before I came to the beach. Surely you didn't think I'd come here to sponge off you?"

She hadn't thought anything. "No, but where did you find bacon?" Closing her eyes for a moment, she inhaled the delicious smells.

"In Volos. It helps if you know where to shop. One egg or two?"

"One," she said promptly. "But you don't have to make my breakfast."

"Why not? I have to eat, too, and you're probably hungry after your swim," he replied, turning back to the stove. "Besides, I've cooked in this kitchen more times than I can count."

It suddenly dawned on her that he might resent the fact that the house where he'd spent so much time was now hers. "Alex, I'm sorry about Katerina. Truly I am. I loved her, too."

His expression softened. "I know you did, Joanna."

"What I don't understand is why she left me this house."

Alex removed the crisped bacon to a paper towel to drain, then cracked eggs into the frying pan. "It was hers. She had the right to leave it to anyone she wanted. She was your godmother, after all. You were like family to her."

"And to you?" Joanna set plates and cutlery on the table just outside the back door. The table stood on a patio that was shaded in the morning by a huge mulberry tree but sunny in the afternoon. She'd gotten into the habit of eating her breakfast out in the fresh air.

"I never felt like your brother, if that's what you mean, Joanna." He dished up the eggs and bacon, and they sat down to eat.

"I was only ten when you came to live with your Aunt Katerina," she reminded him.

Calmly he buttered a slice of bread. "Sure, but you had four brothers. You didn't need another."

Had she thought of him as a brother? Perhaps at the very beginning, but not for long. He'd been thirteen, tall for his age, and to her eyes frighteningly mature. By the time a year had passed, she'd fallen in love with him. The love had remained strong during the four years he'd lived next door, and she had suffered when he left.

The emotion had proved transient, as most youthful passions are, changing to anger when he didn't write. Then it had died. She'd gotten over him by the time she'd completed high school. She'd gone on to university, met other men, relegated Alex to the back of her mind as a bittersweet memory. A memory that too often refused to stay in its place.

"Your aunt didn't come here often in the last years of her life, did she?"

"No, not as much. She felt at home in Vancouver, and cut down on her traveling."

Joanna smiled. "Yes, she was very active in the Greek community there."

"Except for attending her funeral, I hadn't been to Vancouver in years," Alex remarked. "Has it changed much, other than on the surface?"

"The Greek community is bigger and stronger than ever, although I must say its members aren't concentrated in one area as much as when we were kids. But there's still the same spirit and unity." She frowned, then asked, "How is it that your aunt was the only one of your family who lived in Canada?"

Alex pushed his empty plate away. "There were only her and my father, you know. My grandfather had a number of business interests. When he died, the Canadian segments went to Aunt Katerina and the European shares to my father."

"You've never talked about your father much," Joanna prompted when Alex broke off to sip his coffee.

"He was already in his forties when he married my mother. He died when I was thirteen, long after they'd divorced." Bitterness underscored his quiet tone. "I was supposed to go live with my mother, but she had just married again, her third or fourth husband. She didn't want me so I came to my aunt."

Joanna nodded. Alex's mother had visited him a few times during the four years he'd lived with Katerina. Joanna remembered her as haughty and unapproachable, always meticulously groomed and dressed in the latest designer clothes. Hardly the image of a mother.

Joanna remembered something else as well. Alex had always been moody and remote for several days following one of the visits.

"She didn't need a kid around," Alex added tonelessly.

"Alex..." Joanna's throat tightened. She reached across the table to touch him.

He jerked his hand away. "Forget it, Joanna. It's over."

Was it? Curiosity tugged at her but she ignored it. There would be another opportunity for her to explore the dark passages in his life.

Taking the remaining chunk of bread from the basket, she crumbled it and tossed the pieces on the patio. Soon a quartet of starlings were quarreling over the feast, filling the silence that fell over the table. And after a moment the antics of an impertinent sparrow stealing crumbs from the larger birds coaxed a smile even from Alex.

"You passed through Volos on your way here," he said at length. "Why didn't you stop by my office?"

Joanna wasn't sure what to say. "It was Sunday when I arrived," she finally muttered, tracing a pattern on the table with her knife. "I didn't have your home address. Anyway, you weren't there."

"You didn't know that, Joanna," he chided, amusement chasing out his earlier tension. "And I know you didn't come by on Monday morning. My secretary would have said something. So why, Joanna?"

"You're going to laugh."

"Try me."

"Okay," she admitted sheepishly. "I was afraid to."

His black brows lifted. "Afraid? Is this the same Joanna who used to climb the highest trees just to prove she was as good as her brothers?"

"That was years ago. Actually I was afraid you'd grown fat and bald, that you'd changed so much that I wouldn't even recognize you."

"We all change." He smiled and his eyes, those remarkable eyes that were as black as deepest midnight, lit up. For an instant he looked young again, and she saw beneath the adult cynicism the boy he'd been. "You've changed a lot. I can't call you Scarecrow anymore," he said.

She'd almost forgotten the nickname she'd detested. Somehow it didn't sting anymore, rather giving her a warm feeling that he remembered the brief years they'd shared. "No, you can't, and you wouldn't dare."

Alex threw back his head and laughed. "What would you do if I did?"

It was a challenge they'd often thrown at each other. "Oh, I don't know. Turn the water hose on you, or something."

Alex looked at the sky, the burning sun. "Wouldn't be much of a punishment on a day like this."

"No, I suppose not." She wiped her hands with a napkin, taking a second one to mop perspiration from her forehead. "How long have you lived in Volos?" She had a sudden, startling thought. "You're not married, are you?" Surely she would have heard if he had been. The Christmas cards he sent her family were always signed simply Alex.

Alex smiled, his expression easy and relaxed, as he tilted his chair back against the wall. "I've lived here almost seven years. And no, I've never married. I guess I couldn't forget you."

Recognition of a long-ago emotion hit them both at once. Was this the truth? For endless moments they stared at each other, stunned, while the heat and the lazy sounds of a summer morning shimmered around them. Nothing had changed; the sharing of minds was still there.

It was too much, all at once. Neither was ready to deal with the emotion that touched them both.

Joanna blinked once, then twice. "Sure, Alex," she said with a skeptical laugh. "All those years. I'll bet you forgot about me the minute you got to England and started university. But how'd you end up in Volos? It's not exactly the center of the world."

"It's an important shipping port," he answered matter-of-factly. "I specialize in international shipping law. I practiced in London for a while, then I decided to come here, to what I've always thought of as my homeland."

That wasn't answering her question, and she couldn't resist teasing him for his evasion. "What'd you do, Alex the Great—" he'd had a nickname, too

"—murder somebody in England so that now you're forced to hide out in a backwater in Greece?" She began to stack the dishes, not noticing that his face went still, his eyes cold and bleak. "Well, you can relax. I'm not Scotland Yard out to bring you in."

The silence, his lack of response, drew her gaze to him. Lines of tension defined his mouth, making him look older. She could have sworn he had paled although it was hard to tell with his dark tan. "Alex?" she asked tentatively.

He shook his head, lifting his coffee cup to his mouth, and the moment was gone, but not the image of what she'd seen in his eyes, the look of fear. Or guilt.

Mechanically she piled the plates at the edge of the table, pretending that everything was normal. It was, she told herself. Alex was calmly sitting across from her, his chair still tipped at a dangerous angle, his expression neutral. It must have been her imagination.

"It took you long enough to get here and have a look at the house," he said. "The estate was settled nearly a year ago." He met her eyes squarely. "So, now that you're here, what are your plans for the property?"

"This house means a lot to you, doesn't it?"

For a moment, he didn't answer, his gaze dropping to the table as he toyed with a couple of scattered crumbs. Joanna saw the tight line of his mouth and sensed that again he fought some emotion he was reluctant to reveal to her. "Alex!"

He lifted his head. "Yes, damn it. It does. It's always been a place for me to refuel. I don't like to think that that could ever change."

Joanna nodded. "I can understand that."

"So what will you do?"

"I haven't decided." Against her will, her voice sounded evasive. She was guiltily aware that if her business deal next week was unsuccessful, her company might choose to develop this land as a site for Paradise Hotels in the area.

Alex's expression hardened, and Joanna had her first glimpse of him as an opponent. Or enemy. The thought startled her. Alex an enemy? Not familiar Alex.

But he wasn't familiar Alex anymore, his cynical look reminded her.

"You're not planning to tear it down and build a hotel, are you?"

Her hands clenched in her lap. How had he guessed? She remained silent, neither denying nor confirming his statement.

"There's hardly enough land," Alex continued.

She bristled at the hostility in his voice. Despite the ideal location, she viewed development here as a last resort. Even in the brief time she'd spent in the village, she'd come to appreciate its tranquility, and had found herself entertaining a certain reluctance to change the way of life.

But not for the world would she admit this to Alex. She had to maintain a strong front. "The land outside the fenced yard is yours, isn't it? You could sell me some of it. I'd give you a good price."

He stood up abruptly, picking up the stack of dishes. "Yeah, I bet you would. But I'm not selling. I don't need the money and I value my privacy here."

"It's not your privacy anymore," she retorted, angry not just at him, but at the career pressures that forced her to see everything in terms of future development. "Or did you think I'd just let you use the house as long as you wished?"

He paused in the kitchen doorway. "You didn't come to claim it in all this time, so what was I supposed to think? Besides, who kept it up? You or me? Seems to me that gives me some rights." With that, he disappeared into the kitchen.

Groaning in frustration, Joanna let her head drop onto her folded arms on the table. The day had barely started and she had already run a gamut of emotional upheavals. Far from allowing her to escape the stress she'd been under, Alex was generating new conflicts within her. Alex, whose black gaze rested on her with both the warmth of remembered times together and the hostile cynicism of a stranger.

She drew in several deep breaths, willing her agitation to subside. Around her, wasps flew back and forth, buzzing in quarrelsome greed over fallen mulberries whose sticky sweetness permeated the warm air. As she turned her head, a shaft of sunlight found an opening in the canopy of leaves and touched her face. Closing her eyes, she luxuriated in its warmth. So peaceful, or it had been.

Before Alex came back.

CHAPTER THREE

THE LOUD CLATTER OF DISHES in the sink warned Joanna that Alex's anger hadn't abated. She got to her feet, gathering up the cups and the coffeepot onto a tray. No point in putting off the inevitable. Squaring her shoulders, she marched into the kitchen.

Golden sunlight spilled through the uncurtained window over the sink. Alex stood in profile, placing a rinsed plate on the draining board. With the rush of water from the tap muffling the sound of her approach, he was unaware of her gaze on him.

For a moment she indulged herself, allowing nostalgia to well up inside her. He'd been a beautiful boy whose toughness combined with a sense of humor had prevented the teasing he might otherwise have suffered from his peers. Now, he was better-looking than ever, even though his brows were drawn and his mouth sulky with leashed temper.

He turned back to face the sink in a quick graceful movement that shifted the muscles of his buttocks under the wheat-colored denim of his jeans. The tanned skin of his shoulders gleamed while the sun struck burnished highlights in the black curls that covered his head so thickly.

Releasing her breath in a sigh, Joanna pulled her errant thoughts together. If she wasn't careful, she would fall into the sensuous trap of her youth, when she had loved him with passionate intensity and no reservations. With a man like Alex it wouldn't be hard.

But it would be foolhardy.

"Alex," she said hesitantly. "I'm sorry. Whatever I decide to do about the house, I'll discuss it with you first. In the meantime, feel free to stay here, anytime. There's plenty of room." She took a deep breath. "I am sorry. Regardless of what you think, I do feel you have a claim on the house that is just as strong as mine."

"But business comes first now, doesn't it, Joanna?" He shut off the flow of water into the sink but didn't bother to turn around. "You *have* grown up."

His sarcasm was the last straw. Joanna's eyes flashed in a warning her brothers wouldn't have ignored, but Alex had probably forgotten it. "Oh, you noticed, did you?"

He turned, amusement lighting his dark face as his mood changed with the quicksilver swiftness she remembered. "Yeah, I noticed. But some things haven't changed. The way you dress, for instance." His gaze ran over her slender figure, which was clad in electric-blue shorts topped by a loose camp shirt with brilliant red bird-of-paradise flowers on a black background. His scrutiny continued downward, caressing her long tanned legs with a visual touch that was so tangible she trembled.

Defiantly she kept her eyes on his face, but a sensual heat trickled through her veins, quickening her heartbeat and awakening a faint, guilt-induced dismay. No one had ever aroused her with just a look.

She stood before him, tense with anticipation. When he placed his hands on her shoulders, she let out a pent-up breath, relieved that the waiting was over.

His hands were warm, holding her in a near embrace. Her throat suddenly felt parched; she couldn't speak. More than the warmth of his hands, his scent held her—a faint musky aroma that called to all that was female in her. Fifteen years receded and she was young again, a child-woman enthralled by the boy who was almost a man. The remembered scent of grass and the soft pressure of his lips on hers came back to her.

"Joanna?"

She blinked, stepping back out of his reach, abruptly restored to the complex present, the real scent of herbs drying on the windowsill, of sun-warmed dust on the patio outside. Her lips stung as though the kiss had been real, and for a wild moment she wondered if he could read her mind.

Alex appeared puzzled. "Joanna, what is it?"

"Nothing," she said hastily. "I was just wondering how long you're planning to stay."

His grin was quick, spontaneous. "Well, I'm not sure. How long do you want me?" He turned it into a joke but deep inside he knew that getting to know Joanna again was no laughing matter. There was no pressing work to draw him back to Volos in a hurry, shipping being in a slump at the moment. He could stay as long as it suited him. Or her.

"As long as you want," she answered, frowning at his odd, speculative expression. "Do you want your room back?"

"No, you can keep it. There are plenty of other rooms." He grabbed her hand in his, his grin returning in full measure. "But that can wait. Right now, I think it's time I took you to meet Jenny, especially since she practically ordered me to bring you."

Joanna pulled free of his hand but followed him out the door. The heat struck her like a blast from a furnace. She squinted against the glare, wishing she'd brought her sunglasses from her room. Too late now. Alex was striding toward the gate. "Who's Jenny?" she asked, panting a little as she caught up. "This is a small place. I thought I'd met pretty well everyone."

"If you'd met this lady, you'd remember," he said with a knowing grin.

Joanna's house stood on a promontory at the south end of the village, somewhat isolated from its neighbors. During the past four days, she had trod the steep path at least a dozen times.

The village was not large, but the sturdy houses with their neatly swept stoops gave it an air of permanence that highlighted its charm. The first building they passed at the foot of the slope was a small inn built of the local stone and trimmed with wooden balconies that overlooked the pebble beach. Beyond it, two paved streets made up the commercial center. The one along the beach boasted a couple of tavernas, the usual coffee shops, and what was probably Greece's smallest branch of the National Bank. The second street, lined with shops, ran parallel to the first.

At the north end of the village, near the junction with the highway to Volos, lay a public camping ground populated by both tourists and Gypsies. A scattering of houses, thrown with haphazard abandon onto the mountainside and connected by steep, rocky paths, formed the residential area.

On this morning, as on all weekday mornings, the streets were crowded with women shopping for the day's vegetables, children playing and men gossiping, either on the street corners or at tables in front of the

coffee shops. One or two tourists proclaimed their
status by wearing scanty bathing suits off the beach,
and several Gypsies flitted like multicolored butterflies among the more somberly clad villagers.

It was obvious to Joanna that Alex was well known
here, and well liked. Several of the shopkeepers came
out of their open-fronted businesses to greet him, even
to embrace him with all the warmth they might have
given one of their own children.

And in his laughing responses Joanna saw again
glimpses of the boy she had known, carefree, always
ready with a witty and humorous rejoinder.

Near the campground a side street ran off at a right
angle, the end of it forming a cul-de-sac lined mainly
with storage sheds for apples and olives. Joanna, in
her explorations, had steered clear of this area because of its proximity to the often noisy campground.

A tall Victorian house dominated the cul-de-sac, a
gingerbread-encrusted monstrosity completely at odds
with its surroundings. The wood trim, carved in fan-
ciful curlicues and badly in need of paint, formed a
contrast to the sturdy stone walls.

As Alex and Joanna entered the street, she could
hear the sounds of an argument escalating. Three or
four men stood by the open door of a shop that sold
hardware and plumbing supplies. Their loud words
were punctuated by wild gestures. Amusement curved
her mouth in an involuntary smile. No Greek could
hold any kind of discussion without shouting and
waving his arms, she thought.

Then, all at once, the argument was over. Two of
the men climbed into a battered Mercedes truck and
drove off, leaving behind the echo of an unmuffled
engine and an acrid cloud of black smoke. The shop-

keeper turned to reenter his store, and the remaining man walked around the hood of a dusty Datsun pickup, whose yellow paint pockmarked with rust reminded Joanna of an overripe banana.

The man waved to someone across the street and walked over to the fence that surrounded the Victorian house. Joanna saw a woman leaning on the fence, her voice carrying clearly to them as she laughed at something the man had said.

The woman was the oddest sight Joanna had seen yet in the village. Tall and stately despite her obvious advanced age, she was dressed in a lurid pink-flowered dress that even Joanna with her own flamboyant tastes in clothes found excessive. Greek women just didn't dress like this, especially in an out-of-the-way village.

The woman's hair was the color and texture of steel wool, an unruly tangle around a face distinguished by wide cheekbones and an aquiline nose, a face that was not beautiful, but which must once have been handsome.

Close enough now to hear the conversation, Joanna felt her mouth drop open as she understood the words: "Just remember, Manoli, if you don't want to drive all the way home tonight, you know where you can sleep." This was accompanied by another boisterous laugh and a sly wink.

Manoli laughed, too, and chucked the woman under the chin before dropping a brief kiss on her wrinkled cheek. "I know, Jenny, but Maria would be waiting with the frying pan. *Yassou.*"

With that he swung back to the truck and drove off. "Alex!"

Joanna winced. Surely this *loud* woman wasn't the person Alex wanted her to meet. But there were no other houses in sight, and she doubted he was planning to introduce her to any of the camping Gypsies who might be gone tomorrow.

Yes. They were embracing and kissing each other's cheeks like old and dear friends. At last the old woman pulled free, and extended a hand to Joanna, taking her fingers in a firm handshake. "So this is Joanna." Her volume had diminished only marginally, but the switch from Greek to American-accented English took Joanna completely by surprise. "How is it that we haven't met when I know you've been here since Monday?"

The twinkle in her faded blue eyes was irresistible, and Joanna returned her smile with a warm one of her own. She might be loud, perhaps even rude, but the woman definitely had a heart.

"I guess because I didn't need any plumbing supplies. I've never been on this street."

Alex said, "Joanna, this is Jenny Astridis. She knows everyone in the village."

"And everything," Jenny put in with another hearty laugh. "All the eligible men, who is getting married, who is having a baby." She winked as she turned to the gate, which squealed a protest as she pushed it open. "Who's sleeping with whom."

"Jenny?" Joanna said slowly. "That doesn't sound Greek. But you must be—"

Jenny grinned, displaying strong white teeth. "I certainly am, Joanna. I was born in Greece but we moved to America when I was a child. Eugenia seemed like a long name when I was going to school there so my parents simplified it to Jenny."

They followed Jenny up the path through a garden filled with a profusion of roses, marigolds and geraniums. A gigantic purple blossoming jacaranda grew in riotous abandon over the veranda. All the colors clashed like those in a child's drawing but somehow it suited Jenny.

The inside of the house, protected from the heat by stone walls three feet thick, was cool, closed shutters giving it a welcome, shadowed dimness. Jenny led them into a room directly off the entrance hall. Here too the shutters were drawn, but the windows were open and the lace curtains stirred gently in the faint breeze.

"Sit. Sit." Jenny gestured toward a cushion-covered daybed that stood at one side of the room, in a position convenient for watching television. It appeared to be the only comfortable piece of furniture apart from a worn leather armchair. The other furniture was stiff, Victorian, looking as if it were upholstered with horsehair and would be prickly to sit on.

Joanna sat down on the daybed, arranging the cushions comfortably behind her. Alex sat next to her, the springs sagging so that their bodies couldn't avoid touching. Quickly, nervously, Joanna moved over, earning herself a knowing look from Jenny.

The old woman stood before them, rubbing her palms together. "Now, what can I bring you to drink? Coffee? Lemonade? Perhaps some ouzo?" She winked at Alex. "Or is it too early in the morning?"

Alex chuckled. "It is, rather. But you go ahead, Jenny, if you want. Make some coffee for us."

Jenny glanced at Joanna. "Is that all right with you? You look like someone who likes to make up her own mind."

Joanna couldn't help laughing. The woman, despite her boisterous manner, was delightful. "Yes, coffee will be fine."

"Okay, Alex. Who is she?" Joanna whispered as soon as Jenny was gone.

Alex reclined against the pile of cushions, linking his fingers behind his head and crossing his feet at the ankles. "Jenny? Why, she's just Jenny. I've known her since I was a kid, when my dad and I used to stay with Aunt Katerina here for the summer." He frowned, the lines of his face becoming tight, his eyes distant, as if his words had revived a distasteful memory. "Jenny saved my sanity a few times."

A short silence followed, which Joanna didn't interrupt. Then he turned his head toward her and smiled, that brief flashing smile that had melted her bones at fourteen. "She's my godmother."

Joanna lifted one eyebrow. "Oh? And how did that come about? Because of your father coming here?"

He nodded, still smiling. "Jenny and Aunt Katerina were great friends, especially during the war. When I was born it was only natural that Jenny should be chosen for my godmother."

"Okay, but what about her English? She must have spent years in the States."

"She did. She grew up in Massachusetts, married at eighteen. Some years later her husband moved her and their seven children back to Greece, to Volos where he had business concerns. They lived here only in the summer, and for most of the years of the war. The country seemed safer than the city during the German occupation."

A pensive note in Alex's voice told Joanna that the story had been more complex than his abbreviated version. "Where are her children now?" she asked.

"They all live in the United States. And her husband died years ago."

Joanna's brows lifted. "She doesn't wear black, like all the other widows in the village." She smiled, recalling the bright pink dress. "That must have caused a stir for a while."

"Jenny doesn't care what people think. And anyway, after the things she did during the war to help the Resistance, they have too much respect for her to ever say anything against her."

Joanna was just about to ask another question when the older woman reentered the room. She was carrying a tray loaded with cups of thick black coffee, glasses of water, and one shotsized glass of a clear liquid that gave off a scent of aniseed.

Setting the tray on the table in front of the daybed, Jenny picked up the glass of ouzo and sat down in the leather armchair. Lifting the liqueur, she winked at both of them, a roguish look in her blue eyes. "Here's to an eventful holiday."

In one swallow she tossed off the contents of the glass, smacking her lips in avid enjoyment. Setting down the glass, she picked up her coffee cup. "Come on, don't be shy. Drink your coffee." Taking a sip, she pinned her piercing gaze on Joanna. "You speak Greek, Joanna?"

Joanna's smile was wry. "Yes. My parents saw to it. Every Saturday morning, I dutifully went to Greek school. But I'm glad now."

"Good for you," Jenny pronounced before turning to Alex.

Joanna sipped her coffee, inhaling the rich scent. No matter what brand one used, Greek coffee never tasted this delicious anywhere but in Greece. She let Jenny and Alex carry the conversation, content to sit back and allow her mind to wander. She sensed the deep affection and understanding that existed between them despite the difference in their ages, and was glad that Alex had had Jenny during the lonely years of his childhood, the years she knew so little about.

"And what brings you here all the way from Vancouver, Joanna?"

Jenny's question brought Joanna out of her reverie. She glanced at Alex. Hadn't he told Jenny? "I came to see the house I inherited."

Jenny nodded, her eyes bright and shrewd as they studied Joanna. "And what are you going to do with it? You're in the hotel business, Alex tells me. Thinking of building a hotel there? If I were you, *koukla mou,* I wouldn't. There's not enough traffic here to support another hotel. Too far from Volos. No ancient ruins."

Joanna looked at Alex suspiciously. Had he put Jenny up to this? She suddenly saw the purpose of this supposedly casual visit. He'd known she would like Jenny, and with the old woman as an ally, Alex was putting just one more obstacle in her way, shoring up his own position even before war had been declared.

Joanna fought to keep her temper under control. She *would not* make a scene in front of Jenny, especially since the woman seemed to thrive on controversy.

Alex must have sensed something for he looked at her with a challenging light in his eyes. "Jenny's right,

Joanna. The simplest solution would be to sell the house to me. You could use it whenever you like, as long as you let me know ahead of time.''

His complacent expression told her he thought it unlikely that she would require it on a regular basis. Swallowing her anger, she muttered, ''How generous.''

The sudden silence in the room was punctuated by a loud thud from overhead. Joanna started, her knee bumping the table as she sat up. The cups rattled in their saucers and from upstairs sounded another, louder thud. ''What's that?''

''Rats,'' Jenny said succinctly, her mouth turning down at the corners.

''Rats?'' Joanna resisted an urge to peer under the daybed as she pulled her bare feet off the floor.

Jenny laughed humorlessly. ''No, dear, not that kind. What sort of housekeeper do you think I am? No, I'm talking about the two-legged kind of rat.''

Alex grinned, baffling Joanna further. ''You mean Costas is here?''

''Costas and that hoity-toity wife of his.'' Jenny scowled. ''Sleeping till all hours. Expecting to be waited on hand and foot.''

''Who's Costas?'' Joanna asked.

''My nephew, from my husband's side of the family. They come here to stay—free room and board and all—then complain all the time about how dead this place is and how bored they are.''

Alex scowled. ''And how long are they staying this time?''

Jenny shrugged her ample shoulders. ''Who knows? And don't worry, Alex, I'll try to keep them out of your hair.''

Alex got abruptly to his feet. "Then I think it's time we left. Come on, Joanna."

She got up, flexing her cramped legs while groping for the sandals she'd dropped somewhere. She had barely managed to slide her feet into them before Alex was dragging her toward the door.

"Sorry you can't stay for lunch," Jenny called after them without getting up from her chair. "Come again, Joanna, any time."

"Thank you. I will," she said breathlessly, struggling to slow Alex's headlong pace. "Must you walk so fast?" Irritated, she forced him to halt just outside the gate where again a group of men congregated in front of the hardware store.

"You put her up to that, didn't you?"

Alex's eyes narrowed. "And if I did, what will you do about it?"

"You have no right to tell me what to do with my own property."

"It's mine, too, Joanna. You admitted that yourself." The quiet conviction in his voice defused what remained of her anger. Not that she would give up, but she was not about to brawl with him on the street.

One of the men in front of the hardware store called to Alex and he let go of her hand to cross the road. Rubbing her wrist, she followed.

"*Kalimera*, Miss Joanna," the shopkeeper greeted her. To her knowledge they hadn't met but since she was new in town, everyone must know who she was. It was a feeling that made her both comfortable and uncertain. She sensed the caring the villagers had for their own, and for her since she was Greek and had been Katerina's goddaughter, but she also knew everything she did would be under close scrutiny. In a

Greek village there was no such thing as privacy, especially for a young, single woman.

"Kalimera," she answered. She pushed back her hair from her perspiring brow as the sun beat with a tangible force on her head. "It's hot today, isn't it?"

"And you're not used to it," the man said. "Doesn't it rain all the time in Vancouver?"

She laughed. "Not all the time."

"Yassou, Angeli," Alex said, sliding his arm around Joanna's waist, an action that did nothing to cool her.

Angeli nodded, smiling. "Aleko, we don't see you nearly often enough these days."

Alex glanced down at Joanna. "I have a feeling that this summer you will." He tightened his arm at her waist. "Joanna, shall we go get a cool drink? Your face is as red as a lobster."

Trust him to remind her, she thought with a grimace. She loved the heat but it showed on her skin in what she considered a most blatant and unflattering manner.

They started back, taking the street that ran along the beach. The astringent scent of resin from stunted beach junipers stung Alex's nostrils, the faint breeze from the sea doing nothing to cool the stagnant air. The village was almost deserted as the heat drove people indoors for their midday meal and a long siesta.

As the silence between them lengthened, Alex glanced at Joanna. Every time the house was mentioned, she got upset. Why?

Oh, it was legally hers all right. He couldn't argue with that since he'd been one of the executors of his aunt's estate. Nor did he want to. But he'd thought that they could reach some amicable arrangement for its future.

A misplaced hope obviously, if Joanna was not disposed to cooperate. She saw only dollars and cents, and seemed to care not at all for his feelings. She certainly wasn't the same girl he remembered.

That was the problem, wasn't it? The image of Joanna he'd carried in his mind was completely different from the person who walked beside him. Although she seemed happy to see him after all these years, he was frustrated to realize he knew nothing of what she was feeling inside. She had developed a superficiality that shut him out. He hardly knew how to talk to her anymore, which was strange after the easy camaraderie of their youth.

Leading her to a restaurant where he often ate when he stayed in the village, he stepped aside to let her enter the enclosed courtyard.

"Thank you," she said, as he held her chair.

So polite. So distant. Alex stared at her, a heated tension coiling in his stomach. They'd once been best friends; why did she have to be so aloof with him?

The restaurant proprietor greeted Alex with affectionate familiarity, bringing sweating glasses of water and a pitcher for refills to them at once. Joanna gulped down the first glass, then sipped more slowly from the second one he poured for her.

"You'll get used to it," Alex said, still feeling at a disadvantage.

"I know." She held the glass against her forehead, closing her eyes at the blissful cold. "I thought I was but today seems even hotter than usual."

They ate in virtual silence, a light meal of stewed summer vegetables and meatballs, along with a salad of tomatoes that were so sweet and succulent they could have been served as dessert. Replete, Joanna pushed her empty plate away and leaned back in her chair. Above their heads the gnarled tendons of a grapevine twisted over a sturdy trellis, shading the patio. The grapes were small, green and hard, scores of tiny clusters hanging among deep green leaves the size of dinner plates. Wasps hovered above the table, tiger-striped scavengers sampling the remains of their lunch.

"Well?" Alex said, propping his elbows on the table as the restaurant owner gathered up the plates. "What did you think of Jenny?"

She smiled. "She's a delight. Even though at first I wondered."

Alex grinned. "Yeah, she does tend to be a little outspoken."

Outspoken wasn't the precise word, but Joanna let it pass. First impressions weren't always accurate, as she'd found out in this case. "How old is she, anyway? She must be sixty-five at least, to have worked with the Resistance during the war."

"She's eighty-three," Alex said with another grin at the way her jaw dropped. "You wouldn't know it to see her, would you?"

"You certainly wouldn't. She seems years younger." Joanna frowned. "What was all that business about her relatives? If her nephew and his wife are a royal pain in the butt, why doesn't she just tell them they can't come?"

Alex's expression didn't alter. Whether or not he felt displeasure at her questions she couldn't tell. But he took his time answering, picking up the plain tumbler that held his wine and drinking slowly before speaking. "Jenny was very fond of her husband. Before he died she promised him that his family would always be welcome in her house."

"But if they're obnoxious? . . ."

He shrugged. "Doesn't matter. In Greece *philotimou* is everything."

Philotimou, that nebulous, untranslatable quality that colored so much of Greek life. It could mean self-respect, or hospitality, or friendship, or honor, but it actually comprised all of these qualities and many others. You couldn't argue against *philotimou*, nor could you ignore it.

"Does her nephew have any claims to her house? Or is he trying to keep on her good side so that when she dies he'll inherit her estate?"

"Jenny's very cagey on that subject, which nearly drives Costas nuts. And no, at the moment he has no claims on any of her property and it's considerable, so he may be trying to stay on her good side. What he doesn't seem to realize is that Jenny is nobody's fool and she'd see through any of his ploys if he tried them."

"And what's your connection in this?"

His eyes were wide and innocent, if that were possible in a face like his. "What makes you think I have a connection?"

"Oh, come on, Alex. You nearly pulled my wrist out of joint dragging me out of there before Costas made an appearance."

He looked contrite. "Did I? Let me see." Before she could react, he reached across the table and took her hand, turning it palm up and carefully examining her wrist. "I don't see anything wrong, but just in case, I'll kiss it better."

The feel of his lips on the exact spot where her pulse beat under her skin was like ice and fire, cool, yet igniting sparks deep inside her body, in places far removed from her wrist. He circled her wrist with tiny kisses, as if he were stringing a bracelet of pearls. Then he turned her hand again and placed a last, warm, open-mouth kiss in the hollow of her palm, just barely flicking the tip of his tongue against her skin. The effect in her body was instantaneous, as if she'd been touched by an electrical current that robbed her of strength and at the same time wired her with excitement.

She closed her eyes, feeling dizzy. Whether it was from his kiss or from the heat, she didn't know. She only knew she'd never felt like this, light-headed, detached, her senses swirling around a pivot formed by the pressure of his mouth in her palm, his long, hard fingers holding her hand.

It had to be the heat, the blatant sensuality that wrapped her in a drugging embrace, embodied by the burning sun, the rich wine, the lush foliage over their heads.

Alex still held her hand, but when she opened her eyes, he was staring at her face, his eyes black and unreadable. His expression told her even less but almost at once his mouth tilted in what could have been a sardonic smile. "About Costas. I didn't want to run into him. If I had, we'd still be there. Every time he sees me he's got some deal he wants me to invest in. He goes on and on. I didn't think you'd want to hear it."

Joanna nodded. She'd met people like that in her own business dealings. Gently she removed her hand from Alex's and picked up her glass of water, drinking slowly from it. "Tell me what Jenny did during the war."

Alex's eyes twinkled. "Do you have the rest of the day?"

She grinned. "I have, if you do."

"Okay. You asked for it." He leaned back in his chair, closing his eyes for a moment, as if to gather his thoughts. "You have to understand that I got a lot of this from different people in the village. Some of it may have been elaborated on."

"I understand." Joanna planted her elbows on the table, her chin resting in her palms. "Go on."

"As you know, the German army invaded Athens and occupied Greece from 1941 to 1944 in spite of the strong resistance the Greeks put up. You see, controlling this country was vital to the Germans. The railroad that runs from northern Europe through Yugoslavia and into Greece was one of the main supply lines to bring goods and munitions to Rommel's troops in North Africa. They had to keep it open, no matter what the cost. Of course, the Greeks and the Allies made it as difficult as possible for them, even managing to blow up a couple of bridges."

"So where did Jenny come in?"

Alex put up his hand, drinking the last of his iced coffee. "I'm getting to that. It was in this area and all down the center of Greece toward Athens that the Resistance forces were the strongest. Later their strength led to more trouble but that's another story. Anyway, people like Jenny's husband, who were prominent in business, had the money and the connections to sneak in arms under the noses of the Germans. The tricky part was getting it up to the Greek fighters hiding in the mountains. That's where Jenny came in. Many times she and other women from the village carried guns and ammunition up the mountains on their backs or on donkeys while they were supposedly going to tend sheep or gather wood.''

Joanna's eyes widened as she took in the implications. ''And if she'd been caught?'' she whispered.

''Firing squad,'' Alex said succinctly. ''There were no second chances. Fortunately Jenny was never caught, although she had some close calls.'' He smiled faintly. ''Ask her about it sometime.''

''She doesn't mind talking about it?''

''No, not after all these years. You know how it is with old soldiers.'' He noted her empty glass and reached for his wallet. ''Do you want anything else? If not, we'll go. I thought I'd take you to see my sailboat.''

Joanna smiled. ''That sounds wonderful.'' A disturbing thought struck her and the smile slid away. ''Jenny's husband didn't die as a result of something during the war, did he?''

Alex laid several bills on the table. ''No. He survived and lived a good many years afterward.'' Taking Joanna's hand, he pulled her from her chair. ''Come on. It'll be cooler on the water than it is here.''

CHAPTER FOUR

THE VILLAGE JETTY LAY DESERTED in the afternoon sun, except for a lone fisherman who nodded to them as they passed. He sat on the concrete seawall, a section of net stretched between bare toes as his gnarled hands wove a wickedly curved needle in and out of the nylon strands.

Alex and Joanna stepped around the fishing nets with their bright yellow cork floats, which were spread out to dry, like displaced cobwebs littering the dock. The water was calm, vivid red, blue and green reflections of the anchored fishing boats shimmering like spilled paint on the surface.

The steps at the end of the jetty were slippery and wet. Joanna removed her sandals, letting them dangle by their straps from her fingers as she stepped into the rubber dinghy Alex used to get from his anchored boat to the dock. With the agility of long practice Alex followed her, steadying himself with a hand on her shoulder as he moved to the outboard engine in the stern. The little boat rocked wildly, splashing water over Joanna's bare thighs.

"Sorry about that," Alex said, pulling on the cord to start the engine.

"It's cool," Joanna replied, dipping her hand in the water and dabbing her perspiring forehead. In this heat she was almost tempted to swim to the sailboat.

Alex's boat rode at anchor in a small bay just north of the village, where the water was a deep blue, like a shadow of the sky. The boat swayed gently, a white bird resting with folded wings. Along the bow, as they neared it, Joanna could make out the name *Meltemi*, inscribed in blue cursive letters. Glossy white, with blue trim accentuating its long slender lines, the boat looked alive, even with furled sails, ready to take flight to some unknown and exciting world.

Inexplicable emotion tore at Joanna's heart, sending tears into her eyes. She blinked them back but could not shake off the sensation that the boat, so attuned to the element that cradled it, represented freedom and escape, choices she'd never had, and truthfully hadn't missed until lately. She stared at the far horizon, the faint line where violet sea joined azure sky, her vision blurred.

Why was she feeling this sadness, this sense of loss? It didn't make sense. She had a successful career, a loving family, good friends. It seemed wrong to question her blessings.

The high roar of the little outboard reverberated off the rose-hued cliffs surrounding the bay, the echoes dying as Alex cut the engine and glided to a stop. The abrupt silence jolted Joanna back to the present.

She eyed the hanging rope ladder with a certain trepidation, but Alex clambered up the wooden rungs with the ease of one who is at home on boats. Securing the painter, he called down to her, "Come on, Joanna. It's easy. I'll catch your hand when you get up here. It's only a couple of steps."

The dinghy bumped with little thuds against the side of the boat. Joanna timed its movement for a moment, then reached for the bottom rung. Clumsily, feeling as if she had six unwieldy legs instead of two, she managed to put her foot on a rung, shift her hands higher, and then groping with her bare toes find the next rung. The ladder swayed. The sandals, which she had been clutching in one hand, fell with a thump into the dinghy. She looked down at them in dismay. Great.

"Leave them," Alex said. "You won't need them." Leaning over, he gripped her wrist and, with no apparent effort, hauled her aboard.

Joanna let out her breath in a sharp puff, at the same time sweeping her hair back from her face with one hand. "Guess I need more practice at that."

Alex watched her with amusement. The motion of her hand pulled her shirt tight across her breasts, outlining their soft curves. She was small and firm, not at all voluptuous, but perfect in his eyes. When she turned slightly, the breeze molded the faintly damp cotton to her body, delineating her nipples. With surprise he realized she wasn't wearing a bra. Joanna might have flamboyant tastes in clothing but her mother had been strict about the propriety of her attire in public.

Obviously her mother no longer had a say in her wardrobe.

"Haven't you sailed?" he asked, to put his mind on a less hazardous track. "I thought everyone in Vancouver sailed."

She smiled. "I don't know about everyone. But I haven't sailed for a long time. And the few times I did, I could step directly from the dock to the boat. None of this scrambling up swaying ladders."

She glanced around, noting the uncluttered deck, the brightly polished brass trim and the satin of the wood under her feet. No wonder Alex had told her to leave her shoes; it would be sacrilege to scratch the beautiful finish. "This isn't teak, is it?"

She traced an invisible curve with one toe, drawing Alex's eyes to the flawlessly smooth skin of her foot, its tawny brown tan set off by bright pink polish on her nails. Desire stirred within him. He wanted to kiss those pretty toes. His gaze moved up. And a hell of a lot more.

Ruthlessly he pushed the urge away. "No, it's cherry. It's hard and supposedly just as durable as teak." He took her hand in his. "Come on. I'll show you the rest."

The cabin below was small but exquisitely designed and finished. The galley at one end of the combination sitting and eating area contained a refrigerator, stove and even a microwave oven. Beyond it lay a sleeping area, which could be closed off with a sliding partition to ensure privacy. The tiny bathroom consisted of a shower, sink and toilet, along with space for storage.

"All the comforts of home," Joanna said, half joking. Alex's nearness in the confined space was making her short of breath. She was aware of his breathing, even imagining she heard the beating of his heart.

"Yes." His tone was quiet, even. He appeared completely unmoved by her proximity. "It's comfortable. I've lived on it, sometimes for weeks cruising the islands. And if I want company, the seats next to the table fold out to sleep two more."

Afterward she was never sure how it happened but as she turned, her foot caught on the raised doorsill. Off balance for the barest second, she fell against him. At the feel of his hard body aligned with hers, her

breath not only died but so did all desire to ever
breathe again.

She was suddenly aware of Alex in a way that embodied profound mysteries and warned of secrets not
yet explored. As she lifted her eyes to his, she saw their
fathomless black depths and dived in, neither knowing nor caring that she might drown.

"Joanna," he groaned, lowering his head. Dimly
she registered the warmth of his mouth, the taste of his
lips on hers. At first demanding, almost fierce, the kiss
of a man aroused and driven, the movement of his
mouth on hers quickly softened, gentling in a tender
tribute to her sensitivity, her femininity.

When he raised his head the cynicism that so often
marked his features had vanished, replaced by an
expression that encompassed both confusion and
wonder.

They stared at each other, the suddenly stifling air
filled with their rapid breathing. Reality, the creak of
the mast and the rhythmic thump of the dinghy strik-
ing the hull seemed far away.

Alex spoke first, his voice hushed. "Joanna, I'd say
you definitely have grown up. You didn't use to let me
kiss you."

She wasn't sure she could talk but somehow she
found the words, although she doubted they were
prudent ones. "I did once." A memory of that first
time flooded her: the green scent of newly mown grass
and the heat of a different sun, the touch of his lips
and the first, tentative probing of his tongue, shock-
ingly erotic, arousing all the forbidden feelings her
father had warned her against. *If you let them, boys
will take advantage of you. Boys are slaves to their
passions and it's up to the girl to keep a cool head.*

Fine advice, she thought, but experience had taught her that male-female relations were much more complex than that.

"Yes, you did." Alex's voice was soft, his eyes filled with the same memory as hers. "I wasn't sure if you remembered."

Somehow his tender kiss had made her feel vulnerable enough to let down the guards she habitually used. "Of course I remember, Alex," she said quietly. "Do you think there was anything about you, in those four years, that I forgot?"

"Did you miss me, Joanna? I missed you, you know."

"Then why didn't you write? Why didn't you let me know you thought about me once in a while?"

He lifted one shoulder, then let it fall. "I thought a clean break was best. You were young. You would forget."

She was amazed at the depth of his perception of her feelings. Obviously, at seventeen he'd been sensitive far beyond his years. "Well, it didn't make it hurt any less. I thought you were my friend."

"I was, Joanna. Believe me." He reached out and laid his palm on her cheek. "Will you let me be your friend again?"

"For how long this time?" she couldn't stop herself from asking.

"I won't be the one leaving," Alex reminded her. "I live here. You'll be going whenever your holiday is over. It won't be like before." He sighed heavily, turning away from her and heading for the stairs that led to the deck. "It can never be like before."

He was right, Joanna thought sadly as she followed him.

A freshening breeze off the water cooled the deck to a comfortable temperature. Joanna inhaled deeply of the salt-scented air, wishing she'd brought a bathing suit, assuming of course that it was safe to swim in the little bay.

As if he read her thoughts Alex turned to her. "Do you want to go for a swim? It's deep enough to dive off the boat."

"What about swimsuits?"

His white teeth flashed provocatively. "We can always skinny-dip."

She drew herself up to her full height, although a smile tugged at the corner of her mouth. "No, thank you. I haven't skinny-dipped since I was ten."

"I remember. I was there. Your brothers dared you to strip in front of me."

Her face flushed. "Well, I didn't know you very well then."

"But you did it, didn't you?"

"They made me mad when they called me chicken." She arched one dark brow in challenge. "And what did you get out of it?"

"Not much," he admitted. "I already knew what females looked like. You weren't any different. I thought the same as I'd always thought, that girls certainly were deprived in a particular area of their anatomy."

Her color deepened but a crazy urge to provoke him drove her on. "And what about now? Do you still think women are deprived?"

He looked at her and for a moment she wondered if she had gone too far. The heat in his black eyes scorched her, but his tone was mild enough. "No, I think they're wonderfully made."

For the space of a heartbeat she stared at him. "Yes, and I'm sure you speak from plenty of experience." With that she dived off the side of the boat, shorts, shirt and all.

The clear water closed over her head with blessed coolness and for long seconds it was tempting just to float in the limpid world below the surface. Why hadn't she been born a mermaid, with a fish tail and long golden locks languidly flowing around her?

She was soon reminded that she wasn't a mermaid as her lungs began laboring for air. With a strong kick she thrust herself upward, breaking the surface in a rainbow spray of water.

Alex's dark head surfaced beside her and, startled, she treaded water, slicking her wet hair back from her face with both hands. He scowled. "You stayed down long enough. I thought you'd hit your head."

"My mermaid impression," she said, catching her breath. "You said it was deep enough to dive from the boat, so I did." Arching her back, she dived again, swimming underwater in the direction of the shore where a little beach formed a white crescent. Tiny ripples curled against the coarse sand, swirling around her feet as she waded through the shallows.

Alex was right behind her, and belatedly she wondered how he'd managed to change so fast. As he came out of the water, she wondered no longer. He had only pulled off his shirt and jeans. A closer look revealed that all he wore was a pair of black bikini Jockey shorts that left absolutely nothing to the imagination.

Joanna wasn't mystified by male physiology, having grown up with four brothers who'd had no compunction about walking around in various states of undress. But the sight of Alex virtually naked made another blush creep up her cheeks. She spun around, walking rapidly up the beach to the fallen rock that marked the foot of the cliff.

Damn, why was he affecting her like this? She felt as if she were on an emotional roller coaster.

She sat down on a flat boulder, gasping a little as the heat stung her thighs. In a sky burned naked of color, a blazing copper sun hung halfway to sunset. Its furnace breath poured over her, unabated, despite a twisted juniper casting its inadequate shadow on her. The sea was a cobalt blue that stung her eyes as sparks reflected from it.

Sighing, she closed her eyes against the glare, seeing multicolored balls rebounding behind her eyelids. Her head was beginning to ache.

The crunch of Alex's feet on the scattered gravel told her he had again followed. "Why don't you just leave me alone?" she muttered without opening her eyes.

Alex stared at her, noting the flushed cheeks and pale skin. Another few minutes and she would be suffering from heat exhaustion. He was willing to bet she already had one dilly of a headache. And she'd never admit it, never confess to a single weakness.

"Because you have to go back to the boat and sit where it's cool and drink about six glasses of water," he said. "Otherwise you'll be really sick. You've already got a headache, haven't you?"

"Yes," she snapped. She stood up, swaying slightly. "Okay, let's go."

Without looking around she marched to the water, plunging in as soon as she reached waist level. She soon realized she'd made a mistake in not waiting for

Alex. What had been an easy swim minutes earlier now stretched into infinity. Her arms were leaden weights, her head throbbed and she lost all sense of direction.

Where was the boat? It hadn't been this far before.

Too exhausted to lift her arm for the next stroke, she sank below the surface. It was tempting to just keep sinking, slowly spiraling to the bottom, endlessly floating in a vacuum that was wet and safe.

Suddenly Alex was grabbing her roughly by the arm and dragging her up into blinding heat. With one hand holding her soaked shirt, he hauled her into the dinghy, closing his ears to her shrieks of protest.

"You little idiot," he stormed. "Why in the hell didn't you wait for me?"

She heard the anger but also the concern. "I swam out. I could swim back." Feeling nauseated all of a sudden, she clutched her stomach. She started to retch, too miserable to notice that Alex had left her and scrambled up the rope ladder.

He returned almost at once with a glass of water that he thrust into her hand. "Here, drink this. Then you can probably manage to climb up."

Obediently she gulped the water. It tasted flat and stale, making her gag, but she forced herself to swallow. "Sorry it's not cold," Alex said, "but I haven't had time to replenish the tanks."

"Doesn't matter." She coughed and tears filled her eyes. Mortified, she wiped them with the wet tail of her shirt. The dinghy rocked gently but oddly the motion soothed rather than exacerbated her nausea.

After a few minutes Alex saw healthy color come back into a face that had been paper white. "Feeling better?" She nodded. "Okay, then, let's see if you can get up the ladder. Don't worry. I'll be right behind you."

That was what she did worry about, she realized with a flash of humor that bordered on hysteria. Those black eyes of his would be fixed on her soaking shorts that revealed everything, including the outline of her underwear. And being Alex, there was no hope that he would be too much of a gentleman to notice.

With as much aplomb as she could muster, she climbed the ladder, managing the unstable rungs more easily than she had earlier. With practice, she could become good at this, she thought.

She shook her head, marveling that the headache had subsided. Amazing thing, dehydration. She had no doubt that it had been at the heart of her illness. Now she felt fine, if still thirsty.

"Just sit in the shade while I get you some more water," Alex said in a tone that suggested he was giving an order.

"Don't you have any fruit juice?" she asked. "Or even a cold beer?"

"Alcohol contributes to the problem rather than relieves it," he explained. "And nothing is cold. I hadn't planned to eat here so I didn't keep the fridge running. Everything's warm."

"Yuck," she muttered, but when he came back with a glass of tepid water, she drank it dutifully, grimacing only when it was empty.

"And now you can have some juice," Alex said, producing a can from behind his back. "Blood."

For an instant she stared at him in horror. Then, throwing back her head, she gave a peal of laughter that had him eyeing her with concern before he joined in with her. "You remembered," she said when she could talk. "That was a long time ago."

"Of course I remember that we used to call tomato juice blood. It's a wonder your mother didn't order us all to leave the table when we kept asking each other to pass the blood." He smiled at her, the deep affinity they'd once shared back in full force. "Joanna, those years were the happiest of my life."

His expression clouded and he was silent for a moment. "After I left, it was all downhill. I lived a life that seemed glamourous, but I know now we were all pretending to be happy. Nothing was real. When it became real, some of us found we couldn't handle it. It was all bubbles, bubbles that blew away on the wind with no substance at all."

A need to know about that time tore at her. Questions trembled on her lips, but she bit them back as Alex abruptly rose and took the empty glass below. Lost in thought, she popped the top on the juice can and took a long swallow of the thick tangy liquid. It slid down with a welcome saltiness her body craved.

For a long time she sat there, lost in reflection while Alex puttered about the boat, securing the furled sails, wiping brass polish here and there, doing the constant jobs that keep sailors occupied. She watched, content to be lazy. This was the way one should spend a holiday.

She wondered again how long Alex planned to stay at the house. But she couldn't very well ask him since she'd told him to stay as long as he wanted.

They would be alone, just the two of them. Since the house was situated just outside the village, they were isolated from their neighbors. The villagers were inclined to be nosy; total strangers had asked personal questions about her marital status, her family, her job, and even how much money she made. And warned her about the unattached young men of the village. Living with Alex in the same house would cause gossip but her status as a foreigner allowed her some freedom from censure. The villagers might talk but they would have no proof of any impropriety. Nor would they ever be so forward as to mention such a possibility to her face.

She gasped aloud. What was she thinking of? An affair with Alex? She'd really been out in the sun too long.

Alex, who had disappeared below a moment ago, reappeared with a wide, cotton-covered foam pad. He spread it on the deck next to Joanna, where there would be shade for the rest of the afternoon. His hair was drying in tousled ringlets, and he looked warm and sexy, as if he'd just gotten out of bed. "Feeling better?" he asked.

She smiled, glad her thoughts had been interrupted before they led her into deeper trouble. "Much, thank you." Draining the juice can, she tossed it toward a nearby plastic trash basket, smiling again as it landed neatly inside without hitting the edges.

"Nice shot," Alex commented lazily. "Do you ever play now?" Settling himself on the mattress, he lay on his side with one arm propping up his head. He patted the striped fabric next to him. "Move over here. It's more comfortable than the deck."

She did so, aware of the near nakedness of his body but determined to ignore it. "Not often now. But by the time I finished high school, I could get more baskets out of a hundred than my brother Dino."

"I'll bet your team won most of their games."

She saw no reason to deny it. "Yeah, I guess we did. We were district champions."

He closed his eyes, shifting to lie on his back, lazy indolence in every muscle of his tanned body. Thick lashes cast tiny shadows on his cheekbones.

Joanna pulled her gaze away from him, lying back and closing her own eyes. "High-school basketball must have been the farthest thing from your mind in those days, though," she said, having decided talking was safer than looking. "You must have had an exciting life."

"I guess," he said sleepily. "But sometimes I wished I was back in Vancouver, living like a normal person."

"Then why didn't you come back? Your aunt would have been glad to have you."

"I couldn't," he said, his voice harsh. Abruptly he turned on his side, presenting his long, tanned back to her. "Go to sleep, Joanna."

What was eating him? Joanna wondered. He wasn't going to tell her anything. That was clear. But what was he hiding?

Lulled by the heat and the gentle motion of the boat, Joanna didn't speculate for long. Soon she was sleeping, a deep, dreamless slumber.

Alex heard the slowing rhythm of her breathing and turned over, his movements stealthy so as not to awaken her. Sooner or later she was going to have to know the dark secrets from his past, the secrets that might well destroy everything that was beginning anew between them.

But not yet.

And maybe not ever.

She was utterly lovely in her sleep, all long limbs and golden skin, her hair a dark nimbus around her exquisitely flushed face. He wanted her, yet he was still trying to come to terms with his desire. He'd never really thought of her as a sister, yet she'd been untouchable, out of reach.

It was a difficult concept to shake off.

Still, he couldn't deny that she was now a woman, a woman who attracted him. What was he going to do?

With any other woman it would have been simple. Enjoy her for the summer, or until either of them tired of the affair, and then a clean break. But with Joanna there was the complication of the past and his once close friendship with her family.

Joanna had the power to reach out and touch his soul.

And his greatest fear was that she would find out that he no longer had one.

After a time he slept too, but his sleep was restless. He shifted from side to side, muttering. The music was too loud, a painful assault on his ears. Lights strobed through the air, stabbing his brain and searing his eyes. Abruptly they went out, leaving him in a darkness that pulsed with noise. He saw the woman dancing ahead of him, swaying with the languid grace of a sleepwalker. *Stop!* he yelled, but no sound came out of his mouth. He groaned, struggling against a paralysis that froze his limbs. *No, stop—*

"Nooo!"

He jerked awake. Joanna leaned over him, a worried expression on her face. "Alex, wake up."

"Mmm?" He floundered in momentary confusion, his forehead beaded with sweat. "What's wrong?"

"What's the matter with you is more to the point," she said. "You were moaning and thrashing around. Did you have a nightmare?"

His eyes lost their confusion, becoming guarded, as if a barrier had slammed into place. "Something like that." Sitting up, he squinted at the lowering sun. "We should get back."

Aware of the summary dismissal, Joanna shrugged but didn't avert her gaze. He glared at her as if daring her to pry into his mind. Finally she stood up, going below to wash her face. There'd be other opportunities to question Alex.

CHAPTER FIVE

EVERY EVENING it seemed as if the entire village came out to walk along the beach promenade. In contrast to Vancouver, where people either stayed home or went to the movies, restaurants or bars in the evening, Joanna had noticed that here life was lived outdoors. Often as late as midnight children ran up and down the streets, playing tag or hide-and-seek while their elders talked or nursed an ouzo for hours.

She and Alex had gone back to the house to change their clothes. Alex had taken the bag he'd brought from his boat into the room next to hers. They hadn't discussed arrangements, but since he had gone up and closed his door, she assumed he didn't mind if she took first turn in the only bathroom. Later, or in the morning, they would have to work out a convenient schedule.

Alex took Joanna to the restaurant where they'd eaten lunch. The tables were mostly occupied, in contrast to the way they had been during the quiet noon hour. As they drank the Cokes he ordered, the sun extinguished itself in the sea but the memory of its heat lingered in the stone slabs under their feet and in the clear air. From the monastery on the mountain above the village, church bells clanged several times, calling the monks to vespers. As the sky darkened, the fishing boats pulled out, a string of lights stitched across a burgundy sea. In this quiet hour of the evening, when the village seemed entrenched in a deep peace and an almost mystically profound sense of rightness filled her soul, Joanna thought she could stay here forever.

Sometimes ambition was a greedy taskmaster. If only she had the courage to discard it.

She came back to earth as the tantalizing aroma of roasting meat drifted to her nostrils. Her stomach growled. "Excuse me."

A smile tipped up the corners of Alex's mouth. "It's been a long time since lunch. I'm hungry, too." He glanced toward the kitchen where a half dozen chickens and a whole lamb were turning slowly on a spit over a pungent charcoal fire. "It shouldn't be long now."

A couple of Gypsy children with bare feet and ragged clothes came by, holding out grubby hands. *"Kyrie, enna franco? Enna franco?"*

Alex reached into his pocket and tossed them a handful of coins. "And don't come back."

"They don't understand English, do they?" Joanna asked.

He shrugged. "Probably not, but they understood the tone."

Refusing to be intimidated, the children grinned at him, showing surprisingly good teeth. *"Efharisto, Americano."*

Alex scowled in mock ferociousness, waving a hand in dismissal. *"Fighye, pedhia."*

The smiles disappeared, and the children scampered away, clutching the coins in their hands.

The food came and they devoted themselves to eating it, allowing the conversation to lag. But later, over the second half of a bottle of wine, Alex said lazily but with a touch of provocation, "I take it you're enjoying the village, since you haven't gone screaming with boredom back to the bright lights of Athens."

"It's peaceful here, perfect for a holiday."

His eyes, intense and black, probed hers. "Then why haven't you come before? I know you've barely taken any time off since you started working for Paradise Hotels. Are you afraid some other rising young executive will usurp your position in the company if you let up?"

There was no way she was going to admit she lay awake at night sometimes, brooding on just that fear. "Dad still runs the company. He expects everybody to work as hard as he does." She threw him a barbed look. "How'd you know I haven't had a holiday?"

He leaned back in his chair, idly moving his wineglass to precisely fit one of the wet rings on the white paper covering the table. "Oh, I get a letter from Dino every now and then."

"Do you?" Dino lived in Cannes and was a professional race-car driver under contract to a major French auto firm.

Alex nodded. "He seems to think you're totally devoted to your job. And here I find you, taking two whole weeks off."

"Well, if I haven't taken a long holiday before, it's time I did, isn't it?"

"Maybe," Alex agreed lazily. "So what's the bottom line, Joanna? Is your work the most important thing in your life? And while we're on the subject, perhaps you could tell me exactly what it is you do at Paradise Hotels."

That seemed a safe enough subject since he wasn't to know the ambiguity she felt toward her job at the present time. "I'm in charge of new development. I look at possible sites for hotels and resorts, and I preside at the openings of new ones whenever that happens."

He absorbed this in silence, his eyes narrowed. Joanna fidgeted restlessly under that unblinking gaze, wondering what he saw and what was going on behind that cool and sexy facade. "And I suppose how rapidly you climb the ladder of success in your career—" he used the buzzwords with a good measure of irony in his tone "—depends on how many new sites you find and how prosperous they are once they open."

She nodded. "Something like that, yes."

"Are you thinking of putting up a hotel where my aunt's house is now?"

She'd known that was coming but she wasn't prepared for the outright hostility in his voice and attitude. She bristled in resentment. "It's my house now, not your aunt's."

"I still have a vested interest in it."

She waved her hand in assent. "Okay, I wasn't disputing that. As for whether the house would be a good hotel site, I hadn't given it much thought." This was only partly a lie. "As you pointed out this morning, there really isn't enough property attached." She gave him a shrewd look. "Unless you've changed your mind about selling me a piece of the orchard?"

"No way."

She shrugged. "Oh, well, it was a thought."

Alex scowled, his mind working. Much as he tried to convince himself that she was only baiting him with her talk of building a hotel on the property, it bothered him that she was so evasive. That wasn't like Joanna. Of course, she might have changed over the years. The Joanna he remembered had been honest, even blunt, sometimes to the point of rudeness. When she fixed you with that direct blue gaze of hers, you believed her. He didn't think basic personality changed that much.

Or did it? He'd met few honest women in his life. One was his Aunt Katerina, another Jenny. Was Joanna the third?

"Of course, it would help my career," Joanna was saying. "Dad has thought of developing a hotel in this part of Greece."

"Over my dead body," Alex retorted. "Anyway, there are enough hotels in the area. Most of the tourists like to camp, anyway."

Joanna sipped at her wine, enjoying the fruity tartness, the faint heat of the alcohol. And enjoying sparring with Alex. "So I've noticed. And they're almost all European. Paradise Hotels specializes in resorts primarily geared to the well-to-do North American traveler. Still," she added thoughtfully, "Porto Carras seems successful."

Alex set his glass down with a crash. "I wouldn't like to see a group of gray concrete monoliths here in this landscape. Besides, I know you'd get plenty of active opposition from the residents. They like things as they are."

She'd almost forgotten this was only a theoretical discussion, at least as far as she was concerned. "Put to them properly, I'm sure they wouldn't block progress. And it would create jobs, boost the area's economy."

"Along with the noise level, crime and damage to the environment," Alex stated flatly.

Realizing the peace of the evening was about to be shattered, Joanna laid a placatory hand on his. "Alex, it's only an idea. I haven't given it any serious thought at all. Let's not argue about it."

He forced a laugh that sounded more like a snarl, his voice tight as he said, "Who's arguing? As your mother used to say when she disagreed with your father, we're only having a loud discussion. We're not fighting.

"You know, Joanna," he added reflectively, his fingers toying with the keys he had taken from his pocket. "I envied you your family."

Yes, he must have. Although Joanna had taken the closeness among her brothers, herself, and their parents for granted, she suddenly realized now how they must have appeared to Alex with his unsettled childhood. Her family must have represented a haven to him and she was glad they had been able, at least partially, to fill an underlying need in him.

"I liked the order, the predictability," he continued softly. "The way all of you played together and laughed at the same things. The games on winter evenings. The way your mother made sure you were all dressed for church on Sunday."

Joanna pulled a face. "At times we sure didn't want to go."

He laughed. "Neither did I sometimes, but she always dragged me along even when my aunt had other plans." He grew serious. "I enjoyed going with you. I used to pretend I was part of the family."

Joanna covered his hand with her own, her heart aching for the lonely boy he'd been. "Alex, you were part of the family. We always considered you to be."

He nodded, his eyes fixed on a point in the distance. "For a while, I was. When I left I missed you more than I can ever tell you, all of you. Your family seemed to represent stability, the stability that makes for a decent society, a decent world. The closeness, sharing everything, your home, your problems, the interests you all had in common, the religion, your mother's strength, even your father's sometimes autocratic dictates—it made you strong. It was something I'd never had before, and haven't found since."

"Then why didn't you stay with your aunt?" Joanna asked. "You could have gone to university in Vancouver instead of in England."

His face changed, as if a mask had dropped over it. "I had to. My mother wanted me with her. But there were many times that I wanted to fly back, to be with a real family again."

Joanna didn't know what to say. Yes, she'd had an inkling but had never really realized how deeply and emotionally he'd been involved with them. It was a sobering idea.

She fell into a daydream of what her life might have been like had he stayed. Probably she would be a contented mother with several children. Alex would have been their father....

"*Yassou*, Themistocles," Alex greeted someone over her shoulder.

Joanna turned her head and saw the stooped figure of a man she'd noticed around the village on several occasions. He shuffled down the streets, one leg dragging, often muttering to himself. Not knowing how to take him, she had always given him a wide berth although no one else seemed to pay him much mind.

To her surprise, after his rather summary dismissal of the Gypsy children, Alex reached for his wallet and drew out a couple of thousand-drachma notes, folding them and discreetly tucking them into the old man's hand. The man pocketed the money with a furtive gesture, as if he didn't want anyone to witness his acceptance of charity. Then he grinned, showing jagged stumps of tobacco-stained teeth. *"Efharisto,"* he said with an odd dignity. Touching the brim of his cap, he turned and shuffled off into the darkness of an alley.

"And who was that?" Joanna queried.

"Themistocles," Alex replied, drinking from his glass as if the incident hadn't occurred.

When he said nothing further, Joanna reached across the table and pinched the solid muscle of his forearm. "Alex!"

Smiling, he relented, grabbing her hand before she could withdraw it. He held it warmly in his palm, his fingers curling over hers, distracting her and disrupting her breathing for a second. "Your hands," he murmured. "They're so soft, well kept, not at all like the grubby, callused little paws you used to have. As for Themistocles," he went on without missing a beat, "in any North American city he'd probably be the male equivalent of a bag lady, or institutionalized. Here, the whole village sort of takes care of him. He rents a little room from a lady who's a widow with grown children no longer living here. Sometimes she feeds him, more often the restaurants treat him to a meal. He doesn't need much. In exchange he washes dishes or sweeps the floor."

Compassion. It was something she had seen in the village before, an adjunct to what she had first thought of as nosiness and excessive curiosity about one's neighbors' affairs. It now struck her that the entire village was a kind of extended family. They took care of one another.

"What happened to make him like that?" At home she would have passed by a homeless person sitting on a street corner, perhaps throwing a coin or a couple of dollars, but feeling vaguely self-righteous as she did it. The poor were the government's responsibility. Here, apparently, the poor were everyone's responsibility, and she was genuinely interested in knowing why someone didn't have a proper home in a place where home and family were everything.

"He used to be a diver before the market for sponges was decimated by technology. He was crippled and brain damaged in a diving accident."

"How awful," Joanna exclaimed.

"Yes," Alex said. "But here it's accepted and life goes on." He lifted his arm, requesting the check, and they left soon after.

IN THE MORNING, as was her habit, Joanna woke early. Sunlight rollicked around her room from the window where she had left the shutters open. She sat up in bed, listening. Not a sound. Alex must still be sleeping, as well he should be. He'd been up half the night.

Although she'd fallen asleep almost immediately, she'd been awakened sometime after midnight by the sound of footsteps in the hall. She had known it was Alex; the cadence of his walk was distinctive and familiar. A moment later the light thump of the back door closing had told her he'd gone out.

It had been over an hour before she'd heard him in the hall again, and then sleep had eluded her for another hour.

Alex, an insomniac?

The thought stayed with her as she washed and dressed and went into the kitchen. She poured herself a bowl of cornflakes and milk and ate it while she stood at the window, watching the sky slowly lighten as the sun's rays crested the mountain behind the village.

Alex had changed. Of course that was to be expected, but the manner in which he had changed was not. It wasn't just the cynicism—lawyers were bound to become a little cynical—he seemed possessed with a deep melancholy, as if he had lost all hope of happiness in his life. His sense of humor still surfaced at times but the presence of haunting shadows remained, a new and disturbing part of his personality.

He'd never been moody as a teenager. She stopped short, her spoon in midair as she frowned. No, that wasn't quite true. He had had moments when he grew silent, lost in introspection, but these moods had passed quickly, as if he hadn't wanted his friends to know of them.

Putting the empty cereal bowl in the sink, Joanna wondered what his childhood had been like before he'd come to live with his aunt. He'd never talked about it.

ALEX WOKE with a heaviness in his body, and an urgent sense of lateness. Although his run through the orchards at midnight had tired him, he still hadn't fallen asleep until nearly morning.

He squinted against the bright sunlight, regretting that he'd left the shutters open last night. Hours of heat had already poured into the room. It was a fair exchange, he thought with a grimace. Total darkness was definitely not a friend to him. Heat was preferable.

He wondered belatedly if he'd disturbed Joanna last night. He'd forgotten that she was in the house until after he'd blundered down the dimly lit stairs.

Swinging his legs over the edge of the bed, he buried his head in his hands, pressing his palms to his aching eyes. When would those nightmares stop? They'd plagued him for years now, the dreams and the sleeplessness that dogged him after each episode.

He groaned, pulling on his underwear and then his jeans before heading for the bathroom. A psychiatrist would probably have a field day with the guilt inside him, the guilt and the always-present sense of failure that ate at him whenever he let down his guard.

Ruthlessly he pushed his hang-ups aside and splashed his face and chest with quantities of the icy mountain water that issued from the tap. As he mopped up with a thick terry towel, he listened to the familiar creaks of the old house. Where was Joanna? At this hour on a Saturday, probably out at the market, picking up fruit and vegetables for the weekend.

It occurred to him to wonder what she did to pass the time in this community that didn't even boast a library. True, she had brought a goodly number of magazines and books with her but a person couldn't read all day long.

He helped himself to cornflakes from the box that stood on the kitchen table, munching them thoughtfully. Joanna's food. He wouldn't have dreamed of buying cornflakes although dry cereal was becoming more popular in Greece.

A large pot bubbled gently on the back of the stove. He lifted the lid, inhaling the rich aroma of fish soup, his mouth watering as he put it back. Cornflakes suddenly lost all their appeal. Deciding to save his appetite for lunch, he dumped the remainder of his cereal down the sink.

On his way out of the kitchen he spotted Joanna's net shopping bag on a hook next to the door. So she wasn't at the market.

Nor was she in the garden, although the formidable heat outside would have prevented anything more strenuous than lying in the shade. One did not linger in the sun in the middle of the day unless it was absolutely necessary.

He found her at last, glossy hair hanging across her cheek while she stuck her head into the engine of the diminutive Renault that lived in a lean-to at the far end of the orchard. Her face was screwed up in concentration as she pulled at a bolt that had rusted into place. A spate of language that startled him cut through the condensed heat in the shed.

"Joanna," he said softly, his voice laced with amusement.

She jerked up her head, hitting it on the raised hood. "Ouch. Damn it. Do you have to sneak up like that?"

"Sorry, I thought I made quite enough noise." He peered into the grimy engine, taking note of the many little pieces that lay on the floor around the car. "What do you know about cars?"

"A lot more than you, I'll bet," she said grimly, giving the wrench a final twist. "There. I got it." She took a step back, triumphantly holding up the bolt that had given her so much trouble. Pushing back her hair, which he saw had once been confined at her nape by a rapidly slipping length of string, she swiped at her cheek. The streak of black grease she left behind gave her the look of an Indian brave about to go into battle. "Dino taught me."

"Well, I hope." He couldn't keep the skepticism out of his voice. "Are you sure you can put it back together?"

"Of course I can. Dismantling is the hard part when a car has been stored for so long. Once I put it together, it should run fine." Picking up unidentifiable objects from the floor, she inserted them into the engine. Her voice was muffled as she asked, "Why is this car still here, anyway? Why didn't you sell it?"

Alex leaned against one of the posts that supported the roof of the shed. "I thought I'd use it when I came out here on weekends but it wouldn't start."

Joanna laughed, narrowly avoiding another knock on the head as she reached for more parts. "You always were a klutz when it came to anything mechanical, weren't you?"

"Well, I can cook," he said in his own defense.

"So can I," Joanna retorted. "So what?"

He shifted uncomfortably, his cheeks warming. He was glad she wasn't looking at him. Used to dealing with people who saw only his expertise at law and business, he wasn't sure he liked having his shortcomings pointed out so bluntly.

Then he chuckled below his breath. It was obvious that Joanna hadn't changed in some respects. She was still honest to a fault, and she certainly wasn't in awe of him. Not that he would have wanted that, but a little respect would have been nice.

"And if you get it running, then what?" he asked idly.

"Why, I'll go for drives in the country, of course. There are plenty of small villages in the area that all the tourist brochures say are unique. It will be something to do, and just maybe I'll find a wonderful site for a new hotel."

As he'd thought, she wasn't the sort to remain idle for long, nor could she separate herself from her work. Well, let her build a hotel, as long as it wasn't on his land. Correction, next to his land.

He remained standing at the side of the shed, enjoying the view of her neat bottom in faded, shrunken cutoffs. Below the ragged hem her thighs were tantalizingly bare. He wondered if the tanned skin would be smooth under his hands if he touched her.

He managed to talk himself out of the impulse; she'd probably hit him over the head with the wrench she was applying inside the engine to the accompaniment of colorful curses. It was obvious that Dino had taught her more than just the fundamentals of automobile surgery.

The sun was edging around the wall of the shed, increasing the heat to unbearable levels when she finally came out from under the hood. She threw down the wrench. "There. That should do it." The note of satisfaction in her voice was unmistakable.

She turned and her breath seeped out in a silent gasp. Absorbed in the intricacies of the engine, she hadn't really looked at Alex until this moment. Now she couldn't take her eyes off him.

He hadn't shaved and the heavy stubble accentuated the hard bone structure of his face, imparting an irresistible wickedness to his handsome features. The same snug jeans he'd worn yesterday morning hung dangerously low on lean hips. Her mouth was dry and she couldn't look away. Sexy was too insipid a word to describe him.

His arms folded across his naked chest, he stared right back, with a smile that told her he knew what she was thinking, how he affected her.

That superior look did it. While Joanna experienced a sense of satisfaction in knowing Alex desired her, she saw no reason to make it easy for him.

With a snort, she turned back to the car and got behind the steering wheel. She turned the ignition key, letting the engine crank over a couple of times before gently pressing her foot to the gas pedal. With a roar and a cloud of black smoke the little car came to life, settling down to a calm purr after a moment. The smoke cleared away slowly, drifting out into the orchard.

Joanna tossed Alex a saucy "see, I told you" look as she walked around to the front of the car and slammed down the hood. Pushing back her recalcitrant hair and leaving more grease streaked rakishly on her forehead, she glanced at her watch. "I don't suppose you gave the soup a stir, did you?"

"I did," he said. "And I turned the gas down to minimum."

"Well, then it should be all right for a little longer." She got in again, putting her foot on the clutch. "I'm just going to take her out for a little spin. You could set the table if you want."

He walked over to the car. "The soup'll be okay. I'm going with you."

She shrugged as he got in on the passenger side. "Suit yourself." The smile that crept over her face as she stepped on the clutch and engaged reverse should have warned him but the years had dimmed his memory of the mischief Joanna had so often instigated as a child.

Bucking slightly on the rough track, the car settled down once they reached the paved road. Joanna drove sedately through the village, waving a greeting at several of the shopkeepers who hailed her. But once she passed the campground, she sped up, careering around the tight curves through an olive orchard. Alex checked his seat belt, then as she narrowly missed the thick gnarled boll of an olive tree, hunched down in the seat and began to pray.

"Now, wasn't that pleasant?" Joanna asked brightly a half hour later as she skidded to a stop in a cloud of dust in front of the house. "It'll be so much fun to be able to get out and explore the country-side."

Alex opened his eyes cautiously, hardly daring to believe they had returned in one piece. He was sure his stomach was still back there on that stretch of road that overhung a sheer cliff above the sea. Now he knew why he preferred to sail his boat from Volos rather than drive. Not that he feared mountain roads but that section had once been a mule track and hadn't been paved or otherwise improved substantially in the past fifty years.

And Joanna's driving was more suited to the Grand Prix than to the twisting roads of Pelion. He shuddered as he recalled the truck that had nearly shaved the paint off their fender on a curve.

"Next time, I'll drive," he said. "That truck driver is probably still shaking."

"Well, he shouldn't have been cutting the curve like that, way over on our side of the road."

"And you shouldn't have been speeding."

She seemed to realize for the first time what he'd been going through. "Why, Alex, you're all white." Then she burst into peals of laughter. "Alex, I was putting you on. The next time I'll drive like a little old lady on her way to church."

Oh, yeah? he thought derisively. *Fat chance of that.* Her personality and her propensity for getting into trouble apparently hadn't changed a bit.

CHAPTER SIX

THEY HAD JUST FINISHED their lunch of fresh bread and the savory fish soup, when a boy appeared around the corner of the patio with a message from Jenny.

Alex pressed a coin into the small hand despite the child's attempts at refusal, then sent him on his way skipping along the rough path in scarred bare feet. He unfolded the single, lined sheet apparently torn from an old notebook. "Alex," it said in Jenny's spidery handwriting. "Could you please come over during siesta? Costas and Stella are in Volos for the day. Bring Joanna with you if she wants to come."

He smiled. He could just see the gleam in that inveterate old matchmaker's eye as she wrote the last sentence.

"I hope you weren't planning on taking a nap," he said as he walked into the kitchen.

Joanna turned from the sink where she had been rinsing the dishes. "Me? I think sleeping in the daytime is a waste of time. Who was that?"

"A boy with a message from Jenny." He paused, his smile broadening. "She wants to see us both."

Joanna glanced down at her grease-streaked T-shirt. "I'll have to change first."

Rubbing a hand over his beard stubble, Alex agreed. "I'll give you a hand with the dishes."

He let her shower first, and while she was upstairs changing her clothes, he shaved and found himself a clean shirt that wasn't too wrinkled.

The heavy afternoon heat pressed down on them as they walked along the deserted street. Even the birds were silent, and a dog lying panting in a doorway only glanced up, too lazy to bother barking.

Jenny sat in a rocking chair on her shaded veranda, waving an ivory-handled fan before her perspiring face, and occasionally sipping from a tall glass of iced tea at her elbow. To Joanna she looked pale, not nearly as sprightly as she had yesterday. Of course Joanna didn't know her well but her observation was confirmed when Alex addressed the old woman with the candor only possible between good friends of long-standing.

"You look like you should be napping instead of entertaining," he said forthrightly.

Jenny gave a faint laugh that seemed forced. "Those two will be the death of me."

Alex motioned Joanna to the other chair on the porch while he seated himself on the cool stone step a little below Jenny. "What do they want now? More money?"

"You guessed it." Jenny turned to Joanna. "Would you be a dear and get the pitcher of iced tea out of the fridge? And bring a couple of glasses." She winked slyly. "Don't worry. I won't tell the story until you're back."

Jenny was pensively rocking and fanning when Joanna returned. Joanna poured out two glasses of iced tea, also refilling Jenny's glass with amber liquid and clinking ice cubes. Then she sat down again, sipping the tangy brew and waiting for Alex to reopen the subject.

She had to admit she was curious. Jenny struck her as a strong, confident woman, not one to let people take advantage of her. Her nephew and his wife must have some hold over her for her to feel this obligation to them when she clearly did not welcome their presence.

Alex drank half his iced tea in a single gulp, then set the glass down and fixed Jenny with a resigned look. "Okay, Jenny. Let's have it. What's their latest angle?"

"Another apartment building that's supposed to be the bargain of the century."

"Doesn't that idiot know when to quit?" Alex demanded. "Last time he had this kind of a deal arranged and you gave him money for the down payment, he lost it all gambling."

Jenny exhaled noisily, her gaze fixed on the rough floorboards of the veranda. "He says this time will be different."

Alex snorted. "How?" he asked rhetorically. "So are you going to give him the money?"

For a long moment Jenny didn't answer. Joanna waited, realizing there was more to the story, but to her dismay a tear slid down Jenny's wrinkled cheek. "Jenny, what is it?"

Jenny reached over and patted Joanna's hand, as if Joanna was the one who needed comfort. "It's all right, dear. He won't be able to do anything." She lifted her eyes to Alex, the tears firmly under control now. "There is no money."

"No money?" Alex echoed in surprise.

"No money," Jenny repeated. "It's all gone. Every penny. What I gave him last time was the end of it."

Alex's eyes blazed, his body radiating tension and a towering anger. "Then why did you give it to the deadbeat?"

"Because dear Ari asked me to look after his relatives. He made me swear I wouldn't abandon them if they were ever in need."

Joanna sank back into the chair from which she'd half risen. At home such a situation would have been beyond anyone's belief. Here it was all too common, the famous *philotimou* carried to the ultimate degree. If Jenny had promised her husband she would not turn away his relatives, no matter how obnoxious and grasping they turned out to be, she could no more go back on her word than command the sun to stand still in the sky.

"Well, tell them," Alex said bluntly.

Jenny twisted the ivory handle of the fan between age-spotted fingers. "I have. They don't believe me. They say Ari had a cache of gold coins stashed away during the war, to hide it from the Germans."

"Do they have grounds for this idea?"

She resumed fanning, slowly moving the accordion-folded paper in front of her face. "Not as far as I know. Ari never said anything about it. If it was true, I can't believe he wouldn't have told me."

"I can't either," Alex declared, although having been a child when Ari died, he had only Jenny's stories about her husband's character to go on. By both Jenny's and the villagers' accounts, Ari had been a sterling character who was still well thought of. He'd helped anyone in need, especially during the civil war that had turned the already battered country into a scene of chaos after the retreat of the Germans.

He drained his glass, his expression thoughtful. "Give me a little time, Jenny. I'll try to come up with something to get rid of Costas." He grinned suddenly. "Maybe we can organize a plan to get the whole village to make things thoroughly uncomfortable for them. I'm sure all your friends would be only too happy to cooperate."

Jenny emitted a pale ghost of her usual hearty laugh. "I'm sure they would, but I don't really think it's fair to involve them in my problems."

Alex stood up, moving across the warped floorboards to give Jenny a hug. "Just put them off the best you can. I'll see if I can come up with something to send them hiking back to Athens."

Tears again stood in her eyes. "Alex, you're a dear."

He regarded her seriously. "No, I'm not, and you know it."

She leaned forward and bussed him firmly on his lean cheek. "That's all in the past. It's over, *pedhi mou*. What counts is the person you are now."

A frown creased Joanna's forehead. What had happened in Alex's past to give him this guilt complex? She had the impression that he felt he'd committed sins that put him beyond redemption, sins that he could never atone for. What could have been so terrible that it still haunted him?

She filed her questions away in the back of her mind. Jenny would probably know. She'd come one day and ask her.

Alex took Joanna's hand and she, puzzling over what he had inadvertently revealed, clasped his firmly.

Somewhere deep inside him lived a demon, and the least she could do was not add to the torment in his mind and heart. If he wanted to hold her hand, if it gave him comfort, she would reciprocate.

"Goodbye, Jenny," she said softly as they went down the steps.

"Goodbye, Joanna," Jenny said. "Come and see me again."

"Thanks, I will."

They were at the gate when Jenny called after them. "Oh, Joanna, the postman told me he had a registered letter for you. He was by your house this morning but no one seemed to be home." The question she must have been burning to ask lay on her face.

Hiding a smile, Joanna said, "I was working on Katerina's car."

It appeared that Jenny possessed none of Alex's doubts about Joanna's mechanical ability. "The Renault? Did you get it going?"

"Did she ever!" Alex put in with a wry grimace.

Jenny looked from one to the other, her eyes bright with curiosity. "Anyway, you can pick up the letter at the post office."

"Sure. Thanks."

"I didn't know the post office opened on Saturday afternoons," Joanna said as they walked slowly down the street. With one hand she shaded her eyes against the glare of the sun, intensified to an excruciating degree by the whitewashed walls of the buildings around them. Sweat trickled down her back. Not a creature moved in the entire village, and she was reminded of Kipling's poem about mad dogs and Englishmen. Then, as if to dispute her thoughts, a rooster, blatantly out of tune with the time of day, crowed raucously.

"The post office is in the back of the pharmacy. I know the man. He's usually there, working on his books. He should let us in long enough to pick up the letter." He turned his head and looked at her. "I thought you were on holiday. What would be so important that the sender would register the letter?"

"Probably some emergency and Dad figuring I'm the only one who can take care of it." But the bored note in her voice told him this was not a situation she'd anticipated.

THE LETTER WAS FROM TONY. She knew that black scrawl from a hundred interoffice memos. Thanking the pharmacist, she walked outside, clutching the thick envelope. What could he have to say that was so important? Nothing about work, she decided, so it must be personal. In light of their last conversation, she could imagine the letter's content. This was an aggravation she would rather postpone.

"Well, aren't you going to open it?" Alex asked.

"It's my letter. I'll open it if and when I please."

He stared at her. "Well, excuse me," he said with dry emphasis.

Even back at the house he didn't leave her side long enough for her to open the letter in relative privacy. She could have gone to her room and closed the door but she was afraid that would whet his curiosity further. Instead she tossed the letter on the kitchen table and moved to the fridge in search of inspiration for their supper, a rather obvious procrastination since they weren't planning to eat for some hours yet.

Feigning casualness, Alex picked up the letter. "This isn't from your father," he said. "Who is Anthony Stamos?"

"It's none of your business." Her head was still in the fridge, although her mind was far from the plastic sack of vegetables she'd bought that morning or the neatly wrapped packet of meat. They could have the rest of the fish soup, she decided, and if Alex was still hungry after that, he could fix himself a couple of eggs. Slamming the fridge door shut, she went over to where Alex stood studying her letter. "Give me that. It's mine and you're snooping."

"I wouldn't have to snoop if you'd tell me who is so important to you that he sends you a registered letter. Who is this guy?"

She glared at him with eyes that could have bored holes in steel. "A friend."

His brows rose. "A friend?"

"Yes, a friend." Anger seethed inside her. "Is that so hard to understand? We work together."

Alex stared at her. He looked as immovable as one of the ancient pillars of the Acropolis. "There's more to it than that, isn't there?"

"He's talked about marriage," she admitted reluctantly, aware that she had previously given Alex the impression that there was no particular man in her life.

"He? What about you?" Alex apparently wasn't going to rest till he had the whole story.

"What is this, a cross-examination by the prosecution?" she retorted, hiding her distress behind a strong offense.

Alex made a sound she couldn't begin to interpret, and wasn't sure she wanted to in any case. "No. It's just strange that you never mentioned this Tony before when it seems you're so close."

Joanna drew a deep breath. "I like Tony a lot. The projects we've worked together on were among the most enjoyable and productive of my career."

"Sounds like a good basis for a relationship," Alex said more calmly.

"Sure, but that's as far as it went." She gestured impatiently. "Dad said Tony's in love with me."

"Is he?" Alex asked without particular emphasis.

"I didn't want to see it, but Dad's probably right. The problem is I'm not in love with Tony, but there's no denying he'd make a perfect husband. Dad says so, too."

She stared past Alex out of the kitchen door, hearing the loud crow of a rooster nearby, and the more distant bark of a dog. The musical tinkle of sheep bells carried across the orchard, conveying peace, a peace she was far from feeling.

"Do you have to listen to him?" Alex asked.

"No. Of course I don't," Joanna blurted out. "But you can understand the pressure it puts me under." She slammed her fist against the doorjamb in frustration. "Oh, if I had a normal family, I wouldn't have these problems. I wouldn't feel honor bound to work in the family corporation." She stopped, appalled at what she had just admitted. That was it, wasn't it? That was why she stayed even though her satisfaction with the work had lessened. Throwing away restraint, she plunged ahead. "I'd like to do something on my own for once."

"But Socrates would be hurt if you left Paradise Hotels." Alex knew all about the intricate honor and pride in Greek families.

"Yes." She sighed and went over to sit down on the bench next to the kitchen hearth. "Remember, Alex, how I used to say I'd like to someday run a quaint little country inn."

"Yeah, I remember. Why didn't you?"

She picked at a loose thread on the hem of her shorts, her face pensive. "I joined the company."

"To please your father."

She lifted her head, tossing back her hair. "No. Not entirely. It was what I wanted at the time, to prove I could do it. You see, everyone's a success in my family."

That was true, Alex knew. Although they had followed careers more conventional than Dino's, the others also were outstanding in their endeavors. Joanna's oldest brother James was a noted geologist who could find oil where no one suspected it hid. Michael was a partner in a major Vancouver law firm, and Nicholas had made a name for himself as a pediatrician.

"If I quit," Joanna said, "they'll think I'm a failure."

"Perhaps, perhaps not," Alex said reasonably. "Depends what you followed it up with. Joanna, did something happen before you left? Is that why you're here?"

"Nothing happened." *Except for some soul-searching,* she added to herself. "No. I just needed a holiday."

His expression concerned, he sat down beside her. "Tell me, is this Tony the first man who's been seriously interested in a relationship with you?"

"Of course not. He's not the only man I've dated."

"But you like him better than the others. So why the uncertainty? Why are you dithering?"

Getting up, she paced from the door to the table and back again. "Because I'm not sure, damn it. And I think I should be sure before I marry anyone." She raked her fingers through her hair in agitation. "Tony and I are friends but sometimes I feel there's something missing."

"Friendship can turn to love," Alex said without much conviction. What was love anyway, besides a romantic notion that inexplicably supported a billion-dollar network of books, movies and soap operas? "You wouldn't want to marry someone who wasn't your friend, would you?"

"No," Joanna agreed. "That's what makes it so hard. I don't want to hurt Tony."

"You don't want to hurt Socrates. You don't want to hurt Tony." Alex's patience had obviously run out. His voice was heavy with sarcasm. "What *do* you want, Joanna?"

"Oh, you're a hell of a lot of help," she snapped. Crossing her arms over her chest, she turned away from him. "What do I want? A little happiness. That's what I want, with no pressure from anyone."

"Doesn't everyone?" Alex muttered to himself. He got up and handed her the letter. "Why don't you open this? See what friend Tony has to say?"

A great deal, Joanna thought, judging by the bulkiness of the envelope. "Okay," she said with a peculiar fatalism.

Inserting a fingernail under the flap, she ripped it open, extracting the thin airmail sheet. Ignoring the thicker envelope that fell onto the floor, she unfolded the letter, scanning it rapidly. Oddly, it was short and contained little of any consequence. Below the signature was a cryptic message. Joanna stared at it, perplexed. "Your dad says hi and that you might want to consider the enclosed. Love, Tony."

A sound from Alex drew her attention from the letter. He looked angry.

"Mr. and Mrs. Socrates Paradisis request your presence at the wedding of their daughter Joanna Eleni Katerina Paradisis to Anthony Stamos, et cetera. The date is blank." His eyes bored into hers. "What is this, Joanna? Some kind of joke? Looks to me like the noose is already around the neck."

Feeling the blood drain from her face, Joanna reached out her hand. "Give me that."

In mounting horror she scanned the embossed gold letters on the thick cream paper. The word *sample* had been stamped across the engraving. She clenched her fist around the letter still in her other hand, loosening her fingers when she heard the crackle of the flimsy paper. "So this is what Dad decided to do." She now understood the remark he'd tossed over his shoulder as he left her office last Thursday. Something about making up her mind.

Well, he wasn't going to make up *her* mind.

Hurling both the invitation and the crumpled letter across the room, she allowed her temper full rein. "He's trying to railroad me. That's what he's doing!"

"Who, Socrates?" Alex asked, surprised by her outburst. "Or Tony?" He didn't know who made him angrier, Socrates and Tony for their manipulations, or Joanna for allowing it.

"My dad," she said tonelessly, her anger giving way to an icy detachment. "But I've no doubt that Tony knew about it. He seems to talk more to my father about his feelings than he does to me."

Alex's eyes flashed. "Maybe you intimidate him."

Tony intimidated? The idea was so ludicrous that she nearly laughed. "No. That's not it."

"Then why didn't he talk to you?"

"He did, Alex, in a way." A guilty expression appeared on her face. "But I sort of put him off."

"But without slamming the door on his hopes," Alex said bluntly. "Which makes me think you're not sure. Joanna, if you knew there was no possibility of a future with Tony, why didn't you tell him? You never used to be so coy, so sparing of other people's feelings."

"Maybe I've developed a little sensitivity along with growing up," she retorted, stung by his reference to her old habit of speaking first and thinking later.

"It wasn't sensitivity you lacked and had to develop. You always had plenty of that. But you were assertive, knew what you wanted and went after it. Just let anyone stop you. You were all over them like a steamroller. So what happened to take the starch out of you? I'm beginning to think this Tony isn't the man for you after all. He'll stifle you."

"And what do you know, Alex? You don't even know Tony."

"Do you love him, Joanna?"

Did she? If she did, would Alex have the power to fill her with a yearning every time he came near her, or touched her? Maybe Tony was just a comfortable habit she was reluctant to break.

"I told you. No, not that way."

"Did you tell Tony that?"

"Yes." She lifted her chin in defiance. "As a matter of fact, I did."

"But you're still keeping him around, just in case nothing better comes along." Alex shook his head. "What's happened to you, Joanna? You never used to be afraid to take a few chances. You used to have such dreams. What happened?"

"I grew up, Alex," she said, her voice tight with resentment. "This is real life, not a fantasy world. I've learned it's safer to plan things, think them through rather than going off the deep end on impulse."

"Sometimes a person has to take chances, to use an opportunity when it presents itself, to grab a rainbow before the sun steals it away."

"Is that how you live your life, Alex?"

That made him pause. "Not any more," he admitted after a moment. "But perhaps I should, once in a while."

He took a step toward her, and she backed away, not trusting the look in his black eyes. "Alex, don't you dare lay a finger on me."

"Finger wasn't what I had in mind," he said with a sardonic grin. "Just a little experiment I want to try."

"Don't you dare," she warned, her pulse speeding with an excitement she tried to tell herself was fear.

"What will you do?" he asked with arrogant challenge.

"I—I—I'll never forgive you." She hated the way her voice wavered, knowing he heard the ineffectiveness of the threat.

"Well, I guess I can weather that. I've got thick skin. So I might as well be hung for a sheep as a lamb." With that he laid his hands on her shoulders, drawing her into the heat of his body.

She knew it would be useless to struggle, nor, after a moment, did she want to. As she felt the touch of his lips on hers, emotions crowded in on her, making it hard to distinguish reality. The long suppressed memory of that kiss he had given her the day he'd left Vancouver rose in her mind. In the midst of the confusion of loading his bags into the taxi, he'd pulled her into the dark hall closet and there among the moth-ball-scented winter coats he'd kissed her, once more arousing forbidden passion in her teenage breast.

But in an instant the memory faded, replaced by a breathless reality that left her weak and trembling in his arms, her hands clinging to his shoulders. This was real, the now, the forever.

Rapturously she opened her mouth to him, absorbing the anger that still simmered under the passion, feeling it vanish as the kiss grew deeper, more demanding. She welcomed the demand, answering it with her own need, as she gloried in the sweet entry of his tongue into her mouth.

"Alex," she moaned when he paused to drag in a labored breath. "Alex."

He kissed her again, feather-light caresses over her downswept eyelids, a hot tongue tip grazing her cheeks, teasing the corners of her mouth before delving deeply inside once more. Spreading both hands on her rounded bottom, he pressed her close, moist heat pooling in the center of her body as she felt his arousal. She wanted him, all the passion she had once been too afraid to express flooding through her like a spring-swollen river out of control.

"Alex," she whispered again, pushing closer to feel the hardness of him against the place that ached to receive him.

"What is it, Joanna?" His voice was low, harsh, as if he could barely speak.

"I want you," she said, mindless with the hunger raging in her. "Alex, I want you."

To her complete and utter astonishment, he pushed her away, keeping his hands on her shoulders but putting distance between their bodies. "Do you, Joanna?" he said with cynicism turning his eyes as hard as anthracite. "Are you so sure after one kiss?" He paused, his expression sober and thoughtful. "But at least you reacted, you responded. *You didn't plan it.*"

Stung by the vehemence of his words, Joanna pulled herself free. She hugged her arms around her chest, shivering with overwrought nerves. Yes, she'd responded, as if they'd never been apart.

"Joanna." The sudden gentleness of his tone washed over her like a soothing ointment. "Joanna, I think you need some time. I'm going back to Volos." He stepped close and touched his fingertip to her cheek. "I'll be seeing you."

CHAPTER SEVEN

JOANNA'S EYES BURNED but she refused to cry. She reread Tony's letter, which said nothing, and sat for a long time with the wedding invitation in her hand, staring sightlessly at the gold leaf that formed the elegant engraving.

Of course she couldn't marry Tony. Alex had shown her that once and for all. His methods had not been subtle but the doubts she'd had before had finally crystallized in the smelter of Alex's anger and passion. In the kisses she'd shared with Tony, she hadn't experienced a fraction of the stunning emotion she had in one moment with Alex.

She had always been proud of her control. All her previous dealings with men had been strictly on her terms. Although she'd been involved a couple of times in promising relationships before meeting Tony, neither had worked out. Each time she'd emerged with both her heart and her pride intact.

She wasn't a virgin although her father probably lived with the illusion that she was. She could just picture what he would say if anyone dared to hint otherwise. "My daughter? Why, she's as innocent as the first snow of winter." She was content to let him keep the fantasy that women only succumbed to passion after the priest's blessing; fathers were fragile where their daughters were concerned. Men were, of course, ruled by different ethics. They were allowed to have their little flings. It was a double standard that would have infuriated Joanna if she hadn't loved her old-fashioned father the way she did.

But this business of ordering wedding invitations in an attempt to force her into line with his wishes, this was going too far.

She had half a mind to place a call home, blistering the telephone wires. Wisdom prevailed, however. She would write and send the letter registered, giving her and them more time. Knowing she was again running, she still realized that it was better than giving in to pressure. From the time she was born, she had always attempted to keep up with four older brothers, had always lived with the specter of potential rejection. She had to achieve; she had to make her own decisions. She couldn't let either her father or Tony coerce her into any hasty moves.

Yes, that was what she'd do. Write a letter. Now, while her thoughts were clear and fresh in her mind. She would mail it tomorrow, no, Monday, since the post office would be closed tomorrow.

The sun went down, and darkness had lessened the heat slightly by the time she'd completed her task. She sealed the letter in an envelope and licked the flap after inserting the sample invitation with ''Not possible'' scrawled across it.

Placing the letter on the china cabinet next to the door, she glanced around the kitchen. The lamp above the table made a soft pool of light in the center but the corners were dark and shadowed. The slowly ticking clock on the mantel indicated that it was past ten.

No wonder her stomach rumbled. She hadn't eaten since noon. Hurrying to the fridge, she pulled out the saucepan of soup and lit a burner under it.

Alex had left hours ago. She'd hoped he might change his mind, but he hadn't returned. He was right about one thing. She needed time to think.

Turning from the pot she was stirring, she stared at the letter. Had she been firm enough? She certainly hoped so.

THE SUN WAS ALREADY HIGH in the sky when Joanna woke the next morning. Rolling out of bed, she wandered over to the window. Another beautiful day, she thought. Sonorous bells tolled out the first call to prayer in the village church. Obeying a sudden impulse, Joanna decided to go. If she couldn't find the answer to her problems within herself, perhaps an hour of meditation in the cool, dark sanctuary would give her insight.

The measured cadence of the bells played a background to her disquieting thoughts as she washed in the bathroom, then went back upstairs to make her bed and put on a dress suitable for church. She finally settled on a white knit that covered her shoulders and her upper arms and accentuated her tan, enhancing the rosy glow of her cheeks. Not quite the effect she would have liked; an ethereal paleness would have been a much more accurate portrayal of her mood. Still, there was something to be said for keeping up a bold front.

Jenny was in church, a beacon in a youthful dress printed with pastel flowers, standing among her peers who wore the unrelieved black of village widows. Joanna hurried forward and lit a candle, then paid for

and took another for good measure, genuflecting before the stand that held the church's most treasured
icons.

Any remarks Jenny might have made to her were
postponed as the congregation knelt for the solemn
high point of the mass. Joanna closed her eyes, allowing the mellow chanting of the priest to flow over
her. As always, the hot scent of melted wax and the
drifting aroma of incense gave her a sense of peace.
She recalled her childhood when she had sat in church
every Sunday next to her mother, father and brothers.

After the service Jenny insisted Joanna come to her
house for coffee and biscuits. In summer, mass was
held early, ending by midmorning. The coffee shops
were barely opening, taking advantage of the after-
church trade.

"The Terrible Couple didn't come back from Volos," Jenny said with a droll expression as they walked
along. Her ebullient mood was a complete contrast to
yesterday's anxiety. "Maybe they'll stay there."

"Maybe they've given up," Joanna replied but
Jenny's expression told her there wasn't much chance
of that.

"Where's Alex this morning?" Jenny asked,
glancing behind them as if she expected him to appear at any moment.

"He's gone back to Volos." Joanna was proud of
the steadiness of her voice. "He left yesterday."

Jenny accepted the explanation with surprising
equanimity. "Well, I'm sure he'll be back." She gave
Joanna a sly look as they entered the house. "Who is
Anthony Stamos?"

"Isn't anything private around here?" Joanna
snapped.

Jenny gave her a broad smile that effectively disarmed her and compelled her to smile back. "No. Nothing is. I received four suggestions just this morning that I should warn you about the impropriety of sharing the house with Alex."

Joanna's eyes narrowed. "I asked him to be my guest. It's none of anyone's business."

"I reminded the concerned parties of that. Also of the fact that you are both adults. But they still said that you should be warned." Jenny affected a scandalized tone. "'Men take advantage of these situations. You must tell her to be careful.' Of course, Maria is the biggest gossip in the village and was probably delighted to have something to talk about. So, who is this man who sends you special-delivery letters?"

"A friend." Even to Jenny she wasn't going to reveal all the complications of her life.

"Okay. Don't tell me," Jenny said placidly, giving Joanna the unmistakable impression that the old lady would ferret out the whole story sooner or later and that she could afford to wait.

Over coffee Jenny related the latest village gossip. There was plenty that had nothing to do with Joanna or Alex, but eventually his name came up again. "He's done so much for me, Alex has," Jenny said with deep fondness in her voice. "And he refuses to take a single drachma in compensation."

Alex was an enigma. There was no doubt about it. "How did he happen to settle here?" Joanna asked, with only a fleeting thought that Alex might resent her questioning his friend.

"You mean why isn't he a big shot in Athens or, for that matter, in any major city of the world? After his turbulent youth I suppose he values peace and privacy. His law practice isn't his only source of income. Alex came into a number of investments from his late father when he turned twenty-one. He's also involved in several businesses, both here and in England."

Joanna nodded. It had occurred to her that Alex's family might have fallen on hard times, despite her memory of his mother's extravagant wardrobe. But, if he was still reasonably well-off, why had he chosen to live in a quiet place like Volos?

And the anger in him, the cynicism and the restlessness—what was behind them? What had happened to drive him away from London and the lifestyle he'd seemed to enjoy once? She couldn't believe it was as simple as appearances made it.

"What happened to him about seven years ago?" she asked.

Jenny regarded her with a bright, unblinking stare, a severe expression lining her face. "What makes you think anything did?" *Cagey,* Joanna thought. Okay. Jenny hadn't known her long. Why should she divulge Alex's secrets even though she made no bones about her own? "His life seems to have changed suddenly."

"Maybe he got nostalgic for his mother country. That's a condition that strikes many expatriate Greeks to judge by the number who return to live out their retirement."

"Maybe." Joanna didn't bother to hide her frustration. "And maybe something happened to wake him to that view."

Jenny seemed to take pity on her. "Joanna," she said gently. "I'm afraid it's not my story to tell. You'll have to ask Alex."

"So there *is* a story."

Jenny inclined her gray head, making a business of arranging the cups on the tray. "I'm not saying anything more. I've said too much already. Ask Alex."

Sighing, Joanna said, "I tried, but he just pretended he didn't know what I was talking about."

"When he's ready, he'll tell you." Jenny patted Joanna's hand, tightening cool fingers around it for a moment. "I'm sorry. I may give the impression of being brash and noisy sometimes. It's an old lady's privilege to be eccentric. But I don't betray anyone's secrets, not even when I feel it's for their own good. I can't tell you about Alex." She rose with a lightness that belied her years, and picked up the tray. "Stay to lunch, dear. Keep me company."

But Joanna was no longer in the mood for anyone's company. "Thank you." She forced a smile. "But could I make it another time? I'd like to be alone."

Jenny took no offense, merely fixing her with another of those bright, penetrating looks. "I understand, dear. But do come by tomorrow morning when you've done your shopping. I always keep a pot of coffee going."

"Thank you. I will."

Outside the heat had increased to awesome proportions. Nevertheless, instead of walking toward her house, Joanna headed up the path that lead to the bay where Alex kept his boat.

The water was calm. Tiny ripples caught the sun and sparkled like a field of diamonds. She wondered how long it would be before he returned. She was missing him already.

Volos was hot and humid. Although he'd given his secretary the week off, Alex had decided to return to his office. But the odds and ends of work on his desk failed to hold his interest. He was bored.

He'd been content with his life even if it wasn't very exciting. He'd even been moderately happy, never missing any of the frenetic activities he'd found vital to his existence in his youth. His present life had fulfilled him, he thought.

Until he'd met Joanna again, and disturbed the sleeping memories of an ardent love.

He'd told her she needed time to think, an insufferably arrogant assumption on his part, no doubt. However, it was true, as far as it went. But he now admitted his abrupt departure had been a knee-jerk reaction that had its roots in jealousy. She'd seemed happy to be with him, free with her affection, and, he'd assumed, honest. It hadn't occurred to him that she might have a man waiting for her in Vancouver. He'd thought they could have a good time together, and at the end of her holiday part friends, no complications.

His reaction to the letter from Tony warned him that things were already complicated.

He exhaled slowly, turning his chair and staring out of the window at the shimmering, heat-burdened city. What he ought to do was go on a cruise of the islands, just him and his boat, the mistress who was safe, who made no emotional demands on him.

But he knew that for once his usual escape was not going to satisfy him. Without Joanna he would still be empty. He needed her, the quick wit honed by years of sparring with a lively family, the sharp intelligence that shone from her eyes, the femininity that had matured and become womanly.

He needed her and it frightened him. He'd vowed no woman would ever make him feel that way again.

Joanna put him off his stride. He was attracted to her in ways unfamiliar but strangely exhilarating. Although he'd tried to analyze the feeling, tried to take it apart and really look at it, it had proved frustratingly elusive. He wasn't even sure if it was the present Joanna who attracted him, or some half-baked desire to relive the past.

It had to be more. He didn't think he'd ever forget the sick feeling that had invaded him when he'd seen the name on the envelope she'd received Saturday. Although reason told him it was highly unlikely that a woman of Joanna's age and appearance had no men in her life, since she'd mentioned no one, he'd assumed she wasn't involved at present in a serious relationship. The letter indicated otherwise.

Why hadn't she told him about Tony?

He'd had a right to know.

He snorted in self-disgust. What rights did he have? It was presumptuous of him to think he did.

Spinning the chair back to face his desk, he determinedly rifled through the papers lying there. Everything was up to date, no new cases pending. Summer was slow at the best of times, this year particularly so.

He had contacted a private detective he knew in Athens to look into the life of Costas Astridis. It might be weeks before he heard from him.

There was nothing to keep him in his office. He thought of the village with its soft nights, gentle sea breezes, and Joanna.

Was she ready to see him again?

Was he ready to see her? Or was he putting off their next meeting because he was scared?

He stood up, squaring his shoulders to hide the uncertainty that was stronger now than when he was seventeen. He was a man. Men weren't scared.

JOANNA HAD FORMED THE HABIT of rising early and taking long walks before the sun began to scorch the land. Her walks were seldom solitary; there were always villagers going to the orchards, or to their fields, or up to the mountains with flocks of sheep or goats. She would walk with them until their ways parted, talking as she went about the price of produce or wool, the insular limits of their community, and she would always answer their avid questions about life in Canada. Other areas of Greece were dimly known to them; the outside world seemed a vast paradise to which they could never aspire, a Disneyland too fantastic to imagine.

She'd done a lot of thinking in the past three days, about her career, her family, Tony, her future. And about Alex. She'd made one firm decision, putting the other considerations on hold.

She had to see Alex again. If he didn't return to the village before Friday, she planned to drop by his office after her morning appointment with Mihalis Samaras.

ON WEDNESDAY MORNING, under a pearly dawn sky, she found Jenny working in her garden, and stopped to talk.

"I don't sleep well, Joanna," Jenny said, leaning on the handle of her hoe and rubbing her lower back. "One of the infirmities of old age."

"Neither does Alex," Joanna said impulsively.

Jenny's eyes gleamed slyly. Before she could voice one of her outrageous suggestions, Joanna added hastily, "No. It's not what you think. The nights he stayed at the house, he seemed to be up half the night. I heard him."

Jenny was not to be stopped. "Maybe he'd sleep better beside you."

Joanna had no reply although the images that sprang into her head would have shocked even Jenny.

The older woman spoke again, quietly, seriously. "He'll be back, you know. And soon."

"What makes you say that?" Joanna tried to still the sudden leap of her heart.

Jenny leaned on the hoe, staring off at the mountain where rose-and-amethyst scarves of mist heralded the rising sun. "Just a feeling. I think seeing you again opened up a lot of memories he'd thought safely buried. When he's ready to face them, he'll be back."

Joanna laughed lightly. "Should I barricade my doors?"

Jenny regarded her seriously although a twinkle edged into her eyes. "Might not be a bad idea."

Whether or not Jenny possessed the power to predict the future, Joanna wasn't sure. But that evening, just before sunset, Alex was back.

He greeted her with cheerful nonchalance and no undercurrents that spoke of dark secrets. "Is the offer to stay in the house still open?"

"For as long as you like." She decided she would take her cue from his easy mood, even though her body temperature shot up a notch when he walked past her with a small duffel bag. A moment later he went out again and then returned, carrying a large cardboard box that seemed to move when he set it on the floor.

He pulled up the flaps and from the interior extracted the largest orange cat Joanna had ever seen, an ugly, lean, sinuous beast that promptly bit his thumb to show its gratitude for the long confinement. Cursing, he dropped it on the floor, putting his thumb to his mouth and sucking at the wound. "Ungrateful beast," he muttered. "He's never liked me."

Joanna felt a lump in her throat. Instinctively she knew he'd brought the cat as a peace offering. When she was about eleven her pet cat had been killed by a speeding car. Alex had gone out and bought her another. Then, as now, the gesture had been endearing and unexpected, a side of Alex's complex nature that he revealed only to her.

The cat might not like Alex but apparently he had no animosity toward Joanna. He sniffed at her ankles, then wound himself around her, rubbing his sleek sides against her legs and purring as throatily as a Ferrari.

"I didn't want to leave him alone at my place," Alex added, feeling a little awkward when Joanna didn't speak. He didn't deem it necessary to mention that he was often away and the cat had always managed on his own before.

Joanna lifted her eyes to his. "But will he like it here? I thought cats oriented themselves to places, not people."

Alex shrugged. "This cat seems to make his own rules. I got him in Rhodes or maybe it was he who got me. He jumped on my boat one morning and just stayed, making himself at home just as easily in my apartment in Volos. So I don't think he cares much where he lives."

Joanna leaned over and stroked the cat's rich fur. Her action seemed to increase the decibel level of its purrs. "What about when I leave?"

"I'll take him back, or give him to Jenny." He sounded supremely indifferent as he walked out of the room.

When he came down again she was laying the table for supper, a tomato salad, bread fresh from the bakery that morning, a plate of tiny fish she'd fried for her own lunch. She always prepared more than enough for a meal as they were delicious and savory even after being refrigerated.

Alex downed the food with gusto, thanked her for the coffee she poured them both afterward, and helped her to clean up. "How's your friend Tony these days?" he asked as he put the clean plates in the cupboard.

And so it starts, she thought, experiencing a sinking feeling in her stomach. She'd known the peace, the unspoken truce, wouldn't last. Wiping the sink with the dishcloth, she pretended she hadn't heard in order to give herself time to think of an answer that would stop him in his tracks.

"No more letters, Joanna?" Alex gave a sweeping glance around the room. "Or do you keep them under your pillow, to sleep on at night?"

"No more letters, Alex," Joanna said evenly. "There has hardly been enough time."

"So what are you going to do about dear Tony? You can't keep him dangling forever."

"Tony can take care of himself."

"I'm sure he can." Alex stepped close to her, tweaking her nose between his forefinger and thumb. "I think I'll go down to the coffee shop for a while." Lightly he kissed the spot he'd touched. "Don't wait up."

"You can bet I won't," Joanna muttered darkly as soon as he was out of earshot.

However, she was still awake, reading in bed, when she heard his steps in the hall. Holding her breath, she waited as he passed her door but the even rhythm didn't alter, and a moment later she heard his door close. After that she found the book didn't hold her attention and she turned out the light.

She slept, only to awaken when the floorboards squeaked in the hall. Alex?

The other night a reluctance to violate his privacy had restrained her from going to him but tonight she obeyed the impulse to get up. Although she often slept naked on hot nights, she kept an ankle-length cotton robe next to her bed. Pulling it on and securing the tie around her narrow waist, she stealthily opened her door and stepped into the hall.

Alex had already gone downstairs. Even as she walked on bare feet to the head of the stairs, she heard the click as he released the lock on the back door. Quickly she ran down, reaching the patio just as he was about to go around the corner of the house.

"Alex," she called in a loud stage whisper.

He jumped, then turned, his expression thunderous as he saw her. "Joanna, what are you doing up?"

"I might ask you the same."

"I saw a light out on the side of the mountain above the orchards. I was going to see who's out there."

"Another insomniac?" Joanna suggested with a grin. "Wait a sec. I'm going with you."

"In that?" he asked, brows lifting. "You look like the heroine of a Gothic novel."

"Give me a minute. I'll put on some clothes."

"Well, hurry." He sounded irritated.

She ran up the stairs, whipping off the robe before she was halfway to her room. She pulled on a T-shirt and shorts, stuffing her feet into sturdy sandals as she zipped up.

To her relief Alex was still waiting, the cat beside him. It deserted them as soon as they reached the street, streaking off up a rocky path in pursuit of some unfortunate rodent.

Joanna and Alex walked through the sleeping village. They crossed the lighted islands beneath the street lamps and plunged into the larger seas of darkness between the widely spaced poles. At three o'clock in the morning no one was abroad although a rooster crowed raucously, startling Joanna.

"Shh!" Alex hissed, scorching her with a frown. "We're getting close now."

"That rooster doesn't know how to tell time." Joanna couldn't suppress a giggle at Alex's serious demeanor, the way he clung to the shadows as they bypassed the last streetlight.

The campground was quiet, the Gypsies having moved on. Only one tent remained, a yellow nylon affair occupied by a couple of Italian girls who Joanna had observed swimming topless during siesta when the village was asleep. Two elongated bumps lay on the ground in front of the little tent.

They skirted the fenced area, moving up a rocky goat path on the mountain's flank. Joanna bit back an exclamation as her bare leg suffered a painful introduction to a thornbush. Straining her eyes, she scanned the mountain. Starlight cast an eerie radiance over the landscape, creating gray highlights among deep shadows.

There was no sign of any light.

"Ouch!" she exclaimed again, beneath her breath, rubbing another scratch on her leg just as Alex stopped in front of her.

She ran right into him, her face mashing against his back. In the split second of contact all kinds of sensations rushed to her brain: the clean soap scent of his cotton shirt, the warm resilience of his muscular shoulder, the faintly astringent aroma of his sweat.

He put out one hand to steady her, keeping his fingers on her forearm as he stood there listening. She could hear it, too, a large body crashing through the bushes not far from them.

They heard a pungent curse, followed by the crackle of breaking twigs and louder curses. Apparently deciding the risk of being seen at this hour was minimal, the figure about fifty feet away turned on a flashlight.

Alex pulled Joanna behind a thicket of holly oak, cautioning her with a finger across her lips to be quiet.

They huddled together, listening to each other's breathing and to the crashing in the bushes that drew nearer and nearer. Alex laid his arm protectively around Joanna's back, the scent of her sweet in his nostrils. Shadows enclosed them, thick as coal dust.

He found he couldn't let her go, not even when moments passed and his muscles began to cramp. He wanted her even closer. He wanted that soft body lying beneath his.

Joanna felt his arm tighten around her, the rhythm of his heartbeat speed up. Her own heart pounded so loudly in her ears she was sure whoever was coming down the path toward them would hear it. And it certainly wasn't fear that afflicted her.

Alex's nearness, the sense of privacy in the dark, even the danger, made her excruciatingly aware of every breath he took.

She shifted to ease the stiffness in her legs, and felt the sharp intake of Alex's breath, realizing only then that in an effort to maintain her balance she had grasped his upper thigh.

A deep erotic heat flooded her. They were dangerously close. Under her hand the muscle tensed, and she didn't dare move, lest she draw attention to its position.

Circumstance saved them both.

Costas, clearly illuminated by the flashlight he waved before him, wandered by, muttering to himself. He'd obviously decided quiet was useless.

As soon as the light receded to a pinpoint, Joanna eased to her feet. Carefully avoiding each other's eyes, they stretched their cramped muscles and quietly followed Costas, although where he was heading now was no mystery.

They lost him going around the campground. Behind Jenny's house was a field planted with rows of lush grapevines. Costas took a shortcut through there, made it to the shadows of a group of storage sheds behind the house, and disappeared.

"There must be another way in," Alex whispered to Joanna as they reached the sheds. The open paved yard before them was lit by a light high on a pole, but no furtive figure crossed it to the back door.

"Maybe he beat us and made it inside."

"We'll see."

Sticking to the shadows in case their quarry was watching, they circled the yard, and silently climbed the back steps of the house.

Oddly, the door wasn't locked. They entered what seemed to be a pantry although the kitchen lay at the far end of the house. Joanna could smell the pungency of garlic and oregano. The interior was a black void.

"Shall we risk a light?"

Alex's hand was on the switch when a voice came out of the darkness. "Stop right there or I'll shoot."

CHAPTER EIGHT

"JENNY, DON'T SHOOT. It's us," Alex yelled. Fumbling along the wall beside the door, he flipped on the light.

Jenny, clad in a voluminous nightgown printed with lurid purple cabbage roses, pointed the business end of a shotgun right at them. "Well, why don't you knock at the front door then, like civilized people?"

Joanna swallowed her heart back down into its normal place. Beside her, Alex was making peculiar choking noises that finally erupted into a rafter-shaking laugh. Joanna rolled her eyes although she was hard put to keep from joining his laughter. If the neighborhood hadn't wakened from his shout, they'd surely be up now.

"Oh, Jenny," Alex finally said, wiping his eyes. "You caught the wrong ones. Didn't Costas come through here?"

Jenny let the gun slide through her fingers until it was aimed at the floor. "Not in the past five minutes, no. What's going on?"

"I saw a light on the mountain and I went out to see who was prowling around. In this heat wave we're having it would be a tragedy if some arsonist set a fire in the brush. Anyway, it turned out to be Costas, but we lost him when he came into the yard."

"Humph," Jenny said. "He must have gone in by way of the cellar."

"Cellar?"

"Yes, there's a sort of secret entrance to the cellar. We used it during the war."

"Yeah. I remember," Alex said. He frowned. "I thought it'd been boarded up years ago."

"It was for a while but later we opened it again." Jenny sniffed. "I didn't know that some dark night you were going to be hot on the heels of a rat of the two-legged variety. Do you want to go up to his room and see if he's there?"

"No." Alex grimaced. "That won't be necessary. But I do have a question. What would he have been looking for on the mountain?"

Jenny shrugged. "The pot of gold at the end of the rainbow?"

"Yeah. Probably," Alex agreed in an ironic tone while keeping his thoughts to himself. Was there something Jenny wasn't telling him? They were friends; he trusted her, but sometimes she could be a cagey character. He turned around. "Come, Joanna. We'd better let Jenny get back to bed. Sorry to have disturbed you, Jenny."

"That's all right." She grinned saucily. "Haven't had this much excitement in years."

He took Joanna's hand and led her outside, turning back to the older woman when they reached the step. "Lock this door, Jenny. It wasn't locked before."

She gave him an odd look but moved to close it. "Okay, Alex. But I never have before. What's to steal anyway, a few strings of garlic? *Kali nichta, pedhia.*"

The streets were still deserted as they walked home; the neighbors must sleep more soundly than Joanna had given them credit for. Only a couple of cats scurried to shelter in the shadows at the sound of their feet on the pavement. The mountain was silhouetted against a sky just turning light with false dawn.

"And how did you just happen to see Costas prowling over the mountain waving a flashlight?" Joanna asked at length. She already suspected the answer but she wanted to provoke him into a discussion of his sleeplessness.

"I was awake." Period. Full stop.

Never one to give up on a challenge, Joanna tried another tack. "You don't sleep well, do you?"

He kicked at a stone as they climbed the incline toward the house, sending it flying off into the dense thornbushes that lined the path. "So I've got insomnia. So do lots of people. It doesn't mean we're weird."

"Did I say that?" Joanna asked mildly. "Have you talked to anyone about it?"

"Why should I?" He sounded sulky. "It's my problem. I'll handle it."

Sure you will, Joanna thought. "What do you do when you go out at night?" She waved her hand at the thick blackness on either side of the path. "You certainly can't be sightseeing in the dark."

"I go running. It's the way I keep in shape for sailing."

"And how long have you had this problem?" Joanna asked, as they entered the house.

"Keeping in shape is a problem?" He was being deliberately obtuse.

"No. The problem of not sleeping."

Seeing she wasn't going to quit, he rounded on her, eyes flashing. "Just get off my back, will you, Joanna?" Spinning around, he stamped down the hall and up the stairs.

"Pheww!" Unsure whether to laugh or yell, Joanna let out a long breathy sigh. *Face it,* she said to herself, *he doesn't want you to know.*

Keyed up after all the excitement, Joanna decided against going back to bed. She would do some cleaning in the kitchen. When it grew light enough, she went out and worked in the garden for an hour.

Back in the house later she found that Alex had cooked breakfast and she saw at once that his mood had improved considerably.

"I thought you might like to go out on my boat, Joanna," he said as if his earlier testiness had never occurred. "Do you have anything planned for today?"

The two of them alone on an endless blue sea, the wind singing in the rigging, intimacy in isolation; the images beckoned, sending little shivers of excitement through her. "Nothing that can't wait until another day. Yes, I'd like to go.

THE HEAT WAVE, which had lasted over a week already, continued unabated, but out at sea a breeze swept refreshingly across the decks and sent the boat skimming along the water with exhilarating speed. "Sunburn weather," Alex warned.

Joanna knew that; one experience with a day like this, on a boat in the Caribbean had taught her a lesson she would not forget. Over her bikini, a brief confection of shocking-pink triangles, she wore loose white pants and a matching gauze shirt.

They sailed along the coast, never really out of sight of land. Around them the deep blue sea glittered like a field of crushed sapphires. Once a trio of dolphins broke the surface next to the boat, their elongated snouts seeming to smile as they chortled a greeting. With graceful leaps they dived under the hull, only to surface on the other side, spinning on their tails and uttering birdlike chirps.

Joanna clapped her hands, laughing like a child in her enjoyment. The dolphins, in perfect formation, arced their gray bodies out of the water, and then, single file and looking like a multicoiled sea serpent, they leapt away.

When the sun hung straight over the main mast, a molten copper ball in a colorless sky, Alex dropped the anchor in a sheltered cove surrounded by precipitous cliffs. At the foot of the cliffs lay a tiny crescent of fine white pebbles. The Pelion coast was riddled with such picturesque bays, and Joanna suspected that Alex knew them all.

Alex had packed a picnic lunch while Joanna had been upstairs changing her clothes after breakfast. They loaded the basket, a bundle of towels and Joanna's beach bag into the dinghy. The bay was deep, the sailboat anchored so close they could have swum to shore except for the problem of keeping the food and towels dry.

Alex rowed the dinghy; starting the engine would have been a sacrilege in this peaceful setting. "I've been here before," he told Joanna. "We won't be too hot even though it faces west. The cliffs are close enough that there's always a strip of shade."

"How many people know about this place?" Joanna asked, idly trailing her fingers in the water.

His eyes narrowed. "Don't you mean how many women have I brought here, Joanna?"

She drew up her hand and flicked water at him. He broke into that hearty laugh that had always pleased her so much. She heard it too seldom from him these days. "Am I that transparent?"

"Like a child." He leaped out of the dinghy as it scraped onto the shore, pulling it higher before Joanna could get out to lighten the load. It rolled easily on the pebbles.

Straightening, he offered his hand to her. She took it, jumping lightly to the ground. Instead of releasing her at once, he reeled her in close, until they were standing only inches away from each other. "But you're not a child anymore, are you, little Jo?"

Her breath caught in her throat, turning her voice low and husky. "Alex, you keep saying that. Is it so hard for you to see me as a woman?"

"No," he said quietly. "But I can't forget how it used to be when we were kids. I see so many things about you that haven't changed, and so many things that have."

"In fifteen years we're bound to change. You've changed too, Alex."

"How?" he asked, as if he really wanted to know.

"You've gotten older," she teased.

"Oh, really. I hadn't noticed."

As if the laughter that lay just under their talk had broken some spell, he let her go and picked up the picnic basket. She followed with the towels, hitching her beach bag over her shoulder.

The tiny pebbles were warm and pleasantly resilient under her bare feet, beautifully clean, washed by centuries of lapping waves. She dumped the towels and her bag in the shade next to the basket, then stepped back to gaze up at the sheer cliffs rising a hundred feet above them. A goat couldn't have climbed either up or down. They were as isolated here as they would have been on the moon.

She glanced at Alex. He was calmly tugging at the drawstring that held the waist of his pants. "Want to go for a swim before we eat?"

Her mouth was dry as she watched him undo the pants and slide them down his long legs. She could only nod. He was magnificent, she thought again. She was a fool to be so obsessed with him. In spite of his kindness with Jenny, and his thoughtfulness with the crippled Themistocles, she couldn't ignore the cynicism that seemed an ingrained part of him.

"What's the matter, Joanna? Sun getting to you?" He scowled, almost in anger.

She jerked back to the present, stripping off her shirt and trousers and tossing them on the towels. "Last one in washes dishes for a whole week."

"Starting tonight or tomorrow?"

The unexpected question threw her off just long enough for him to get the jump on her. Although she raced after him, he leaped into the water just ahead of her, propelling himself away from the shore with powerful strokes of his arms.

HE HAD BECOME A MAN of the most maddeningly fluctuating moods, Joanna thought later as she tidied up after their picnic lunch. He'd looked almost angry when he'd leaped ahead of her into the water, but during lunch he'd filled the space between them with cheerful banter. Superficial chatter that belonged at a cocktail party, not in a conversation between two friends.

After a while she felt like telling him to either pick something meaningful to discuss or to shut up. He was wearying her brain while subtly keeping her at a distance.

He had been mercifully silent for the past five minutes, to her relief. Closing the picnic basket and pushing it to one side of the blanket on which they rested, she looked over at him.

Her heart skipped once, then galloped forward at a headlong pace. The expression in his eyes would have burned the clothes off her at forty feet. Nervously licking her lip, she glanced down. Her bikini, what there was of it, still covered her. But the way he looked and the way it made her feel, she might as well have been naked.

The devil had finally burst out of its bonds. "Have you ever sunbathed topless, Joanna?" His voice was silky, sliding over her skin with the same artless ease as the water during her swim.

Going along with his little game, she said lightly, "Of course I have. On the French Riviera and on many Caribbean beaches, everyone does." Reaching behind her neck, she pulled the string that held her top. The twin triangles of fabric clung damply to her breasts for an instant but as she released the string at her back, the skimpy bra fell loose.

Three decades of summers spent on public beaches all over Europe had not prepared Alex for his reaction to the sight of Joanna deliberately and casually removing her bikini top. All breath died in his throat.

Her breasts were small and firm, uniformly tanned. Desire slammed through him, an agony of need that was mixed with jealousy. Other men had seen her like this. Inwardly he cursed the unfairness of it. Joanna was his.

The primitive need for exclusive possession rocked him. He'd never felt anything like it before. He'd always enjoyed the company of women, their femininity, and the intricate and often baffling female mind. But he'd never laid claim to any of his companions. They had remained free of emotional entanglement, and so had he.

With Joanna, everything was different. There was so much more.

But this was hardly the time to figure it out. He rolled over on his stomach, bearing her down to lie next to him and swinging one leg over her thighs.

She lay on the blanket, looking calmly at him with those lapis lazuli eyes that seemed a distillation of the sky. Her lips, moist and luscious, parted as if she were about to speak. He never found out what she would have said for he covered them with his own, drinking of her taste, feeding on the exquisite sensation of knowing she was here, she was real, she was his.

"Joanna, Joanna," he whispered, caught in the wonder of her skin, silk and velvet, her scent, sea and flowers.

Joanna closed her eyes and her hands clasped his shoulders, savoring the sleek resilience of his skin, the vibrancy in the hard muscles. She couldn't speak but when he released her mouth to start a journey over her cheeks and down to her throat, she tightened her fingers, holding him closer.

"Joanna, you've no idea how it makes me feel to touch you like this, to know you're here, in my arms."

"I do know," she said quietly, lifting her hand and lazily running her fingertip along his sweat-dampened upper lip and over the full curve of his lower lip. He nipped playfully at the wayward finger, pulling it into his mouth and sucking on it with a pressure that set up a renewed aching deep in her body.

"Alex, do you remember the time you kissed me that last summer? It was on a summer day like this, in your aunt's backyard. We were lying on the grass beside the pool, just the two of us. No one else was home at either your aunt's or our house."

He removed her finger although he didn't release her hand as he twined their fingers together. "Yes. Of course I remember. You were so sweet."

"But at the last minute you pushed me away."

"You were far too young, only fourteen. I suddenly realized how alone we were, how easy it would be to take advantage of you."

"If I was willing, it wouldn't have been taking advantage."

"No. But I was old enough to know better, Joanna. And you weren't."

That was true and perhaps she should have been grateful, but at the time she had only felt the hurt of rejection. Now she realized the rejection could have hurt even more, if he hadn't handled it with such sensitivity and gentleness.

Alex propped his head on one elbow. "I never forgot that day," he went on softly, lost in reminiscence. "You were wearing a bikini, like this one." His finger traced the edge of the fabric at her hip, toying with the tie. "Only yellow. When you came out of the water, the yellow was much darker." He skipped over the knot and began a path across her thigh. "I wanted to touch you, to kiss you, right here." His warm fingers closed on the faint mound concealed by the pink triangle of nylon.

The pleasure that pierced her was shocking, and when he replaced his hand with his mouth, she squeezed her eyes closed and helplessly allowed her thighs to relax on the blanket. His breath was hot, his mouth wet, and she felt the gentle nip of his teeth through the thin fabric.

"Alex," she whispered.

"Yes?" he asked, his breath fanning the moist spot he'd made, cooling and heating at the same time.

"Nothing. Just... Alex."

Just Alex. Tenderness rushed through him and his eyes stung. He had a sensation of balancing on a precipice. This moment had been hanging between them for fifteen years. Wasn't it time they finished what had started in that summer garden with the smell of grass and roses all around them?

"Joanna, do you want me?"

The uncertainty in his voice startled her. She would have expected him to be sure of himself, overpowering in his sexuality, in his desire. Yet he waited for her.

Filled with confusing emotion, she could only say one thing. "Yes, Alex. I want you."

He let out the breath he'd been holding in a sharp gust. Quickly, as if fearing she would change her mind, he jerked at the ties on her hips.

The strings released their hold. She lay naked before him, golden in the summer afternoon, uninhibited even though he knew he was staring as if he'd never seen a woman before. Only an inch of skin above the dark thatch of hair was white, a stark contrast to her tawny brown tan. In an ecstasy of discovery he kissed that pale strip, over and over again, nuzzling her, inhaling the fragrance of her, the clean sea smell mixed with the flower perfume she must have applied that morning. He was drunk on the flavor of her, moving up her body, lingering only briefly at her dimpled navel before continuing over the taut stomach to the delicate underside of her breasts.

He took one rosy pink nipple in his mouth, suckling deeply, his tongue a gentle tormentor. Tangling her fingers in his crisp hair, she arched her body up to his, welcoming the abrasive roughness of his chest hair against her tender skin.

Alex lifted his head for a moment, his eyes hot, gleaming with anticipation. "Do you like that, Joanna? Tell me what you like."

She was beyond speech, nearly beyond thought, her blood a river of fire. "Please." Her mouth formed the word with a sound like a sigh. "Please, come to me."

He chuckled deep in his throat. "Not yet, my sweet, but soon. Soon we'll fly off the edge of the earth and into space. Soon. You'll see."

Standing, he pulled off his swimming suit. For a moment he stood silhouetted against the glare of the sun outside their patch of shade, his body an even bronze without a trace of tan lines.

He came back, lying down beside her again. With exquisite sweetness he kissed her, his tongue exploring her mouth, dancing along her tongue. Joanna gasped at the deep surging desire that pulsed in the secret places of her body. Her hands tightened convulsively on his shoulders.

The knowledge of her pleasure ran through him in a current of warmth. She flushed under his gaze, tilting her head to one side, and he smiled gently. "Sweet Joanna, it's okay. You dòn't have to hide from me."

She wanted him, and yet the intensity of her feelings frightened her. This was Alex. If she made love with him, there would be no going back. Was she ready for an intimacy that might change her forever?

He felt her hesitation. Tenderness flooded him, mellowing his passion. "Joanna, there are no secrets between the two of us. There can't be." His black eyes searched the sea-blue depths of hers. "Joanna, do you trust me? Do you trust me not to hurt you?"

She wasn't sure. In the dried grass nearby, the musical chirring of a cicada fell silent. The scent of Alex embraced her, warm skin, sweat, and elemental male, luring her with a mating call she desperately wanted to answer.

Alex studied her flushed cheeks, the hair in disarray around her temples, her mouth pink and moist from his kisses. In her eyes he saw acceptance, but also a lingering uncertainty.

He brought his hands up to frame her face, willing them to stop trembling. "What is it, Joanna? If you're worried about pregnancy, it will only take me a moment to swim out to the boat for something to take care of that."

Always prepared, like a Boy Scout. Joanna choked down a laugh. "No. That's not the problem. I'm on the pill."

"For Tony." He said it aloud, feeling as if he'd stepped into an icy sinkhole in the sea bottom. Damn. He'd never poached on another man's territory. He wasn't about to start now.

He half sat up, looking at her. Her eyes were wide and shocked, guilty he thought. She opened her mouth to speak but he didn't give her a chance. "Forget it."

Standing up, he stalked to the sea. He lunged into the gently curling surf, and surged through the water, leaving behind a foaming wake that slowly settled into glassy calm.

CHAPTER NINE

JOANNA SAT UP, wrapping her arms defensively around her raised knees, not bothering to pull on her bikini. Somehow it didn't seem to matter any more that she was naked.

For Tony. Alex's conclusion was obvious, and she hadn't answered him, hesitating because of her own uncertainty. Not with regard to Tony, as Alex had thought. It was Alex she was uncertain about.

He had asked her to trust him. Intellectually she had agreed, yet when the moment of intimacy came, she had let him down. She had to prove to him that she did trust him, did love him.

Getting up, she pulled her shirt and pants on over her bare body, bundling the bikini into a towel and stuffing it into the beach bag. She loaded the dinghy and laboriously rowed it back to the sailboat, wondering where Alex had disappeared to.

She found him as soon as she staggered into the cabin burdened with the slipping load of the picnic basket and beach paraphernalia. He lay on his back on the bed that filled the curved bow of the boat. He was naked, his body glistening with water droplets, fresh water she surmised as there was no bloom of salt on his skin. Evidently he'd swum straight here and taken a shower.

"Yes, Joanna?"

She couldn't read his expression; his arm lay over his eyes. His tone was uncompromisingly hard.

"I'm sorry," she said simply. "But it isn't what you thought." She took a deep breath. "Whatever you may think, Tony and I are really just friends. I don't sleep with him."

Alex lifted his head, shifting his arm. She caught a glimpse of his eyes but couldn't read their message. "Oh?"

"Believe me, Alex." She bit her lip, keeping her voice steady.

He sank back, resuming his original position. "I believe you, Joanna. I'm sorry, too. I overreacted. I should have trusted you."

"Both of us," Joanna murmured, more to herself than to him. The dark, unsettled emotion that gripped her when she was with Alex was far too complex to resolve in a promise of trust. But she was finally sure of one thing. She wanted to be with him now, in the deepest intimacy possible. She wanted to live this moment of madness.

The sun slanted into the window in the bow. No portholes for Alex's boat but wide windows opened to receive the sea and the light dancing off its sparkling surface. A golden ray lay across his body, giving the bronze skin the sheen of satin. Suddenly Joanna couldn't wait any longer.

Quickly, ignoring the shaking of her fingers, she stripped off her shirt and pants. Naked, she padded across the space that lay between her and the bed.

Gently, softly, she touched his ankle. He made no reaction, not a sound. She traced the hard bone with her fingertips, feeling a surge of elation when she realized he was far from indifferent. The pulse, steady and slow at her first touch, sped up, heating the smooth skin.

Almost fearfully, amazed at her own boldness, she allowed her eyes to move up the long, hair-sprinkled length of his legs. His heart wasn't the only part of his body that acknowledged her presence. He was aroused, turgid and erect.

Forgetting her inhibitions, Joanna sat on the edge of the bed, pressing her mouth to the wildly beating pulse above his ankle bone. A sharp inhalation was his only response but it was enough. With a boldness she knew she would never have dared with any other man, she allowed her lips to move higher, delighting in the tickling of the crisp hair against her skin. He smelled of soap, he tasted of salt, he aroused a terrible heat in her that had to be quenched.

When she touched him with the tip of her tongue, he jerked convulsively, a deep shudder chasing over his skin. When she placed her mouth against him, he groaned in an agony of pleasure. "Joanna. *Joanna.*" His fingers clenched in her hair, as if he would pull her away, but then the pleasure overcame him and he pushed her into even greater contact.

"Joanna, Joanna, oh, love. Oh, please. Please stop . . . or it's all . . . over. . . ."

Recklessly she increased the pressure—and the pleasure—of both her mouth and her caressing hands, but he forced himself to remain under control.

Heaving to a sitting position, he grasped her shoulders and brought her mouth up to his. Deeply, on a sigh of profoundest passion, he kissed her, tasting the mingled flavor of himself and her on her lips, delighting in it. It was a symbol of the greater union they would shortly share.

He trailed the fingers of one hand down her throat, caressing the velvet skin, the quick beat of her pulse in the tantalizing little hollow. He placed his mouth there, inhaling the fragrant traces of her perfume that lingered. Her skin was salty from the sea, silky with a sheen of perspiration. He was suddenly ravenous, wanting to devour all of her, to absorb every sensation.

When he touched her breast, she gasped. When he took one tight nipple in his mouth, she moaned, tangling her fingers in his hair. "Alex."

"Mmm," he murmured. "You taste so delicious. I want to kiss you all over, every inch of you. Will you let me?"

The images his words evoked were so incredibly erotic she couldn't control the shiver that rippled through her body.

"Will you let me, Joanna?" he repeated. As he uttered the soft but relentless words, he ran his hand down her body, skimming over her hipbones, moving across the flat plane of her stomach to her thighs and between them. "Will you let me kiss you here, Joanna?"

Heat rose in a pink flush on her skin. She twisted her head to one side, avoiding the piercingly direct gaze of his eyes. *Alex.* Her mouth formed the word but no sound came out as the burning tide threatened to engulf her.

She struggled for sanity, fought to hold back something of herself, but as he smiled and kissed her again, she lost the battle. For the first time in her life she was ready to let go, to allow someone else to take command. For the first time she understood that love was the deepest act of sharing.

```
****************************************************
* You may have already won a lifetime of cash payments *
* totaling up to $1,000,000.00!  Play our Sweepstakes  *
* Game--Here's how it works...                          *
****************************************************
```

Each of the first three tickets has a unique Sweepstakes number.
If your Sweepstakes numbers match any of the winning numbers
selected by our computer, you could win the amount shown
under the gold rub-off on that ticket.

Using an eraser, rub off the gold boxes on tickets #1-3 to
reveal how much each ticket could be worth if it is a winning
ticket. You must return the <u>entire</u> card to be eligible. (See
official rules in the back of this book for details.)

At the same time you play your tickets for big cash prizes,
Harlequin also invites you to participate in a special trial of
our Reader Service by accepting one or more FREE book(s) from
Harlequin Superromance.® To request your free book(s), just rub
off the gold box on ticket #4 to reveal how many free book(s)
you will receive.

When you receive your free book(s), we hope you'll enjoy them
and want to see more. So unless we hear from you, every month
we'll send you 4 additional Harlequin Superromance®novels. Each
book is yours to keep for only $2.74* each--21¢ less per book
than the cover price! There are <u>no</u> additional charges for
shipping and handling and, of course, you may cancel Reader
Service privileges at any time by marking "cancel" on your
shipping statement or returning a shipment of books to us at our
expense. Either way your shipments will stop. You'll receive
no more books; you'll have no further obligation.

PLUS-you get a FREE MYSTERY GIFT!

If you return your game card with <u>all four gold boxes</u> rubbed
off, you will also receive a FREE Mystery Gift. It's your
<u>immediate reward</u> for sampling your free book(s), <u>and</u> it's yours
to keep no matter what you decide.

P.S.

Remember, the first set of one or more book(s) is FREE. So rub
off the gold box on ticket #4 and return the entire sheet of
tickets today!

*Terms and prices subject to change without notice.

"GIVE YOUR HEART" TO HARLEQUIN SWEEPSTAKES

"GIVE YOUR HEART TO HARLEQUIN" SWEEPSTAKES

1 If this is a winning ticket, it could be worth

$1,000,000.00

Rub off to reveal potential value if this is a winning ticket: ▶ $35,000

UNIQUE SWEEPSTAKES NUMBER: 5B 214933

2 If this is a winning ticket, it could be worth

$1,000,000.00

Rub off to reveal potential value if this is a winning ticket: ▶ $10,000

UNIQUE SWEEPSTAKES NUMBER: 5C 214675

3 If this is a winning ticket, it could be worth

$1,000,000.00

Rub off to reveal potential value if this is a winning ticket: ▶

UNIQUE SWEEPSTAKES NUMBER: 5D 214656

4 ONE OR MORE **FREE BOOKS**

HOW MANY FREE BOOKS?
Rub off to reveal number of free books you will receive ▶

1672765559

Yes! Enter my sweepstakes numbers in the Sweepstakes and let me know if I've won a cash prize. If gold box on ticket #4 is rubbed off, I will also receive one or more Harlequin Superromance novels as a FREE tryout of the Reader Service, along with a FREE Mystery Gift as explained on the opposite page.   134 CIH KA6V

NAME

ADDRESS   APT.

CITY   STATE   ZIP CODE

Offer not valid to current Harlequin Superromance subscribers. All orders subject to approval.   PRINTED IN U.S.A.

DETACH HERE AND RETURN ENTIRE SHEET OF TICKETS NOW!

Gasping as he touched her more deeply, she whispered on a note of desperation, "Oh, Alex, I feel so strange, as if I'm floating but at the same time about to explode."

He laughed again. She heard the gentleness, the understanding. "That's the way you're supposed to feel. You must have felt this way before."

She looked confused. "Not like this. It scares me. I don't like the feeling of not being in control. Please, Alex, help me."

On some cosmic level Alex was aware of the gift she was giving him, perhaps more aware even than she was. Joanna had not only allowed him to see her softer, vulnerable side, but she trusted him to cherish it. Even though he couldn't entirely understand what this must cost her, he felt humbled. At the same time he knew that when she came to the realization of her unequivocal surrender to him, she might well reject him. With the fatalism that had been part of him for the past ten years, he accepted that condition to loving her.

Chances. That was all one had. And risks.

He risked it all on a single stroke as he joined their bodies into one.

Conscious thought fled from him as he absorbed the feel of her closing around him. She was hot and tight, and he thought he would die of the pleasure surging in ever-increasing waves through him.

She moved against him and he bit his lip to stop the imminent explosion. "Easy," he whispered, although he couldn't hold back his elation at her uninhibited response. Gently he touched her, mindful of the excruciating sensitivity of her skin. She stiffened involuntarily, her eyes squeezing shut.

"Easy," he said again, keeping his touch so light she could only yearn for more. "Trust me, Joanna. I won't hurt you."

He wouldn't, not that way. But he knew her too well, as no one else did. She was afraid of the power this gave him.

But then thought was suspended as he surged deeper into her, until she was caught in an undertow from which there was no escape. She poised on the brink of release but some remnant of self-preservation still held her back.

Sweat dripped from Alex's brow and the mingled rasp of their breathing filled the hot cabin. "Go with it," he urged. "Let yourself go. You have to let yourself go."

"I can't," she cried, her nails digging into his shoulders.

"Can't? You mean you've never—"

She made a sound that was half laugh, half groan. "Of course I have." She didn't meet his gaze; hers remained fixed on his shoulder where the dark skin glistened with sweat. "But never with anyone who counted."

He looked startled, then thoughtful. "Well, you're about to. Just forget everything but the feeling. Let yourself go completely. I won't let you fall."

And suddenly she found she could. She arched into his caresses, moving with him in a rhythm that echoed the faint rocking of the boat beneath them. Then she was aware of nothing but him as the joyous, soaring ecstasy caught them all at once, flinging them to the stars where they hung for endless moments before drifting slowly back to earth and sanity.

They lay in a tangle of limbs and sheets, spent and exhausted, yet strangely exhilarated. Joanna felt like shouting from the top of the mast the happiness she felt, the glorious feeling of having shared the ultimate intimacy with someone who was gentle and understanding, who didn't judge her. If only her legs weren't so weak, the consistency of warm rubber. At the moment she wondered if she would ever be able to get up again. At the moment, with Alex's arms wrapped around her, she didn't care.

She looked at him and he smiled, his mouth curling against the tender skin where her neck joined her shoulder. She used one finger to trace a path down his straight nose, over the slightly parted lips. He chuckled and nipped at her.

She laughed lazily, enjoying the sight of his lean, naked body sprawled in comfortable relaxation, his bronze skin a dark contrast to the white sheets. Sunlight caressed them, and tiny golden dust motes shimmered in the slanting rays.

"If I don't get up soon," Alex murmured, "we'll both expire from dehydration." He rolled to the edge of the bed, patting her familiarly on the rump. "I'll be right back."

She must have dozed off even though he was back within minutes.

"Joanna."

Sitting up, she blinked sleepily. She was about to grope for a sheet to cover herself when she saw what he held out to her. Forgetting her nakedness, she reached for the tall glass. Thirstily she lifted it to her lips, gulping down the orange juice. It slid down her parched throat, icy cold, tart, refreshing.

"Ohh," she sighed, handing back the empty glass. "That's even better than sex."

Alex grinned, his eyes crinkling at the corners as he sat next to her on the bed. "Sure?"

She tilted her head to one side. "Well, maybe not."

Alex regarded her with a disconcerting seriousness. "It was good, wasn't it? *We* were good together."

But Joanna didn't want to be serious. If she kept it light, she was safe. "Yes, but I'm sure lots of people are good together. That's why sex never loses its popularity."

Was that all it had been for her? Alex asked himself. Sex? A simple roll in the sack to satisfy her curiosity? The idea infuriated him.

Keeping his temper in check, he slanted her a look. She had turned her head to stare out the window and the pure lines of her profile distracted him from his anger. She was hiding again, that trait she had lacked as a child, which she had acquired and honed to such perfection in adulthood. A vulnerable quality he saw in the droop of her mouth told him more than the flippancy of her tone.

She needed time.

Well, he decided, getting up from the bed and picking up the scattered clothes from the floor, he would give her a little time. But she needn't think that this was the last time for them. There would be more.

THE EDGE OF THE SAIL snapped in the breeze as Alex ran it up the mast. Joanna watched as he secured the lines. The midafternoon sun was hot.

"Need any help there?" she called, not that she particularly wanted to get up from the foam mattress on which she lay. But talking kept her from thinking about what had happened between them earlier.

"No, thanks." A grin came and went on his face. "I've got it."

The boat skimmed buoyantly over the gentle swell of the waves, running before a freshening wind. They sailed up the coast, coming in parallel to the pebbled beach that separated a long narrow village from the sea. At the end of the village the blue-and-white colors of a naval station guarded a headland.

The sea was deep enough here so that they could come in close. Between the village and the naval station Joanna could see a dusty campground populated by a crowd of tents. A couple of young men raced motorcycles in the narrow lanes dividing the campsites, raising clouds of acrid smoke and dust while shattering the siesta quiet with the snarl of engines.

"Why doesn't somebody stop them?" Joanna exclaimed.

"Apathy, probably," Alex replied, making an adjustment to the tiller to bring them around the end of a jetty whose stone structure jutted out into the water. In the silence broken only by the wind song in the rigging, Joanna could clearly hear the shouts of the men on the motorcycles, and the curses of campers rudely awakened by the noise.

"That, Joanna, is what can happen in the name of progress. Development without controls, a village where they see only the short-term benefits. The trouble is, in a few years, its reputation will become widespread and campers won't come anymore. Would you camp in a dusty olive grove where there isn't a blade of grass left on the ground?"

"No, I wouldn't," Joanna agreed. "But our resorts aren't like that."

"Granted." Alex nodded. "But this wasn't like that five years ago, either."

They left the village behind and Joanna inhaled the fresh sea air untainted by exhaust fumes. Alex had a point, but Paradise Hotels had a reputation for looking after its investments. She would never be part of a devastation of the environment such as they'd just witnessed.

But what if the wrong kind of people came in and no one stopped them? She was reminded of one of their resorts on an island off the coast of Florida. The manager had gotten involved in drug running and by the time word had reached the head office, the resort had been trashed in a gang war. That sort of thing wasn't likely here but what she'd seen was bad enough.

"This is an example of how it can be," Alex suddenly announced, bringing her out of her reverie.

To her surprise they had reached another village, similar in size and aspect to the first.

Alex brought the boat up to the end of a long jetty, tossing a line to a fisherman who secured it with several loops around the heavy iron cleat.

"I'm getting good at this," Joanna remarked as she negotiated the rope ladder with quick agility.

"I'll say." Alex, already on the dock, caught her around the waist as she jumped the space between the boat and the jetty, holding her close for an instant before letting her slide down his body.

"Alex," she said breathlessly as he ignored the amused stare of the fisherman to drop a kiss on her mouth.

"Alex," he mimicked playfully, winking at the fisherman who made some probably ribald remark that Joanna wasn't quick enough to catch. "Are you going to stop me?"

He was looking at her with that impossibly sexy gleam in his black eyes. "Think I should?" she challenged.

"Naw," he said, throwing his arm across her shoulder and leading her toward the land. "Live dangerously, little Jo, for once in your life."

She pulled a face. "Yeah, I remember. Your philosophy."

They walked along the beach where brightly painted orange-and-blue paddleboats were drawn up on an expanse of pebbles as clean and smooth as those in a Japanese garden. Farther down was a campground, planted with oleanders and marigolds, with the parking lot neatly fenced off and separated from the campsites. Trash barrels encouraged tidiness, and the area was well kept and orderly. Properly spaced rows of tents looked as if they'd settled in for the summer. Beach towels and swimming suits hung to dry on clotheslines stretched between tent poles and trees.

What struck Joanna most during the walk back to the little store/coffee shop where the paddleboats were rented, was the absence of litter, the general air of pride in the appearance of the houses, businesses and streets. Mikrohori also had that meticulous European cleanliness but it was small and hosted few tourists. Here, even with the flocks of campers she'd seen, there was order, a vivid contrast to the village they'd seen earlier.

"Why the difference?" Joanna mused aloud as Alex pulled a chair out from a table so that she could sit down. He took the seat opposite her.

"Planning. That's the difference. And a refusal to let a transitory population disturb the order of life." He looked past her shoulder, lifting his hand in greeting. *"Dhio limonathas, parakalo."*

The man who brought the frosted bottles of lemonade wore only a black bikini swimsuit. A wool fisherman's cap perched on the shock of gray curls that covered his head. He set down the bottles and greeted Alex by name, laughing uproariously as Alex patted the enormous hairy belly that overhung the swimsuit.

"Join us, won't you?" Alex invited, and the man went back inside for a third bottle, not lemonade but beer, which explained his expansive waistline.

"This is a charming place," Joanna commented after taking a sip from her drink.

"Yes," Yannis Psaras agreed. "We like it that way." He waved one large hand in the direction of the campground. "Now we have the tourists; in the winter we fish." He shrugged. "It's not a bad life."

And sitting there, absorbing the quiet ambience of the village, Joanna agreed. The excitements of cities might be compelling and addictive but there was something to be said for an undemanding existence where contentment took precedence over success.

EVENING FOUND THEM back in the little bay outside Mikrohori. Alex lowered the anchor into a glassy sea suffused with the tangerine hues of sunset, his face thoughtful as he moved along the deck to secure the sails. "Joanna, if you and Tony got along so well that you considered marriage, how is it that you never slept with him?''

The question took her by surprise. She dropped the picnic basket and beach bag she was carrying abruptly on the deck. Why did he feel he could pry into her personal life when his own was strictly off limits to her? It wasn't fair.

''We just didn't. That's all. It would have complicated things at the office.''

Alex jerked at a rope, the end of it snapping like a whip and startling a gull perched on the rigging. The bird swooped over their head, shrieking.

''Yes, I suppose it would have,'' he said after a moment. ''Better not to mix business with pleasure.'' He came and stood before her, his callused hand cupping her chin. ''But then you wouldn't have wanted to waste the time, would you, Joanna? Tell me something, has your work been so important to you that you've never had time for men?''

Her anger seeped away. ''I've been busy, yes. But I go out. I've had a couple of fairly serious relationships. But there was something missing, some spark I felt was necessary for permanence.'' She hesitated, then added frankly, ''Maybe I didn't give enough. It was nothing like with you and me.''

Under her bare feet the deck was smooth and cool, rocking gently. The masts creaked faintly, the evening breeze singing in the lines, a siren's lullaby. The gull was silent, watching them with yellow eyes from a perch on the brass rail at the bow.

''And what about you?'' she asked when Alex didn't reply. ''You've known a lot of women. Did any of them mean anything?''

A suggestion of a smile played around his mouth. "There haven't been as many women in my life as you might think. In the past few years, they've been few and far between."

His eyes on her were steady, as if he were gauging her reaction. Uncomfortable, afraid that again she had opened herself too much to him, Joanna stooped to pick up their gear. "It's not my business, anyway," she muttered.

Alex took the beach bag from her hand, hoisting the straps over his shoulder. "We're involved whether you want to admit it or not. That makes it your business."

Not having a witty reply ready to parry the truth of his statement, she started down the rope ladder, arranging the equipment in the dinghy as he handed it down to her. He had started the engine before she spoke again. "Why do you anchor out here rather than tying up at the village jetty? The water's deep enough there, isn't it?"

He adjusted the throttle down to a low idle. "Sure it is, but I like the privacy. I always keep the boat here, and at night if it's too hot in the house and I can't sleep, I come out and lie on the deck and listen to the quiet."

As he opened up the engine and sent them in a wide, foaming arc away from the sailboat, she sat bemused by the image of sleeping in the open under a night sky, in which stars glowed like tiny lamps. Listening to the quiet. She hoped they could do that before she went back.

Which reminded her of the purpose of her trip. "By the way, I'm going to Volos tomorrow. I have an appointment."

"How are you planning to get there?" he shouted above the roar of the outboard.

"I thought I'd drive."

"I'll take you in the boat, if you like."

She hadn't been looking forward to driving the Renault for a couple of hours in the heat although by starting early she would have avoided most of it. Still, her clothes would have been wrinkled, and she considered it a matter of pride to present a groomed, businesslike appearance. She couldn't afford to fail with Samaras. The meeting was important, not only in light of the pending promotion, but also, should she decide to resign from Paradise Hotels, she would leave on a high note.

"I wouldn't want to inconvenience you, Alex." But both of them knew her protest was only courtesy.

"No inconvenience," he assured her. "I can stop by my office at the same time."

Why hadn't he told her? Alex asked himself as he steered the dinghy around the headland. Sooner or later she would find out he was the owner of the hotel Samaras managed.

It was a question he couldn't answer, except on a superficial level. He didn't want talk of business to disrupt the present harmony between them, as it surely would.

He wanted tonight.

CHAPTER TEN

HER HIGH HEELS CLICKING on the marble floor, Joanna walked across the lobby of the Hotel Meltemi. Odd, she reflected, that the hotel bore the same name as Alex's boat, the Greek equivalent of the Provençal *mistral*, the capricious wind that played havoc with interisland shipping schedules at certain times of the year. To Alex it might be a symbol of freedom, but to tourists whose journeys were delayed and interrupted it must spell inconvenience. Still, she could appreciate the romantic overtones of the name.

The hotel appeared to be well kept, quiet, and recently remodeled, featuring modern amenities married to nineteenth-century architecture and charm. The manager's office was spacious, with comfortable furnishings that escaped pretentiousness. Mihalis Samaras extended a genial smile and a firm handshake to her, at the same time running an appreciative eye over the crisp white linen suit she wore. She returned his smile, knowing she looked efficient and competent, in spite of the slight ruffling of her hair from the motion of the boat and the drive afterward.

Alex had dropped her off after docking the boat in his private slip just outside the city and driving her to the center in his black CX Turbo. She had commented on the car, somehow having expected a Ferrari such as he'd driven in his youth, or perhaps a

Jaguar. He admitted the Citroën was a concession to his new life, his adult respectability, and his position as an attorney.

"But I can open it up if you want," he teased her as he put his foot on the accelerator, causing the tires to squeal around a curve in the beach road. "She's got enough horses under the hood to blister pavement." But when they reached the main road and the early-morning traffic, he'd slowed to a conservative pace.

Mihalis motioned her to a seat as he sank into the leather chair behind his broad oak desk. He leaned back, steepling his fingers beneath his chin. Outside the open window, a motorcycle sped through the intersection, and a truck honked a warning.

Mihalis tipped his head toward the window and asked in his excellent English, "Does that bother you? I can close the window but in the mornings when it's still cool, I like the fresh air."

Not that fresh if the traffic was heavy, Joanna thought with a smile, but the nearby sea generated a breeze that had more aesthetic appeal than air conditioning. "I like it, too."

The man's broad face took on a serious expression. "Miss Paradisis, I know you want to discuss the possibility of buying this hotel but, although the owner has given me full authority to conduct the negotiations, he still has the final decision."

Joanna nodded. "So I understand." She reached into the slim briefcase she had brought with her, extracting a file. "If you could give me a rundown on assets and liabilities, any changes that might have occurred since we originally contacted you, I'll show you what we're prepared to offer."

"Fine," he agreed. "But first, wouldn't you like to have a look around the facilities?"

"Of course, although the photographs you sent were very comprehensive. But I would like to see firsthand."

An hour later they were back in the office. Joanna was pleased with what she'd seen. The entire hotel appeared meticulously in order, updated where necessary as in the case of equipment, but retaining the old-fashioned charm of an inn in the bedrooms and in the bathrooms with their claw-footed tubs.

The only thing that bothered her was the nagging feeling that Mihalis was not anxious to sell the hotel. She didn't like the idea that she might have come here on a wild-goose chase. For her, the urge to acquire the hotel grew stronger, the more she saw of it. Only she wanted it for herself rather than for the company. Except for its somewhat less than ideal location—in a city—the building almost exactly conformed to her dream of an inn she could run on her own, one with a regular clientele to whom she would give personal attention.

"What would you do with the hotel if you bought it?" Mihalis uncannily echoed the tenor of her own thoughts. Perhaps he was also concerned about his job. A change of ownership often meant a change of staff. "Would you be making major changes? I understand that Paradise Hotels caters mainly to the wealthy North American traveler who likes to visit out-of-the-way places, yet demands the comforts he's accustomed to at home. In our present form, I feel we don't fit those criteria."

"That hasn't been finalized. We try to be flexible, treating each project individually. But I will say that in this case, my father is considering converting to time-share condominiums." She arched her brow questioningly. "I don't know if you're familiar—"

Samaras waved his hand with a touch of impatience. "Yes, yes. They have a lot of those in Hawaii."

Joanna nodded. "All right, then. You have to agree that this building, the size of the rooms and the fact that there's a bathroom connected to each one, would be simple to convert."

The man frowned. "Yes, but we have a steady clientele of business people—the port of Volos is a center of shipping to the Middle East—and also a good number of European tourists who return year after year. We're never empty, Miss Paradisis, not even in winter."

"The changes haven't been decided on," Joanna said diplomatically while feeling she was losing ground with every moment that passed. She didn't want to fail in this venture.

"Even so," Mihalis said, clearing his throat, "I think we would require a clause to insure there would be no major changes for a certain number of years." He paused. "If we decided to sell. The owner made that clear to me."

"Who is this owner?" Joanna asked, unable to restrain her impatience. "Can't he deal with me directly? I'd like to meet him."

"You already have, Joanna." Alex's voice came from behind her so unexpectedly she jumped. "I'm the owner."

"Oh." She couldn't stop the astonished exclamation. Then anger submerged her surprise as she leaped up from the chair. "And I suppose you knew exactly where I was going this morning, didn't you? Why the hell didn't you tell me? Does it give you a feeling of power to make me deal with your manager when we could have discussed it between the two of us?"

The half smile on his lips infuriated her but before she could form an even stronger indictment of his behavior, he spoke. "Joanna, I knew about the appointment. But I wasn't planning to get involved in the negotiations. Then yesterday..." He paused. "Yesterday, well, I should have told you but I didn't want to spoil the day."

Joanna sank down into the chair. "You could have told me last week."

"Yeah. I could have, but I was curious to see what kind of a businesswoman you'd become. And I figured you'd want to inspect the hotel firsthand."

"If you'd said something, I could have come to inspect it before this."

Alex stepped closer, trailing one fingertip over the curve of her cheek. Joanna jerked her head away but she was trapped in the chair. Out of the corner of her eye she noticed that they were alone. She'd barely been aware of Mihalis rising with a muttered excuse and leaving them, closing the door as he went out.

"So quickly you're back in your business mode, Joanna," Alex said softly. "You needed your holiday but it doesn't seem to have had any lasting effect."

Determinedly Joanna got to her feet. "That's nothing to do with you, Alex." Going to the window, she stared blindly at the street, hearing but not really registering the noise of the incessant traffic, the shouts of a sponge vendor.

Damn, this was a complication she hadn't counted on. First the clash with Alex over the house, and now this. "You're not going to sell, are you?"

Alex came up behind her and placed his hands on her shoulders. The scent of her perfume teased him with memories of the night just past. Jasmine. In the heated darkness of the night when he'd been deep inside her, her feel and scent had been the only reality in the world. Even now he was aroused at the thought of her soft slender thighs parting so sweetly for him.

Did she notice? A long shudder rippled through her body, and he knew she did.

Did she want him again? Or had this business destroyed the wonder of it for them, stolen the possibilities?

She turned in his arms and pressed herself against him, nestling her head in the hollow of his shoulder. "Oh, Alex, why does life have to be so complicated? Why can't it be simple, like when we were young?"

"Probably because we're not young anymore."

It would be so easy to give in, to forget the reason she was here. He held her against him, his hand firmly spread on her hip. She was acutely aware of his arousal and of the responsive softening of her own body.

He brushed his lips over her forehead so lightly it was more the ephemeral ghost of a caress than a kiss. "Tell me, Joanna, is getting this hotel so important to you?"

She pulled away, moving back to lean on the windowsill, her arms crossed over her chest. "If it is, would you sell it to me?"

Alex didn't miss the hardening of her tone, the rejection obvious in her pose. Important apparently wasn't the word; crucial appeared to be a more accurate term. "I might," he said with deceptive laziness, hitching his hip up on the corner of the desk.

Joanna's chin tilted up and she eyed him imperiously. "Don't do me any favors."

"A profitable business deal is not a favor." Her attitude baffled him. With Mihalis, she had been prepared to wheel and deal on equal terms, one business executive to another. Now the whole situation had taken on the most personal overtones. In fact, she was acting as if he'd insulted her. "And don't kid yourself, I'd make a nice profit if I sold."

"Why would you want to, if the place is making money?"

He hesitated, then plunged ahead, deciding the risk was worth it if he could goad her into revealing the real story behind this. "Perhaps because it means so much to you."

She straightened to her full height, her face flushing with anger. "Whatever success I have, I made on my own," she snapped. "People think that because my father is my boss he gave me a cushy position in the company. The truth is just the opposite. I had to work up from the bottom, like anyone else. Dad doesn't believe in handing out favors. *My* work, and mine alone, got me where I am." She walked up to the desk and fixed Alex with a hard stare. "If I were a stranger, would you sell the hotel?"

No answer yet but some glimmerings of light, Alex thought. "Maybe," he said carefully. "As Mihalis said, I haven't decided. Depends on the deal I'd be offered."

She leaned over and picked up her briefcase from the floor. "Then let's pretend we just met today, and talk about what Paradise Hotels is offering."

Alex gently took the case from her hands and with a light push on her waist, steered her toward the door. "Let's not. Let's go and get a drink, and then you can tell me why you're so desperate."

Desperate? Joanna fumed as she shook off his touch. She threw a tight smile toward Mihalis as they passed him in the hallway leading to the lobby.

"Is everything all right, Miss Paradisis?" he asked courteously.

"Fine," she muttered through clenched teeth. She might as well resign herself to the worst. She had just kissed the promotion goodbye. Without the hotel, or a location for a new one, she had lost that little bit of leverage that would make Socrates choose her over Tony. And suddenly, as it appeared to be slipping away from her, she wanted the promotion.

ALEX LED HER DOWN a flight of stairs a block from the hotel, into a bar that was dim and cool after the burning sun outside. The early-morning freshness had given way to a blinding heat that seared everything it touched. Over the mountains north of the city livid mauve clouds were massing, emitting low rumbles of thunder muted by the cacophony of the heavy traffic in the streets. After weeks of the unrelenting heat wave, tempers were short. During the short walk they had seen a butcher and his customer come to blows over a cut of meat.

Joanna sank down gratefully in the deep leather chair Alex pulled out for her. "What can I get you?" he asked politely.

"Oh, coffee, I guess. And a pitcher of water." Resting her elbow on the table, she pressed her thumb and forefinger against the bridge of her nose, massaging away the headache she'd thought she'd left behind in Vancouver.

After giving their order to the waiter, Alex took her hand. "Joanna, talk to me. Tell me what's wrong. You used to be happy, laughing in the face of whatever might be bothering you. Now you look tense so much of the time." With one finger he smoothed the furrow between her brows. "Is it worth it, Joanna?"

She straightened in the chair. "Of course it's worth it. I wouldn't be doing it otherwise."

"Wouldn't you?" Alex asked seriously. "Isn't it true that you feel you have to prove something, that you're just as good in business, or whatever, as your brothers?"

Angry with herself, she regretted giving Alex even a hint of that deep-seated insecurity. "Don't be ridiculous."

He stared at her. "But you said—"

"Never mind what I said. It's not that simple. I love my work, the challenge of it. And I'm doing this for myself, not for anyone else. I don't have to prove anything. I've already done it. I *am* a success."

"Nobody's disputing that," Alex said, looking up and thanking the waiter as he brought a tray with coffee, and glasses of water in which ice clinked refreshingly. "So why all the heavy weather over a hotel in a non-*touristico* city in Greece? I don't understand it."

"You would if you knew what was at stake," she retorted before picking up her water glass and drinking thirstily.

Alex grinned as he watched the undisguised look of pleasure on her face, the vivid contrast to her determinedly businesslike demeanor. "Better than sex, huh?"

A fluid warmth ran through her at the reminder of last night, her room with the windows open to the sea air, the distant murmur of thunder and the blue flashes of heat lightning that had illuminated Alex's face as he had made love with her. In those moments when they had been tightly joined and climbing to the farthest reaches of ecstasy, they had been as close as it was possible for two people to be.

Regret clawed at her heart even as she flashed him a smile that conveyed a hint of youthful spirit. "Only rarely," she said softly.

Lifting her hand, she toyed with the pearls that hung in the low neckline of the crimson silk blouse she wore with the white suit. "Alex, a couple of days before I left, Dad called Tony and me into his office and told us he was considering both of us for a promotion. He likes Tony, and I think he favors him for the position because he thinks I work too hard already and he'd like me to get married. It's not that he doesn't think women should have careers but . . ." Her voice trailed off.

Alex nodded, remembering her dismay at the sample wedding invitation. He recalled that Socrates had always run his household in an autocratic manner even when Joanna and her brothers were young. He had demanded much of his children, and they had not disappointed him, all of them achieving enviable success in adulthood.

Only Joanna somehow didn't seem to feel she'd done enough, and continued her driven search for more.

Alex understood her fears and motivations in a way he suspected would shock her if she sensed just how deeply he saw inside her. Yet, even as he understood, he seriously doubted that her ambition and her success made her happy. Even though he had long ago discarded any hope of real happiness for himself, he wished nothing more than for Joanna to realize it.

If he sold her the hotel, would that allow her to achieve her dreams? It would be so easy, a couple of words, their signatures on a legal document, and it would be done.

And Joanna would resent him forever, for not letting her accomplish her own achievements.

"He'd like you to marry Tony," Alex said in a neutral tone that gave no clue to his inner ruminations.

Closing her eyes, Joanna allowed her head to fall against the padded back of the club chair. "I think he's trying to force the issue. If I agree to marry Tony, he can give Tony the promotion with a clear conscience. He'll just assume that I won't mind because I'll be happy for Tony and then I'll settle down and have babies." She lifted her head, her eyes popping open. "Can you imagine such an attitude in this day and age?"

Alex, who had never led a sheltered life, could very easily. "Joanna, have you thought how you would handle it if you got the promotion and then got married?"

"I told you. I'm not marrying Tony." She fixed him with a hard stare. "Do you think I'd have made love with you if I was serious about Tony?"

Alex hoped not but the realistic fatalism he accepted as part of his basic psychological makeup told him it could easily be otherwise. Women, especially ambitious women, a group in which he was forced to include Joanna, went to bed with men for any number of reasons.

"You might have," he said, cynicism giving his voice a cutting edge. "You wouldn't be the first woman to use her body to get something she wanted."

Joanna reared up from her seat. "I resent that, Alex!" She bit off the words, teeth clenched so tightly her jaw ached. "I might also question your motives. Maybe you thought I'd meekly let you keep your aunt's house if you softened me up. Well, let me remind you, no one softens me up that way."

Alex closed his eyes wearily. "Sit down, Joanna. You're making a scene."

She glanced around at the dim room, the unoccupied tables, the waiter out of sight in the kitchen judging by the sound of glass and cutlery clattering. At this hour, she and Alex were the only occupants of the bar. "Who would care?" she retorted.

"Joanna," Alex said quietly, "we could argue motives and repercussions forever but it would get us nowhere. I made love with you because I wanted to. I hope you felt the same way, but that's between you and your conscience. I had no intention of insulting you with what I just said. It was a legitimate question."

Joanna sat down, her anger draining away. "You wouldn't say that if you knew me."

"That's just the point, isn't it? We don't know each other any more, not as we once did. We've both changed." He put his forearms on the table and leaned toward her. "Even this, our meeting here, is an artificial situation. When you get back, you'll remember it as a pleasant interlude, a holiday fling. 'Alex? Yes, I saw him. He's gotten older but he still looks pretty good. How he can bury himself in that place, I don't know.' Your mother will ask about me, you'll tell her, and that will be that.''

Joanna listened to this in silence. She wanted to protest that their lovemaking had meant much more than a casual fling to her but if this was how Alex saw it, she would only make a fool of herself if she argued with his assessment of the situation. It was clear that Alex entertained no thoughts of her beyond the present.

To give herself a moment to digest the unpalatable truth, Joanna lifted her coffee cup, making a face as she tasted its bitterness. "Ugh, it's cold."

"I'll order some fresh." Alex tapped on the table, bringing the waiter from the kitchen. When the man had left them again, he said, "Suppose, just for the sake of discussion, you get the promotion, and you marry Tony."

"I told you it's out of the question," she said sharply.

Alex put up a hand. "This is a theoretical discussion, okay? Suppose you marry—we'll leave Tony out of it—it could be someone else. When will you find time to spend with a husband and children? Are you going to make appointments with your husband to ensure conception, and then give the children to a nanny to raise as soon as they're born?"

"Other career women do," she said, aware that her words lacked conviction. To her dismay, an image of an infant with wrinkled pink skin and Alex's black hair and eyes had leaped into her mind as he'd spoken. And even more startling, the vision didn't seem to represent entrapment but conveyed a feeling of content, of rightness.

"Sure they do," Alex agreed. "And more power to them. But is that what you want, Joanna? That's the question you have to ask yourself. I think you're so busy trying to please everyone that you forget about yourself. As long as you find it impossible to separate duty from your own needs and desires, you'll be caught in this position."

In virtual silence they drank the fresh coffee the waiter brought. As it neared noon, more customers drifted into the bar, men in shirtsleeves, wiping perspiring faces with large white handkerchiefs. Women who ventured into the predominantly male enclave wore thin silk dresses and the look of money. Volos was a city with a well-established upper class, riding on its prosperity as a flourishing international seaport centrally located in a thriving agricultural region. Smaller than Athens but hardly less sophisticated, it had none of the provinciality Joanna would have expected. She was beginning to see why Alex had settled there.

Alex paid for their coffee and they ascended the shallow flight of stairs to the street, blinking against the painful assault of light from an incandescent sky.

"Let me show you a little of the city," Alex suggested.

"In this heat?" Joanna asked as sweat popped out on her forehead. "And in these shoes?" Sightseeing usually involved walking. Driving in the narrow crowded streets gave one no chance to concentrate on anything but negotiating a safe course.

Alex grinned, accepting the indication that harmony had been restored between them. "I'll buy you a pair of sandals." He glanced at the sky, squinting as he avoided the copper sun. "As for the heat, we'll only walk a short distance and then we'll have lunch."

"If we're not going far," Joanna declared, "I can manage in these shoes."

"Just in case, I'll hold your arm." Secretly pleased at the opportunity to reestablish physical contact, he took her briefcase and the suit jacket she had taken off in one hand, and slipped his other arm into the crook of her elbow.

"Where do you live, Alex?" Joanna asked as they started down the street. "Oh, I suppose in one of the quaint villages just above the city."

"Wrong. I have a waterfront apartment a couple of blocks from my office."

"So close? Then you hardly need a car."

He smiled. "I need it for drives into those quaint villages on the mountain," he said, gently mocking her. "And for trips to Larissa or Athens or Thessaloniki. I do get out sometimes." As they waited for the traffic light to change, he touched her with his fingertip, collecting the beads of sweat nestling in the little indentation above her upper lip. "It's too hot to walk. We'll just go to a restaurant and eat lunch, then start back. It'll be cool on the water."

Yes, the boat. In her mind Joanna could feel the breeze sweeping across the deck, spray washing over them as the billowing sails sent the boat skimming over the sea. With sadness she realized this might be the last time she sailed with him. Her business accomplished, however unsatisfactorily, she had to get home.

COMING OUT OF THE RESTAURANT later, they were hit by a blast of heat and humidity that felt as solid as a wall. Thunder, closer now, rumbled ominously and the sky had an odd green luminosity, like a two-day-old bruise. A fitful wind, fiery as a breath from hell, whipped Joanna's skirt against her knees.

Alex glanced at the threatening sky. "Looks like we're in for it."

"Will it be safe to sail?" Joanna asked.

"For a couple more hours, sure. We'll be close to shore so if it turns bad we'll put in to a harbor. It's not as if we're venturing into the Pacific or something."

They took a shortcut through the courtyard of Agios Nicholas, a massive brick church with impressive carved wooden doors. A wedding party stood at the top of the steps, smiling for a photographer, the female members chattering and fussing like hens on a roost.

"Didn't most weddings used to be held on Sundays?" Joanna asked, smiling as a little boy in a blue velvet suit ran across to the water fountain, forcing the photographer to wait until he returned.

"Times have changed, Joanna. A Friday wedding gives a couple the weekend for a honeymoon. And then it's back to work on Monday."

A gust of wind blowing around the corner of a tall apartment building buffeted Joanna, and Alex took her arm to steady her as she stumbled. She glanced at him, seeing the set expression on his face. Was it the impending storm, or the sight of the happy wedding couple that had darkened his mood?

"Odd you never married, Alex," she said with deliberate provocation. "You must have had plenty of opportunities."

"Yeah, plenty," he said abruptly. "They saw the Ferrari, the apartment, and the money, and I was fighting off proposals. Yeah, I had opportunities."

His hand clenched her arm, loosening only when she made a low sound of discomfort. "From users," he said. "That's all they were. Users."

The vehemence in his tone silenced her, but only for a moment. "Sounds like you had some bad experiences," she said with casual calm.

They stopped at a traffic light, watched as the cars rushed by, the tangle of vehicles more frenetic than ever. Drivers yelled at one another as they braked and swerved to avoid an elderly Mercedes wheezing with an overheated radiator.

"You might say that," Alex said without looking at her.

Another dead end? Joanna asked herself. In her family, feelings had been aired, not buried, a much healthier state of affairs than Alex's stoic reticence.

"I suppose you never fell in love," she asked bluntly as they got into the car.

He turned the key in the ignition, giving a cynical laugh that hurt her. "Love? What's love? Something women invented to glamorize the reasons for marriage?"

The hurt faded, and she hid a smile. This was a typical reaction from a man put on the defensive. "So? Is that bad?"

He looked startled and almost ran a red light. Eyeing her with new respect, he laughed a little uncertainly. "No, I guess not. I just hadn't thought of it that way." He wheeled the car into the parking area. "Here we are."

Casting anxious glances up at the sky, they scrambled onto the boat. Alex ran up the sails, his movements quick and efficient, and set a course for

Mikrohori. Riding before an increasing wind, they made good time.

They were perhaps a half hour from home when the storm clouds reached them, looming ominously overhead. The wind whistled among the lines, and the sea rolled beneath the boat like a restless dragon about to waken. Alex's knuckles were white on the tiller as he fought to keep on course. When a blue arrow of lightning shafted from the billowing clouds into the sea just ahead of the bow, Joanna learned the metallic taste of fear.

"Get below," Alex shouted over the crash of thunder that followed. "And close the hatch."

"What about you?" she yelled back.

"I'll be okay. This isn't my first storm."

Reluctantly, knowing she was too much of a novice sailor to help and only a worry to him out on the open deck, she turned away. But as she faced the open expanse of the bay to the west of them, she saw it coming: a curtain of gray, a solid wall of water stretching from the sea to the angry sky.

CHAPTER ELEVEN

"ALEX, LOOK!" Joanna cried.

He turned his head, then gave his attention back to wrestling with the tiller. "Get below, Joanna. And don't worry. We'll make it. There's the headland."

The curtain of rain advanced, chasing before it a wind heightened almost to hurricane force. A giant wave rolled under the boat and the craft pitched and wallowed before miraculously righting itself. The first raindrops slammed as hard as pebbles against Joanna's face.

"Get below," Alex yelled again.

"I'll stay here." She huddled in a corner seat, hugging her arms around her knees. Better to take her chances out in the open than to have the boat capsize with her trapped inside.

The rain hit them, drenching their clothes in seconds. At the same time a wave driven by the howling wind lifted the boat nearly free of the water. Alex swung the tiller hard around and sent *Meltemi* flying into the relative calm of the little cove.

Moving quickly, he dropped the anchor and secured the rigging. The boat rocked on the rolling waves while the wind shrieked among the lines like a demented beast deprived of its prey. "We'll have to climb the cliff," Alex said, turning to Joanna. "But the boat is safe here. Why don't you go down and look in the locker under the bunk? You should be able to find something dry to wear.''

Joanna glanced down at her sodden suit. The linen would never be the same again.

The cabin, with its watertight hatch, was dry and held a residual warmth from earlier in the day. Even so, Joanna shivered as she peeled off her suit and blouse before unsnapping the catch that secured the locker. Inside she found an assortment of shorts, cut-offs and jeans, as well as T-shirts and sweatshirts in all sizes, probably the lost and found of numerous sailing trips with various passengers. Had some of them been women?

Squelching the thought, she pulled a pair of cotton rugby pants and a fleece sweatshirt over her damp underwear. The sleeves covered her hands and she rolled them to the middle of her forearms. Catching a glimpse of herself in the mirror, she burst out laughing. ''Definitely something the cat dragged in,'' she muttered, pulling a face at the sight of her straggly hair and the oversize sweatshirt hanging shapelessly from her shoulders to her hips.

She was applying a brush vigorously to her hair when Alex came in. He was soaked to the skin, his cotton shirt and pants clinging and delineating every contour and muscle. He looked masculine and sexy, the grin on his face and the reckless gleam in his eyes enhancing the triumphant air of his having fought the elements and won.

''Told you we'd make it,'' he said jovially as he stripped off shirt, pants and underwear without even bothering to turn his back. Joanna couldn't take her eyes off him. He returned her gaze, never losing the grin that gave him the look of a successful pirate.

Moving toward her, he extended one hand and cupped it around her cheek. "Joanna." He lowered his head to kiss her and she felt the hardening of his body against her thigh.

A fresh gust of wind sent the boat heaving under them. Alex lifted his head. "I guess it's not over yet. We'd better make shore."

He pulled on a pair of cutoffs over his naked body, topping it with a striped fisherman's shirt. From another closet he pulled bright yellow hooded slickers. Apparently they came in only one size, extra large. The one he handed Joanna enveloped her like a shroud.

Alex laughed as she straightened the rubberized fabric on her shoulders. "You look like you're wearing a tent."

Grinning, she took a couple of steps, the slicker flapping around her calves. "Feels like it, too." She followed him up the steps. "How will we get to shore? I'd say it's a bit rough for swimming. Besides, we're dressed wrong."

He groped in the locker for a small knapsack to carry their shoes. "It's not as bad here in the cove as out in the open. We'll make it in the dinghy."

On the exposed deck, the wind was a rapacious demon that whipped Joanna's hair across her face and tore at their clothes, belling out the slickers, diminishing their protection from the driving rain. An ominous green-hued gloom hung around the boat, made eerie by the frequent flashes of lightning. Thunder reverberated across the sky like a battalion of celestial cavalry.

Joanna clung to the rail as she made her way aft to the rope ladder, struggling against the wind and the heavy rolling of the deck under her feet. When her fingers slipped for an instant, only Alex's steadying arm around her waist saved her from being washed overboard.

The dinghy bobbed on the roiling water like a rubber duck, and looked about as safe. "As soon as you get into it, sit down," Alex cautioned as she clambered down the rope ladder, the wooden rungs slippery under her bare feet. "Keep the center of gravity as low as possible."

The rubber boat rebounded wildly as she landed off balance, but by crouching down at once, she managed to avoid being dumped into the sea. A second later Alex landed next to her, concern in his eyes. "Are you okay?" he shouted over the wind.

"Fine," she yelled. "But I think I'm soaked again."

He gave her a thumbs-up signal as he turned away to start the engine. It snarled to life but Joanna saw they hardly needed it as the breakers drove them toward the shore. Moments later the bottom of the dinghy scraped on sand and Alex jumped out and pulled it higher.

The scramble up the cliff, arduous as it was, seemed almost anticlimactic after their battle with a sea gone mad. Rain pelted them, and lightning and thunder bombarded them with dazzling light and ear-splitting noise. The prolonged heat wave must have built tension in the stratosphere that finally erupted with a force that was awesome and terrifying.

But Joanna had no time for fear or contemplation of the power of nature as she clung with her hands and knees to the cliff face, climbing with dogged persistence. Hiking up the flapping tails of the slicker, she gained level ground just ahead of Alex.

"We made it," he said, coming up next to her.

"Yes, we did." Around them the storm still raged but they were safe. Far below, the sailboat was barely visible as it rode out the battering of the waves against its sturdy hull.

"It's letting up a bit," Joanna added, flicking a glance at the charcoal clouds. As if to prove her wrong, a flash of lightning crackled across the sky and stabbed to earth nearby, setting fire to a thornbush. The flames were immediately extinguished by the drenching rain.

Alex grabbed Joanna's hand. "Let's get out of here," he yelled over the vengeful roar of thunder.

Hand in hand, they ran along the cliff path, keeping as close as possible to clumps of beach junipers and outcroppings of rocks. The wind and rain assaulted them with increased violence.

"Some storm," Joanna gasped as they reached the relative shelter of the warehouses at the edge of the village. "And here I thought Greece was a hot, dry country."

"Not always," Alex conceded, his chest heaving as he caught his breath. "Sometimes these storms come down. It's exciting after the boredom of one sunny day after another."

"Well, I could live with the boredom," Joanna declared. Charged with adrenaline at having survived the worst of the storm, she threw her head back and laughed aloud. Grabbing Alex around his neck, she gave him a smacking kiss. "No, you're right. It's exhilarating. I wouldn't have missed it for the world."

Jenny was out on her porch when they passed her house, rocking serenely back and forth in her chair. She was smoking a thin black Turkish cigarette, the exotic smoke an odd counterpoint to the aroma of parched earth soaking in water, and of green, growing plants. The perfume of the roses in the garden overlaid every other scent with an exotic top note.

"*Yassas, pedhia,*" she called casually. "Got caught in it, did you?"

"Sure did," Alex said, stopping and leaning on the gate. "But we made it."

"Were you scared, Joanna?" Jenny asked, tapping the ash off her cigarette.

"When I saw that wall of water coming toward us, filling the sky from top to bottom, I was for a minute. But after that I had too much to do—" she cast Alex a laughing glance "—hanging on to the rail to keep from being swept overboard."

Alex ruffled her hair. It was soaked through as the hood of the slicker had fallen back during the scramble up the cliff. "She's quite a sailor. Almost anyone would have been hanging over the rail, throwing up their lunch. But not our Joanna."

"Hang on to her, Alex," Jenny admonished with a sly laugh as they started down the narrow, deserted street outlined by feebly glowing street lamps.

"Don't worry. I will."

Jenny called something else after them, which was lost in a rumble of thunder.

"What did she say?" Joanna asked.

Alex stopped in his tracks, causing Joanna to wrench her arm as she skidded in the mud that yesterday had been choking dust. She rubbed the muscle, giving him an aggrieved look. "What did she say?"

Deviltry gleamed in Alex's eyes. "Well, now, I don't know if I should tell you."

"Tell me, or I'll belt you."

Her belligerent stance sent him into gales of laughter. "Okay. You asked for it. She said 'have fun.'"

Joanna's eyes grew round, vividly blue against the muddy streaks that turned her face into a parody of a warring Indian's. "She knows."

Alex laughed again, a full-bodied bellow of pure enjoyment. "By this time, the whole village probably knows. And they no doubt approve. They see a happily-ever-after for both of us."

Joanna's high spirits began to deflate. They both knew that a storybook ending was not possible for them. "Then why did they make such a fuss before? Why did little old ladies tell Jenny to warn me about madness under the moon, to tell me in a kind but direct way that it wasn't proper for an unattached man and woman to share a house?"

"Because, my dear Joanna, they didn't want bad lecherous me taking advantage of innocent tourist you."

She regarded him thoughtfully. "Well, we both know you didn't take advantage of anything I didn't offer, don't we?"

He stared back at her, his own eyes black and smoky, a promise in the sudden sweet curve of his mouth. "Then why are we standing here in the rain discussing it?" He lowered his mouth to her ear, nipping at the lobe and whispering a suggestion that made her burn despite the dank clinging of her wet clothes to her body. "Would you like that, Joanna?"

Setting aside all thoughts of making haste only to repent at leisure, Joanna smiled. "I can hardly wait."

JOANNA REALIZED she had never fully appreciated the size of the old-fashioned claw-footed bathtub in her godmother's house. Up to her neck in hot water, the storm firmly shut out but still faintly audible, she reveled in the feeling of security imparted by thick stone walls.

And she reveled in the voluptuous pleasure of Alex seated behind her in the tub, his legs stretched out on either side of hers.

He pulled her snugly against him, nuzzling her nape and letting his hands slide up to her breasts. She smelled of flowers, a heady scent that made the blood sing in his veins. He loved how she smelled. He loved how she felt, her firm breasts exactly the right size for his palm, the nipples hard and pink, like rosebuds about to open.

Joanna leaned back, her hair tangling with his chest hair, causing a wonderfully erotic sensation that made her close her eyes and stifle a groan. The tub was full and she lifted her foot to turn off the water with her toes. Twisting her body, she moved to flip over but he restrained her.

"Stay like that, Joanna. It feels so good, better than anything. And I can touch you."

She wriggled against him, the sleek slide of her skin on his exacerbating the heat in her abdomen. "But I can't touch you."

His chuckle reverberated against her ear, tickling so that she shivered. "You'll get your turn. Don't be greedy."

Working up a lather between his palms, he soaped her breasts, kneading them in a way that turned her insides hot and liquid. Again, Joanna tried to turn but his legs clamped around her.

"Wait," he breathed.

She couldn't. She had to hold him, to give in to the hot flood that was about to burst over her. Her breath came in gasps. Then she forgot to breathe entirely when his soapy hand traveled further down, his fingers coming inside her, stroking, caressing, in and out, round and round, advancing, retreating—

"Alex!" she cried frantically as heat washed up her. She clutched his hand to her as her body convulsed wildly, beyond her control, beyond reason or reality. The waves subsided and she lay limp against him, gulping in air.

"Good?" he asked teasingly, his fingers beginning to move again.

She held them still, sated, unbearably sensitive where he touched her. "So good," she sighed. "But no more for a moment. I can't breathe."

He turned her so they were face-to-face, the water a buoyant cradle for their bodies. "Will you scrub my back?" he asked, giving her a wet kiss. His mouth lingered on hers. "Or shall I give you mouth-to-mouth resuscitation?"

Joanna laughed, still shaken by the incredible climax he had triggered in her. "I don't think that will be necessary. In fact, it might make matters worse." She reached for the soap. "My turn. Let me wash your back."

"My front is much more interesting."

She allowed her gaze to follow the line of wet hair that bisected his stomach. "I'll say. But we'll get to that, too."

Kneeling, she rubbed the fragrant lather over his back, relishing the supple play of muscles under the silky skin, and the little groans of pleasure he made whenever her fingers touched a particularly responsive area.

She started on his chest, her hands alternately gentle and provocative. Every movement made her thighs stroke against his, the friction of her soft skin driving him crazy.

With a muscular twist that sent water sloshing onto the floor he lifted her, at the same time pushing his legs under her. Slowly, he lowered her, burying himself in her hot wetness, groaning uncontrollably at the deliciousness of it.

Joanna gasped, clenching her fingers in his hair. "Alex!" She cried out his name just before his mouth covered hers. His tongue was everywhere, probing the depths of her mouth, playing with hers, licking at her parted lips, washing over her cheeks.

With sure instinct she began to move into his rhythm. They fit so closely and it felt so good, the hardness of him deep inside her, the delicious friction of his chest hair on her sensitized nipples.

Suddenly, incredibly, she felt it again, that headlong blaze that started in her toes and moved swiftly to the center of her body. Her movements became frantic, her mouth against his chanting raggedly, incoherently. "Oh, Alex, please. Yes, like that. Alex!"

The final spasm of completion hit them both at once. Caught in the grip of a force beyond their control they slid under the water, coming up gasping for air.

For a long moment they stared at each other, stunned. "Joanna," Alex said at last, his voice strangled by the emotion he felt. His hands cupped her flushed cheeks. "Joanna, I've never, ever—" He shook his head. Language hadn't invented the words he needed to describe what he'd felt.

But Joanna understood, even though confusion warred with elation inside her. "I know, Alex," she said. "I know."

The water had cooled and they shivered as they stood and grabbed towels from the rail, wrapping them around each other.

Alex yawned widely. "Why don't we go up to bed? I could sleep a week."

Joanna laughed although her wobbly knees and the lassitude weighting her body reinforced the wisdom of his suggestion. She flicked him with the end of a towel, scoring a stinging hit on one lean buttock. "Worn out already, Alex?"

He whirled and flicked her back, the towel snapping harmlessly as she danced out of reach. "I'll show you who's worn out."

Laughing, they ran up the stairs, arguing about whether to eat now, or later, after a nap. As they tumbled onto Joanna's bed, "later" won although it was a long delicious time before they napped.

At midnight they dined on grilled-cheese sandwiches made by Alex, washing them down with the remnants of a bottle of wine Joanna had found at the back of the fridge. The wine was strong and astringent, a local vintage she used for enhancing stews, but in their mutually besotted state it could have been nectar.

After cleaning up the kitchen, they went back upstairs and made love yet again before falling asleep, soothed by the patter of raindrops on the slate roof.

CHAPTER TWELVE

ALEX TOSSED AND TURNED in his sleep. Someone was calling him. A woman. Suddenly he was a boy again, running across a lawn. A group of people dressed in white summer clothes were sitting at a table. He ran too quickly, and bumped the table, spilling a cup of tea into his mother's lap. He stood, mouth open in horror at what he had done. *I'm sorry.* No sound came out. His mother glared at him; the fierce blue of her eyes cut him like razors. She got up, and the scene changed. She was on a balcony, near the low railing. *Come away,* he wanted to scream. He saw her tip over the edge, as if in slow motion, and fall silently through the air, her white dress billowing.

Alex jerked awake, his heart racing out of control, sweat cold and clammy on his skin. Bewildered, he searched the room. Beside him Joanna breathed quietly. A dream.

With a sigh, he left the bed and walked to the window, skirting the little heaps of the clothes they'd shed after their midnight snack.

The rain had stopped; the air was fragrant with the pungency of wet soil and fecund plants. He breathed deeply, inhaling life and sanity, pushing away the nightmare. The exotic sweetness of jasmine drifted into the room, mingling with the warm muskiness of the sheets and their bodies.

"Alex?" Her voice was low, faintly rough with sleep, wrapping around him with sweet entreaty.

Slowly he turned, seeing her face, arms, and bare breasts bathed in pearly moonlight. "Joanna, I'm here."

He moved back to the bed and lay down beside her. Joanna felt tension in his body. Turning her head, she studied the face on the pillow next to her. His eyes were open, a frown etching two vertical lines between his brows.

"Alex, what is it?" She snuggled closer, laying her arm across his bare chest, her fingers stroking lightly along the smooth skin of his side. "You had another nightmare, didn't you? Isn't it time you talked about it, to somebody?"

He shifted uncomfortably, as if by avoiding her gaze he could avoid her questions. "It has nothing to do with you."

"I know, but I can see you're hurting. It might help to talk about it."

He sat up abruptly, throwing off her arm and wrapping his own around his raised knees. "I don't see how. It happened a long time ago."

"But you haven't let it go," she said gently, hiding her frustration at his continued refusal to open up to her.

He turned his head, the frown deepening. In the semidarkness of the room she could not see his eyes, but it seemed to her they glittered with cynicism. "As I said, it happened a long time ago. There was no point then, and there's no point now, blubbering over what can't be changed. I'm a man. I'm not a child who goes bawling to his mother every time something hurts. I can handle it."

Not very well, from what I see, Joanna thought with a rush of compassion. The rigid carriage of his body, his stubbornly defensive declaration, showed her clearly that he was suffering. "I'm not your mother," she said mildly. "I hope you realize that."

The laugh that erupted from him was brief and bitter. "No. You're not. At least I hope not." But deep down, he wondered. Didn't all women possess some of the qualities of his mother?

"She died soon after you went back to live with her, didn't she?" Joanna asked gently. "I'm sorry."

He looked at her, his face tight with suppressed anger. "Why should you be sorry? You might have met her a couple of times but you didn't know her." He gave another harsh laugh. "You should be grateful for that. I often wondered what kind of a human being she was. She had no feelings at all. She wasn't any kind of a mother. She had me, an unfortunate accident, as she never forgot to remind me, and gave me to a nanny. If I'd been a kitten or a puppy, she would have drowned me at birth. I don't remember one time that she kissed me or gave me a hug."

Tears welled in Joanna's eyes as she pictured an unloved, unwanted little boy. No wonder Alex had so wholeheartedly embraced the noisy closeness of her family when he'd stayed with his aunt.

She also understood the moodiness he had shown after each of his mother's visits during the years he'd lived next door. Those had been the only times Joanna hadn't been able to talk with him. He'd shut himself away even from her.

"What happened to her?" She had to keep him talking, not only to satisfy her own curiosity and to foster her deeper understanding of the man he was, but to provide a catharsis for him through the telling of his story. He could not begin to heal until the festering wound was excised.

"They said it was a heart attack but I've always wondered. There was more than drinking going on at that party where she collapsed. They tried to cover it up. They might have fooled the press and the police, but I knew that crowd. I should have. I was part of it once."

His eyes were fixed on the rectangle of window, silvered with moonlight that bathed the room in a soft glow. "I drank too much, drove too fast and played too hard, but somehow I managed to stop short of burning out my brain."

Joanna felt her stomach muscles tighten. Her life had been so different, ordered, secure, something she hadn't appreciated. While Alex's... "But you left that life. Was it hard?"

Slowly he turned toward her, sliding down until he lay beside her. He pulled her close, aligning her body with his, until their faces were next to each other on the pillow. Gently he stroked her hair, fanning it out with his fingers until it lay spread around her head. "Yes, Joanna. It was hard to make the break. My friends were the only family I had after I left Vancouver."

"You could have stayed. Your aunt often said how much she missed you."

"I know she did, but my mother had said she needed me. For the first time in my life, she needed me. When I got to London I found out that she was between husbands. She'd been ill. She wanted me around, but don't kid yourself. She never became the ideal mother nurturing her long-lost son, even at the end." He frowned. "You know, now that I think about it, maybe she was lonely. Not that she ever let on. It was one party after another. And after she died, I continued what you might call the family tradition."

"But you stopped."

Alex nodded, his fingers still playing with her hair, as if threading through the silky strands soothed him. "Yeah, I stopped. One day I decided this was no way to spend the rest of my life. I was about to be kicked out of law school so I knew it was time to shape up."

"Just like that." Her voice held a note of disbelief.

"No, Joanna. Not just like that." He left off his caresses and just held her head, his palm warmly enclosing her skull. "You know, there's a theory that some people, either by personality or physical chemistry, are addictive types. I guess I wasn't. Oh, it was hard to quit drinking but I just said one day, who's the boss around here, me or the bottle? I still have the occasional drink or a glass of wine, but that's it. The fast driving—well, you saw the other day how I feel about that. I've learned to value my life."

"Don't we all, at some point in our lives?" Joanna said soberly. "Particularly when something happens to point out the fragility of that life. What happened to you?"

"It's not important," he started to say but she interrupted.

"I know it is, Alex."

He was silent for a long moment, then sighed heavily. "Yeah, it is. This girl in our crowd killed herself. She fell off a balcony twenty-two stories up."

"An accident."

"That's what the police said, but they didn't know the whole story. Some of the guys had dared her to walk on the rail. She did it. We were all laughing. She made it to the other end of the balcony, jumped safely down. We all went back into the apartment. We'd been drinking and fooling around. Some of the people there were flying pretty high. The next thing we knew she was out on the rail again. This time she fell, screaming." His voice broke. "I still hear that scream in my dreams."

She could feel him shudder as she wrapped her arms around him. He pushed his face into her neck, and she held him close, cradling his head against her shoulder. "Was this girl special to you? Did you love her?"

"No." The word was muffled. "No. I didn't. She was someone on the edge of our crowd." His voice strengthened into brutal honesty. "We used her. Maybe if one of us had cared, the whole thing wouldn't have happened. But it was only a game, a game we all played at the time. We thought we could do what we wanted when we wanted."

Her heart ached for him, for the sterility of his childhood, the mother who had paraded a succession of husbands through his life, denying him any anchor, and who had rejected him when he needed her. He had had so little love.

Joanna could no longer deny her own love for him. But at the same time she knew he wasn't ready for it. It was a secret she clasped to her heart. "This isn't a game. This is real, Alex," she whispered.

"Yes," he murmured. "This is real. You are real. My Joanna." His gaze shifted to the window. The night was fading, the sky changing from a predawn colorlessness to a delicate pink.

He took Joanna's hand, throwing aside the sheet and pulling her up from the bed. "What is it?" she asked.

He smiled. "Come and see."

She shivered in the cool, rose-scented air coming from the open window but only until he wrapped his arms around her. Together, they faced the window. "I love the way the sun paints the sea when it comes up over the mountain, like the dawn of creation. When I used to sleep in this room, I'd often get up for the sunrise and then go back to bed."

Joanna pulled back to stare at him. "If I'd known how much it meant to you, I would never have let you give me this room."

"Joanna, I wanted you to have it. It's your house now."

Yes. Technically. But emotionally? "Alex—"

"Shh," he said. "It's all right. Watch now."

The sky had cleared overnight. Puddles were drying along the beach road, and Joanna knew that by noon all trace of the storm would have vanished. In the orchard a multitude of birds, hidden among the leaves of the apple trees, sang an ecstatic ode to the morning. Joanna snuggled close to Alex, shivering a little. He was warm against her, and getting warmer, she noticed, the shiver becoming one of pleasure.

He kissed her again, smiling as she touched him. "See what you do to me?" He took her hand, holding it in his. "Don't, or we'll miss the sunrise."

Like the rising crescendo of a symphony, the sun crested the mountain and laid a wash of gold and amber on the sea, giving it the sheen of new brass. Daylight and the promise of warmth spilled into the room. Joanna looked from the window to Alex, her eyes shining with blue fire, her sleep-tousled hair shimmering in a nimbus of light. Alex thought he'd never seen anyone more beautiful in his life.

He'd told her the secrets that haunted him. She hadn't judged him, only listened and accepted. There had been no trace of pity in her demeanor. He couldn't have stood it if there had been. He felt cleaner, lighter, but he was too much of a realist to believe that the nightmares and the restlessness were over.

Hungrily he let his eyes move over her, memorizing the moment. She met his gaze boldly, her lips parting as she responded with her whole being to the naked longing he knew must be in his eyes. He shuddered with the force of his desire, yet for an instant fear clutched at his heart. It was dangerous to feel this depth of emotion, dangerous to open himself to her, safer by far to insulate his feelings by keeping a distance between them. He'd tried to love, so long ago, and been rejected. With the young Joanna, he had loved but circumstances had been against him. Since then, he'd been careful.

But when he saw the awakening passion in her eyes, the shimmering blue that rivaled the June sky, the fear faded into oblivion. She was temptress, flame, unlike any woman he'd known, enticing him, drawing him toward what? Ecstasy?

Or destruction?

Swinging her up into his arms he carried her to the bed. What did it matter? Perhaps they were ultimately the same.

CHAPTER THIRTEEN

JOANNA AWOKE to the realization that the sun was high in the sky and that there was an inordinate amount of noise outside. She rubbed at her eyes, glancing with affection at Alex who lay on his stomach, his sleek skin a dark contrast to the white sheets. Tiny droplets of sweat lay in the shallow dip of his spine, and a ripple of pleasure shot through her as she remembered the erotic feel of their damp bodies sliding against each other.

He snored gently, undisturbed by the pounding that was becoming more than intrusive. She frowned in annoyance. Who would be hammering so close to her house? There were no other buildings nearby.

Then, with a shock, she realized it was someone banging on the door. She jumped out of bed, grabbing her robe and her watch as she headed for the stairs. Ten-thirty-seven. She gasped. It couldn't be that late.

But it was. The sun hung in a flawless blue sky, a benign guardian of life rather than the ravenous presence it had been for the past weeks. Downstairs, closed shutters darkened the rooms, and Joanna shivered as she hurried to the door where a renewed pounding shook the wooden panels.

Muttering imprecations at the persistence of her caller, she unlatched the door and threw it open, only to stagger back as she saw who waited outside.

"Tony," she gasped, her heart catching in her throat. "What are you doing here?"

Tony tossed her a rakish grin, his dark brown eyes sparkling. "I thought I'd join you for a few days."

"Join me?" She leaned on the doorframe, unsure that her trembling legs would support her. After their discussion before her trip, Tony was the last person she had expected to see here.

Suddenly comprehension dawned, and red color washed up her cheeks. The letter she'd sent special delivery. Stifling a groan, she rested her forehead against her arm. Impulse. She should never have given in to impulse, never have given free rein to her temper as she had in that letter.

"Your mother and father are here, too," Tony went on cheerfully, as if it were a normal day and Joanna were behaving in a normal fashion.

"They're here, too?" she repeated stupidly, her eyes widening as she peered around him.

He gestured down the path. "They're waiting in the car. I wasn't sure if it was advisable to drive up that track, so I came to make sure you were still here."

Joanna took a deep breath, fighting to recover her equilibrium. "A long way to come without knowing, wasn't it?"

"Well, I phoned Mihalis Samaras and he thought you'd come back here with his boss." For the first time the smile slipped, and Joanna saw what she hadn't noticed sooner, that Tony's cheerfulness was a thin veneer that hid a wire-tight tension. "What's going on, Joanna? Your father was very hurt by the tone of your letter."

"What about you?" she couldn't resist asking.

"I was hurt, too, but I assured him it was only a lover's quarrel." He half turned from her. "Shall I go and tell them to come up? What about the car?"

"It's safe enough down there." Joanna's head whirled with the implications of the arrival of more guests just when she and Alex had made some headway in understanding each other.

"Joanna?" Tony prompted her.

"Yes, tell them to come up."

He jumped down the step and strode away, a tall athletic man whose demeanor struck lust into the hearts of all the female employees in the executive offices of Paradise Hotels. The endearing thing about it, Joanna thought, was that Tony never capitalized on his good looks. He was a thoroughly good-natured man who liked women. He wasn't complex and full of dark shadows like Alex.

Alex. She closed the door in a state of near panic, almost severing the cat's tail as it sneaked in past her legs. She had to get him out of her room before her mother and father came in and found him sprawled in her bed. Old-fashioned as he was, Socrates would find a shotgun and a priest, and Alex would find himself hanged by the marital bonds before he even woke fully.

If it hadn't been so serious, if it had happened to anyone else, Joanna might have laughed at the ridiculousness of the situation. It had all the ludicrous, comic elements of a Victorian melodrama.

She ran up the stairs, bursting into the room just as Alex sat up in the twisted sheets. "Quick," she said frantically. "You have to get out of here."

"Now, is that any way to treat your lover?" he asked in a lazy voice rough with sleep.

She was scrambling around on the floor, trying to find all his clothes. "If my father catches you, he'll make it impossible for you to be anyone's lover ever again."

That got his attention. He threw back the sheet, and leaped from the bed, his thigh at Joanna's eye level as she squatted on her heels with the bundle of clothes in her hand. "Your father's here?" He grabbed the clothes, thrusting his legs into his jeans and zipping them up.

"Yes." Joanna nodded. "And so is Tony."

Alex stared at her and swore succinctly.

"Exactly," Joanna agreed dryly.

"And what brought them here? Some misguided notion that your virtue was in danger? How would they know?"

Joanna ducked her head, glad of the need to make the bed. She knew Alex's eyes must be filled with censure, and she didn't want to see it. She wanted to remember him as he had been earlier, a contented lover sprawled in her bed. "My letter," she admitted miserably. "But I was so angry."

The sound of voices drifted up the stairs. "Hell!" Alex took his clothes from the end of the bed where she'd dropped them and strode into the hall, closing the door of his room with a bang Joanna fervently hoped was inaudible to the trio downstairs.

Sinking down on the edge of the bed, she pressed the heels of her hands to her temples. "What am I going to do now?'' she groaned. The cat, who usually minded his own business, poked a cold nose against her calf, then jumped into her lap and settled down to purr.

Joanna laughed shakily and buried her face in the soft fur, bringing an interrogatory ''meow?'' from the animal. ''Oh, cat, it's simple for you, isn't it? Just follow your instincts with no worry about feelings.''

Realizing her parents must be getting impatient while she dithered upstairs, she put the cat in the middle of the bed where he lay watching her with translucent, pale green eyes as she dressed. Finally, unable to procrastinate any longer, she opened the door and went out, glancing at Alex's closed door as she went by. With a wry grimace she continued down the hall. If he was smart, he'd go back to bed and sleep until noon, pretending he hadn't heard the commotion.

Her parents, standing rather awkwardly with Tony amid an untidy heap of suitcases and totes in the front hall, looked relieved to see her.

''Joanna,'' her mother exclaimed, enfolding her in a warm embrace. ''You look good, so tanned.''

Joanna hugged her mother, her eyes going past her to meet Tony's shuttered, enigmatic expression. She wondered what he was thinking about the long delay before she'd come downstairs, the no-doubt-easily-heard banging of Alex's door. Of course they had no reason to suspect she was sleeping with Alex but apparently Mihalis had indicated Alex was there. And with faint horror, she recalled her unkempt appearance when she'd answered the door. Had she looked like a woman just arisen from her lover's bed?

Hurriedly she kissed her mother on the cheek, noting that Mary looked cool and well-groomed despite the two-hour drive down from Volos. It was from Mary that Joanna had inherited her slender, fit body and height. Socrates was almost a head shorter than his wife but that minor detail had never undermined the love and respect that had sustained their marriage for nearly forty years.

Joanna turned to her father, kissing him on either cheek. "Dad, it's good to see you, but who's minding the store? You didn't even leave Tony in charge."

"Delegation, my dear." He shook his finger at her. "That's one thing you haven't learned yet, but you'll have to if you want to succeed. You can't do it all yourself." His severe expression faded, and he grinned, throwing his arms around her shoulders. "You can have next week off, too. We'll have a nice holiday together. And don't worry, Joanna, I haven't come to interfere in your deal with Samaras."

She looked at him in amusement. "I wouldn't have dreamed of such a thing." A couple of years ago she might have but these days he rarely supervised her closely. Joanna turned to her mother. "Have you had breakfast?"

Mary nodded. "We drove up from Athens yesterday. We stayed at the Hotel Meltemi overnight and had breakfast there this morning before we started out."

"What about coffee then?" Joanna felt her face stretching as she gallantly retained a smile, but she was unable to keep from glancing up the stairs at intervals. Forcing her attention to her guests, she tucked her arm into her mother's elbow. "Come and help me make it. We can talk in the kitchen."

The men followed since she, in her distracted state, hadn't given them any idea where they could take the luggage. She measured coffee, sugar and water into the little *briki* before setting it on the burner and lighting the gas.

"How did it go with the Hotel Meltemi?" Socrates asked. "Samaras didn't say much about it. You know, Joanna, I found out—"

"Good morning." Alex's deep voice cut into the conversation as incisively as a scalpel into a diseased patient.

The abrupt silence went almost unnoticed as Mary ran up and embraced Alex. "Alex, how good to see you after all these years!"

"I expect I've grown some since those days." Alex laughed easily.

Mary stepped back, surveying him with a happy smile. "You certainly have. I might not have recognized you."

"Well, you're prettier than ever, Aunt Mary," he said, causing a becoming flush to rise in her smooth cheeks.

Socrates came forward and took Alex's hand. "Good to see you, my boy." But somehow, to Joanna, his heartiness had a false note in it, as did his mercifully brief introduction of Tony.

"Yes, Joanna has told me about Tony," Alex said with cool aplomb. But Tony didn't smile as he shook Alex's hand, and Joanna received the distinct impression that they were carefully taking each other's measures as rivals for the same woman. After her stormy rejection of the sample wedding invitation, Tony had no reason to feel sure of her.

Neither did Alex, since she had never given him any indication of the depth of her love.

Under the guise of stirring the foaming coffee, she studied the two men. Both were dark and handsome although Tony's looks had a more rugged cast than Alex's. Tony was the taller but only by a couple of inches. Their major differences lay in personality. Tony's demeanor was cool and relaxed although not as relaxed as he normally was, Joanna saw. Alex, under the facade of social niceties, simmered with a dangerous undercurrent of suppressed emotion that put Joanna in mind of a leopard coiling its muscles for the killing leap at an unsuspecting gazelle. Was she the gazelle?

She shook off her fancies, pouring the coffee into the small cups her mother had taken from the cupboard, grateful for the task that kept her hands busy and gave her an excuse to let the conversation go around without her active participation.

They all trooped out onto the shaded patio to drink their coffee, Mary exclaiming about the charm of the place and wondering why they'd never visited Katerina years ago when she'd stayed here regularly. Alex's aunt had invited them often enough.

The question that burned in Joanna's mind was why they had come to visit now. She glanced at Socrates, his sturdy body relaxed as he tipped his chair against the house wall, balancing it on two legs. Was it because of the angry letter she'd sent home? Or was there another, deeper reason?

CHAPTER FOURTEEN

THEY ALL WENT OUT to Alex's favorite taverna for lunch. Because of her late rising, Joanna hadn't done her morning shopping. She could hardly make three eggs stretch to feed five people.

Mary was the only one who seemed oblivious to the undercurrents between the younger men, and to the questioning glances Joanna cast her father.

"So how long have you owned the Hotel Meltemi, Alex?" Socrates asked with deceptive nonchalance. He seemed like just a man making polite conversation, but Joanna, having seen her father in action at hundreds of board meetings, felt her inner warning system come to life. Get 'em disarmed by coming on all folksy and friendly and then move in for the kill, was Socrates's motto. Not that he misused it. Business was a game to Socrates, to be played with as much enjoyment as possible. And if he made money doing it, so much the better.

"Nearly five years," Alex answered.

"You going to sell?" Socrates asked bluntly. "It would mean a lot to Joanna's career."

Alex's expression didn't alter but Joanna saw the cynicism that had been absent since yesterday come back into his eyes. He lifted one brow. "Oh?"

"It could mean the promotion she's been wanting," Socrates went on, blithely driving nails into the coffin of their infant relationship.

A slight movement drew a glance from Joanna to Tony. He was leaning back in his chair, smiling faintly, as if the discussion amused him. And well it should, she thought. If she failed, he would get the promotion.

Joanna ground her teeth in helpless rage. Her appetite for the food still on her plate vanished.

"Well, I haven't decided about the hotel," Alex said calmly. "And I had no idea it was so important to Joanna."

Liar, Joanna fumed. Even a man with a lot less sensitivity than Alex would have realized just what it meant after the way she'd described the situation in the Volos bar yesterday.

Whether Socrates would have continued and whether she would have exploded into a reckless scene, she was never to find out. Jenny, accompanied by a man and a woman Joanna knew could only be Costas and his wife, sat down at the next table.

Alex immediately jumped up and performed introductions all around, presenting Costas and Stella with a note of irony in his voice that effectively distracted Joanna from her anger. She vowed to deal with her father later. As for Alex, well, she would just have to convince him she didn't use her body to succeed in her career.

Costas was a gangly man with wire-rimmed glasses, whose lank brown hair kept falling over his forehead. His wife Stella was comfortably rounded, fluttering in her mannerisms, and overzealous in supporting the cosmetics industry. Her heavy eye makeup was already melting, leading Joanna to wonder if she'd resembled a raccoon constantly in the much-more-intense heat of the past weeks.

"We decided to go out to eat, in celebration of the cooler weather," Jenny explained. "Besides, I wanted to meet Joanna's parents."

Joanna's brows flew up. The village grapevine had been even busier than usual.

Jenny leaned closer to Joanna, whispering, "Actually Costas insisted. He wanted to meet your father. Business, you know."

Presumptuous of him, Joanna thought. Costas appeared to be an opportunist of the most pushy sort. Well, Socrates could handle him.

Jenny seemed her usual self, although she looked somewhat harried on the rare occasions when Costas addressed her. It was clear that Costas must be putting on the pressure, and the injustice of it chafed Joanna. Couldn't Alex do something? He'd promised, but in the week that had gone by since, she'd seen no results.

Jenny, as was her nature, immediately made fast friends with Socrates and Mary, questioning them about Canada, and the social and economic changes that had occurred since she had last lived on the North American continent. To Joanna's relief, no mention was made of hotels or resorts.

"So this is your Tony," Jenny murmured as an aside to Joanna at one point. "Quite a hunk, as they say on American television. If I were fifty years younger, I'd steal him from you."

"I don't own him," Joanna snapped, instantly regretting her tone when Jenny gave her a startled look that quickly became thoughtful.

"No. But you own Alex." With that cryptic remark, the old lady turned and presented a charming smile to Socrates, leaving Joanna biting her lower lip in frustration.

After the meal, Joanna's parents accepted Jenny's invitation to continue the conversation at her house. Tony, restless for the past hour, declined with thanks, and Joanna impulsively invited him to go for a drive in the countryside, sightseeing. Anything to put off the storm she sensed brewing between her and Alex. She had to escape from the hard, cold look that turned his black eyes to obsidian whenever they rested on her.

ALEX WATCHED Joanna and Tony drive away in the Renault, wincing as she recklessly flung the little car down the rough driveway. A spray of gravel spun out from under the wheels and the tires squeaked a protest as she peeled out of the track and onto the paved road.

He was glad to be alone, he told himself. All these people suddenly invading his holiday was a shock to the system, especially since he'd counted on a few idyllic days alone with Joanna.

Only it wasn't idyllic any more. Her *friend* Tony had shown up. And, right away, she was putting herself out to make sure he felt welcome. Alex was obviously dispensable now that Tony was here.

Which raised a question that bothered him even more. Had she made love with him only to make him amenable to her plans to acquire his hotel and thus insure her promotion? Once he would have dismissed the idea as preposterous, but Joanna had never made a secret of her ambitions. Socrates's remarks only reinforced the notion that Joanna would do almost anything to succeed.

He turned sharply and headed for the house. Women. Did they always have ulterior motives for their relationships with men? Did they ever consider what they could give rather than what they could get? It appeared that even his sweet, generous Joanna had joined the band of female mercenaries who cared only about money and prestige.

Of course, he could just sell her the hotel. She would get the promotion. He would lose her but she would be happy, realizing her ambition.

Or would she be happy? With a flash of insight he realized that she would know at once why he'd done it, as a favor to an old friend. What would that do to her self-esteem?

Scowling, he slammed the door shut before stalking up the stairs to his room. Why should he care? Once she achieved the success she wanted, she wouldn't have time for him, anyway.

What he had mistaken for emotion in her had merely been nostalgia heightened by expedience, he decided bitterly. She'd slept with him out of a need to relive old times, to consummate a situation started that last summer in Vancouver. She didn't care for him as a man, no more than poor Lindsay had when she'd taken a dive off the balcony, no more than his mother had cared for any of the cavalcade of husbands and lovers, all with obscene quantities of money, who had paraded through his childhood.

Damn. He threw himself on his bed in the guest room. To hell with them all.

"JOANNA, DO YOU THINK you could stop abusing this car and park someplace so we can talk? Hey, watch it." Tony blanched as a flock of goats poured down a cliff and onto the road in a torrent of sharp horns, shaggy multicolored coats and jauntily waving ears and tails.

Swearing, Joanna hit the brake, skidding to a stop just as a black goat with curling horns slammed against the side of the car. It scrambled to its feet, shook its skinny body and, giving her an inimical stare, stalked after its companions. Shakily Joanna got out of the car. Except for a faint scratch on the paint that could have been there before, there appeared to be no damage. She sagged against the vehicle, her legs as weak as stretched-out rubber. An acrid scent of goats and hot dust filled her nostrils.

"That was close, Joanna." Tony stood beside her, a frown knitting his heavy brows.

Joanna took a deep breath, willing her frantic heartbeat to subside. "I'm sorry, Tony. I should have been more careful."

"Yes, you should have. Come here." Gently he folded her into his arms, holding her until the trembling stopped. Joanna rested her head on his chest, grateful for his support and for his sensitivity in not giving her a lecture, as Alex would no doubt have done.

At the thought of Alex, she pulled back and, although Tony's arms tightened for an instant, he let her go. Leading her around to the passenger side of the car, he opened the door and let her in, fastening her seat belt securely. "I think you'd better let me drive."

He got in behind the wheel and expertly engaged the gear. After driving down the twisting road for several miles, he spotted a track into an orchard. Pulling off the road, he stopped the car in the shade of a tree laden with green, unripe apples.

Silence blanketed them as he turned off the engine. Gradually the disturbed insects came back to life, cicadas chirring their monotonous summer music, a bee buzzing among the weeds that grew under the car's wheels. Joanna laid her head on the back of the seat and closed her eyes.

"Isn't it about time you told me what's going on, Joanna?" Tony said in a firm voice that brooked no evasions. "I think I have a right to know exactly what brought on that letter you wrote. Your father was on the warpath, especially since he'd just found out that Alex is the owner of the Hotel Meltemi. I thought he'd have a stroke. Good thing your mother walked into the office to take him out for lunch. She managed to calm him down by suggesting that they fly over here, take a few days off."

"And they dragged you along." Joanna opened her eyes and stared through the windshield, noting that it could stand a good washing after the dusty roads she'd driven.

"They didn't drag me. Socrates suggested that I might want to come along, said that—are you sure you want to hear this?"

"I'm sure I've heard it all before," Joanna said dryly.

"Yes, probably. Anyway, he said that what you'd written was only said in anger, and that now that you'd had a little time to think, you'd do the right thing."

"I've had time, Tony. And nothing's changed. You know I can't marry you." Still Joanna did not look at him.

"Why? Because of Alex? Are you really going to give up everything you've worked for for a quixotic adventure with the man you had a crush on as a teenager?"

"Dad *has* been busy, hasn't he? I suppose he told you all the gory details of how I was gaga over Alex fifteen years ago." Tony made a sound of protest and she suddenly felt sorry for her acerbic tone. Turning toward him, she laid her hand on his, squeezing his fingers. "No, Tony, I'm not planning to throw away my career, nor do I see any future with Alex. He's changed. I'm not sure any woman could live with the man he's become." She took a deep breath. "At any rate, that has nothing to do with my feelings for you. You're a wonderful friend. We have a lot in common, but I'm not sure there's enough passion between us for marriage."

"But that will develop," Tony said stubbornly. "It does for other people. Even when there is a mad passion, I doubt if it lasts long in the day-to-day grind."

"It has in my parents."

"Yeah," he agreed. "It has. But I'm sure they're the exception."

He turned toward Joanna, grasping both her hands in his. Her breathing was suspended momentarily as she waited for the hot rush of desire she felt whenever Alex touched her. But it didn't come, only the warm, comfortable sensation that told her Tony cared. Even when he leaned over and brushed his mouth across her lips, the reaction in her body was fleeting and superficial. *Oh Tony,* she thought, *I haven't been fair to you. I took advantage of your friendship.*

Tony understood her and admired her. He didn't mind her hours, often taking her out for a hamburger when they'd stayed at the office late. He was safe, an undemanding companion who was there when she needed someone to talk to. She didn't want to hurt him.

Just for a second she indulged the tenderness that swept over her, freeing one hand and laying it on his cheek. "Dear Tony, I'm sorry. I'm so sorry."

"Don't be, Joanna. It's not over yet. And when it is, I'll be waiting for you."

Just what he meant by that only became apparent later. It didn't take long for Joanna to realize that Tony had made up his mind to seriously court her. Away from the office, he was prepared to go beyond the comfortable relationship they'd always maintained when they worked together. For the first time, Joanna saw the determination beneath his easygoing manner.

At dinner, which Mary had cooked, and which they ate on the patio, Tony behaved as though she were a princess and he an avid suitor for her hand. He pulled out her chair, made sure she had the best cut of meat when it was served, and never let her wineglass become empty.

Dessert consisted of a plate of early peaches and Tony carefully peeled hers, cutting it up and feeding her the succulent slices. When Joanna would have made a protest, he, oblivious to the interested gazes of her parents and Alex, planted a firm kiss on her lips. When Tony lifted his head, Joanna was acutely conscious of a condemning stare from Alex that flashed from her to Tony and back again.

Since there weren't enough bedrooms to go around, Tony offered to sleep on the couch in the living room. This was fine with Joanna. It would prevent Tony from making a midnight visit to her bedroom for Alex's benefit, once he had realized Alex was a restless sleeper. As it was, Tony settled for a good-night kiss, a close embrace and a bit of whispered nonsense in her ear that must have looked to the watching Alex like a tender lover's promise.

That apparently proved too much for him. Joanna watched in dismay as he stalked out the door.

Alone in her bed, she was still awake at midnight and had not heard Alex walk past her door on his way to his room. She had to talk to him, to explain, but Tony had never left her side the whole evening, giving her no chance. Alex wouldn't get on his boat and just leave without saying goodbye, would he?

Tense, she sat up in bed, turned on the light and opened a book. After an hour, her eyes were heavy as the day's emotional upheavals took their toll. At last she fell asleep.

Alex had not returned.

BY SUNDAY EVENING Alex was going crazy. Tony never left Joanna's side, and she gave every indication of liking his attentions.

During the night as he had spent hours walking in the orchards, accompanied by a chorus of crickets and his own turbulent thoughts, he had made up his mind that he would not let her go just like that. His anger had cooled, and in its place had come cold, logical reasoning. Okay, Joanna was ambitious, but her innate pride made it impossible for her to use sex as a means of advancing her career. On the other hand, she certainly didn't seem to be repelling Tony, even though she had told Alex she couldn't marry Tony.

Alex had no way of knowing what they had talked about on their drive yesterday. They'd been gone so long that a sick jealousy that disgusted him had gnawed at his stomach. When they'd returned, they had appeared to be on friendly terms, laughing and talking. Joanna spent all her time with Tony, ignoring Alex. Had she become so fickle, so just like his mother, that she could go without compunction from one man to another?

No matter how Alex looked at it, Tony had the advantage, the inner track in Joanna's affections. He told himself he shouldn't care since his own relationship with her could, by her own definition, be only temporary, but the hurting truth was, he did care. A lot. And not only about his own pride and satisfaction but about hers.

He wanted her to be happy, and Tony looked capable of bringing her that happiness. He was a good man, perhaps a little too easygoing by Alex's standards, but he would balance Joanna's impulsiveness. He would make her a perfect husband, a fact that Joanna might well come to realize before long.

And why that should bother Alex, he hadn't been able to figure out during the night. Was he taking a classic dog-in-the-manger attitude? If he couldn't have her, no one could?

Well, he had decided he wasn't going to just let it lie. He would make a play for her as well. Perhaps Joanna would come to know herself and whether she was really ready for marriage.

That afternoon he made the first advance in the counter battle.

"Joanna, you wanted me to take you up to look at the monastery library," Alex said as the entire household drank coffee on the patio after siesta. "Would you like to go now? We'll be back in time to join the others for dinner at the taverna."

Joanna hesitated. She recognized Alex's suggestion as a legitimate way for him to be alone with her but she wasn't sure it was a good idea. A future with Alex was impossible. She couldn't stay here when her life was in Vancouver. They had had a rapturous few nights together but it was only a holiday romance. Common sense told her Tony was a much more viable prospect. Would it be so bad if she didn't have fireworks for the rest of her life?

Damn. Why did life have to be so complicated? Why couldn't she know her mind, instead of vacillating between the two men?

Before she could respond to Alex's question, the decision was taken out of her hands. "Oh," Mary said, innocently unaware of the undercurrents, "is it a good library?"

"Yes, it is," Alex answered reluctantly. "This area wasn't bothered much by the Turks during the Middle Ages so they have a number of early Byzantine manuscripts that are in excellent condition."

"That's interesting," Socrates put in. "I'd like to see them."

So it was settled, much to Alex's chagrin. They put the coffee things in the kitchen and all trooped out to follow the path up the mountainside, Joanna sticking close to Tony's side.

SEVERAL UNEASY DAYS PASSED, during which Joanna did her best to play the gracious hostess. But by midweek, the constant strain of entertaining three people of assorted tastes in a place where there just wasn't much entertainment was beginning to get to her. Thankfully they all took siestas, which relieved her for a couple of hours each afternoon. She had gotten into the habit of taking a solitary swim at that time, to regroup.

But on Wednesday afternoon, to her annoyance, Tony followed her to the beach.

"Go home and take a nap," she told him, not bothering with even minimal courtesy. "I want to be alone."

"She vants to be alone," Tony mimicked. "Why? Does Alex meet you here?"

"I haven't been alone with Alex since you came." She was dismayed to hear the note of wistfulness in her voice.

Gravel crunched under their feet as they neared the beach. "Why is he still hanging around, anyway?"

"It's his place as much as mine," Joanna said, stripping off the shirt she wore as a coverup with her bikini. "He has a right to be here."

"Well, it's not going to get him anywhere." Tony sprawled on the towel Joanna had spread on the beach. Linking his fingers behind his head, he lay back, squinting against the glare of the sun. "You know what you should do, Jo? You should forget about the hotel in Volos—I don't think Alex is very anxious to sell it to you, anyway. Even if he'd intended to, he'd probably refuse now out of spite."

Joanna couldn't deny that the same thought had occurred to her but she remained silent, torn between wanting to hear Tony's analysis of the situation and her desire to lose herself in the buoyant cradle of the sea.

Tony lifted himself up, propping his head on his raised palm. "If you tore down the house and built a kind of a deck over a section of the beach, there would be enough space to build a hotel. It could be small and exclusive, catering to a limited clientele who would come here to experience the real Greece."

"If tourists came here in numbers, it wouldn't be the real Greece for long. Look what's happened with Agios Nikolaos on Crete, and what's happened on Mykonos. Wall-to-wall tourists and the loss of most of the local ambience. Besides, Alex would never stand for it."

"Alex, my dear lady, wouldn't be able to do anything about it, would he? The house and this piece of land are yours, aren't they? If you came in with a bulldozer tomorrow, he couldn't stop you."

Joanna shivered despite the heat. "I can't do that to him, Tony."

"But think what it could mean to your career. On the way here, all Socrates could talk about was what a coup it would be if Paradise Hotels opened the first major resort on Pelion. Why, it's practically the last attractive area of Greece that hasn't been developed extensively. You'd be sure of getting the promotion."

"What about you?" Joanna asked, fighting the chill that invaded her. Sure, she would probably win as far as her career was concerned, but Alex would be livid.

And disillusioned. Could she do that to him?

Tony shrugged. "There'll be something for me."

"You seem pretty confident." Joanna felt sick. With all of them ganging up on her, what chance did she have?

He jumped to his feet with lithe grace. "Oh, I am. Socrates and I had an interesting discussion on the way down. It'll all work out. You'll see." He kissed her briefly on the cheek before turning to walk back to the house. "Have a nice swim, Joanna. And think about what I said."

CHAPTER FIFTEEN

ALEX RAN UP THE STAIRS, taking them three at a time. If he changed quickly, he might just catch Joanna before she came back to the house for a brief nap.

He had to get her alone, to talk to her. There never seemed to be any chance to do so, thanks to Tony's persistence, and Joanna's elusiveness. He was beginning to suspect she was deliberately avoiding him. He had racked his brain to find a plan to separate her from her guests for even half an hour, entertaining highly fantastical scenarios such as throwing her over his shoulder and carrying her off to his boat. The thought of her screams of outrage had made him reluctantly discard the idea.

For several days he had observed her movements, and then inspiration had struck. The siesta hour, when everyone retired to their rooms to escape the midday heat. He noticed Joanna had developed the habit of taking a solitary swim after lunch.

Monday and Tuesday he'd missed the opportunity to meet her on the beach. She always waited until the others had settled down for their siesta. He'd stretched out on his bed to wait until she left the house but he'd fallen asleep, the consequence of his restless nights. Oddly, the nights he'd shared a bed with Joanna, he'd slept fairly well, but since Tony and her parents had come, his insomnia had returned. The only positive aspect had been the absence of his nightmares since he'd discussed them with her.

Difficult though the nights were, his wandering had convinced him of one thing that gave him a peculiar and selfish satisfaction. No matter how chummy Tony and Joanna appeared, she slept alone. In his midnight rambles Alex had always been aware of Tony snoring gently on the living room couch.

Damn. He looked out the window. He could see a small segment of the beach. Today she wasn't alone. Tony was with her, lying on Joanna's beach towel as if he meant to settle in for the afternoon.

That did it! Pulling off his clothes, Alex flopped onto his bed, the springs twanging in protest.

He had almost fallen asleep in the drowsy heat of the afternoon when his door opened. Instantly alert, he kept his eyes closed, his breathing even and measured. With a faint squeak the door closed. Then the room was silent once more, except for the soft swish of the lace curtains moving at the open window.

Joanna stood beside the bed, poised in indecision. Should she wake him? He looked so peaceful, his hair tousled on the pillow. He needed the sleep since he was up so much of the night.

Never in her life had she felt so torn between opposing problems. Tony was sweet, but a nuisance. As his hostess she was obligated to take him sightseeing, take him for drives in the spectacular hills surrounding the village. But all the time the memory of the lovemaking she and Alex had shared remained, as pervasive as the flowers in a potpourri conjuring up the scents of summer on a wet winter day.

But Alex looked so ferocious these days, she didn't know how to approach him.

"Alex," she called softly. "Are you awake?"

He shifted in the bed, the single sheet twisting around his hips so that she knew he was naked. A torrent of heat flowed through her in bittersweet remembrance of how his body had felt against her, inside her. The driving power of him, the ecstatic finale when they were two souls fused into one.

She'd never have that with Tony.

Ruthlessly she forced the thought away. She would never have it again with Alex either unless she took the initiative, unless she had the courage to risk revealing her love. And on the outside chance that he didn't throw it in her face, there was still the problem of her career.

"Ahem."

Joanna started. She came out of her disquieting thoughts to find Alex's eyes fixed on her with all the concentration of a hawk about to plummet from the sky onto a rabbit.

"Oh, you're awake," she stammered, almost forgetting what had brought her to his room in the first place. The sight of his dark skin against the white sheet, the glistening of perspiration on his sleek shoulders, the faint scent of musk that emanated from him proved nearly overwhelming, swamping sense and will.

From somewhere she found the resolve to maintain aloofness. "Alex, I saw Costas just now, at the end of the orchard, near the car shed."

Alex regarded her with a lazy, studious look. "What was he doing? Picking apples? He may have a problem when he tries to eat them."

Joanna gestured impatiently, her hands going to the belt that secured her shirt around her waist. The bi-

kini she wore beneath it was drying, but the damp-
ness lingering in the lycra under her breasts and
between her thighs drew disconcerting attention to
these areas. Her skin tingled inordinately and inap-
propriately. "He was sort of sneaking around, looking over his shoulder all the time, as if he were worried
that someone would see him."

"Did he see you?"

"I don't think so."

Alex sat up, putting his feet over the edge of the bed
and reaching for his clothes. Joanna wanted to avert
her eyes when he let go of the sheet to step into his
underwear but to her shame, she found it impossible
to turn away.

Alex looked up to find her eyes on him, burning.
"You haven't forgotten, have you, even if we haven't
had a moment together? Maybe later?" He scowled as
he pulled on his jeans and zipped them. "If you can
ever shake off Tony."

Joanna drew herself up to her full height, spinning
around toward the door. "Tony and my parents are
your guests as much as mine. We have an obligation
to them."

"Yeah," Alex drawled. "But I'm finding it hard to
remember that."

"Nobody's keeping you here. You can always go
back to Volos."

"What, and miss the sight of Tony fawning over
you?"

Joanna's eyes flashed. "Tony doesn't fawn."

"No?" He lifted his arms to pull his shirt over his
head, muscles flexing in the pale gold light of the
room. Joanna's palms itched with the urge to touch

that sinewed chest, to run her hands over the crisp curling hair.

She sagged against the closed door, her breath escaping in a lengthy sigh as Alex turned toward the dresser to run a brush over his hair.

"Do you suppose Costas would still be there?" Alex asked as he turned around.

She blinked owlishly at him. He waved a hand in front of her dazed eyes. "Wake up, Joanna."

Shaking her head, she straightened away from the door, turning to grasp the knob. *Get your act together,* she told herself sternly. "I don't know. By now he might have left."

Alex gave her a little push out the door. "Well, let's have a look, shall we?"

They tiptoed down the stairs, each instinctively avoiding the one that creaked. In the living room closed shutters gave the light an eerie underwater effect. Tony lay sprawled on the couch, one bare, hairy leg hanging over the edge. A sheet precariously covered him but the sight of his lean, nearly nude body moved nothing more in Joanna than a detached appreciation of his fitness.

They had nearly reached the shed where the Renault was housed when Alex hissed a warning to Joanna and pulled her behind the thick trunk of an apple tree. Costas appeared a moment later, his eyes fixed on the ground in front of him. His lips moved, and as he drew closer they could hear him counting. "Twenty, twenty-one, twenty-two."

He broke off, standing in the middle of a faint path, his mouth twisting in frustration. Scratching his head, he squatted, examining the ground around him. He got up and they heard him swear. Turning, he moved back toward an abandoned well that had once been used to water the orchard.

Again he paced, slow measured steps in another direction. Reaching twenty-two once more, he kicked viciously at the tree trunk that stopped his progress.

"What's he looking for?" Joanna whispered.

"Buried treasure?"

"But why here? This isn't Jenny's land."

"No," said Alex. "But it used to be. It was only after the war that my aunt bought it from Jenny's husband."

"Well, I think he's suffering from delusions," Joanna declared.

Costas moved away from them and reached the edge of the orchard where a path curved down the slope toward the village. Having apparently given up, he continued purposefully down the path, his stiff, lurching gait reminding Joanna of a heron. She smothered a fit of laughter behind her hand.

Alex gave her an acerbic look, and the giggles erupted from her mouth. "Perhaps you'll share the joke?"

"Oh," she gasped. "He looks so funny, just like a long-legged, skinny heron." And she burst into renewed gales of laughter.

Alex stared at her for a startled instant, then joined in, his deeper voice mingling with hers in a shared merriment that recalled the closeness of their youth. They had always laughed a lot, seeing humor in things and situations that passed her brothers by. Her brothers had regarded them in baffled pity. Idiots, their looks had said, but Alex and Joanna hadn't cared.

Costas was almost out of sight down the path. Alex wiped his eyes, and tugged Joanna's hand. "We'll lose him if we don't get going."

The streets were just coming to life after the siesta, shop owners raising the heavy metal grills that protected their stores. The greengrocer was lifting the tarpaulin that kept the sun off the fruit and vegetables, folding it carefully as he wished them a good afternoon.

As he had the previous week, Costas entered Jenny's yard from the rear, disappearing before Alex and Joanna could catch up with him. But this time they had the advantage of daylight, and they could easily make out the door that must lead to Jenny's cellar, a wooden panel that appeared to be part of the wall of a storage shed.

"So that's how he got in the other night," Alex muttered as he examined the panel.

Around them the whitewashed courtyard lay under a blinding sun, the nearby house drowsing in the heat. From somewhere inside Joanna could hear voices, the tinkle of china tea cups, an occasional burst of laughter.

"I think it's high time we had a look at this mysterious cellar of Jenny's," Alex said.

"Won't she mind?"

"Naw." He wrinkled his brow in thought. "What day is this? The last Wednesday of the month? Yeah. This is the day she has her regular monthly meeting of the Daughters of the Resistance or something. They won't notice us."

Shrugging, Joanna followed him through the narrow doorway and down a steep flight of stone steps that lay beyond it. Slimy moss glistened in the dim light that fell on the concrete walls, and a dank, musty scent assaulted Joanna's nostrils. She stifled a sneeze as cobwebs caught in her hair, wrapping gossamer tendrils stickily around her face.

At the bottom of the steps Alex halted Joanna by placing one hand on her thigh. One step above him, she leaned over his shoulder to peer into a passage filled with assorted boxes, crates and discarded furniture, and lit by a single bulb suspended from the ceiling on a black cord.

They crept along the passage, skirting the bulk of an old-fashioned armoire that would have been at home in a castle, before they finally reached a large room also filled with furniture and the accumulated paraphernalia of years of living.

Joanna let out a low whistle. "She could start an antique shop with all this." She ran one hand over the inlaid surface of a table, wiping away the dust to uncover the glossy patina of the wood. "Some of this stuff is worth a fortune."

"Sure is," Alex agreed. "And they must have dragged it all the way from America." He glanced around. "It looks different, somehow."

"What does?"

"This room, and the passage. I used to hide in here when I was a kid, especially when Aunt Katerina wanted me to weed the garden."

"Really?" Joanna said dryly. "And here I thought you were a perfect little boy."

He pulled a face, the corner of his mouth turning down. "Seems to me there was another passage." He shrugged. "Maybe not. Or it collapsed. With all this furniture in here, it's hard to remember, and I was pretty young at the time."

Together, moving stealthily in the gloom barely pierced by the light of a dusty bulb, they advanced into the room. Suddenly there was a crash ahead of them. Alex pulled Joanna with him into a space between a capacious sea trunk and a cedar chest that at close range still gave off the pungent fragrance of the wood.

For the space of several heartbeats there was silence, then a muttered curse and another crash so close at hand that Joanna couldn't suppress a startled cry.

"Shh," Alex hissed, his fingers coming up to rest on his lips. "Somebody's coming, and three guesses who it is."

Costas came into view from the other side of the room, bent nearly double as he sidled along. One hand clutched his shin, which he had apparently smacked against the object that had crashed to the floor. The man was cursing, his expression disgruntled in the extreme.

A moment later they heard a door opening with a deafening groan. It thudded shut, and the sound of irregular footsteps stumping up a wooden staircase faded into the distance.

"Into the house, I would imagine," Alex said. "What's eating you, Joanna?"

Her face was red. Even in the dim light he could see that. Her eyes were streaming with tears, not of distress he was quick to note, but of laughter. It occurred to him briefly to wonder what euphoria-producing drug had been present in the sea that afternoon but all thought fled as she buried her face against his neck.

Her breath was warm, her mouth moist and so evocative that swift, scalding desire seized him. His body hardened and he knew she felt it as she gasped.

All the laughter fled, to be replaced by a look that almost frightened him with its intensity.

Driven beyond control, he kissed her, fusing his mouth to hers and smothering whatever protest she might have made. Her body was rigid, but as his tongue sought and found the sweet depths of her mouth, she grew soft and pliant, kissing him back with a heady deliciousness that made him dizzy.

"Joanna," he whispered. "It's been so long."

"Mmmm." Dreamily she burrowed her head against his chest.

The scent of her spun in his brain, turning his thoughts to mush. He wanted to make love to her, but this wasn't the time or place. He fought to keep his feelings under control.

The tread of feet over their heads brought both of them back to reality. Joanna pulled away from him, turning and smoothing her tangled, salt-stiffened hair. "Let's go see what Costas was after over there." Only a faint tremor in her voice revealed her agitation.

They found an old rolltop desk, the cover jammed halfway open. In the slots were old letters, none of them of much interest since they had been postmarked within the past twenty years and the return addresses were in the New England states. Correspondence from Jenny's children, obviously.

The contents of the drawers looked more promising. Several newspapers dated in the late forties, with glaring headlines mentioning *andartes*, a term Joanna knew referred to guerilla fighters. There were yellowed old maps and charts, none of which meant much; they were on such a large scale that without a reference it was impossible to tell what part of the mountains they covered.

"Nothing that wouldn't be available in any library." Alex threw back the papers and closed the drawers.

"What does this newspaper say?" Joanna held one up with a particularly large headline. "It's a Volos paper."

Alex scanned the faded print. "It refers to a village where the Germans apparently slaughtered all the men."

"Around here?"

"Possibly." Alex frowned. "The name isn't familiar but that may not mean anything. They've changed quite a few of the place names since the sixties." He tossed the paper on the desk. "I think we're going to have to talk with Costas."

"Now?" Joanna asked, looking down at her wrinkled shirt and salt-stained legs.

"Not now. I don't want to upset Jenny. We'll catch him away from the house."

No more was said as they walked back up the stairs, looking out the door before opening it wide enough to permit their exit from the cellar. Jenny's courtyard was deserted except for a stray chicken pecking in the flower bed. The flagstones were white and hot in the late afternoon sun. Quietly they crossed to the other side, skirting the storage sheds to reach the path that led to the house.

To Joanna's horror, Tony greeted them from the living-room door as they stepped into the hall. *"Kali spera."* He peered closely from one to the other, taking in their dusty appearance, the wrinkles and smudges on Joanna's shirt and the tear in the knee of Alex's jeans. "I hope you'll pardon my crassness in noticing but you two look like you just came back from a war.''

Joanna found it impossible to control the hot color that ran up her face. It was obvious what conclusions Tony was drawing. And he wasn't far wrong.

"We followed Costas who was snooping around in the orchard,'' Alex said coolly. "Jenny's cellar is packed with odd pieces of furniture, some of which have sharp edges.'' He gestured at his torn pants.

Tony's lifted brows were the only indication of his disbelief.

DINNER, although perfectly cooked and beautifully served by Joanna and her mother, seemed to Alex to drag on interminably. Tony was his usual witty self, telling little stories of his adventures in the hotel business, from when he'd started with Paradise Hotels as a troubleshooter. Alex could have topped the stories with some of his own but he figured why bother. Joanna seemed to be hanging on Tony's every word.

What was going on between them, anyway? Alex wondered, not for the first time. She seemed to be changing in her attitudes more often than Vancouver's notoriously unreliable weather. She'd let him kiss her in Jenny's cellar, in fact she'd responded with her usual warmth and ardor. He ached when he thought about it. But now she looked as close as ever with Tony, laughing at the same stories, and apparently not even noticing Alex's scowl when she let Tony throw his arm around her shoulder.

As soon as politeness allowed, Alex excused himself, intending to go down to his boat.

To do what? a nasty little voice inside his head asked.

To sulk, he told it.

What? And leave the field clear for Tony? the little voice said snidely.

She wants him, not me.

But he had barely rounded the corner of the house when Tony called after him. "Alex, wait up. I want to talk to you."

Stifling an impulse to tell him to go to hell and take Joanna with him, Alex stopped without turning around. "What do you want to talk about?" he asked shortly as Tony caught up to him. He continued walking down the path, but Tony kept pace.

"Maybe it's none of my business . . ." Tony began after a short, awkward silence, during which he seemed to be nervously weighing his words.

"You're right. It probably isn't," Alex snapped.

A flush stained Tony's cheekbones, anger tightening his mouth. "Well, since you keep coming between Joanna and me, I'd say it is my business," he retorted. "I'm concerned about Joanna's happiness, and any fool can see she's not happy now. I think you're the cause. She's eating her heart out over you and I'd like to know what you're going to do about it."

"So you're taking the role of her father now, are you?" Alex sneered.

Tony clenched his fists. "A real bastard, aren't you?" he said with conversational softness, but the steely undertone warned Alex that he was only seconds away from violence. "Joanna can speak for herself. She doesn't need me or her father to be her advocate. Maybe you don't realize that."

"Think not? I knew Joanna long before you came on the scene."

"That so?" They had stopped at the end of the path where it joined the road and were facing off like two wolves fighting for the same territory. "Well, I've known her for four years now and I'd say that's as long as you knew her. So we're even. In fact, I'd say I'm ahead because my time with her is more recent."

This very fact was what had put Alex at a disadvantage all week. Tony did know the present Joanna better than he did. And Tony, with his good nature and their common interest in Paradise Hotels was imminently more suitable for her. He remained silent, hoping Tony would take the hint that he didn't want to talk about it.

Tony was not so easily intimidated, however. "So what are your intentions toward Joanna, Alex? Are you going to sell her the hotel? Are you thinking of marrying her?"

Alex had not expected this bluntness, nor this perception. For an instant he stared at Tony with new respect. "I thought you intended to marry her."

Tony shrugged. "Her father would like that. And I'd hoped that Joanna would, too. But I'd never force her. I'll give her the time and the space to get over this little fling if necessary." He planted his feet apart and took an aggressive stance. "So what about it, Alex?"

Alex raked his fingers through his hair. What could he say? Where Joanna was concerned he hadn't formed any concrete decisions beyond the present. And he realized he'd probably underestimated Tony. Perhaps Joanna would be happy with him after all. What right had Alex to interfere? "I don't know," he said honestly. "Can you make her happy?"

Tony met his eyes with a forthright look that spoke of sincerity and integrity. "I'd sure give it my best try."

"But sometimes our best isn't enough, is it?" Alex said sadly. "Joanna has her career. I could make it easy for her now by selling her the hotel, but she'd see it as an insult to her abilities if I did that."

"Giving her a free hand to build a resort here would be an even better solution to the problem," Tony said.

Alex frowned. "That's one thing I can't do."

"Well, then," Tony said. "I guess that's the dilemma you face with her. If you sell her the hotel, she'll know why and you'll damage her self-respect. If you don't, and she loses the promotion, she'll blame you. Take your choice, Alex. I'm glad it's not me. I'm willing to have her back whenever you're through. And in case you think that's a wimpy attitude, remember that I love her. When you love someone it's not hard to sacrifice a little of your own pride." He began to walk away, then turned. "But I don't suppose you've ever had to face that."

FROM THE WINDOW above the sink where she rinsed the plates before stacking them, Joanna saw Tony catch up with Alex. The conversation looked heated, with agitated hand gestures from both men. She would have given anything to know what they said, especially Tony's end of it. She would never have suspected Tony would fight for her but to judge by his attitude toward Alex that did seem to be the case.

Two men practically coming to blows over her. She didn't like it. It was demeaning somehow.

Long ago in high school, she had entertained fantasies of being so popular men would be willing to duel at dawn for her hand in marriage, much like the heroines of the historical romances she and her friends liked so much. But during this week she had found that the supposedly enviable position of having two personable males vying for her attention bred only frustration and anger. She was not a piece of merchandise; she was a human being, with feelings of her own.

And she was torn between the feelings she had for both men. Tony appealed to her practical self; he understood her, was completely dependable and respectable. But it was Alex she loved. It was Alex who needed her, who made her go wild in his arms, whose touch could drive her to ecstasy.

She gripped the edge of the sink, staring into the stream of water running into the drain. She had to make a choice.

"What is it, Joanna?" Behind her, Mary spoke gently.

Joanna lifted her head. "Mother, have you ever been in a situation where no matter what you did, you'd hurt somebody?"

Mary came over and hugged her. Joanna, her tears already at the point of falling, allowed herself one moment of giving in.

"Alex and Tony?" Mary asked, running one hand soothingly up her daughter's back. "I wouldn't worry so much. They're not that fragile."

Joanna hiccuped forlornly, rubbing her face with the back of her hand. Turning, she snapped a paper towel from the rack beside the sink, mopping her cheeks. "Mother, Alex is."

Mary cocked her head to one side, her eyes warm and, to Joanna, wise. "Yes. I suppose he is. So you know who you want, don't you, Joanna? Tony may seem safe, but it's Alex, isn't it?" She squeezed Joanna's hands. "I'm glad—you'll be good for him. Of course, your father may not be so happy."

"I know." A residual sob worked its way up her throat, making her voice break. "He used to warn me about him."

"Not just about Alex, if you'll remember. But Joanna, you're not a child now. It's your decision, and I think you've made it. It's only a matter of working out the details."

"Mary," Socrates yelled from the front hall. "Are you coming?"

Mary winked at Joanna. "Coming, my love," she called. She turned back to Joanna. "Will you be all right? We can talk another time, or would you like me to stay now?"

Joanna shook her head. "No. I'll be okay. I'll just finish these dishes."

When her mother was gone, she looked out the window again. Alex and Tony had gone their separate ways. The path was empty.

CHAPTER SIXTEEN

THE FOLLOWING MORNING the sun had barely cleared the crest of the mountain when Joanna woke with a start. She sat up in bed, rubbing her eyes, her head thick with the need for more sleep. She had lain awake for hours, and had dropped only off shortly before dawn.

A stiff breeze sent the curtains billowing like sails at the window. The sea-fresh air was welcome but on it rode the noise that had disturbed her much-needed slumber. Voices, raised in argument.

At this time of the morning?

With a groan, she pulled the pillow over her head. But even then, the angry urgency of the voices penetrated. Dragging herself out of bed, she wandered over to the window. Only a corner of the orchard was visible from her room but at the end she could see two figures, their outlines blurred by a ground mist that was rapidly dissipating. Costas and—she squinted— a man much shorter. With a start she recognized Themistocles.

Outside her room a door crashed against the wall, then she heard the thud of Alex's running feet along the hall. She listened as he landed on only three of the stair treads on his way down before slamming through the outside door.

The men were yelling at each other. Joanna saw Costas raise the shovel he held. Enough was enough. Even if Alex was on the way, she wasn't going to stand by and let that rat threaten an old man.

Forgetting she wore only a thin cotton nightgown, Joanna pulled open her door and headed for the stairs.

She arrived outside just in time to see Alex charge up to the two men. He tore the shovel out of Costas's hands and threw it aside. It clanged against an apple tree, sending up a flurry of startled sparrows from its branches.

Alex's voice, tight with anger, carried to her, a low counterpoint to the continued heated words of the other two men.

The crunch of footsteps brought her head around. Tony and her parents came up behind her, in assorted states of dishabille. Tony wore only a pair of running shorts, Socrates was unexpectedly resplendent in a sapphire-blue silk robe that sported a red dragon on its back, and Mary clutched a lacy negligee closed over her bosom. Both men were barefoot but Mary had on high-heeled sandals that looked particularly incongruous in the circumstances.

"What the hell is going on?" Tony demanded. "And what is Costas doing here? Why, the sun's hardly up."

"That's what I'm going to find out," Joanna said grimly, marching forward. Tony and her parents followed.

Costas and Themistocles were still shouting at each other, despite Alex's attempts to make peace. To Joanna's amazement, the previously quiet, unassuming Themistocles lifted his fist and shook it in Costas's face, almost landing a blow before Alex intervened.

"What's going on?" Joanna demanded.

"We'll find out," Alex said tightly. As he pulled Costas away, something fell out of the man's pocket. Stooping, Alex seized the object before anyone else noticed and slipped it into his own pocket.

But Joanna had seen Alex's furtive movement. She was about to speak when he bent lower, examining the ground carefully.

"Well, well, well," he said after a moment. He looked up at Joanna. "Could you hand me that shovel, please?"

She retrieved it and placed it in his hand, her mind filled with questions. Setting his foot on the metal edge, Alex dug into the ground, clearing the packed earth next to the pile of rubble. He dropped the shovel, and pushed the dirt aside with the edge of his palm. "Now, what's this?"

Joanna bent down. She could see a line of weathered stones the size of ordinary bricks, too precisely placed to be there by chance. Under Alex's hands, a pattern of small colored stones was emerging. It didn't take an archaeologist to recognize what he'd unearthed: a mosaic floor, probably ancient.

"You know," Alex said too softly for the others to hear, "I think Costas found a treasure after all, although we won't know for sure until we confirm it."

He got to his feet, dusting his palms. Placing one arm around Themistocles's stooped shoulders, he murmured something to the old man, before turning to Joanna. "Joanna, will you go and get Jenny?" He paused, noticing for the first time how she was dressed. The grim set of his features softened marginally. "After you put something else on, of course. I have to make a phone call. When I get back we'll hear what Costas has to say." He looked at the silent group. "In the meantime, don't mention any of this to anyone."

JENNY WAS SITTING on her veranda, drinking the inevitable black coffee when Joanna pulled up in the Renault. "Hello," she said in surprise. "What brings you out so early?"

"Alex sent me." Joanna debated how she could break the news of Costas's latest transgression, finally deciding on naked facts. "Costas was in our orchard this morning, digging with a shovel. He and Themistocles were having a terrible argument that Alex broke up. He says you should come."

Jenny grew pale, her fingers plucking at her dress. "Won't he ever give up? It was bad enough when it only affected me, but now he's going too far." She stood up, squaring her shoulders. "Trespassing. No, it can't go on. Come, Joanna."

Jenny slipped into the passenger seat while Joanna got behind the wheel. They headed home through the quiet village, each lost in her own thoughts.

When they arrived, the others were all gathered around the table on the patio, drinking coffee and demolishing a plate of biscuits in lieu of breakfast. Only Themistocles had set himself apart from the group, sitting on the kitchen stoop with the cat on his lap. Costas, the guilty one, sat with his head lowered, silent for once.

"Ah, Jenny," said Socrates. "Sorry to get you up."

"I was up." Jenny sat down, reaching for another cup of coffee. She glared at her nephew. "Costas, what's all this about?"

Joanna took the coffee Mary handed her, grimacing at the taste as she took the first sip. Mary's remedy for stress was strong, overly sweet coffee.

"Yes, Costas," Alex said. "Let's hear your story. Now," he added threateningly.

The man looked miserable, his hair uncombed and sticking out in spikes at the back of his head. He twisted his fingers together as he straightened in the chair, crossing one leg over the other in a defensive gesture. "There is supposed to be a cache of gold hidden around here," he said at last.

"Ari's gold," Jenny said, fixing him with an icy stare. "I've told you Ari didn't have any gold. He spent it to help the Resistance."

Costas shook his head. "There was more."

"Oh, you mean the Turkish gold. That old story!" She turned to the others. "There's been a rumor around for years that a wealthy pasha, fleeing from the approaching Greek army in 1821 left behind a treasure. There's no proof. It's just a legend."

Costas drew himself up straighter, a flush staining his cheekbones. "The Nazi occupation isn't a legend. Neither is what happened afterward." He looked at Jenny, his voice dripping with venom. "I only wanted what I was entitled to. If it hadn't been for Uncle Ari and others like him, we would be in power."

"Power?" Jenny's voice faltered. "I knew your father Leon was a member of that Communist fringe group but there was no hope they would gain any power."

"Yes, there was. If my father hadn't died before giving them the gold, they could have bought their way into one of the larger groups."

Joanna began to understand. In her childhood Greek classes they had studied the twentieth-century history of the country. As soon as the Germans had retreated in 1944, the Greek guerrillas, many of whom had communist leanings, possibly as an overreaction to the fascist Nazis, had seen an opportunity to take over the country. To save it from further turmoil, Joanna assumed. They must have meant well, these ardent patriots. But not everyone had been of the same mind, and in the resulting bitter civil war, more Greeks died than were killed by the Germans.

"They would have brought the country to ruin," Jenny declared passionately.

"They were patriots." Costas's voice rose.

"Traitors." Jenny leaned forward. "We would have traded one kind of tyranny for another, here in the birthplace of democracy."

"There would have been order," Costas insisted. "It can happen now, if I find the gold."

"Over my dead body." Jenny settled back in her seat. "Besides, how many times do I have to tell you? There is no gold, not a single drachma."

"And I say there is. It's all in my father's diary." He patted his shirt pocket, dismay flooding his face when he found nothing there. "Where is it?" His hands fluttered in agitation.

"It's here," Alex interjected. "You dropped it."

Costas snatched at the small black book but Alex held it out of his reach. "It's mine. You have no right."

"But maybe Jenny has," Alex answered, his eyes narrowing. "Most of the diary is in code, but I've no doubt you've managed to decode some of it."

Joanna heard Costas's muttered affirmative but her attention strayed to Jenny. An odd expression crossed the older woman's face. Perplexity? No. More than that. Joanna was sure of it. More as if a light had suddenly gone on, and she didn't particularly like what it revealed.

"Let's have it, Costas," Alex said. "What's in the diary?"

Costas glared at all of them, but seemed to know he had no choice. "The Germans paid my father well for a couple of pieces of information they needed very badly at the time," he said sullenly. "Do you remember the plan to blow up the railway bridge in the Vale of Tempe?"

"That's more than sixty kilometers north of here," Alex said. "They came from here to do that?"

Jenny turned very pale. Her hand flattened on her chest, as if she were suddenly in pain. "Through the mountains, over Ossa, it's closer. Less chance of getting caught, too." Her lips tightened into a straight line. "The plan failed. I always wondered how they knew. But maybe now we'll find the answer. Why, Costas?"

He squirmed under her condemning stare, his bravado shredding. "My father warned the Germans."

Jenny slumped in her chair. "I can't say it's entirely a surprise. We knew someone had betrayed us. But for it to be Ari's own brother." She shook her head. "So he worked for both sides? How could he have?"

"His group needed the money the Germans would pay for information." Costas showed no sign of remorse. "They were sure they would ultimately win since the Germans were already retreating."

Jenny suddenly gave a cry that cut through to Joanna's heart. Jumping up from her chair, she went to her, taking the old woman's hand in hers. It was limp and cold, lifeless, as were her eyes. The sparkle had gone out; they were sunken into blue sockets. "Jenny, what is it?" Joanna's heart pounded in alarm.

"Leon betrayed us to the Germans. That makes him responsible for the death of all the men in Petra," Jenny said in a low voice that shook with anguish.

"Petra?" Joanna frowned.

"The village on the other side of the mountain," Alex supplied.

Joanna looked at him, her eyes wide. "It was in the newspaper we found, wasn't it?"

She remembered something else, an incident that had puzzled her at the time, but which now became clear. On one of their drives during the week, Joanna and Tony had passed through a tiny village that seemed populated solely by elderly women dressed in stark black. That must have been Petra, endlessly mourning its dead.

The story was not unfamiliar, she knew. Senseless slaughters had taken place in a number of towns in Greece, especially in the winter of 1944 when the occupying army had become aware that it couldn't win, and had been determined to extract a last, cruel revenge from the beleaguered people of a battered country.

Jenny swayed back and forth in her chair, her arms wrapped around her. "They marched through the whole area, looking for the explosives that were to be used. When they found nothing, they used Petra as an example, since it was on the route used by many of the guerrilla fighters." She rose to her feet, pointing a vengeful finger at Costas. "Your father killed those people."

"It was war. They paid him in gold. He was going to use it to help the country." He glared defiantly at Jenny as she sat down again, her head falling onto her chest. "He did what he thought best."

"Where is the gold now, Costas?" Alex asked.

"He hid it somewhere nearby. But when he was killed—"

"Poetic justice," Jenny muttered fiercely.

"If you and Uncle Ari had helped him, none of this would have happened," Costas burst out. "Apparently he'd trusted no one for it wasn't until last year when my mother died that I discovered in his desk a key that belonged to a safety deposit box. In it, I found his diary. Even my mother never knew about his collaboration."

"At least she was spared," Jenny said. "It would have killed her to have known. Why, she and I carried guns and explosives on our backs to the guerrilla camp beyond Petra. If I had known what Leon was up to, I would have killed him with my bare hands."

And Joanna, seeing the angry glitter in her eyes, had no doubt that she was capable of it.

Jenny leaned forward, bracing her hands on the arms of her chair. "Why didn't he betray the rest of us, Costas? Why only that village where, in spite of its strategic position, most of the people were innocent?"

Costas shrugged. "I guess because you were family and they were strangers."

Joanna was aware of this odd aspect of Greek country life. In the insular world of the village, everyone was close, like an extended family. Outsiders, even those in the next village, were often referred to as foreigners. And the oddest thing of all was that the word for foreigners and guests was identical. Being brought up in Canada, Joanna had never really explored all the ramifications of such attitudes.

"They were still Greek," Jenny retorted, before subsiding once more in her chair.

Costas looked away, crossing and uncrossing his legs nervously. Much of his earlier bravado was fading, the effort he made to sustain his self-righteous defiance crumbling. "The diary was full of cryptic notes, references to the cellar, to an apple orchard, even to a shepherd's hut halfway up the mountain. I went there one night but all I found was a heap of rubble. The wooden frame had rotted long ago, causing the stone walls to collapse. But I felt it was the least likely place he would have hidden the gold. Too far from the village and too easy for any sheep or goat herder to find."

"But our orchard?" Joanna said when no one else spoke. Tony, Socrates and Mary sat silently, their attentive expressions overlaid with horror. Alex looked angry, especially when his gaze slid to Jenny. Her chin rested on her chest but as Joanna squeezed her hand in sympathy, she smiled briefly, then pulled out a handkerchief and wiped her eyes.

For someone who had just had a dreadful shock, she was holding up remarkably well. Joanna knew she drew on the same inner strength and courage that had cast her in the forefront of the Resistance movement. However, she couldn't help wishing Jenny had been spared this final revelation of treachery.

"Let's have the rest of it, Costas," Alex said, growing impatient.

"I guess it doesn't matter any more," Costas said dispiritedly. "I searched the cellar several times, since it seemed the most likely place to hide something. The maps in the desk were interesting but they didn't help my search. They only showed the secret paths the men used. I found nothing else but old furniture and dust and several nests of mice. So it came down to this orchard."

"Why this one?" Alex asked.

"Because it used to belong to our family. And there was a reference to heaps of rocks, which this has plenty of, and none of Aunt Jenny's other fields have. Also a mention of an ancient olive tree. I asked Themistocles if there had ever been an olive tree in the orchard. He said yes, once, but it had died. He showed me where it had been."

Costas stared at the old man who sat quietly on the steps. As if he felt the hostility, Themistocles lifted his head. For the first time he spoke, vehement words pouring from his mouth, his speech impediment rendering them unintelligible to Joanna.

But not to Alex.

Alex got up and spoke quietly to the old man, who briefly displayed a gap-toothed smile as he gestured with his bony, gnarled hands. After a brief exchange Alex came back to the table. Instead of sitting down, he stood behind his chair, resting his hands on the back of it.

"Themistocles says Costas only asked him where the olive tree was. He showed him. He says why didn't he ask him about the gold if that's what he was looking for."

Joanna looked at Themistocles with new respect. What else did he know?

"Shut up, will you, old man?" Costas shouted, jumping up from his chair. Alex hurriedly intervened.

"Sit down." He pushed him roughly back in the chair. Costas, after a murderous glare at them all, settled down. "Jenny," Alex continued in a milder tone. "Do you remember another passage in your cellar, a narrow one going off from the main one? Seems to me there was one when I was a kid."

Jenny nodded. "There was, but in that quake we had five years ago, much of it collapsed. It's been closed, from both ends." She winked at Alex, in a ghost of her former teasing. "Yes, I knew you kids got in from the sea cave. But that's all blocked now."

"Where was the blockage?" Alex asked.

"About twenty meters in from the cellar entrance. But nobody's been in there for years, even before the quake. The ceiling wasn't shored up there. It was the emergency escape."

Alex nodded. "That's what I thought."

He walked over and took Themistocles by the arm. "We're going to look at Jenny's cellar now."

To Joanna's horror the old man turned white, and shrank back against the wall, his hands extending out in front of him as if in defense.

"You won't have to go inside," Alex assured him.

"Ever since the diving accident that crippled him, he's afraid of confined places, especially if they're dark," Jenny explained to Joanna.

They took both cars, Socrates driving the rented Mercedes and Joanna the Renault. Moments later they arrived at Jenny's house.

Themistocles, his posture miraculously straighter as he savored a position of importance for once in his

life, led them to the door through which Alex and Joanna had entered the cellar the day before. There he
balked. He sat down on the flagstone floor, adamant
in his refusal to enter.

The passage was the same, dim light, dust and cobwebs, but, swarming with people, had none of the
spooky aspect that had caused Joanna to shiver yesterday.

"I tell you I looked everywhere," Costas muttered.
"There's nothing here."

"The armoire," Jenny said. "There's a doorway
behind it."

The exact spot where Alex had speculated on the
changes in the cellar yesterday, Joanna realized.

"It's heavy," Jenny warned.

"Not with four of us here," Alex said. "Come on,
men, grab a corner and heave."

Even so, shifting the heavy piece of furniture wasn't
easy but at last enough space appeared that they could
get behind it.

"Jenny, do you have a crowbar or something?"
Alex asked, examining the oak planks that had been
used to board up the entrance.

She produced one out of a tool chest in the storage
room. In short order Alex had removed a number of
the planks, revealing another passageway, narrow and
dank, and smelling of rotting seaweed. Cobwebs
formed an almost impenetrable barrier but Alex swept
them summarily aside as he led them into the tunnel.

Only Mary declined to follow. "I'm not going into
any dark passage where there are probably tarantulas
and mice." She shuddered.

Joanna resolutely closed her mind to the thought of the exotic wildlife that must inhabit this place, holding tightly to Jenny's hand.

They didn't have to go far. The passage was blocked by a rock fall, preventing further exploration. "From here it connected to the sea. We used to play all sorts of games in here as kids. Great scope for the imagination," Alex said. "And handy for smugglers and such." He looked at Jenny by the light of the flashlight he held, but she merely smiled and said nothing.

"Now let me see. Where would someone hide a bag or box of gold?" He shot Costas a look, but the man only glared at him.

Alex played the flashlight around the passage. The beam glistened on the damp stone-and-earth walls. "Aha." A shadow appeared over their heads, near the ceiling.

"Here, Joanna, you're the lightest. Let me lift you."

The fresh scent of Alex's after-shave dominated the mustiness of the passage as he hoisted her in his arms. She was aware of his strength as he lifted her higher, then closed her mind to the warmth of his hand under her hips as she felt the indentation in the wall.

She held her breath, banishing images of snakes and scorpions. Closing her eyes, she groped inside, at first encountering only dust, a thick layer soft as powder. Then she felt it, the hard edge of metal. Using both hands, she slowly withdrew the heavy object.

"Got it."

The chest was battered and rusty, about twice the size of a safety deposit box. Alex held it out to Jenny, and she lifted the lid. Gold. The heavy coins gleamed dully in the faint light. A treasure, but Joanna doubted

that Jenny or any of them felt it was worth the price
paid for it in lives.

"ISN'T IT AMAZING?" Jenny said later that afternoon
as they were all sitting on her veranda enjoying their
after-siesta coffee. "All these years nobody ever paid
any attention to Themistocles, and yet he knew about
Costas's father. Of course that's probably how he
knew. Since he couldn't talk very well and he was
crippled before the war, he probably was present at a
lot of secret meetings but nobody noticed. It's too bad
he's so hard to understand. I wonder what stories he
could tell."

Joanna noticed that Jenny seemed to have re-
covered most of her natural exuberance. Costas and
Alex had spent the remainder of the morning at the
police station. Since Costas had technically not been
guilty of any misdemeanor other than trespassing,
Joanna had wondered why a report was necessary.

"Any find of gold has to be reported," Jenny explained. "It happens more often than you'd think.
Shepherds often find hidden caches in the mountains,
some of them dating back to the days of the Turks
when wealthy Greeks couldn't trust banks because
they were controlled by the enemy. But you can't just
take it to the bank. In this case, at least, where they
know the source and the rightful owner, however
wrongfully he may have acquired it, the process
shouldn't take long. The government will make the
final decision on who gets it."

By late afternoon, it was all over. The Terrible
Couple, as Alex had once termed them, had packed
and fled, never to return he hoped, since Jenny had
made it clear they were no longer welcome. Family was

family, but ostracism was the only way to treat traitors.

"I guess we'll never know the full story, though," Jenny added. "I lived through it and this went on without my knowledge, too." She leaned back in her chair and stretched her arms over her head. "Ah, it's a relief to know that Costas won't be back, sniveling about needing money. Do you know that that was all a pretext, just to give him an excuse to keep coming around to look for the gold?"

She patted Alex's knee and he grinned and covered her hand with his. "Alex found out that Costas is the owner of a number of apartments in Athens and makes a very comfortable living off the rents. Sure, he gambles a little at Mount Parnes on the weekends, and he did lose the last money I gave him that way, but generally he manages to keep out of trouble. By all accounts, he and Stella live a good life, the rats."

"That's right," Alex said. "There was no excuse for the kind of harassment they put you through."

"Just goes to prove that old proverb about the apple falling under the apple tree," Jenny said. "Like father, like son." Her face saddened momentarily. "I still can't believe Leon could be a traitor. And I wonder now about the circumstances of his death. Do you know he was found in a field, shot in the head at close range, several weeks after the Germans had pulled out of the area? We always knew they couldn't have done it."

"Maybe his activities weren't as secret as they appeared to be," Socrates suggested. "One of his own countrymen might have decided that justice must be done."

There was a brief silence as they thought about war and how its cruelties could twist people. Then Jenny slapped her palms on her thighs, pulling the bright pink dress taut across her lap. "Well, it's all over now. What do you say we break out the ouzo I've been saving for an occasion?" Her voice lowered conspiratorially. "It's a very good brand. Costas brought it from Athens as a gift, and he always brought the best, to butter me up, of course."

Alex put up his hand. "There is one more thing, that will affect some of us." He looked straight at Joanna, then at Socrates, his face unreadable. "The place where Costas was digging this morning—well, you saw it. I've just come back from having another look at it with a representative of the Volos museum who was kind enough to drive down after I phoned him this morning. Costas didn't find the gold there but he discovered something that might have even greater significance. He uncovered a portion of an ancient wall."

"An ancient wall?" Jenny asked. "How ancient?"

"Probably Roman, early AD, possibly during Christ's lifetime. The colored stones look like part of a well preserved mosaic floor."

"That's all very interesting," said Socrates. "But how will that affect us?"

"It means that building a resort hotel on that site is out of the question. You know how I felt about it all along, but now it's no longer my decision. The government does not allow development on an archaeological site."

So that was the end of the matter, thought Joanna. Although developing a resort would have excited her on a professional level, part of her was relieved to have the decision taken out of her hands. Her time here had shown her the value of a simple life and she didn't want to be the one who ended the peace of the village, no matter what Alex thought. She had some scruples.

CHAPTER SEVENTEEN

"HELLO, JOANNA."

At the sound of Alex's voice, Joanna nearly jumped out of her skin. He stepped out of the shadowed corner of the room where the light from the bedside lamp didn't reach. "It's after midnight," he murmured. "Late for you, isn't it?"

"I wasn't sleepy. So much has happened today. I went for a walk."

Yes. With Tony, Alex thought. He'd seen them from the window.

He cleared his throat, feeling incredibly awkward as he carefully weighed his words. "I wanted to talk to you, Joanna. For days, actually, but there never seemed to be time."

"What about?" Joanna moved around the room, straightening the curtains, fastening the loose shutter at the window. Her tone was only mildly curious, and he realized with dismay that she had already distanced herself from him.

He shifted his feet, crossing his arms over his chest. "I just wanted to say that I hope there won't be any hard feelings between us. Since you've been here we've had some good times, but I also was presumptuous enough to judge you. I accused you of putting ambition and a need for power before personal considerations. I shouldn't have done that. It's your life. Just because I decided a few years ago that I wanted a quieter life without pressures doesn't give me the right to decide for you or anyone else."

Her blue eyes were very direct and serious as she absorbed this but he couldn't tell what she was thinking. "If you think power is all that is important to me, Alex," she said with quiet dignity, "you don't know me very well."

He inclined his head, acknowledging the truth of her words. "That's the trouble, isn't it? I thought I knew you but all my ideas about the person you are now were colored by the past. I remembered you as a carefree child just coming to grips with the adult you would be. But I saw you as the competent business executive who came to buy a hotel. I couldn't reconcile the two images."

"Have you now?"

Had he? In his head, he had. But deep inside, in his heart, he wasn't sure. When he was with her, his loneliness, and the fear of the dark demons that lived inside him, receded. But he was much too aware of the limits of her time with him. She was leaving tomorrow and nothing he said would prevent it. "I don't know, Joanna."

She nodded, the ponytail into which she'd drawn her hair bobbing. "No, you don't, do you? Otherwise you'd never have said that power is all that's important to me. I think you've known more than your share of cold, greedy people but I'm not like that."

Pain wrenching him, he closed his eyes for an instant. He would have given anything to be able to throw out all the negative conditioning of the past and believe her, have faith in her. But trust wasn't something that came like a blinding flash from the sky.

"Aren't you, Joanna?" he said sadly, looking at her calm face and wishing he could see it alive with passion once more. "You must admit that you certainly emphasized your ambitions and your practicality."

"She really did a number on you, didn't she, Alex?"

"Who?"

"Your mother, with all her marriages and her denial of you as her child. How many husbands did she have, anyway?"

Distracted, he pinched the bridge of his nose between his thumb and forefinger. "Five or six. I don't know. After the fourth, I sort of lost track. But in the end she had no one. None of them even came around when she died, and she didn't even seem to recognize me that last day in the hospital." His tone was bleak.

A wave of compassion made tears sting Joanna's eyes, and she wanted nothing so much as to go and put her arms around him and take away his pain.

The fierce, defensive look on his face stopped her. "Forget it, Joanna. I'm an adult. I've come to terms with the situation. It doesn't affect me now."

How could he be so blind? she thought. "Doesn't it? Then why do you find it so hard to trust, to love? I realize your mother left a lot to be desired as a parent and role model, but surely you've come to see that not all women are like that."

"Too many of the ones I knew are like that, Joanna." He spoke with a quiet conviction that tore at her heart.

"And now you feel it's safer to reject them all. Including me."

"I didn't reject you," he protested, but he knew he had, simply by not *accepting* her.

"You did, Alex. Because I'm a success, you thought I was just like all the rest, putting my career ahead of everything else in my life." She walked away from him to the window, and stared at the calm sea. The rhythmic surge of the water lapping onto the beach echoed faintly in the room. "And where my relationship to you is concerned, you never even gave me a choice. You just judged me by your biased standards."

He wanted desperately to deny it, but the lie stuck in his throat.

"You know, Alex," Joanna said reflectively, "I really would like to quit my job and go somewhere and run a little inn, all on my own. But it doesn't seem practical at this stage of my life. I've got responsibilities I can't give up."

Success is addictive, Alex thought harshly. Aloud he said, "I suppose you're leaving with the others tomorrow."

Her fingers clenched the curtain. The sweet scent of jasmine drifting up from the garden suddenly seemed cloying, like an overabundance of flowers at a funeral. "Yes. There's nothing more to keep me here."

"A holiday fling. That's all it was, wasn't it?" he said flatly.

Something moved in her eyes. A trick of the light? Or an emotion she quickly hid? "That's all it could be."

If only she'd argue, yell at him, behave with the fire he expected in Joanna. Even now, his breath caught in his throat as he looked at her, so beautiful despite her casual sleeveless blouse and wrinkled, smudged shorts. Wispy little tendrils, straggling loose from her ponytail, clung to her temples and delicately flushed cheeks.

A reaction, that was what he wanted, not this passive acceptance.

He tried another tack, frustration edging his voice. "You were in love with me when you were fourteen, weren't you?"

"Yes." She refused to dissemble. "But I was very young. And very innocent." She half smiled. "It amazes me sometimes to think back and realize just how young I was."

"Are you now?" His voice was totally serious, intense, and she knew it wasn't her youth he referred to.

She turned back to the window, torn with sorrow for what he could not see. He *could* trust her; she would never let him down. But telling him so would not lay his doubts to rest. He had to find that trust for himself, the belief that he was worthy of being loved. For she knew that despite his appearance of total self-confidence, arrogance even at times, it was this insecurity, the knowledge that no one had ever loved him deeply and constantly, that lay at the bottom of his ambivalence toward her.

And until he came to terms with it, and trusted her, there could be no love.

She didn't hear him move but suddenly he was so close that his breath fell warm on her bare nape.

"Are you in love with me now, Joanna?"

He placed his hands on her shoulders, but she shook them off. "Of course not."

The lie almost choked her but what use was it to admit the truth? She loved him deeply, with a love that had all the fervor of her youth but was strengthened by the stability and maturity of a woman's passion.

She kept her eyes fixed on the horizon where a slim crescent moon rested lazily on its back and cast a faint glow on the sea. If she looked at him now he would see that she was as besotted as she had been those many years ago.

"When you go home, are you going to continue seeing Tony?"

"I work with Tony, remember." Her voice was chilly.

"You know what I mean."

She sighed. "Yes, Alex. I know. And no, it will be strictly work between us."

"He loves you, you know," Alex said after a moment. "The other evening he had the nerve to ask me what my intentions toward you were. He'll still be your friend."

"I hope so," Joanna said. "Tony's a thoroughly nice man."

"I agree," Alex said promptly. "A lot nicer than me. He called me a bastard although I'm not entirely sure why. Did you tell him you slept with me?"

Again Joanna moved away from him but he followed, almost as if he stalked her. "Of course not," she said heatedly, this time unable to control the color that washed over her cheeks.

"But he knows, doesn't he, Joanna?" Alex said softly, stopping right in front of her. "He's not stupid."

Although he didn't touch her, she was trapped in the corner of the room, aware of the increased tempo of his breathing, the heat emanating from his body.

"He's taking it remarkably well, isn't he?" Alex went on in a soft voice that contained a dangerous edge. "He's very good at hiding his jealousy. I'm afraid I wouldn't be, in his position."

"But you're not in his position, are you, Alex?"

He was only a foot away. "I could be. Couldn't I, Joanna? We still want each other. When I get close to you, fireworks go off all around us, don't they? We should have a proper goodbye." His low tone became a husky whisper that seared her already sensitive nerves. "Like now. Tell me. What are you feeling right now?"

She stared at him defiantly, daring him to come closer. When he remained standing where he was, a half smile on his mouth, she dropped her eyes, against her will allowing her gaze to slide down his body.

His shirt was only half-buttoned, revealing his darkly tanned chest covered with the black curls she loved to touch. Had he dressed like this in the hope that she would be overcome with lust at the sight of him, enough to give him one last night in her arms?

Her eyes moved lower. His lean hips were encased in tight jeans so old they were faded almost white in places, especially—

With a shock she realized that he was rampantly, blatantly aroused, and making no attempt to conceal that fact from her.

His smile broadened. "You see, Joanna, what we do to each other? And don't try to tell me you feel nothing." He reached out with one hand and touched her shirt, the nipple that rigidly strained against the cotton cloth.

Stepping closer, he pulled her into his arms. "Tell me, Joanna," he whispered, his breath hot against her mouth, "in the years ahead, will you think of me? When you're in some other man's bed, will you be able to forget the passion we shared?"

"No!" she cried, turning her head before his lips could brush hers. A tear slid down her cheek. "How can I, when it's you I love? Still, after all these years."

There, she'd said it. She hadn't intended to but now that the truth was out, she was conscious only of relief.

It was about time there was some honesty between her and Alex, and she knew it had to come from her. She was used to speaking her mind but with Alex she had prevaricated. Not her usual mode of behavior at all. Feelings were meant to be laid out in the open, not buried. Even if Alex had never been taught that, perhaps it was time he learned that open discussion was the first step toward complete communication.

"Yes. I'm in love with you, Alex." She hugged her arms around herself, bereft as he moved abruptly away. "So now that you know, what are you going to do about it? Are you going to leave me alone for the next fifteen years as well?"

He looked at her, torment in his face and eyes. "Joanna, you have to believe me. I thought it was for the best. I had to go, and you were far too young. I couldn't ask you to wait for me."

"And now you're not going to do anything, either, are you, Alex?" She knew it was futile to even hope; the answer lay in the bleak remoteness that carved harsh lines in his face. "You're afraid that if you allow yourself to feel deeply, you'll be hurt. Alex, you once told me my life was too rigidly mapped out, leaving no room for chance, but it's yours that's like that. And you won't change because you're afraid to."

He bowed his head, accepting her judgment. "I'm sorry, Jo. There are things I have to work out."

What things? she wanted to scream. *We could try working on them together.* She whipped up rage to combat the spreading pain tearing at her chest. "You know what I think, Alex? That you just don't have the guts. You're a coward. That's what you are."

He lifted his head, anger kindling his dark eyes. "Joanna—"

She ignored the warning. "Come on. Prove it," she goaded. "Take a chance. Prove you've got what it takes to love someone."

He walked over to her, pressing his body against hers. "I'll prove it all right." Slowly, suggestively, he rolled his hips, letting her feel his hardness.

With a frustrated sound, Joanna pulled away. "That doesn't prove anything. It could be lust."

"Well, it's sure as hell something that's eating at me."

She regarded him with dispassionate eyes. "That's your problem. Not mine." She gestured toward the door. "Go, Alex. Just get out of here."

For a long moment he stared at her. She stared back, showing no sign of backing down. Finally, shoulders slumped as if he carried an overwhelming burden, he walked to the door.

"Tell me this, Alex." Her peremptory tone halted him in his tracks. "Do you love me?"

He turned his head and the stunned look on his face told her more than she wanted to know. Anger flared anew, although at whom it was directed she didn't know. For the first time she understood the impenetrability of the barrier Alex had erected to keep his vulnerable heart safe.

But when she thought he would just walk out, he surprised her. "Do I? It would be easy to say yes. I did once, or rather I felt what passes for love when I was seventeen. But now—I guess that's one of the things I have to work out."

"Okay," she said, battling against growing futility. "Let's try this. Do you trust me now? You thought I was a grasping female, a piranha in a business suit—"

"Joanna." He was indignant.

She put up her hand. "Don't deny it, Alex."

He shrugged, his expression rueful. "Okay. I wondered. But I've also seen the other side of you, how you are with your parents and with others. With Jenny. I don't think you'd ever put yourself ahead at anyone else's expense."

"But you're not convinced. Haven't you ever trusted your instincts and done what they tell you?"

"My instincts haven't been too swift as barometers in my relations with people. I think they're underdeveloped."

"Then perhaps you should give them a chance to develop," she said in a tart voice that concealed an enervating sense of failure. "Think about it, Alex. Isn't it time you took a risk?"

THROUGH THE BLACKNESS of the night he ran, finding his way by instinct and faint starlight. His only companion was the rhythmic pounding of his feet on the summer-hard ground beneath the apple trees. His heart hammered in his chest, reminding him he was alive, a man who could feel.

Then why couldn't he feel love?

Gasping for breath, pain searing his throat, he stopped, bracing his hand on a tree trunk for support. His knees shook with the weakness of exhausted muscles, barely able to hold him upright. He let his head hang down, drawing in air to fill tortured lungs, gradually allowing the dangerously rapid beat of his heart to subside.

A man who had no soul could not love. And he had lost his. He had stood by and watched Lindsay and his other friends continue on a path of destruction, and had done nothing about it. Only poor Lindsay had paid the ultimate price, but how many others could he have helped if only he had been willing? He had been the leader; the others had looked to him for guidance, and he had failed them.

He had seen how Lindsay felt about him, how obsessed she had become, but he had first ignored her, then cruelly spurned her. It was only a day or two later that she had taken her final dive from the balcony. There was no way that he could absolve himself of responsibility. Or guilt. The drugs that had destroyed her judgment weren't responsible; he was.

Pushing himself away from the tree, he began to run again, reaching a meadow where dew-wet grass clung to his ankles, soaking his shoes and plastering the hairs on his calves to his skin. The long muscles of his thighs strained and tensed as he leaped a dry irrigation ditch, his heavy, off-balance landing scaring a covey of sleeping birds into raucous flight. His heart hammered in his ears, deafening him to the sound of crickets in the grass, a night bird's shriek.

But it could not drown out the sound of his own thoughts.

Joanna loved him, just as she had fifteen years ago. He should have suspected it. Joanna wouldn't have tossed away the mores of a lifetime to sleep with a man for no other motive than a nostalgic desire to close the books on an unfinished episode of puppy love.

He had hoped that that was all it was for her. He hadn't intended her to be hurt. The last thing he needed in his life was another Lindsay.

His chest heaved like a bellows, his breath coming in labored gusts, but still he ran, the pain in his limbs a diabolical companion who would not let him rest.

But Joanna wasn't Lindsay, was she? Joanna was strong. Joanna knew herself. She would carry on with her life. When one door closed for her, she would open another. Joanna didn't need him.

He could have pretended. For one heartbreaking moment in her room tonight, he had almost blurted out that he loved her, too. It would have been easy to lie, to tell her what he knew she wanted to hear.

But in the final analysis he had been unable to. If he had said the words, she would have accepted them, but after a year or two she would have found out the truth, that inside he was dead, without a soul. The traumas of his childhood had mortally wounded the part of him that had once loved so innocently and trustingly, and Lindsay's death had delivered the final blow.

The night was dark and hot, and he was near collapse, sweat pouring down his bare chest, soaking through the thin running shorts he wore. He reached another meadow as pale ribbons of dawn unfurled across the sky. There, in a fragrant hollow of grass he let himself drop, falling flat on his back with his face turned up toward a sky that slowly lightened.

There was one thing he could do for Joanna. If he couldn't guarantee her happiness, at least he could ensure her success. On that thought, he burrowed into the sweet green grass and slept.

JOANNA STOOD at her bedroom window, open suitcase on the bed, clothes scattered in colorful heaps on every surface in the room.

She had never felt less like packing. The truth was, she didn't want to leave the village where she had found, if not tranquillity, at least a realization that there was more to life than money and ambition.

And Alex. How could she leave him? But he would never ask her to stay. She knew that as surely as if he'd slammed a door in her face last night.

Tony poked his head around her open door. "Do you have any room for a couple of things in your suitcase, Jo?" he asked cheerfully. "My stuff seems to have multiplied. Must be all the clean air."

Joanna laughed. In front of Tony and her parents she was managing to keep up appearances. "I was about to come and ask you the same thing. I don't suppose Mother has any extra space."

Tony rolled his eyes. "Not likely. She bought a couple of flokati rugs in Volos the other day. The big one she's having shipped, but the small one has to go in a suitcase."

"I suggest you look in the shed across the patio and see if you can find some kind of box. If there's nothing there, try the grocery store."

After Tony left, Joanna sat on the edge of her bed, her hands clasped loosely in her lap. Although she tried to tell herself she was waiting for Tony to return, she knew the real reason she couldn't get down to business was that she needed more time.

"Joanna."

She jumped. Alex had come back? She hadn't expected him.

"Alex, what do you want?" He wore only running shorts, thin nylon that bared his muscular thighs and made the most of his lean hips and buttocks. His hair was wet, clustered in tight curls on his head and around his ears. Sweat glistened on his body and a green stain decorated one shoulder. He smelled salty, tangy, like a fresh sea wind, and her nostrils flared.

He must have seen the subtle movement for he waved his hand in front of his face. "I know, I know. I could use a shower, but I have something important to tell you."

"The shower can wait. I don't mind." She stood up, determined to be businesslike although a treacherous weakness ran through her. For a wild instant she acknowledged that she would have liked nothing better than to press herself against his warm damp skin and inhale his fragrance. And sink into blissful forgetfulness.

"I'll sell you the hotel," he said without further preamble.

"Sell me the hotel?" For an instant she was stunned, then reason returned, along with a sickening despair. She had told him she loved him. Because he was unwilling or unable to offer her his love in return, he was offering his hotel instead.

"It's what you want, isn't it? If you get it, you'll be sure of the promotion, won't you? From what Socrates has said, he wants this hotel and he'd be sure to reward you."

Damn him. Nothing she had said last night had penetrated his thick skull. He saw her only as a woman driven to succeed, not as a woman who loved him.

He didn't even realize that by offering the hotel he was making a subtle statement that questioned her abilities to succeed without anyone's efforts but her own. She closed her eyes, fighting the tears that welled hotly in them.

"What's the matter, Joanna?" he said tauntingly. "Overwhelmed by the offer? Don't be. You haven't heard the terms yet. But you won't refuse, because it will guarantee your future."

"Is that why you're making the offer?"

"Of course it is." But he sounded a little unsure, obviously puzzled by her refusal to look at him. "I'd decided long ago to sell it, but I was particular about the buyer. Let's just say I'm convinced that Paradise Hotels won't exploit the building or do anything to ruin the neighborhood." His voice softened. "Don't worry about what I just said, Joanna. I think you won't find the terms too difficult."

"And why did you decide to do this now?" The urge to scream at him to go, and then to lock the door and bawl her eyes out, was nearly overwhelming but a morbid compulsion to do an autopsy on their dead relationship gave her control.

"Because it's the only thing I can do. I know you would have liked to build a resort on this land but at least this way you'll salvage something. I didn't set out to hurt you, Joanna, but I'm afraid I did. This is all I can offer to make up."

You could offer your love, she wanted to shout at him, but pride, and the realization that his love was the one thing he'd never offer, forced her to hold her tongue.

He reached out one hand and gently ran his knuckles over her cheek. Lowering his head, he kissed her lips, tenderly but with an underlying fierceness. "I hope you'll be happy with your promotion, Joanna. You'll have what you've worked for.''

Through blurred eyes, she saw him turn away. "Wait!"

He paused, looking back over his shoulder. "Yes, Joanna?"

"I—I can't take the hotel."

He stared at her, his eyes piercing. "You what?"

"You heard me. I can't take the hotel."

"You can't take the hotel." He was outraged and his voice echoed around the room. "You won't let me do this one thing to help you?"

"This isn't what I need from you, Alex," she said crisply. "Besides, I haven't gotten to where I am by ever hanging on someone else's coattails."

The anger drained out of him as quickly as it had arisen. "That's not why I did it."

She sighed wearily, wishing he would just go. "I know, Alex. Maybe it's because of what we shared as children, but I don't want business between us. Not like this. I've also thought about what Dad said the other day, what he tried to make you believe. You see, he wanted me to marry Tony so he thought he could cause trouble between you and me. Making me think the promotion hinged on getting your hotel was only another way to manipulate the situation. He thrives on that kind of thing. But he knows my work; I don't need this to prove it. I know you meant well by offering but I can't take a substitute for what we could have had."

He bowed his head, yearning to touch her but somehow knowing it would be cruel. Her pallor and the tense lines of her body told him she had reached the limits of her control. The slightest move toward her would send her over the edge. He had no wish to see his strong, vital Joanna break down. For her to do so in front of him would be her final humiliation. "Well, then, I guess this is goodbye."

"I suppose so." Her heart ached for him but she knew he didn't want her pity any more than he could accept her love. "Do you think it'll be another fifteen years before we see each other again?"

The laugh that came from him was harsh and strained. "I hope not, Joanna. I hope not."

CHAPTER EIGHTEEN

"WHAT'S THE MATTER, JOANNA?" Tony's solicitous question brought Joanna's head up. She glanced around the room with its piles of unpacked clothes, then at Tony who stood in the doorway holding a cardboard box that had once held evaporated milk. Had only moments elapsed since Alex had gone and taken her heart?

"Alex was just here, wasn't he? If he hurt you . . ."

Joanna laughed faintly at his belligerent tone. "There's nothing you can do. There's nothing anyone can do, except Alex himself."

He took her hand, squeezing it. "I'm sorry that it didn't work out with him." He shrugged. "I know there were times I wanted to ship him off to some far-off island so I could keep you for myself, but since you'd made the choice, I had to accept it. I want you to be happy, Joanna."

"I know, Tony, and I'm grateful." She smiled at him a little sadly.

Tony looked uncomfortable for a moment. "Well, I'd better get out of here and get packed." He gestured around the disordered room. "From the looks of things, you've got quite a job ahead of you, too." He paused at the door. "Just for the record, I think Alex is a fool."

Her and Alex, both. As if the words had flashed on in neon letters, Joanna saw the truth clearly.

"Wait, Tony." The decision was an easy one, as if it had been in her mind all along. "I've changed my mind about leaving today. I need a few more days. I'm going to sign the house over to Alex. That will simplify things." She passed her hand over her face, wiping away an errant tear. "After all that's happened, I don't think I want to come back here."

"Okay." He remained at the door. "Do you want me to tell your parents?"

"No. I'd like to go out for a while but I'll talk to them first."

JENNY SAT ON HER VERANDA, the air around her pungent with the scent of one of the Turkish cigarettes she smoked on rare occasions. Seeing Joanna coming up the walk, she stubbed it out in an ashtray before tossing the butt into a rose bed.

"Well, Joanna, I thought you'd be gone by now." There was no sign of the upheavals of the past few days in Jenny's cheerful manner or hearty voice.

"I wouldn't go without saying goodbye to you." Joanna sat down on the top set, leaning back against a supporting pillar and wrapping her arms around one uplifted knee.

"I like your shirt," Jenny said. Joanna wore the tropical print she'd had on the day Alex had first brought her to meet Jenny. "But you didn't come here to hear me say that, did you? Come on, Joanna, out with it. You look like the donkey snatched your last piece of bread."

Even in her misery, Joanna couldn't help but laugh at the old Greek saying, which her godmother Katerina had used so often when she was a child. "I feel like it, too," she admitted.

"Alex? Or Tony?"

Joanna sighed. "Tony's such a nice man. And he's in love with me. Why couldn't I be in love with him?"

"We can't always order these things. Alex was always the one, wasn't he?"

"Yes. Always."

Jenny nodded, her finger tapping the side of her nose. "And you were the only one for Alex. As for Tony, don't worry about him. He's a very secure man. He'll get over it. And while we're on the subject, I might say that I don't think he was ready to settle down, in spite of the pressure he was putting on you."

"He wanted to marry me," Joanna insisted. "We even quarreled about it a couple of times."

"Yes, but I think it was a combination of proximity and expediency. Tony likes his job, and he likes your parents. And he loves you, but not, I think, with a grand passion. All of it gave him a comfortable feeling that he wanted to hang on to. Nothing wrong with that but with time, he'll get over you and then he'll be ready for a grand passion."

Joanna listened, fascinated by the conviction in the old lady's voice but also half-amused by her uncomplicated philosophy. "Does everybody need a grand passion in their lives?"

Jenny cocked her gray head. "Not everyone, but Tony, being the man he is, will have one."

"Did you, Jenny?" This time Joanna was utterly serious, needing to know.

Jenny sighed deeply, her eyes closing as her thoughts turned inward to the memories stored in the far corners of her mind. Around the two women bees hummed among the roses, and in the damp mint bed near the garden faucet, a frog uttered a drowsy croak. The sound of men's voices in the plumbing store carried across the street, a reminder that there was a world outside the peaceful garden.

Jenny's eyes opened, and she gave a little push to set her chair in motion, the rhythmic tap of her toe on the floor forming a counterpoint to her quiet words. "Yes, I had a grand passion, with Ari, my husband, a passion that lasted through poverty and wealth, seven children, and two wars. It remained strong for forty-four years. Even when it wavered sometimes, we always managed to weather the bad spots."

"What made it last?" Joanna asked.

"Love," Jenny replied. "A deep, abiding love. And compassion. And tenacity, never losing sight of the fact that this relationship is the union of two partners who are in it together, no matter what. No bailing out if the sea gets rough. And no going to bed in a sulk. Whatever it is, fight it out and negotiate a compromise you can both live with."

"The trouble is, Alex won't negotiate."

"You've told him you love him?"

Joanna nodded. "For all the good it did. He's got this notion that he's not worthy of being loved, or something. It's stupid in an adult who is successful in all aspects of his life."

"Stupid, maybe," Jenny agreed. "But not so far-fetched. Alex had a terrible childhood."

"I know. He told me."

Jenny shook her head. "He probably hasn't told you half, and he probably never will, but that's neither here nor there. The important thing is that he has to believe in you."

Joanna made a rude noise. "He doesn't. He even offered me his hotel as a sop to my feelings, and then he couldn't understand why I wouldn't accept it. He's blind."

"Not blind, just a little offtrack."

"Too far off the track for me," Joanna declared. "And it's such a waste."

"So you're leaving, giving him up without a fight."

Joanna couldn't hide her despair. "Jenny, I've fought but I can't seem to get through to him."

"Maybe he just needs more time," Jenny suggested.

"Well, he can have a couple of days. I'm not leaving just yet. I've decided to give the house to Alex. I can't see myself coming back here on holidays, certainly not if it means I'll keep running into him and raking up dead ashes."

"Are you sure they're dead?" Jenny asked slyly. "Watch you don't get burned."

Joanna gave a rueful laugh. "The weird thing is, it's so unfair. Alex got angry with me at the beginning when he accused me of wanting to build a resort here. Okay, the idea had crossed my mind but I didn't seriously consider it. Then he accused me of being so involved with my work that I would have no time for marriage or anything else. He couldn't be more wrong. If it wasn't for letting my father down and disappointing my mother, I'd have bought a little inn in some quiet place and settled to running that long ago."

"You work to please your parents?" Jenny's brows rose.

Joanna flushed, her fingers pleating the cuff of her khaki shorts. "No, of course not. I wanted to go into the hotel business ever since I was a teenager working for my father on weekends and in the summer. It's a job I enjoy. But I didn't realize just how much my career had taken over my life until I learned that Dad was considering me for a big promotion. A few years ago I would have thought it the achievement of my ultimate goal, but when I heard about it a couple of months ago all I could think was how much more responsibility I would have if I got it."

"You could handle it."

Joanna gestured impatiently. "Sure. I could handle it. I wasn't afraid of that. It was just that I felt I needed less pressure. I'd wanted to succeed but it suddenly didn't seem worth it to sacrifice my whole life to work."

"So quit," Jenny said with typical decisiveness. "You're the only one who can decide what you want, Joanna. Happiness comes from within, not from someone else. Even if you are hesitant to resign your job, take a leave of absence, trying running a small hotel for a year and see how it goes. You may find you don't want that after all."

"I can't, not just like that. It's not that simple. Dad would think I was a quitter. He's already something of a chauvinist about women in business. He's proud of me, but I think he would have been just as happy if I'd married straight out of school and had babies for him to spoil. So you see, if I quit, I'd lose face."

"Just because you're a woman doesn't mean you have to feel you represent all women," Jenny said with a touch of acerbity. "In my day, we didn't have as many choices but plenty of women still had careers. They worked for them. Doesn't the increased opportunity for today's women mean they have more choices, including the freedom to give up their career if they want to, and if it suits their life-style? And wouldn't it be worth it for Alex?"

Joanna wasn't even surprised at the question. "Yes, it would be, for Alex. He wouldn't expect me to give up everything. I would just make a few changes. But Alex doesn't want me."

"He doesn't know he wants you."

"It amounts to the same thing." Joanna fell silent, losing herself in thought, only half hearing the tap of Jenny's foot on the wooden floor and the faint creak of the rocker.

The slam of a car door on the street startled her. She looked at her watch, jumping up from the step. "Oh, is it that late? I must run and say goodbye to Mother and Dad and Tony. They wanted to get to Volos by lunchtime and it's almost that now."

"Well, don't bother with your own lunch, Joanna," Jenny called after her. "I'll treat you at the taverna. We'll kill a bottle of wine or two. That ought to make life look rosier for a while."

"And give us plenty of regrets in the morning." Joanna laughed as she ran down the path. "Wait for me, Jenny. I'll be back."

AT THE HOUSE, Tony and Mary were loading suitcases and assorted boxes tied with twine into the Mercedes. "So much to pack," Mary said, wiping her perspiring face with the frail lace handkerchief she pulled from her skirt pocket. "I swear it multiplies."

She glanced around. "Now where is Socrates? They say men always have to wait for their women but in this family, it's the opposite. Even when you were small, you and I were always waiting for your father and brothers." She planted a fond kiss on Joanna's cheek. "Are you sure you want to stay longer, dear?"

Joanna wrapped an arm around her mother's slender waist. "Yes. I have to. But I'll be home by the end of next week. I promise."

Mary looked at her with shrewd eyes that had seen far more of the human condition than most people. "Will I sound too motherly if I say I hope it works out with you and Alex?"

Joanna's eyes stung. "Mother, there's no hope of that."

They walked back up the path to the house, arm in arm. All the time Joanna was growing up, she and her mother had had to form a united front as the only females in a household dominated by five noisy and outspoken men. The bond still existed.

Joanna suddenly realized she'd confided her feelings about Alex to Jenny when normally she would have talked with her mother. Her mother was too close to the situation. She'd had to talk to someone with whom she had fewer emotional ties.

In the kitchen Socrates barely looked up from something he was industriously writing. Around him lay contracts and brochures, the scattered contents of his open briefcase.

"Are you ready to go?" Mary asked. "The car is packed."

Socrates scribbled another word, muttering to himself. "Is Tony ready?"

"He's waiting at the car."

"And Jenny's waiting for me, to meet her for lunch," Joanna added.

"Why don't you go then," Socrates suggested. "I'll be a few more minutes. We'll lock up when we leave."

He presented his cheek for her kiss, at the same time sliding a book on hotel management over whatever he was working on, hiding it from her eyes.

"Bye, Dad. I'll see you next week."

Socrates merely grunted and went back to his writing.

Mary's eyes met Joanna's as she pulled a wry face, making laughter bubble up inside Joanna's throat, laughter that was perilously close to tears.

"Bye, Mother." They embraced warmly, Joanna kissing her mother's cheek and breathing in the familiar scent of face powder and Shalimar.

"Bye, Joanna." Mary released her, then pulled her close once more, whispering in her ear. "If you want Alex, fight for him."

Through renewed tears Joanna smiled. "That's what Jenny says. Maybe we can gang up on him."

Tony stood leaning against the open door of the car, his arm resting along the roof. "Are they coming? I've never known Socrates to dither. You should have seen him in Athens, organizing everything like a tour guide who has to visit sixteen cities in six days."

"He's writing something he wouldn't let me see."

"He's grandstanding, no doubt, giving us time to say goodbye in private. You'll see, as soon as I get into the car, he'll be down here, shouting about the delays." His voice softened, his face becoming pensive. He put out one hand and rested his palm on her cheek, and for a moment, she nestled her face against it, absorbing the warmth of his skin. "So, Joanna, this is goodbye."

"But not forever."

"Oh, I don't know. After Alex has a chance to think, he might realize what he's giving up."

It was a subject that Joanna felt had been sorely overworked this morning. "Goodbye, Tony," she said quietly. "Be happy."

"You, too, Joanna." He brushed his lips over hers, a kiss that conveyed regret and the fragility of the emotion that had once joined them. Then, abruptly he turned and walked back toward the house.

"Goodbye, Tony," Joanna whispered as tears trickled down her face. "I'm sorry."

ALEX, FOR THE FIRST TIME in his life, was receiving no pleasure at all from sailing. The day was perfect, a seamless blue sky with a snapping breeze that sang in the rigging and sent the boat flying over the burgundy-dark water. Gray dolphins frolicked around the bow, sounding like happy children with their piping calls.

None of it touched him. He felt cold and empty and hollow all the way down to his toes.

He couldn't rid his mind of the look on Joanna's face when he had left her early this morning. That stunned expression that conveyed a mix of anger and pain, and echoed the feeling in his own heart, haunted him, superimposing its image on everything he saw.

He anchored the boat in the bay where they had picnicked. Was it only last week? It seemed forever. And another empty forever loomed.

Throwing himself naked into the sea, he swam to the little beach, only to prowl up and down it like a restless tiger. The imprint of their bodies on the sand had been obliterated by the storm the other night but between two rocks he found an earring Joanna had only missed when they'd returned home. She'd had no idea of where she'd lost it.

He held the trinket between his fingers, then enclosed it in his palm, clenching his fist on it as pain ripped through him.

"Joanna," he groaned. Everything reminded him of her. This place was the most evocative of all, the way she had looked at him when he'd stripped down to his swimming suit. She hadn't been conscious of the look, he was sure, but he had seen it. He remembered the casual way she'd discarded her bikini top, the action made all the more seductive by her nonchalance.

Had she been nonchalant? No, she had been burning, as he had found out the moment he'd touched her. His face grew hot as he recalled the way he'd left her lying on the beach.

And then she had come to him on the boat, had pleasured him with a generosity that he knew now was love, the profoundest, deepest love.

How could he ever have accused her of being a grasping female, lumped his unique Joanna with the hordes of women who did not share at all her giving spirit and tender heart? *She* had never used him. Even when he'd given her the opportunity, she had turned it down. Flat.

She didn't need him. Perversely, he wanted her to need him, yet wasn't her fierce independence what he admired most in her?

She could make it on her own, but she had told him she loved him. She was willing to share her independence with him.

And he had refused her.

With a hoarse cry he flung himself back into the water.

On the boat, he ran back and forth, arranging the sails for the return trip. The wind belled out the blue-

and-white canvas, against him now. Unless he hurried, she would be gone. Socrates had been planning to leave today, and the day was already far advanced.

Desperately fighting his own despair, he brought the boat around, tacking against the wind, calling on the sailing skills honed by years of battling *meltemis* and treacherous island currents.

Disjointed thoughts tumbled through his mind as he worked. Was it possible that Joanna had struck on a truth about his life; that it was too ordered, far more than hers? He thought of what he had accomplished since his return to Greece and faced facts with a brutal honesty that he should have applied years ago.

He'd been marking time. Hiding out. His career was successful. His business associates admired his work, envied it even, since several large European shipping companies relied exclusively on his talents.

But what had he really done for himself, other than take the coward's route to avoid—

To avoid what? Pain? The agony of rejection that had slapped him in the face so often as a child? He was a big boy now; he should be able to handle anything life tossed him.

And yet he had run from involvement, from Joanna. To what purpose? By running away, hadn't he also avoided the possibility of joy as well, and love, which Joanna would give him in abundance?

Urgency drove him. He had to get back before she left, to beg her to give him—them—another chance.

THE BREEZE HAD DIED after sunset. Joanna walked home from Jenny's house at midnight. Smoke from the charcoal fires hung in the air, carrying the savory aroma of oregano-flavored *koukouretsi*.

Jenny had been in excellent spirits, telling the most outrageous jokes, but at times Joanna had caught her looking sly and mysterious, as if she had a secret. Joanna shrugged. That was Jenny. Whatever it was, sooner or later it would come out.

Joanna skipped up the path to the house. The tranquillity of the warm jasmine-scented night seeped into her, filling her with renewed optimism. She decided to take a quick swim before going to bed.

Alex would be back soon. That he might go straight to Volos without bothering to pick up his things was a thought she banished to the same hell she had consigned the fear that he might never come to love her.

Retrieving her key from under the third flower pot on the stoop, she opened the door. The house was empty, tidied, as if no guests had ever been there. Her mother's work, no doubt. After a peek in the living room she ran upstairs, the cat greeting her in the upper hall.

He sniffed around her legs and she picked him up, ignoring the token struggle he put up before beginning to purr. "Bad cat, you're not supposed to be in the house."

He stared back at her, disdain in his translucent green eyes. "Surely you don't expect me to follow the rules, do you?" he seemed to be asking as he arranged himself on the bed where she set him.

"Just like your former master, aren't you, cat?" Joanna said aloud as she stripped off her clothes and pulled on the pink bikini. Slinging a towel around her neck, she slid her feet into thongs and headed downstairs.

But in the kitchen the sight of a legal-size envelope propped against the sugar bowl on the table stopped

her. Puzzled, she picked it up. Socrates's untidy black
scrawl. Her name. Inserting a thumbnail under the
barely glued flap, she tore it open.

"My dear Joanna," Socrates had written. "You
must know that in spite of the fact that I always spent
more time with the boys than I did with you when you
were children, you were my favorite, my little lamb."

Fleetingly she smiled. He hadn't called her his lamb
since she was eight or nine.

"It was just that after four sturdy rambunctious
boys, I wasn't sure how to handle a girl. Girls were an
unknown quantity, delicate, fragile. Only you weren't
like the image I had in mind. You could hold your own
with the boys, and that confused me more. I was so
afraid of doing the wrong thing that instead of trying,
I just kept a distance between us, let your mother have
all the say in your upbringing.

"I'm sorry now that we weren't closer. I've been
proud of your work in the company, and remiss in not
telling you so often enough. I haven't always been fair.
I've given you difficult assignments, but you handled
them beautifully. You proved yourself in everything
you did, over and above my expectations, and I'm
proud of you."

For an instant the words blurred as Joanna's eyes
flooded with tears. All the years of blustering and this
was what he'd really felt.

"I know I was wrong to push you and Tony to-
gether. Call it a father's instinct to protect his little girl,
but I know now that you have to make your own decisions, especially in this. Your mother and I have had
a long and happy marriage and that is what I pray
you'll have, but I know now it won't be with Tony. I
hope it might work out with Alex but if it doesn't, you

know you can come home to talk it out with your mother. Me, too, if you want.

"Lastly, I'd like to say that I'm giving you the promotion you've worked for. You deserve it."

An odd frisson ran over her skin, the sweet flavor of victory in her mouth, but only for an instant. What should have been the fulfillment of dreams was now only a pleasant stop on the road through her life. Against simply living, against the fullness, the *oneness*, she could have had with Alex, it was still a prize but not the pinnacle of achievement. It felt like the consolation prize.

Still, the warmth of the letter, the simple statement of love from her father, the words that he would never have uttered aloud, spoke to her heart. Even if she had lost Alex, she had been, and still was, loved.

The last paragraph of the letter contained only a promise that Tony would also receive a promotion, perhaps not as prestigious as hers, but equal in many respects. Joanna was glad. Under his often crusty exterior, Socrates hid a heart that contained a deep understanding of his fellow humans.

She laid the letter on the table, and went out into the night. The slender crescent moon, low in the sky, tracked a faint light across a sea as calm as a mirror.

Joanna ran across the beach, laughing aloud as she jumped high in the air, swinging the towel once around her head before tossing it aside. Kicking off her thongs, sending them flying in opposite directions, she cast herself into the sea.

CHAPTER NINETEEN

THE MOON WAS SETTING by the time Alex arrived back at the house. Reluctant to start the dinghy's outboard so late at night and disturb the quiet, he had anchored the *Meltemi* in the cove and come up by the cliff path. Wincing, he rubbed his shin. Climbing up a cliff at night wasn't a great idea. A bush had let go under his hand and he'd slipped, scraping his leg painfully on an outcrop of rocks.

Late in the afternoon, knowing he'd never make it back before dark, he'd put into a village and given Jenny a call, asking her to keep Joanna, not to let her leave with the others. Jenny had told him that Joanna had remained behind. Excitement surged through Alex's veins, despite his realization that her staying behind might mean nothing. "Don't tell her I called," he told Jenny. "I want to surprise her."

Joanna was not in the house. He'd imagined coming into her room, finding her sleeping, her cheeks flushed, her hair spread on the pillow, perhaps one breast peeking out from the inadequate bodice of her nightgown. He would have joined her. They would have talked—it was always easier to reveal one's inner emotions under cover of darkness—and they would have made everything all right.

But she was gone. Only the cat lay on the neatly made bed, blinking drowsily at him when he opened the door.

Bitter disappointment ached in his throat. She had gone without saying goodbye. The fact that she couldn't have said goodbye when he'd been out on his boat all day escaped him completely.

But then he noticed the piles of folded clothes on the dresser and chair in the room, and the opened suitcase she'd pushed onto the floor in order to clear her bed.

Her shirt and shorts and tiny lace briefs lay crumpled on the floor next to the bed. He picked up the garments, held them to his face and closed his eyes, inhaling the scent of perfume and woman that was uniquely hers.

She must have gone to the beach. Even as the idea occurred to him, he went cold inside at the thought of her swimming alone, especially at night, in a sea known to have treacherous currents.

He set a new record for least number of treads he landed on going down the stairs. Running down the path, he called her name, his voice breaking on the syllables. "Joanna. Joanna!"

He tripped on one of her beach thongs, then saw the towel and the other thong at a little distance, and tracks in the wet sand at the edge of the water.

"Damn it, you'd think by now she'd know better." Swearing, he ripped off his own clothes, and threw himself into the water.

Where could she be? A hundred feet offshore he stopped, treading water as he scanned the dark, glassy expanse of the gulf. Not a sign of anyone. Only a fish nearby leaped up and landed with a muted splash.

He struck out once more, his arms powerfully cleaving the water as he instinctively made for the headland that protected the cove where he'd anchored the boat. Was it possible that she'd gone there?

Terror knotted his guts. Around the headland unpredictable currents made swimming dangerous in daylight. At night—

"Joanna," he cried, choking as he swallowed a mouthful of brine. Muscles straining, he drove himself through the water.

SHE REACHED THE COVE, the white mast of the sailboat a beacon visible even in the starlight. For a moment she paused, treading water. Alex was back. Elation gave her new strength.

She had her hand on the lower rung of the dangling rope ladder when a hand closed around her leg. Flailing madly with her arms, she fought to get away, sinking beneath the surface, only to be hauled up coughing and gasping.

"Joanna! You're okay."

Alex. His voice was ragged and hoarse and he was saying things that were garbled and almost incoherent.

"Alex, calm down." Her own voice was thick, and she coughed to clear it. "I'm fine, unless you drown me. Let go."

Clumsily, her arms heavy after the time she'd spent in the buoyant sea, she climbed up the rope ladder. Alex followed, going below at once to get a blanket, which he wrapped around her. In the light from a single lamp mounted on top of the cabin she could see that he was naked but since he hadn't spent half the time in the water she had, his skin was rapidly regaining its normal heat.

He held her against him, rubbing his free hand up and down her back. Joanna closed her eyes, tiredness seeping into her bones.

He was swearing. "Damn it. You scared me. I saw your towel on the beach and knew you were in the water, and I couldn't find you."

She laughed a little uncertainly, flustered by the vehemence of his tone. Reaching up, she touched his face, feeling the beard stubble crisp under her palm. "Alex, I'm okay. I wasn't drowning."

Rage born of the worst fright he'd had in his life erupted from him as he pulled her even closer. "Don't ever do that to me again. You nearly gave me a heart attack. I was never so scared as when I was in the sea and it was dark and I couldn't find you anywhere."

"Well, you've found me now." She struggled against the painful grip of his hands on her shoulders. "And I'm not sure I'm grateful. Alex, you're hurting me."

His fingers relaxed marginally, and the anger drained from him as the slender length of her body against his assured him she was really all right. Their eyes met and she saw tears in his. His cheeks were wet, too, but whether with tears or the residue of seawater she couldn't tell. He looked like a man who had undergone the most grievous torture, his face white and haggard, drawn into lines she'd never seen before.

"Joanna, if I'd lost you..." he whispered brokenly.

"You didn't want me," she reminded him but the gentleness of her tone took the sting out of the words.

"I wanted you, but I felt things that went beyond simple wanting, and I didn't know how to deal with them." He looked straight at her. "I think I love you."

She choked back a hysterical laugh. "You *think* you love me?"

He dropped his eyes, one hand plucking at a loose thread on the edge of the blanket. "Well, the problem is I'm not sure how it would feel to love someone, but I know that if I lost you, my life would be empty."

"And when did you decide this?"

Some inkling of the happiness burgeoning inside her must have conveyed itself to him for he shifted restlessly. "Joanna, you're not taking this seriously."

"Oh, but I am, Alex," she assured him. "I'm just so overwhelmed that you're finally being honest."

"I realized it today on my boat when I kept thinking about how it was when we sailed together, and how all the pleasure was gone when I was alone. I couldn't face that loneliness for the rest of my life." He looked at her beseechingly. "And if you laugh, so help me, I'll belt you."

"Romantic, aren't you?" But elation sang inside her. It might not be the stuff of dreams, the way he put it, but she knew it was a start. And from this start could come endless possibilities. She cocked her head, arching one brow. "Anyway, I'd rather you kissed me."

He needed no further invitation. Lowering his head, he covered her lips with his, kissing her with a tenderness that conveyed the deep emotion he finally acknowledged in himself. But when she responded with gentle thrusts of her tongue in his mouth, tenderness became a rampaging excitement that inflamed them both.

A warm pine-scented breeze caressed them as Alex unwrapped her from the blanket and pulled off her bikini. He barely took time to suckle first one breast and then the other before he parted her thighs and entered her. Joanna gasped and cried out at the exquisite sensation. She was still cold and the feel of his heat inside her sent her spinning toward a relentless climax she fought desperately to prolong.

He touched her, his fingers cool against the sudden warmth that suffused her skin, and she was lost. The powerful shudders of completion crashed over her, rainbow lights bursting behind her closed eyelids. She had only time to call his name before she felt the intense surges of his body that told her he had reached the same pinnacle.

For a long moment they lay still. But the hardness of the deck beneath them finally penetrated the haze of contentment. Joanna groaned, taking her hand from Alex's neck to rub her back. "Mmm, I think this deck has gotten harder." She pushed at him, trying to dislodge his weight. "And you're not getting any lighter."

He lay with a silly smile plastered on his face. "I like it right here. I may never move again."

"Oh, yes, you will." She gave a heave that tumbled him off her. "Like right now."

He lay flat on his back, legs sprawled wide, and her heart lurched at the sight of him. But before she could say anything, or fling herself on his body, he surprised her by rolling on his side and breaking into uninhibited laughter. "Oh, Joanna, you're such a delight. I can see it's never going to be dull."

What was never going to be dull? She had no chance to ask as he stood up, scooped her into the blanket and carried her into the cabin where he dumped her on the bed.

"Now, we'll talk. It's long overdue, isn't it?"

Head propped on his lifted hand, he lay beside her. With one finger he traced down her nose and across her cheek, savoring the flawless texture of her skin, leaving in his wake a delicate flush that told him she was no longer chilled. "Joanna, I'm glad you didn't go. What changed your mind?"

She snuggled into the crook of his arm, inhaling the cool, sea scent of his skin, nuzzling the crisp hairs on his chest, loving him, his closeness. "I realized I needed more time."

"For me?" he asked. "Or for yourself?"

She frowned briefly. "For both of us, I guess. Jenny said I was giving up too quickly. Besides, I didn't know what to do with the house." She broke off, then added a little hesitantly, "Dad gave me the promotion."

Alex stilled, his hand tightening in her damp hair. "Then you *are* going back," he said slowly.

"What would you do if I said yes?" More than curiosity lay behind the question. He had to learn to open up.

"I think I'd lay in provisions and then sail out into the Aegean someplace and keep you there until you changed your mind."

She chuckled. "How barbaric."

"Sometimes a little of that is called for, just so you remember who's the man around here."

She cast her eyes up and down his body, taking in the sleek tanned skin, fascinating islands of hair, and the splendor of his masculinity, flushing a little as she saw his instant response. "I don't think there's any doubt as to who's the man around here."

She paused for the space of several heartbeats. "I'm not taking the promotion." The words fell between them like a rock into a puddle.

Alex's mouth dropped open, his face a study in astonishment. "What?"

"I've decided to stay here, at least for a while." She burst into laughter. "If you could see your face.... Yes, I'm officially on a leave of absence, a leave that may become permanent."

Alex wore an amazed look. "And what are you going to do?"

"Run your hotel if you'll sell it to me."

"Sure, I will," he said promptly, without questioning her change of heart. "It's not the small country inn you dreamed about but Volos is a pleasant place, not too busy. You'll have plenty of spare time, maybe spend some of it with me."

Smiling silkily, she traced a finger down the center of his body. "I'm sure we can think of something to pass the time."

A night bird called to its mate, and the sky slowly lightened with the pearly pink of dawn as they savored their new closeness.

"Are you going to stay here or in Volos until we make the arrangements for you to take over the hotel?" Alex's quiet words aroused Joanna out of a delicious reverie in which they lay in a deserted meadow with flowers waving in a summer wind and only the sky to cover their naked bodies.

"I don't know. I can't think right now," she said, feeling incredibly lazy and teetering on the edge of sleep.

"Will you come and live with me?"

That shook her. She jerked to a sitting position. "What?"

He sat up, too, his eyes gleaming in the dim light as he turned his head toward her. "I said, will you come and live with me, for always?"

Hearing the intensity in his voice, she didn't hesitate. "Yes."

He took her hands in his, holding them so tightly she feared for her circulation. "Will you marry me?"

This time she really jumped. From distrust to marriage in a few hours? Well, he'd often been impulsive as a teenager; she'd lost count of the number of scrapes they'd gotten into. Her eyes were wide as she stared at him. "Did you say marry?"

"Yes, as in a priest and a church and a *koumbaros*."

"Alex, are you sure?"

One broad shoulder lifted, then fell. "No, I'm not sure. Of myself. But I am sure of you." With gentle hands he grasped her upper arms, his face sober, the light in his eyes passionate and sincere. "Joanna, you have to understand. I'm not innocent. With the childhood I had, perhaps I never was. But when I'm with you, when I know I have your love, I feel new again. Everything I ever experienced seems superficial when I compare it to what I feel when I'm with you." He sighed. "I know there'll be times when I'll have doubts, but not about your feelings for me." He cupped his hands around her face, capturing her gaze. "Joanna, it's a lot to ask, but can you live with that?"

She closed her eyes, tears springing to life at the tenderness in his voice, his gesture. "I love you, Alex. Trust will come. I'll help you."

He was silent for a long moment. Then he said, so quietly she had to strain to hear, "Yes, you will. You gave me back my soul."

THEY WAITED to get married. Alex, thinking of her and the hurt she might cause her family by living openly with him, wanted an immediate wedding. But Joanna knew he needed time to fully realize his love, to trust her completely.

But she was no longer afraid he would leave.

On a Indian summer day in October, under a seamless cobalt sky, with the changing leaves painting the hills in a tapestry of orange and yellow, they invited her family, Jenny, and a few close friends to an ancient chapel in a village high above Volos.

Mihalis Samaras, as *koumbaros*, placed the ribbon-connected crowns of white flowers on their heads, and they exchanged vows they'd written themselves, in English and in Greek.

"I pledge you my love, always," Joanna whispered, her heart full as she looked into his eyes.

Alex paused, returning her gaze, knowing there were no more secrets. Joanna would never betray him. Or leave him.

"And to you, Joanna, I give my love and my trust. For always."

And then, standing before a solemn priest in a cloth-of-gold robe, and surrounded by those closest to them, they were united according to the rites of man and society. In the eyes of God they had been one from eternity.

"GIVE YOUR HEART TO HARLEQUIN" SWEEPSTAKES

OFFICIAL RULES

NO PURCHASE NECESSARY TO ENTER OR RECEIVE A PRIZE

1. To enter and join the Harlequin Reader Service, rub off the concealment device on all game tickets. This will reveal the values for each Sweepstakes entry number and the number of free books you will receive. Accepting the free books will automatically entitle you to also receive a free bonus gift. If you do not wish to take advantage of our introduction to the Harlequin Reader Service but wish to enter the Sweepstakes only, rub off the concealment device on tickets #1-3 only. To enter, return your entire sheet of tickets. Incomplete and/or inaccurate entries are not eligible for that section or sections of prizes. Not responsible for mutilated or unreadable entries or inadvertent printing errors. Mechanically reproduced entries are null and void.

2. Either way, your Sweepstakes numbers will be compared against the list of winning numbers generated at random by computer. In the event that all prizes are not claimed, random drawings will be held from all entries received from all presentations to award all unclaimed prizes. All cash prizes are payable in U.S. funds. This is in addition to any free, surprise or mystery gifts that might be offered. The following prizes are awarded in this sweepstakes:

(1)	*Grand Prize	$1,000,000	Annuity
(1)	First Prize	$35,000	
(1)	Second Prize	$10,000	
(3)	Third Prize	$5,000	
(10)	Fourth Prize	$1,000	
(25)	Fifth Prize	$500	
(5000)	Sixth Prize	$5	

*The Grand Prize is payable through a $1,000,000 annuity. Winner may elect to receive $25,000 a year for 40 years, totaling up to $1,000,000 without interest, or $350,000 in one cash payment. Winners selected will receive the prizes offered in the Sweepstakes promotion they receive.

Entrants may cancel the Reader Service at any time without cost or obligation to buy (see details in center insert card).

3. Versions of this Sweepstakes with different graphics may appear in other mailings or at retail outlets by Torstar Corp. and its affiliates. This promotion is being conducted under the supervision of Marden-Kane, Inc., an independent judging organization. By entering the Sweepstakes, each entrant accepts and agrees to be bound by these rules and the decisions of the judges, which shall be final and binding. Odds of winning are dependent upon the total number of entries received. Taxes, if any, are the sole responsibility of the winners. Prizes are nontransferable. All entries must be received by March 31, 1990. The drawing will take place on April 30, 1990, at the offices of Marden-Kane, Inc., Lake Success, N.Y.

4. This offer is open to residents of the U.S., Great Britain and Canada, 18 years or older, except employees of Torstar Corp., its affiliates, and subsidiaries, Marden-Kane, Inc. and all other agencies and persons connected with conducting this Sweepstakes. All federal, state and local laws apply. Void wherever prohibited or restricted by law.

5. Winners will be notified by mail and may be required to execute an affidavit of eligibility and release that must be returned within 14 days after notification. Canadian winners will be required to answer a skill-testing question. Winners consent to the use of their name, photograph and/or likeness for advertising and publicity in conjunction with this and similar promotions without additional compensation. One prize per family or household.

6. For a list of our most current major prizewinners, send a stamped, self-addressed envelope to: WINNERS LIST, c/o MARDEN-KANE, INC., P.O. BOX 701, SAYREVILLE, N.J. 08872

LTY-H49

Harlequin Regency Romance™

Romance the way it was *always* meant to be!

The time is 1811, when a Regent Prince rules the empire. The place is London, the glittering capital where rakish dukes and dazzling debutantes scheme and flirt in a dangerously exciting game. Where marriage is the passport to wealth and power, yet every girl hopes secretly for love....

Welcome to Harlequin Regency Romance where reading is an adventure and romance is *not* just a thing of the past! Two delightful books a month, beginning May '89.

THIS BOOK BELONGS TO:

W9-AFH-697

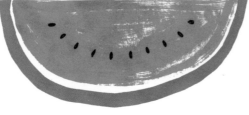

"A simple yet thought-provoking read that will change the way you think about, and define, happiness."

—Marc and Angel Chernoff,
New York Times–bestselling authors of
Getting Back to Happy

"This little book had a big impact on my heart.
Not only do I now have a better understanding of
the language and nuances of happiness,
I can express the feelings I never had words for before.
Every page made me smile."

—Courtney Carver,
author of *Soulful Simplicity*

"Delightful!"

—Martin Seligman, PhD,
bestselling author of *Learned Optimism*

HAPPINESS—FOUND in TRANSLATION

HAPPINESS – FOUND in TRANSLATION

A Glossary of Joy from Around the World

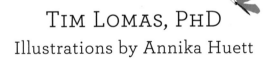

TIM LOMAS, PHD
Illustrations by Annika Huett

TarcherPerigee

tarcherperigee

An imprint of Penguin Random House LLC
penguinrandomhouse.com

Illustrations © Annika Huett, 2018

Most TarcherPerigee books are available at special quantity discounts for bulk purchase for sales
promotions, premiums, fund-raising, and educational needs. Special books or book excerpts also can
be created to fit specific needs. For details, write: SpecialMarkets@penguinrandomhouse.com.

Library of Congress Cataloging-in-Publication Data

Names: Lomas, Tim, author.
Title: Happiness—found in translation: a glossary of joy from around the
world / Tim Lomas, PhD; illustrations by Annika Huett.
Description: New York: TarcherPerigee, [2019]
Identifiers: LCCN 2019008665| ISBN 9780525538080 (hardcover) |
ISBN 9780525538097 (ebook)
Subjects: LCSH: Happiness. | Emotions.
Classification: LCC BF575.H27 .L653 2019 | DDC 152.4/2—dc23
LC record available at https://lccn.loc.gov/2019008665

Printed in China
1   3   5   7   9   10   8   6   4   2

Book design by Laura K. Corless

For Kate and the whole family

contents

contents

contents

Introduction

The language of happiness

Happiness is a many-splendored thing, a dazzling kaleidoscopic wonder. Few words, in fact, harbor as many delights and treasures. To appreciate this, take a moment to consider all the beautifully varied experiences that make you happy . . .

Cuddling up with your partner, perhaps, wholly content and cocooned from the outside world. The giddy joy of reuniting with a loved one after a time apart. Breaking bread with close friends, drinking and laughing long into the night. Switching on your out-of-office e-mail and disappearing from view on holiday. Lying on golden sands, the sea breeze on your skin, with nothing but the sound of lapping waves rippling through your mind. Savoring a perfectly delicious butterscotch ice cream. Watching your child graduate after years of toil. Seeing your parents smile, and knowing that you've done them proud. The list is infinite.

This exercise shows the bountiful nature of happiness, but it also raises a strange issue: the limitations of language. If we can use "happy" for all the experiences above, and many more besides, then what on earth does the term mean? I'm not suggesting it means nothing. Rather, it means *too much*. It's a crazily broad label, sheltering within it vast realms of feeling and experience. And fair enough: sometimes a broad label is useful. A person can like reggae, ska, jazz, blues, swing, funk, punk, rock, and soul, but it can be handy to simply state that they're really into "music." Likewise, sometimes it can be sufficient, and greatly reassuring, to just say, "I'm happy."

At other times though, more precise language is immensely valuable. Just as it is useful to distinguish between different music genres, so do we benefit from being able to conceptualize our happiness with greater precision. For doing so can help us better identify, understand, remember, communicate, discuss, and cultivate these precious experiences. Recognition of this fact underlies recent research into the value of emotional "granularity" or "differentiation"—our ability to appraise subjective experience with greater or lesser degrees of specificity. Indeed, this ability can even influence happiness itself. Generally, the more awareness and understanding we have of our emotional lives, the greater our well-being.

Fortunately, the English language is fairly rich and detailed in that respect. In thinking and talking about happiness, we're blessed with a wonderful array of relevant terms. When it comes to its calmer glades, for instance, we can call upon labels such as relaxation, peace, tranquility, serenity, quietude, and repose. These are all nearly synonymous, but crucially not quite—hence the value of such differentiation. Or again, with more energized forms of well-being, it is useful to be able to speak variously of delight, joy, elation, enthusiasm, ecstasy, euphoria, and so on.

Yet English does not provide labels that perfectly suit *every* nuanced feeling. Have you ever experienced something you couldn't quite describe—a subtle physical sensation perhaps, or a strange, unfamiliar emotion—because you lacked a suitable word? It's an odd, uncanny event. Without being able to label the experience, we may struggle to register it at all, and certainly to understand and articulate it. It hovers nebulously at the fringes of consciousness, before ebbing away irretrievably, like a dream that dissipates upon waking. It was for such reasons that the philosopher Ludwig Wittgenstein argued that the limits of our language define the boundaries of our world.

What is to be done in such instances? Luckily, a solution may be at hand. Even though English may not have coined a word for the experience in question, *another language might have*! These are known as "untranslatable" words—those that lack an exact equivalent in our own tongue—and they are at the heart of this book. For I have been on a quest to collect untranslatable words—those relating to well-being in particular—from across the world's languages. The result is an evolving "positive cross-cultural lexicography" that now includes more than a thousand words. And this book features an enticing selection of one hundred of the most evocative and interesting of those terms, each brought to life by a gorgeous illustration.

First though, let's dwell a little longer on this very notion of untranslatability. For it is my contention, and my hope, that we can use these words to augment our vocabulary of happiness, and even to enrich our experience of life itself . . .

The allure of untranslatability

Untranslatable words possess considerable power and potential. For a start, they allow us to give voice to sensations we've hazily experienced but previously lacked the ability to vocalize. In that way, they enable us to conceptualize familiar feelings, such as happiness, with greater clarity by helping us to sift these into finer-grained elements. More intriguingly, they may even introduce us to new phenomena that had previously been veiled to us and that we perhaps hadn't suspected existed. Truly, such words can expand our horizons, and even usher us into new worlds.

Indeed, the power of untranslatable words has been harnessed throughout history, and is at the heart of language development. Consider the sentence a few paragraphs ago, where I differentiated the realm of brightly positive feelings into such qualities as delight, joy, elation, enthusiasm, ecstasy, and euphoria. The strange thing about those words is that none of them are English! Or to be more precise, although they are *now* fully part of our lexicon, all were borrowed from other languages in the distant past. The first three originated in Latin (as *delicere*, *gaudere*, and *elatio*, respectively), while the latter three hail from classical Greek (as *enthousiasmos*, *ekstasis*, and *euphoria*). They then entered English, sometimes via French—brought over to the British Isles following the Norman invasion of 1066—at various points in the centuries leading up to the present day (from the adoption of "joy" around the eleventh century, to the appearance of "euphoria" in the eighteenth).

In fact, English is full of words that have been "borrowed" from other languages in this way—as much as 41 percent of our lexicon by some estimates. The majority derive from French, which in turn drew on Latin and Greek as noted above. But besides these, we've borrowed from scores of other languages. For instance, Arabic alone has provided numerous terms, from algebra and alcohol to zero and zenith. In the early stages of assimilation, such borrowings are referred to as loanwords. Over time, once their usage is widespread enough, they generally cease to be regarded as "foreign" words and simply become accepted as natural constituents of the lexicon—as with the brightly positive words above, from delight to euphoria.

This process of borrowing raises a fascinating question: *Why* does it happen? Well, as alluded to already, mainly because our own tongue is found to lack a suitable word for the phenomenon in question. In linguistic terminology, our language has a "semantic gap," an area of experience that is not wholly "covered" by any word (even if some existing words may cover *part* of it). However, if we then discover that another language *does* have a precise word for that area of experience, *voilà* . . . we often enthusiastically borrow it, giving voice to what we previously struggled to articulate. In that respect, this book offers you a wealth of untranslatable words with the power to greatly enrich your lexicon of happiness.

I will get to the words themselves shortly. First though, to emphasize the significance of untranslatable words, I'd like to introduce a theoretical metaphor concerning the power of language more broadly: cartography, the drawing of maps.

Experiential cartography

Language is essentially a map that allows us to chart and navigate our experiential world—the world around us, and also our private "inner" world of thoughts and feelings. Indeed, language has much in common with conventional geographical maps, sharing (at least) three deep principles that make both so powerful and effective.

First, the boundary principle. The world is dazzlingly complex and vast, and both maps and languages help us make sense of it by carving it up into small, manageable pieces. Geographical maps segment the planet into countries and regions, for instance. Similarly, our language parses our experiential world into cognitively digestible elements, doing so by identifying distinct entities such as objects (via nouns and pronouns), processes (with verbs), and qualities (through adjectives and adverbs). As I sit here now, for example, my senses are continually assailed by a dizzying river of

6

multidimensional stimuli. But I can bring order to this flood of data by identifying and labeling objects (dog, table, cup), sounds (music, kettle, rain), sensations (breathing, heartbeat, smiling), and so on.

Secondly, and related, is the granularity principle. Think about Google Maps. You can zoom in on specific areas, and as you do, the level of detail becomes ever more precise, showing the world in finer-grained complexity. Language allows something similar. Take a noun such as "music." This encompasses a vast swath of our experiential world—as if it were an entire country on a global map—enfolding a multiplicity of genres, techniques, sounds, and so on. But if we were so inclined, then we could zoom in on specific regions and label these individually, differentiating reggae from rock, country from classical. And we could zoom in further still, perhaps segmenting classical by chronological periods into medieval, renaissance, baroque, romantic, and modern. And then zoom in further still . . .

This process of zooming in can apply to any phenomenon, including . . . most importantly here, our experiences of happiness. And as we zoom in, we develop a more refined map that can allow us to see more clearly, hear more keenly, taste more sensitively, understand more deeply, and appreciate more fully.

Which brings us to the third principle: guidance. Maps and language are indispensable guides to our experiential world. They help us navigate a path through our immediate surroundings, and moreover they also invite us to venture into new territory. Such is the profound potential of language.

But how do untranslatable words fit into this picture? The answer lies in a theory known as the "linguistic relativity hypothesis" (or alternatively the Sapir-Whorf hypothesis, after the theorists most closely associated with it). Essentially, this idea holds that different languages map the world in different ways. In turn, this influences how people who speak those languages experience and understand life. The key to appreciating this theory is the notion that the process of boundary creation is somewhat arbitrary, and often a matter of social convention. For myriad reasons—from climate to tradition—the world's cultures have linguistically carved up the world in unique fashions, usually based on what is salient in that culture (i.e., what it is useful to pay particular attention to).

Consider the popular notion that Eskimos—a widely used umbrella term for indigenous peoples of the northern circumpolar region, albeit one that is not universally endorsed—have many different words for snow, more so than English speakers. This is actually a contentious claim, since Eskimo-Aleut languages create complex words by combining nouns and adjectives, whereas English usually just keeps the adjectives separate. As such, English can in theory harness a panoply of adjectives to qualify "snow," and so isn't necessarily lacking lexical richness in that regard. Nevertheless, in practice, there *are* many more snow-related words in Eskimo-Aleut languages, since snow is so central to their speakers' existence. As a result, per the granularity principle, these cultures have a highly detailed linguistic map in relation to snow.

This map helps people in those cultures understand, navigate, and even *perceive* their snowy world with greater accuracy than they would without such a map. Conversely, given that it rarely snows in the regions where English initially developed, why would we bother with such detail? Our snow-related map is thus relatively crude and undefined, lacking detail and granularity. The consequence of this is that Eskimo-Aleut languages will have many words we don't have in English, which are therefore "untranslatable." And maybe that's fine. Unless we actually find ourselves immersed in a vast snowy landscape, or are especially interested in snow for some reason, perhaps we don't need a particularly detailed snow-related linguistic map.

But the central point here is that many types of untranslatable words *will be* of great relevance to us. In particular, there are a wealth of words that pertain directly to happiness. And these matter to everyone. For instance, in English, the word "love" covers a vast range of feelings, relationships, and experiences. By contrast, classical Greece developed a detailed map of love, differentiating its terrain into more granular regions—from the sensual passion and desire of *érōs* to the benevolent compassion of *agápē*. In each case, these words highlight a region of our experiential world that has not been similarly delineated in English. These more specific labels are therefore untranslatable, since rendering them as "love" is too crude to capture their wonderful nuances. So we can benefit greatly from engaging with such words, which have the power to enhance not only our understanding of vital phenomena like love, but perhaps even our experience of them. These possibilities are at the heart of my lexicographic project, which this book so beautifully brings to life.

The positive cross-cultural lexicography

My interest in untranslatable words was sparked by a chance encounter back in 2015. In hindsight though, its seeds were planted way back in 1998, when as a wide-eyed nineteen-year-old I ventured to China to teach English before starting university. This trip blew apart my horizons—physically, emotionally, and most relevantly, intellectually. I encountered a wealth of utterly fascinating but totally mysterious (to me) ideas and practices, mainly relating to the great traditions of Taoism and Buddhism. Terms like *Tao* and *nirvāṇa*—which I now understand to be untranslatable—bewitched my mind, intriguing me to no end. I had no idea what they meant, and indeed they're still opaque to me now, if I'm honest. But I nevertheless had enough sense to appreciate that they might be of great relevance to our understanding of the mind, and of life more broadly.

However, when I returned to the UK to study psychology, such ideas were nowhere to be found in my undergraduate textbooks. The view of the mind presented there was almost exclusively filtered through the prism of Western ideas and philosophies, and relatedly was structured according to the contours of the English language. There were some tantalizing exceptions though. My experiences in China had led me to take a real interest in meditation, personally and academically. As such, I was gratified to encounter an emergent research literature on "mindfulness," a concept and practice based on the Pāli notion of *sati*—a valued form of attentive, present-moment awareness—which had developed within a Buddhist context more than two thousand years ago.

Eventually—after some circuitous musical detours—I was given the opportunity to study mindfulness myself, embarking on a PhD looking at its impact on men's mental health. This research also brought me into contact with other untranslatable concepts, like *mettā*, a form of "loving-kindness" that my participants said was powerful in helping them to open up emotionally. And I continued to take an interest in such ideas when I was fortunate enough, right after my PhD, to land a job at the University of East London as a lecturer in positive psychology. This is a fascinating field, one that focuses on all aspects of well-being. And although like many branches of psychology it is relatively Western-centric, it nevertheless takes a real interest in non-Western concepts like mindfulness and *mettā*, and practices like *yoga* and *tai chi*.

In this way I kept encountering words in other languages that, despite not having equivalents in English, seemed of real importance to psychology. But not being a linguist, the concept of "untranslatability" itself was still unfamiliar to me. Then in the summer of 2015 I joined colleagues at an international positive psychology conference. I was wandering aimlessly around when I stumbled upon a fascinating talk by a Finnish researcher,

Emilia Lahti, on the concept of *sisu*. Lahti described this as a form of extraordinary courage and determination, especially in the face of adversity, that is central to Finnish identity and culture. However, although the Finns had the foresight to recognize and conceptualize this quality, Lahti argued that it is a universal potential, common to all humanity.

When I got home to England, I was chatting with my mum about the conference. We were both intrigued by *sisu*, and especially the fact that it doesn't have an English equivalent. Between us we speak a few languages, and soon our conversation turned to other words we could think of that similarly lacked equivalents. Despite the formal notion of untranslatability—and the research that already exists on this topic—being unknown to me at that point, I sensed that this was an area of inquiry with much to offer to psychology, not to mention to English-speaking cultures more broadly. By the end of our conversation, the idea had taken hold that it would be useful to collect as many such words as possible, with a specific focus on well-being, given my affiliation to positive psychology. Thus was the "lexicography" born.

I had a vision of a crowd-sourced endeavor, with people from around the world suggesting words from their languages. The trouble was, I didn't even have a website, let alone a way of drawing attention to the project. I realized I would need to spark it myself, so I conducted an initial search for relevant words, delving into the various websites and blogs you can find devoted to this topic, as well as relevant academic sources. This yielded a modest haul of 216 words, which I analyzed thematically, grouping the words into clusters based on conceptual similarity. Then in January 2016, I published the results in the flagship journal in my field, the *Journal of Positive Psychology*.

Excitingly, the paper generated a fair amount of enthusiasm and interest, mainly due to a lovely article written by Emily Anthes in the *New Yorker*. By then, I had created a website to host the burgeoning collection of words (www.drtimlomas.com/lexicography), and I soon began to receive a generous stream of helpful suggestions. Meanwhile I also continued my own explorations: I would often encounter a new word, then fall headlong into a rabbit hole as it drew my attention to a host of related concepts. In this way, the lexicon blossomed, to the point where it has more than a thousand items at present (and remains an ongoing work in progress).

Eventually, I found myself with the enticing possibility of creating the illustrated book you're holding in your hands.

The journey ahead

So I'd like to take you on a mind-expanding trip through the wonders of the lexicography. To that end, I've selected one hundred of its most evocative, interesting, or profound words for your edification. And I'm truly delighted to pair up with the wonderful Annika Huett, whose beautiful illustrations truly make these words come alive. After all, these terms are by definition untranslatable. Although I've sought to formulate a rough definition for each, these descriptions are inherently limited and partial. They can convey only a fraction of the rich layers of nuanced meanings the words have within their original languages. Hence the value of the illustrations, for visual art can convey great richness and subtleties that elude discursive language.

As for the words themselves, as in my original academic paper—and subsequent publications—I've grouped these together thematically. As a result, there are eleven chapters, covering the eleven most prominent themes in the lexicography. To help us appreciate these different themes, and to see how they interrelate, I'd like to introduce a central motif that will run like a golden thread throughout the book: the notion of journeying through our experiential world. This world comprises numerous regions—each itself made up of smaller areas, as per the idea of scalable granularity—including feelings, thoughts, sensations, character, relationships, and so on. And here we shall focus on three regions in particular.

The first region is the *feeling* of happiness (which is part of the broader realm of feelings in general). This region is a complex landscape, featuring three distinct areas: the calm pastures of contentment (which we'll explore in chapter 1), the dramatic peaks of pleasure (chapter 2), and a mysterious forest of ambivalent feelings (chapter 3). The other two regions then overlap or intersect with this first region in complex, interesting ways. These are not *subsets* of happiness, but significant areas of experience in their own right that are nevertheless important factors in our happiness.

The second region is relationships, arguably our main *source* of happiness. This includes our bonds with other people, involving the intimacies of love (chapter 4), and social bonds more broadly (chapter 5), but also our links to the world around us, encompassing aesthetic appreciation (chapter 6) and our connection to place (chapter 7).

The third region is personal development, which features three key *pathways* to happiness: character (chapter 8), wisdom (chapter 9), and spirituality (chapter 10). Finally, we conclude with flourishing (chapter 11), an all-encompassing notion that enfolds all three regions.

My hope is that this collection will enrich your world and expand your emotional horizons. Each chapter features nine of the most alluring or valuable words within that particular theme, which I invite you to engage with in a spirit of respect, gratitude, and appreciation for the cultures that created them. You might even try to deploy these new words in your daily life. To that end, each entry includes a rough pronunciation guide to enable you to attempt a basic vocalization.

Together, these words have the beautiful potential to expand your understanding and even experience of happiness. Some words may allow you to articulate feelings that are already hazily familiar, but which you've hitherto lacked a label for. Others might entice you into exciting new realms of experience and reveal shimmering possibilities that had previously been veiled to you. Either way, I hope you enjoy the adventure.

Chapter 1

CONTENTMENT

In this book we shall adventure deep into the realm of happiness, reveling in its intricate connections to various subjective experiences, psychological processes, and relational causes. But we begin in these first three chapters by focusing on the heart of the matter: the very *feeling* of happiness itself.

In the introduction I used a metaphor that will run as a central motif through this book: journeying through our experiential world. I suggested that this world contains numerous "regions," one of which is our feeling of happiness (which is nestled within the broader territory of feelings more generally). So in these first chapters, we'll explore this most vital and bountiful of regions. For this turns out to be a complex landscape, featuring several distinct areas.

To begin with are the peaceful valleys and pastures of contentment, which we savor in this first chapter. There we roam languidly at our leisure, quenching our thirst in the refreshing waters of its rivers and lakes, even lying down in its soft green fields, daydreaming in the sunshine. Then in chapter 2 we'll broach the more dramatic peaks of pleasure. These are more invigorating and exciting to ascend, and perhaps more vivid in their impact, but are generally not stable locations upon which we can rest for long. Finally, in a quiet, shadowy corner of the region, is a mysterious and foreboding forest of ambivalent feelings, into which we'll venture in chapter 3. Although we travel there warily, it may yet have hidden treasures to offer.

But we start here with the warm glow of contentment. It can sometimes be difficult though to distinguish this from pleasure. As such, to switch metaphors momentarily, these two broad classes of feeling might usefully be viewed as a spectrum, arrayed along a continuum of arousal. Picture this visually as a rainbow. At its lower half are the calmer, more muted tones of peace and tranquility, the deep indigo and violet of calm contentment. Gradually, as we proceed upward along the spectrum, the colors become warmer, brighter, more energized. Thus, at the other end of the continuum we find the vivid, celebratory colors of excitement and pleasure, the vibrant orange and red of joy and ecstasy.

This is too much ground to cover in one fell swoop. So these first two chapters delicately cleave this rainbow in two. Here we shall luxuriate in the more placid half of the spectrum, dwelling on the cool calmness of contentment. Chapter 2 then embraces the upper half of the arc, reveling in the euphoric energies of pleasure.

I hasten to add though that variations in happiness are not only determined by arousal, as if just amping up some physiological volume control to 11. Rather, such feelings are shaped by the confluence of *multiple* spectra. Especially important is a spectrum of meaningfulness, from the relatively trivial (savoring a decent cup of coffee, say), to the deeply profound (finding your soul mate after years in the wilderness). Also, a spectrum of duration, from the tantalizingly brief (an evanescent glimpse of beauty) to the satisfyingly enduring (a fulfilling career). And so on.

As such, although these first two chapters are configured according to the arousal spectrum, we should also bear these other continua in mind, as even feelings of comparable arousal can differ greatly in weight and depth. With that in mind, let's meander in the lush tranquility of contentment.

Sati

Sati (स्मृति)
Pāli / n.
'sæ.ti: / *sah-tee*

Mindful awareness of the present.

Attentiveness that is uninvested yet kindly and curious.

Being in the moment.

HYGGE

Hygge
Danish / n.
ˈhʊːgə / *hhoo*-guh

A deep sense of warmth, friendship, and contentment.

Physical and/or emotional coziness.

Existential safety and security.

Fjaka

Fjaka
Croatian / n.
fjâ.ka / fyah-kah

Relaxation of body and mind.

Sleepiness, drowsiness.

The "sweetness of doing nothing."

Ataraxia

Ataraxia (ἀταραξία)
Greek / n.
ɑ.təˈɹæk.siə / at-tuh-*rak*-sia

Robust and lucid tranquility.

Deep peace of mind.

Imperturbable, calm stoicism.

wú wéi

Wú wéi (無爲)
Chinese / n.
wuː weɪ / woo way

Doing through "non-doing."

Natural, spontaneous, effortless action.

Skillfully flowing with the currents of life.

Fiero

Fiero
Italian / n.
'fjɛːɹo / fee-*yeah*-ro

Justified pride and satisfaction in one's achievements.

The feeling of a job well done.

Being content with one's efforts.

Uitbuiken

Uitbuiken

Uitbuiken
Dutch / v.
ˈəʊt.bɜːɣən / *oat*-ber-ghen

"Outbellying."

To relax, satiated, between courses or after a meal.

The soporific satisfaction of gustatory plenishment.

Gemütlichkeit

Gemütlichkeit
German / n.
gə'myːt.lɪç.kaɪt / guh-*moot*-lish-kite

The feeling of home.

A deep sense of comfort, coziness, and security.

An atmosphere that is full of heart and soul.

BÉATITUDE

Béatitude
French / n.
beɪˈæt.ɪt.uːd / bay-*at*-it-ude

Supreme, perfect happiness.

A state of profound blessedness.

Being in receipt of redemptive grace.

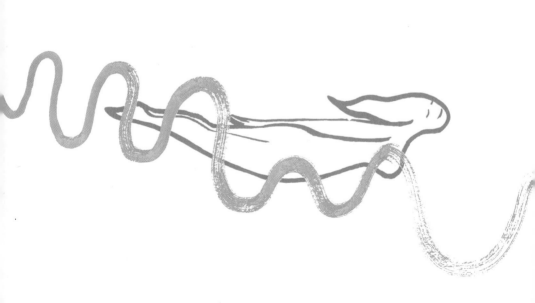

Chapter 2

PLEASURE

Our adventure rolls on as we continue to dwell upon the feeling of happiness itself. Leaving behind the calm valleys of contentment, we begin to giddily ascend the invigorating peaks of pleasure. Or, to switch metaphors, I suggested that one way of differentiating these two realms was according to a spectrum of arousal, ranging—as if climbing a glimmering rainbow—from muted tones of contentment at the base to brighter hues of pleasure at its upper bounds. So having savored the tranquil lower bands of the rainbow in the first chapter, here we reach for the higher arcs of the spectrum, absorbing ourselves in the vibrant and energized colors of pleasure.

But it bears repeating that happiness is woven together from multiple spectra, not merely arousal. Feelings of well-being are not so generic as to differ merely in energy and intensity. Of equal importance are factors such as how *meaningful* an experience is. However, this fact is not always recognized, including within my own field of positive psychology. For there pleasure is sometimes disparaged as mere superficial hedonism, as if shallow, inconsequential, and even suspect in some way.

For instance, a distinction is drawn between *hedonic* and *eudaimonic* forms of happiness. The latter, which is central to conceptions of flourishing—which we explore in the final chapter—hails from the elevated theorizing of classical Greece. In literal terms, it referred to a person being uplifted or ennobled by a benign (*eu*) spirit (*daimon*). But in the hands of Aristotle and other luminaries, it came to refer to people's ability to pursue and attain "higher" forms of well-being, particularly by cultivating virtue. By contrast, Aristotle despaired of cruder forms of hedonism, which he lamented as being little better than a "life suitable to beasts." This attitude persists, to an extent, with scholars frequently elevating *eudaimonic* happiness over more hedonistic strands, emphasizing qualities such as virtue and personal development.

However, critics are beginning to challenge this demarcation of *hedonia* and *eudaimonia* as distinct forms of happiness. After all, many of our most precious experiences are rendered all the more powerful by being a beautiful intermingling of the two. There's all the difference in the world between a merely enjoyable kiss with a casual stranger and the first swooning embrace with one's soul mate. The former may be nice enough, but the latter is what dreams are made of, suffused with divine mystery and meaning.

This is why, in addition to the rainbowlike metaphor of a spectrum of arousal, I like to view happiness as a richly detailed landscape. While contentment is the gently undulating lowlands where we wander calmly, pleasure represents its dramatic, elevated peaks. We ascend these excitedly, enthused by the intoxication of adventure. This metaphor allows us to bring in considerations such as meaning and significance. After all, glimpsing the majesty of the world from a mountain peak can be an awe-inspiring event.

Moreover, the metaphor allows us to account for another key spectrum on which pleasure is differentiated from contentment: duration. For although wild forays into the mountains may be more thrilling than meanderings in the valley, they are invariably more fleeting. After all, mountaineers do not generally set up home on their conquered summits, but return to the comfort and stability of the valleys. Likewise, contentment can be a more languid, enduring state of well-being, whereas the euphoric rush of pleasure tends to dissipate fairly swiftly as its neurochemical messengers subside.

Perhaps that's all for the best. After all, the notion of being permanently turned on by pleasure is strangely unsettling. Life's richness lies in its varied textures and tones. Still, though, pleasure is an undeniable good, and certainly worth celebrating, as we shall do here.

Sólarfrí

Icelandic / n.

səʊ.lɑːfriː / soh-lah-free

Sun holiday.

When workers are granted unexpected time off
to enjoy a particularly warm and sunny day.

The joy of unexpected freedom.

k e f i

Kefi (κέφι)
Greek / n.
ˈkeə.fi / *keh*-fee

Joyful passion and enthusiasm.

High spirits, often accentuated through alcohol.

Euphoric self-abandonment and disinhibition.

Mbuki-mvuki

Mbuki-mvuki
Swahili / v.
mbu:ki: mvu:ki: / mm-*boo*-kee mm-*voo*-kee

To shed clothes in order to move more freely.

To take off in flight and dance wildly.

Uninhibited physical expressions of fun.

JOUISSANCE

Jouissance

Jouissance
French / n.
ʒ'wi.sãs / szh-*wee*-sonse

Physical or intellectual pleasure.

Ecstatic delight.

Sexual climax and orgasm.

Pretoogjes

Pretoogjes
Dutch / n.
prɛtˈoːx.jiːs / pret-*oh*-yeess

Fun eyes.

The twinkling countenance of someone
engaged in benign mischief or humor.

An expression sparkling with joy.

Desbundar

Desbundar
    Portuguese / v.
    dʒiz.bũ'dar / dez-bun-*dar*

Exceeding one's limits.

The liberation of shedding one's inhibitions
(e.g., in having fun).

The pleasure of relaxing uptight self-control.

Bazodee

Bazodee
Creole (Trinidad and Tobago) / n.
bæ.zəʊ.di: / bah-zoe-dee

Euphoric, dreamlike confusion.

Dizzy and dazed happiness.

Bewildered, discombobulated joy.

Njuta

Njuta
Swedish / v.
njʉːta / nyoo-ta

To enjoy deeply and intensely.

To appreciate profoundly.

To revel in life.

TARAB

Tarab (طرب)
Arabic / n.
ˈtɑːrəb / *tah*-rrb

Musically induced ecstasy or enchantment.

Euphoric sensory absorption.

Spiritual self-transcendence through art.

Chapter 3

AMBIVALENCE

Our opening chapters have taken us upon a grand tour of the *feeling* of happiness itself, from the calm pastures of contentment to the dramatic peaks of pleasure. But before we leave this great realm, our path will take an oblique, surprising turn into a quiet, strange corner of this region. For nestled away out of sight is a small area of paradox and mystery. Set apart from the valleys and mountains, we might think of this as a shadowy forest that is dark and foreboding, yet also possibly enchanted. It contains secrets and legends of which we may well be wary yet which might also be of real value.

This area represents certain complex feelings that can be regarded as part of happiness, but which—unlike contentment and pleasure—are not entirely warm, bright, and positive. Instead, they are more nuanced and layered, in which elements of light and levity are interwoven with strands of shadow and shade. They are thus "ambivalent." This term usually has an unfavorable reputation, with a search for synonyms turning up such disparaging qualities as dithering and indecisive, conflicted, and confused. But "valence"—in psychological terms—refers to emotional tone, which can be positive (pleasant) or negative (unpleasant). Significantly, some interesting emotions are a complex mix of positive *and* negative, and are therefore ambivalent (with "ambi-" meaning "both").

We tend to overlook such feelings when we think of happiness, which we naturally associate with the pleasant emotions explored in the opening chapters. However, on closer inspection, it may also involve such ambivalent feelings. A paradigmatic example is longing, which inherently blends light and dark sensibilities. There is pain and sorrow at being separated from a person, place, or object one loves or craves. Yet that very yearning can be precious. For it may contain the sweet, tantalizing possibility and hope that we will be united with our desire. And it can also become an important part of our identity, our soul. A person might be exiled from their homeland, for instance, but these roots, and the ongoing yearning to return, can become central to who they are.

Psychologists are increasingly appreciative of such feelings, as seen in an emergent body of research that my colleagues and I refer to as "second wave" positive psychology. When positive psychology was initiated in the 1990s, it defined itself by focusing on positive emotions and qualities. Before long, however, scholars started to critique this foundational concept of the "positive." After all, some positively valenced emotions can be counterproductive to well-being. For instance, "excessive" or unrealistic optimism might lead to risk-taking, which can be harmful. Conversely, some negatively valenced emotions can be conducive to flourishing. Forms of "adaptive pessimism," for example, may lead one to take proactive precautions that can help life go well.

Such counterintuitive possibilities are at the heart of this second wave. And ambivalent feelings are a prime example. Indeed, while their value has been recognized within Western academia only relatively recently, many cultures have long since acknowledged their significance. Eastern cultures in particular are thought to be especially attuned to dialectical phenomena like these—with "dialectical" referring to a dynamic relationship between opposites, in this case between positive and negative valences. This attunement is symbolized by the legendary *yīn yáng* motif of Taoism, featuring two halves of a circle—one black, one white—in dynamic embrace, with a dash of each color appearing in the other half. ☯

We can turn to the untranslatable words of such cultures—and others besides—to help us develop our understanding and appreciation of dialectical phenomena, and of ambivalent feelings specifically. For although their role in our happiness may not be obvious at first glance, on deeper inspection they may have valuable gifts to offer. Although the forest is daunting, there are treasures to be found within.

Magari

Magari
Italian / adv.
maˈɡɑːri / ma-*gah*-ree

The wistful hope of "if only."

Maybe, possibly.

In one's dreams.

Mono no aware

Mono no aware (物の哀れ)
Japanese / n.
mɒ.nɒ.nɒ.ə.wɛ.reɪ / mo-no noh uh-wah-ray

Pathos toward the world, and particularly its ephemerality.

Delicate appreciation of the transient beauty of life.

A heightened sensitivity toward evanescent wonders.

Charmolypi

Charmolypi (χαρμολύπη)
Greek / n.
ʃɑːməʊˈlɪ.piː / shar-mo-*lih*-pee

Sweet, joy-making sorrow.

Sad, mourning joy.

Happiness and sadness intermingled.

Qarrtsiluni

Qarrtsiluni
Iñupiaq / v.
kʌːrʒ.sɪ.luːnɪ / kartz-sih-loo-nih

Sitting together in the darkness, perhaps expectantly.

Waiting for something to happen
or to "burst forth" (e.g., inspiration).

The strange quiet before a momentous event.

Vorfreude

Vorfreude
German / n.
ˈfoːɐ̯.fʀɔɪ̯.də / *for*-fhroy-duh

Prepleasure.

The enjoyment derived from anticipating future rewards.

Looking forward in keen expectation.

frisson

Frisson
French / n.
fʀi.sɔ̃ / frree-soh

A spine-tingling shiver.

A sensation of thrill, combining fear and excitement.

The ambiguous pleasure of the "chills."

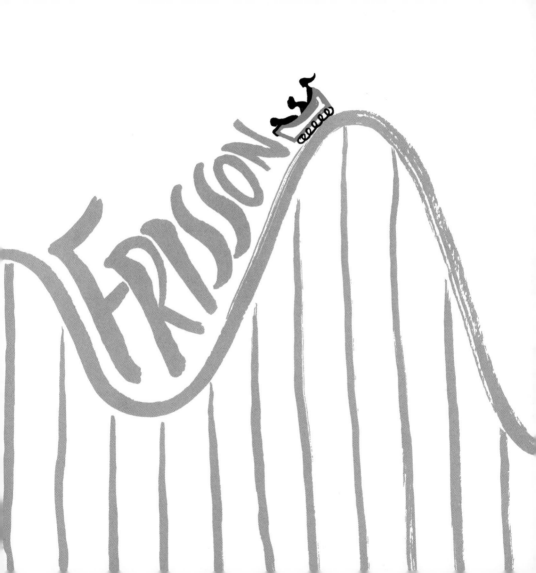

Þetta reddast

Þetta reddast
Icelandic / phrase
'θæ.tæ 'rɛtːast / *tha*-ta *reh*-dst

"It will all work out okay," or "It will fix itself."

A rallying cry of optimism and hope
(used especially when things don't look optimistic).

A mind-set that has faith in good outcomes and in the future.

Þetta reddast

Saudade

Saudade
Portuguese / n.
sɐwˈðaðɨ / sow-*dhadh*

Melancholic longing for someone, somewhere,
or something that is absent and much loved.

Dreamy, wistful nostalgia.

A bittersweet yearning that is connected
to Portugal and Brazil specifically.

Tizita

Tizita (ትዝታ)
Amharic (አማርኛ) / n.
tɪ.ziːtə / tih-zee-tuh

A bittersweet remembrance and longing
for a time, person, or thing gone by.

VIDUNDER

VIDUNDER

Vidunder
Swedish / n.
viˈduːn.də / vee-*doon*-duh

An awe-inspiring miracle or monstrosity.

A vision of the sublime.

A liminal experience that challenges human boundaries.

Chapter 4

LOVE

Our path wends its way onward into one of the most precious regions of our experiential world: the majestic, life-redeeming realm of love. To continue with our metaphor of happiness being a beautiful landscape, we could view love—and relationships more broadly—as a similarly vital region of our world to that traversed so far, one with great significance for happiness.

That is, love is not merely a regional *subset* of the great realm of happiness-related feelings explored in the first three chapters. For love is not only a type of feeling, but is also a fundamentally relational phenomenon concerning our intimate connections with other people. As such, it belongs to a second great region of our experiential world: relationships, which also includes connections with society broadly (chapter 5) and with the world more generally (chapters 6 and 7). So we might view the three great regions pertaining to happiness that we're exploring here—feelings (chapters 1 to 3), relationships (chapters 4 to 7), and personal development (chapters 8 to 10)—as distinct realms that nevertheless overlap or intersect in interesting ways.

What, then, of the landscape of love? Well, we must right away acknowledge this as a realm of astonishing richness and diversity, encompassing an abundance of feelings and relationships. I naturally call upon "love" to describe the profound ardor, care, and respect I have for my wife, and I moreover apply it consistently to our bond across the day-to-day ephemera of shifting moods. I will also invoke it for the unshakable bonds of kinship, loyalty, history, and appreciation I have with my family, and similarly—yet also differently—for the deep connections and allegiances I'm fortunate to find with close friends. But I'll also use it, consciously and deliberately, in relation to our beautiful dog, Daisy; long summer evenings in the park; the music of Tom Waits; the indulgent satisfaction of chocolate; sleeping in on Sunday mornings; and many more things besides.

Clearly, whatever "love" is, it spans a vast expanse of emotional and experiential territory. Indeed, it has been described by theorist Bernard Murstein as an "empire uniting all sorts of feelings, behaviours, and attitudes." And what an empire! A veritable earthly paradise, featuring many of our deepest longings and most precious experiences.

But just as we celebrate the wealth of this realm, we can acknowledge that the word "love" is rather vague, to say the least. As with "happiness" itself, it covers such a broad expanse of experiences that it can be tricky to conceptualize and articulate our feelings with much precision. So as with this book as a whole, we can embrace the lexical richness of untranslatable words to give voice to nuances that in English are airbrushed away by the overarching label "love."

Indeed, psychologists have already undertaken this kind of exercise in developing a subtler understanding of love. In the 1970s, the Canadian psychologist John Lee drew on the classical lexica of Greek and Latin to elucidate six different "styles" of love. He first identified three primary forms: *érōs*, denoting passion and desire; *ludus*, for affection that is playful, strategic, or otherwise "gameful" (a more manipulative variety); and *storgē*, for familial or companionate bonds of care. He then paired these to produce three secondary forms: *ludus* plus *storgē* creates *pragma*, a rational, sensible long-term accommodation; *érōs* combined with *ludus* generates *mania*, signifying possessive, dependent, or troubled intimacies; while *érōs* and *storgē* form the charitable, selfless compassion of *agápē*.

This analysis is a good start but an incomplete one. After all, it mostly just concerns romantic partnerships and doesn't account for many of the intimate feelings and connections that fall within the ambit of "love" in popular discourse. As such, this chapter lovingly showcases a beautiful array of terms which further illuminate the textures and contours of this most precious of human experiences.

ÉRŌS

Érōs (ἔρως)
Greek / n.
'e.rɔːs / *eh*-ross

Sensual desire and passion.

Deep aesthetic appreciation.

Greek god of love.

Retrouvailles

Retrouvailles

Retrouvailles
French / n.
ʀə.tʀu.vɑj / ruh-trroo-vy

Rediscovery, refinding, reunion.

The joy of reuniting with loved ones.

A precious moment of reconnection.

COMPADRE

Compadre

Spanish / n.

kəmˈpɑːdreɪ / kom-*pah*-drray

Godfather or "co-father."

A term of respect bestowed on a close male friend.

An ideal of companionship.

COMPADRE

Mamihlapinatapai

Mamihlapinatapai
Yagán / n.
'mæ.mi.læ.pɪ.næ.tæ'pai / *mah*-me-lah-pee-nah-tah-*pie*

A look between people that expresses unspoken but mutual desire.

A reciprocally imploring gaze, animated by passion.

The frisson of shared urges.

MAMIHLAPINATAPAI

abhisar

Abhisar (অভিসার)
Bengali / n.
ɒb.hiːʃɑː / ob-hih-shaar

Going toward.

A meeting, usually clandestine, between lovers.

The exhilaration of courtship and romance.

JEONG

Jeong (정)
Korean / n.
t͡ɕʌŋ / chung

Deep affection and attachment that doesn't
necessarily imply romance.

Sympathy, compassion, kindness.

Strong affinity, loyalty, and connectedness.

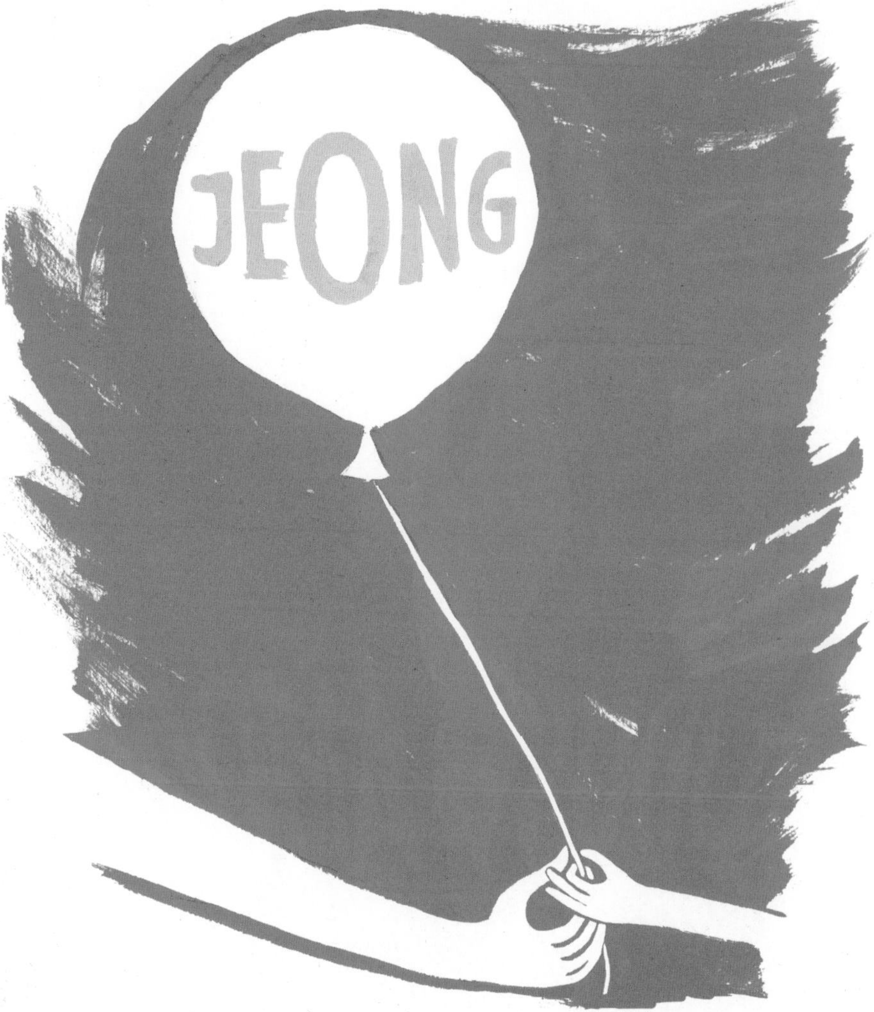
JEONG

Ludus amoris

Ludus amoris
Latin / n.
'ɫuːdʊs aˈmo.riːs / *loo*-dss ah-*moor*-eehs

The game or play of love.

Playful or gameful forms of affection.

A mystical view of the cosmos in which God
eludes, entices, and ultimately embraces the spiritual seeker.

KILIG

Kilig
Tagalog / n.
kɪˈliːg / kih-*leeg*

Butterflies in the stomach.

The nervous intensity of interacting with one's focus of desire.

Exhilaration and elation, shaking and trembling.

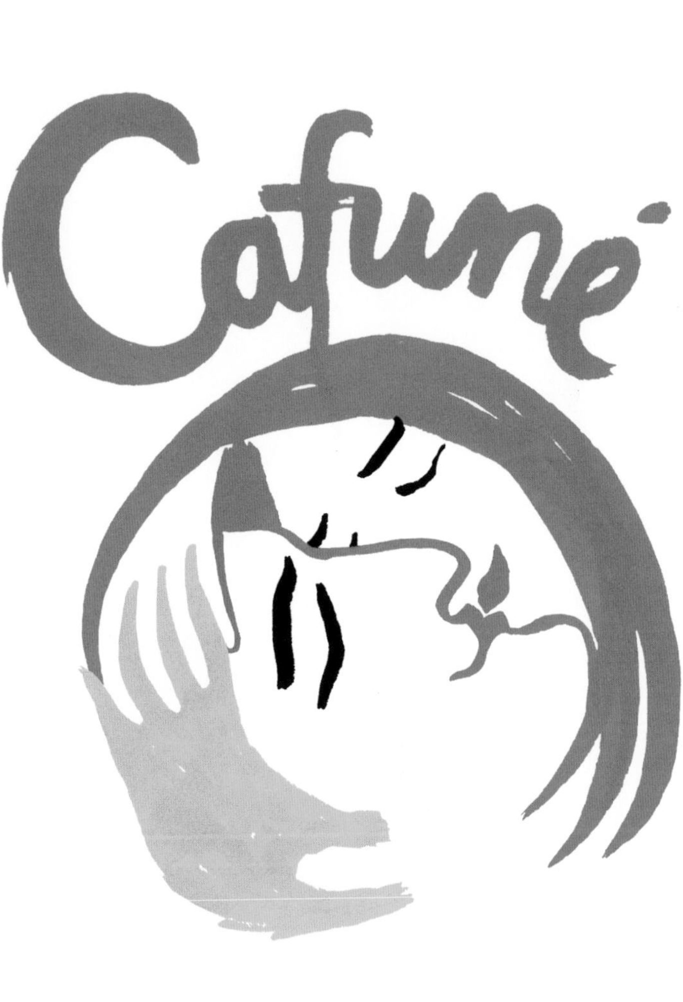
Cafuné

Cafuné

Cafuné
Portuguese / n.
ˌka.fuˈnɛ / cah-foo-*neh*

Tenderly running one's fingers through a loved one's hair.

A loving caress.

The intimacy of touch.

Chapter 5

SOCIAL BONDS

So we've rejoiced in the beautiful majesties and mysteries of love. But that is not the whole tale we have to tell about our fellow human beings. In the great landscape of our experiential world—through which we are traveling in this book—love is but part of the more expansive realm of relationships. Crucially, relationships are not only constituted from bonds with those whom we love in some way. We are also immersed in a far broader human drama.

Our loved ones, of course, play a starring role in our narrative, being—alongside ourselves—its most cherished and well-developed protagonists. But many scenes are replete with a significant and yet often underappreciated and uncredited background cast: extras and supporting players who fill our social world. And even if we are standing onstage alone at some solitary moment, perhaps lost in an internal monologue, signs of our fellow people are everywhere. Our environment is largely crafted by human hands—from architects to electricians—even if we don't see them in person.

The point is, we are social creatures. We exist within vast and multiple networks of other beings. These people range in degrees of intimacy, from our most cherished loved ones, outward to our neighbors in the local community, then inhabitants of our wider city or region, finishing in the countless millions around the world who we'll never meet. Crucially, these networks have the power to greatly shape our happiness, and indeed all aspects of life.

Yet we are often slow or reluctant to recognize this fact. Western cultures in particular are regarded as especially poor at acknowledging the communal nature of our existence, and even poorer at valuing and cultivating it. Many Western countries—with notable exceptions, such as in Scandinavia—have been dominated for centuries by a theory and view of the self known as "individualism." From this perspective, people are mainly regarded and treated as separate, atomistic units, with their connections to others generally downplayed.

That is, humans are universally acknowledged as having a dualistic existence: people are individual beings *and* are situated within broader social groupings. However, cultures differ in the *emphasis* and *significance* they attach to one of these two modes of being. Those that place a greater focus on the latter are known as "collectivist" cultures, with Eastern nations usually seen as exemplars in this regard. Those that prioritize the former are referred to as individualistic, with Western countries like the US and UK being paradigmatic instances.

This perspective was vividly illustrated by Margaret Thatcher's infamous claim that "there is no such thing as society," accompanied by her invocation of self-interest and self-reliance: "It is our duty to look after ourselves." With such messaging dominating the national conversation and consciousness in places like the UK, it is perhaps inevitable that our understanding and appreciation of group solidarity and belonging has become muted in many parts and segments the West.

But all is not lost. We can learn new ways of being in the world, and untranslatable words can play a helpful role in that respect. For many cultures do recognize and celebrate our communal life and have created words to reflect that vision. Through these windows we glimpse the beauty of social connection, and may be enthused to live a little more communally as a result.

Mind you, this doesn't mean *negating* our individuality, becoming submersed and swept away in an onrushing river of collectivity. After all, when human beings are regarded *merely* as replaceable cogs in the vast machine of society, then horrors such as totalitarianism can emerge from the shadows. Rather, we must still salute our individual uniqueness, while also celebrating being part of a larger body of humanity. In the great symphony of life, we each have our own melody to play and yet can also learn to harmonize with others.

Ubuntu

Ubuntu
Zulu / n.
ʊˈbuːn.tʊ / uu-*boon*-tuu

Universal kindness and benevolence.

A spirit of common humanity.

"I am because you are."

Folkelig

Folkelig
Danish / adj.
fɒlˈkɪ.li: / foll-*ki*-lee

Folkish.

Belonging to, or the will of, the people.

Democratic national sentiment.

Inuuqatigiittiarniq

Inuuqatigiittiarniq
Inuktitut / n.
ɪnuːkæt.ɪg.iːtɪɑːnɪk / ih-noo-kat-ig-eet-ee-ah-nik

Being respectful of all people.

Healthy, neighborly communities.

Living in peace and harmony with others.

INUUQATIGIITTIARNIQ

dadirri

Dadirri
Ngangiwumirr / n.
dəˈdɪ.riː/ duh-*dir*-rree

A deep, spiritual act of reflective and respectful listening.

Being receptive and attuned to the world around us,
with a spirit of reverence.

A thoughtful, contemplative way of being.

Simpatía

Simpatía

Spanish / n.

sim.pa'ti:æ / sim-pah-*tee*-ah

Accord and harmony within relationships and society.

Empathic connectedness within a group.

Social attraction and communion.

Shalom

Shalom

Shalom (שָׁלוֹם)
Hebrew / n., interjection
ʃɔːˈləʊm / shor-*lome*

An invocation and salutation of peace.

Wholeness, harmony, and tranquility.

Welfare and prosperity.

GADUGI

Gadugi
Cherokee / n.
gæˈduːgiː / gah-*doo*-gee

Cooperative labor.

Working together for the common good.

A voluntarily undertaken community task.

GADUGI

TUKO Pamoja

Tuko pamoja

Tuko pamoja
Swahili / n.
tuːkə pæˈməʊ.dʒæ / too-kuh pah-*moh*-jah

Literally "one place," "we are together."

Community togetherness.

Shared purpose and motivation within a group.

Hoʻoponopono

Hoʻoponopono
Hawaiian / v.
hɒ | ˈɒ.pɒ.nɒ.pɒ.nɒ / hoh oh-poh-noh-poh-noh

To set in order.

Putting relationships right through prayer, discussion, confession, repentance, and forgiveness.

A practice or interaction of mutual reconciliation and restitution.

Chapter 6

APPRECIATION

In 1927, Max Ehrmann wrote a beautiful poem "Desiderata," which closed with the following lines: "With all its sham, drudgery and broken dreams, / it is still a beautiful world. Be cheerful. / Strive to be happy." These lines resonate for many people. The world can indeed be a terrible place, suffused with suffering, and yet—wondrously, miraculously—it can still astound us with its grace and beauty.

The last phrase is curious though: "Strive to be happy." People often contend that happiness cannot be directly sought, and even that such seeking may make the goal yet *more* elusive, since it means we set ourselves at odds with our current situation, in a stance of non-acceptance that may actually heighten our dissatisfaction. Rather, it's said that happiness tends to only grace us with its divine presence when we are pursuing *other* noble goals, such as developing our character or cultivating our relationships. This sentiment is exquisitely articulated in a saying popularly attributed to

Nathaniel Hawthorne (although its actual authorship is uncertain), namely that "Happiness is a butterfly, which when pursued is always just beyond your grasp, but which, if you sit down quietly, may alight upon you."

Indeed, this book is aligned with that tantalizing idea. The first three chapters may have been about the feeling of happiness itself, but the remainder are focused on experiences and processes that are instead *associated* with it—from relationships to personal development. Crucially, while directly striving to be happy may not be feasible, we *can* work on the factors that engender happiness, endeavoring to make ourselves and our lives the best we can.

Key among these factors is relationships. This includes not only our bonds with other people but also with the world more generally. Which means, here, learning to savor and appreciate the environment around us. For, strangely, to return to the admirable sentiment of "Desiderata," we can even strive to heighten our experience of beauty. That notion may sound surprising to some ears. After all, we can be misled into thinking that aesthetic qualities are simply something that strike us without choice or effort—emanating from stereotypically admired phenomena, such as a great landscape or artwork—as if we are mere passive observers. But that is not true.

To appreciate that, pause briefly and let your gaze roam around your surroundings. Try to find something that you find attractive, however slightly. Even in the drabbest environment, there will be stimuli that are at least *vaguely* pleasing, even if these are not obvious to us at first. A colorful swash of paint on a wall, perhaps. A faded geometric floor pattern. An attractive label on a bottle. Whatever your eyes alight upon, really dwell upon it, savoring its every detail. Pretend it's enclosed in a gilded frame, a long-lost masterpiece by Van Gogh.

The point is that we can find beauty everywhere if we have the presence of mind to look and the curious eyes to see. And again, untranslatable words have much to offer us here, as they can draw our attention to aspects of the world that we had not previously noticed or paid much attention to. They are polite signs that quietly nudge us and say, "Hey, take a look at this, it might be worth attending to."

Moreover, such aesthetic experiences are no mere superficial indulgence, but are intimately connected to happiness. It's all too easy to become trapped inside your own head, caught up in a whirlwind of negative thoughts, spiraling downward in a vortex of unpleasant emotions. As such, lifting your gaze and attending to sights and sounds around you is a powerful antidote to this kind of destructive introspection. Furthermore, appreciating the world in this way can not only help release you from the prison of your own thoughts, it also illuminates life, making it shine with a radiance you may otherwise seldom see. Such is the power of beauty, as this chapter celebrates.

Kulturbärare

Kulturbärare

Swedish / n.

kəl.tuːˈbɑːrɑːrə / kul-toor-*bar*-ah-ruh

Culture-bearer or culture-carrier.

A phenomenon that upholds a culture and/or moves it forward.

The avant-garde of the zeitgeist.

harmonía

Harmonía (ἁρμονία)
Greek / n.
ɑːmaʊˈniːjə / ah-moh-*nee*-yuh

Concordance, union, agreement.

The synchrony of well-matched phenomena.

Empathic resonance between entities.

Harmonia

Fuubutsushi

Fuubutsushi (風物詩)
Japanese / n.
fu.bu.tsu.ʃi / foo-boo-tsoo-shi

"Scenery poetry."

Phenomena that evoke a particular season.

The signifying properties of the natural world.

Sprezzatura

Sprezzatura
Italian / n.
ˌsprɪt.səˈt(j)ʊə.rə / spritz-uh-*toor*-uh

Nonchalant effortlessness.

Art and endeavor concealed beneath a studied carelessness.

The graceful freedom endowed by practice and skill.

LǏ

Lǐ (理)
Chinese / n.
liːi / lee-e

Law, order, rational principle.

The organic order found in nature.

Patterns of symmetry, coherence, and proportionality.

Gourmet

Gourmet
French / n.
ɡʊʀ.mɛ / goor-mehy

A connoisseur of good food and drink.

A person who enjoys culinary expertise.

Someone who prizes gastronomic quality over quantity.

Hugfanginn

Hugfanginn
Icelandic / adj.
ˈhuːfʌŋ.ɡɪn / *hoo*-fung-gin

Mind-captured.

To be enchanted and enthralled by someone or something.

Becoming transfixed, possibly involuntarily.

GESTALT

Gestalt
German / n.
gəˈʃtalt / guh-*shtalt*

Form or shape.

An overall pattern or configuration.

The notion that the whole is greater (or other)
than the sum of its parts.

WABI SABI

Wabi sabi (侘寂)
Japanese / n.
wɑːbɪ sɑːbɪ / wah-bee sah-bee

Imperfect, weathered, rustic beauty.

The aesthetics of impermanence and imperfection.

Discerning depth and significance in phenomena.

Chapter 7

CONNECTEDNESS

We can delight in the world around us, as we've just seen. But in this spirit of appreciation, it is crucial to remind ourselves of a profound but often overlooked fact: We are not merely detached "outside" observers; we are *part* of this very environment. We have an all-too-human tendency to view ourselves as somehow separate from it, as if stranded upon an alien planet that is hostile to our very existence. But we are the fruit of nature too, having in a real sense grown from its roots.

More specifically, we are rooted to certain places, ones we call "home." These places literally produce us. Our physical body comes into being through their combined natural forces of food and water, air and sunlight. We are then formed from biological roots in the guise of DNA, which likewise is epigenetically intertwined with the specific locales in which our ancestors thrived. On top of that, somewhat more abstractly, our hearts and minds are woven together from the precious threads of culture, history, and tradition, and these too are intimately connected to the environment in which they were formed and nurtured.

That is not to say that we are rooted in just one place, mind you. Many people move and migrate, either willingly in a spirit of adventure or unwillingly from necessity. Most people are also the product of a complicated ancestral heritage, with their genetic and cultural makeup traceable to multiple regions across the globe. Accordingly, our roots and affiliations are similarly complex and multifaceted. But they are still very real.

And they are hugely significant, forming a cornerstone of our identity and our happiness. For a deep aspect of our well-being is our connection to the world around us, and especially to places dear to us. Compare the vast distinction between the unsettling feeling of being stranded in an unknown land, and the comforting sense of being in your hometown, and even more so, crossing the threshold of your very own home. The difference in terms of feeling at ease, at peace, and at one is incalculable. Even aside from the question of being on "home turf," the value of a milieu that is safe, peaceful, friendly, inspiring, and beautiful cannot be overestimated.

Thus our connection to place is the fourth and final part of the great realm of relationships we've been exploring over the last few chapters. And it's important to remind ourselves how precious this relationship is. As suggested above, we can easily lose sight of the way we are grounded in, and shaped by, our milieu. There are parallels here with the phenomenon of individualism, mentioned in chapter 5, in which we all too often perceive ourselves as isolated entities, and downplay the way we are situated in networks of other people. Similarly, we are liable to overlook the significance of our connection to nature and to place.

But not always! Some peoples and cultures do manage to successfully recognize and celebrate this connection, and have created words to reflect that. So, as with the other themes here, we can embrace these words and let them illuminate aspects of life that until now we may have perceived only dimly, or perhaps not at all. Which here means our deep interconnectedness to all that surrounds us. To return to the evocations of "Desiderata": "You are a child of the universe, / no less than the trees and the stars; / you have a right to be here." What a beautiful sentiment. For while we draw strength from our connection to specific places, the earth entire is also our home, and we belong in it.

Mana whenua

Mana whenua
Māori / n.
ˈmɑ.nə ˈfɛ.nʊə / *ma*-nuh *fen*-ooa

The power held over a land by those who have acquired,
earned, or demonstrated moral authority.

Territorial guardianship and stewardship.

The responsibility to care for one's environment.

Laadoittuminen

Maadoittuminen

Maadoittuminen
Finnish / v.
ˈmɑːdoi̯.tuːmɪn.ɛn / *mah*-doi-too-min-en

Grounding, earthing.

Rooting oneself in nature.

Connecting with the natural world.

GAIA

Gaia (Γαῖα)
Greek / n., pron.
ˈɣɛ.a / *kheh*-uh

Primordial Mother Earth.

One of the Prōtógonos, the "firstborn" generation of Greek deities.

The contemporary scientific notion of the Earth
as a self-regulating living being.

Cynefin

Cynefin
Welsh / n.
ˈkʌn.nɫ.vɪn / *kun*-uh-vin

Haunt, habitat.

The place where one lives (or feels one ought to live).

The relationship one has to the place
where one was born and/or feels at home.

ELLA

Ella
Yup'ik / n.
ɛl.læ / ell-lah

Awareness and intelligence.

Environment, world, cosmos.

The pantheistic notion that life as a whole
(and all elements within it) possesses consciousness or spirit.

s h i n r i n - y o k u

Shinrin-yoku (森林浴)
Japanese / n.
ʃɪn.ɹiːjɒ.kuː / shin-ree-yok-ooh

"Forest bathing."

Appreciating and harnessing the therapeutic power of woodlands.

The restorative impact of immersion in nature.

Shinrin-yoku

Passeggiata

Passeggiata

Passeggiata
Italian / n.
päs.sād'ja:tä / pa-saj-*yah*-ta

A leisurely stroll, often in the early evening.

An Italian tradition of communal ambulatory savoring.

Wandering aimlessly just for the pleasure of it.

smultronställe

Smultronställe
Swedish / n.
smʊl.trɒnˈstɛl.ɛ / smool-tron-*stel*-eh

A forest berry patch.

A quiet, cultivated place to which one goes to relax.

A nature retreat.

SMULTRONSTÄLLE

Friluftsliv

Friluftsliv
Norwegian / n.
fri:lu:fts'li:v / free-loofts-*leev*

Open-air life.

Appreciation and enjoyment of the outdoors.

Engaging and living in tune with nature.

Chapter 8

CHARACTER

Who are you? You have a name, certainly, along with a host of other identifiers—height and weight, eye and hair color, nationality and ethnicity, and so on. But are these *really* you? Or are they more like qualities and customs we've inherited from our forebears—precious and valued, perhaps, but not accomplishments we can take much credit for, nor unique traits that apply to us specifically and individually. But what about our *character*—whether we are gregarious or reserved, industrious or dreamy, creative or practical, diligent or spontaneous, conscientious or risk-taking? Getting closer now. These things may be inherited too—whether via biology or socialization—but they are certainly more intimately related to who we are personally.

Okay, next question: How do you view the nature of character? Is it fixed and enduring, engraved into our being like a motto carved into stone? Or is it altogether more dynamic and malleable, something we can work at, cultivate, develop? For people who are—perhaps with good reason—more pessimistic about the possibility of human potential and progress, the first perspective might seem more plausible. However, the good news from decades of psychological research—and centuries of philosophizing before that—is that people can and do develop. We can work toward improving our character, and all those other qualities and capacities that distinguish and ennoble us, from wisdom to spirituality.

So we reach the third and final great realm of our experiential world we shall explore in this book: personal development. This is a significant topic, encompassing numerous areas of psychological potential and change—not only character (our focus here) but also wisdom and spirituality (the topics of the next two chapters). In terms of our ongoing landscape motif, these could be regarded as three separate regions within the overall realm of personal development. But on reflection a more productive geographic metaphor is to view this entire realm as one massive, awe-inspiring mountain, with these elements—character, wisdom, and spirituality—as its main "faces."

When theorists think about psychological development, they often invoke metaphors of verticality and ascent—from climbing a developmental "ladder" to progressing upon an upward spiral. In keeping with that tradition, but also incorporating the landscape motif that has sustained us throughout the book, the image of a mountain is apt. It speaks to the idea of effort, determination, and perseverance in making the climb. Just like for a mountaineer, our progress upward isn't guaranteed; we cannot rest on our laurels in the valley, but need the ambition, spirit of endeavor, and grit to start ascending. But this isn't simply some hard, Sisyphean slog. The higher we climb, the better our view of the world and our experience of life. The journey is worth the effort.

How about the notion of these various elements being different faces of the mountain? Well, one could conceivably make the ascent up one face alone—developing personally by just focusing on character, for instance, without paying attention to wisdom or spirituality. However, following this precipitous route is likely to be tougher and more perilous. In developmental terms, this means one's progression is somewhat lopsided and partial rather than an integrative course that draws on all parts of the person.

So a better metaphor of psychological development is a spiral path winding gradually up the mountain—taking in all three faces. In one moment we might be cultivating our character, in the next deepening our wisdom, and then attending to spiritual concerns (or, if the notion of spirituality doesn't resonate with us, then engaging with existential considerations). In that way, around and around we go, onward and upward to the peak, toward the best version of ourselves. This notion aligns with the vision of Carl Jung—one of the world's greatest psychologists—who wrote, "There is no linear evolution; there is only a circumambulation of the self."

And as we climb, we might pause occasionally to glance upward from wherever we are, to contemplate each majestic face of the mountain in turn. We begin here with the promise and potential of character development.

SISU

Sisu
Finnish / n.
ˈsi.su / si-soo

Extraordinary determination and grit,
especially in the face of adversity.

The courage to take action against slim odds.

Having integrity and taking responsibility.

Engelengeduld

Engelengeduld
Dutch / n.
ɛŋ.ɡə.lən'ɣə.dʉlt / eng-uhl-uhn-kher-dult

Angelic patience.

Preternatural tolerance, fortitude, and stoicism.

The capacity to endure with grace.

BILDUNGSRoman

Bildungsroman

Bildungsroman

German / n.

'bɪl.dʊŋs ʁo.maːn / *bill*-doongs roe-mahn

A coming-of-age story.

A narrative of development and self-transformation.

The possibility of finding one's authentic self.

Kintsugi

Kintsugi (金継ぎ)
Japanese / n.
kɪn.tsʊ.gi / kin-tsu-gee

The art of repairing broken pottery using gold lacquer.

Rendering an object's fault lines beautiful and strong.

Metaphorically, finding value, meaning,
and even beauty in our vulnerability and flaws.

Āpramāda

Apramāda (अप्रमाद)
Sanskrit / n.
ʌ.prʌˈmɑːdʌ / uh-pruh-*mah*-duh

Awareness infused with an ethical sensibility.

Moral watchfulness and sensitivity.

Earnestness, alertness, and diligence.

Savoir faire

Savoir faire
French / n.
sav.waʀ.fɛʀ / sav-wah fare

Knowing how to do something (and with flair).

Social and practical intelligence and skills.

The ability to behave adaptively and confidently
in a variety of situations.

Mojo

Mojo
Creole (Gullah) / n.
məʊ.dʒəʊ / moe-joe

A magic charm or spell.

Sex drive and appeal.

Personal magnetism.

orka

Orka
Swedish / n.
'or̩ka / orr-kah

Requisite energy for a task.

Spiritedness and resilience.

The ability and tenacity to start things and see them through.

Solivagant

Solivagant
Latin / n., adj.
səʊˈlɪ.və.gənt / so-*liv*-a-gnt

Wandering untethered and alone.

A solitary being, in one's own orbit.

Engaged in pursuit of individual freedom.

Chapter 9

WISDOM

As we continue to ascend the great mountain of personal development, we take the opportunity here to glance upon the second of its daunting faces: wisdom. This itself is multifaceted, encompassing such near synonyms as understanding, knowledge, insight, and belief. As such, this portion of our climb not only involves *what* we know, but also *how* we know, and in what depth and detail we do so. Such capacities are significant for our happiness. Through these we may learn where to find it, and the best route toward it. Without these, we are essentially lost, fumbling around in the dark.

We are in rather different territory from that in the previous chapter. Whereas chapter 8 concerned the special qualities that make us each unique, this one is more about traditions of knowing that have elevated humanity collectively during our long evolution as a species. This has been an immense journey: from the emergence of Homo sapiens some 200,000 years ago (and possibly far longer), through the spectacular quantum leap in intellectual and cultural functioning around 60,000 BCE, to the brave new world of the present day. And throughout, the human race has steadily developed a powerful set of cognitive apparatuses, thereby increasingly—although by no means perfectly—justifying the label "Homo sapiens": "wise human."

We, today, are heirs to these conceptual resources: We think with the systems and processes forged by our ancestors. As such, this chapter celebrates a curated selection of these tools, and more generally pays homage to human intellectual development. Such progress is valuable in its own right, of course, but it is also supremely relevant to the question of happiness. For to the extent that we can use these tools well—skillfully harnessing and even improving upon the cognitive resources provided by our ancestors—we may be helped in our delicate pursuit of happiness. By thinking clearly, and by understanding what matters to us and how best to attain it, we are empowered to flourish. And that, ultimately, is the purpose and goal of wisdom.

The intellectual resources celebrated here are rich and varied, for wisdom itself is a treasure trove of tools. It includes systems of belief that explain human existence and the mysteries of the cosmos. It features archetypes and symbols that bring such systems vividly to life, including the embodiment of abstract principles as deities. It encompasses innovations relating to epistemology—theories and methods of knowledge—such as new ways of appraising and conceptualizing the world. And it touches upon such jewels of cultural evolution as frameworks of morals and ethics, which regulate human conduct, provide ideals for us to aspire to, and offer pathways for us to *attain* these ideals.

In all these respects, untranslatable words have much to offer. The redemptive promise of wisdom has been valorized across all cultures. The classical Greeks, perhaps, are the most celebrated in this regard, with their veneration of the goddess Sophia and the wisdom she represents (as reflected in the term "philosophy" itself: "love of wisdom"). Furthermore, these legendary thinkers—from Plato to Aristotle—were not merely engaged in the dry, abstract theorizing that often characterizes academic philosophy today. Theirs was a revolutionary quest both to understand the nature of existence and the good life, and moreover, to put their insights into practice and inspire others to flourish.

But our intellectual heritage is not limited to these world-shaping Greek pioneers. Throughout history, all peoples have cultivated wisdom in the hope of bettering their lives. As a result, all have produced precious gifts that still have so much to offer us today. Indeed, as we stand uncertainly upon the perilous vantage point of this troubled twenty-first century, we may need their guidance more than ever.

Ngarong

Ngarong
Dayak / n.
ən.gæ.rɔːŋ / nn-gah-rawng

A spirit guide or protector, who is often an ancestor.

A helper who appears in a dream or vision.

The visitation of an otherworldly being
(perhaps providing a solution to a problem).

MAAT

Maat (mꜥ3t)
Egyptian / n.
mɑːt / maht

Justice, truth, order, and equity, personified as a goddess.

The divine principle regulating the lives of human beings,
and the cosmos itself.

The spirit and enactment of morality and justice.

Shù

Shù (恕)
Chinese / n., v.
ʃuː / shoo

Forgiveness, mercy, reciprocity.

The "golden rule": treat others as you'd like to be treated.

An ethic of common humanity.

Shu

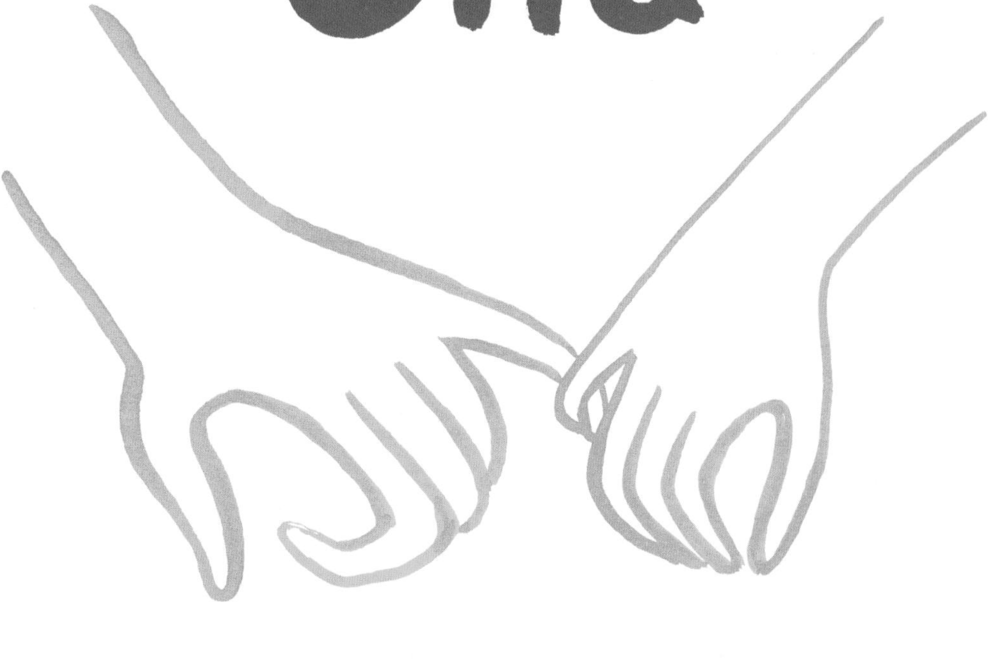

ETTERPÅKLOKSKAP

Etterpåklokskap

Etterpåklokskap
Norwegian / n.
ˈɛt.ə.pək.lək.skɑːp / *eh*-tuh-puk-luk-skarp

"After wisdom."

The knowledge you gain from making a mistake.

Development through trial and error.

X i b i p í í o

Xibipíío
Pirahã / n.
ɪ.biːˈpɪəʊ / ih-bih-*pee*-oh

A phenomenon on the boundaries of experience and perception.

An experience of liminality.

Going in and out of existence or range.

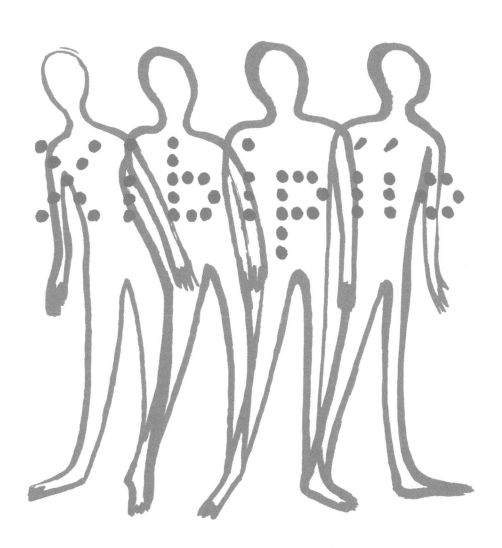

LOGOS

Logos (λόγος)
Greek / n.
ˈlo.ɣos / *loh-yoss*

Word, reason, plan.

The principle of divine reason and creative order.

The power of rationality and consciousness in the cosmos.

Lagom

Lagom
Swedish / n.
'lɑːˌɡɔm / *laar*-gom

Skillful and judicious moderation.

Doing something to just the right degree or amount.

Delicately treading the middle line.

ERSCHLOSSENHEIT

ERSCHLOSSENHEIT

Erschlossenheit

German / n.

ɛɐ̯ˈʃlɔsn̩.haɪt / err-*schloss*-un-hite

World disclosure.

The way life reveals itself to us.

The process by which things become intelligible
and meaningfully relevant to human beings.

Dhárma

Dhárma (धर्म)
Sanskrit / n.
'd̪ʱɑːmə / *dhar*-muh

Principles and laws of the universe.

Teachings and guidelines for living.

The Buddhist path.

Chapter 10

SPIRITUALITY

Finally, we approach, with some trepidation, the third and final face of our daunting mountain of self-development: the mysterious realm of spirituality. Here our path suddenly veers into mist-shrouded territory, through unfamiliar flora, and with an otherworldly wind swirling eerily about our heads. We may well be uncertain of our tread, our footsteps falling quietly on subtly shifting ground. For this is perhaps the strangest region we shall encounter on our journey through the experiential world, and we do not enter lightly.

Nor, it should be added, do we necessarily need to enter here at all. Some people do not like or resonate with the notion of spirituality, which is fair enough. If that's the case though, perhaps one could reframe the notions in this chapter as being more a question of existential considerations. Relatedly, I do not wish to claim that personal development *requires* one to follow a spiritual path. One might well be able to ascend to the peak of one's potential without navigating this particular face of the mountain, doing so by making good progress on the slopes of character and wisdom. So this path is not obligatory. We each need to find a way upward that works for us.

That said, many cultures do hold the view that one must cultivate some form of spirituality to experience life's highest peaks. Consequently, several of their most cherished activities and valued teachings relate to this arena of experience. As a result, some of these languages' most interesting and evocative words pertain to spirituality, as we shall explore here. Together, such terms trace out the manifold ways in which people across the world have conceptualized their ideas around the spiritual life.

More intriguingly still, these ideas may also help us reevaluate or reinterpret what we take spirituality to *mean*. And this may be very useful. After all, people who dislike the notion of spirituality do so based on a particular interpretation of this term—perhaps viewing it as inextricably intertwined with religion. And fair enough, since the two are often viewed as intimately connected. However, if one is put off by religion, then spirituality will likewise be rejected. Crucially though, many cultures have conceptions of spirituality that are quite different from traditional theistic forms of religion.

If spirituality is distinct from religion, what exactly is it? One answer is that it hinges upon the notion of the sacred. "Sacred" is itself a profound and complicated term. People certainly use it for phenomena associated with religion, such as deities and places of worship. But we also use it for that which is personally precious to us, whose value not only exceeds its ostensible material worth, but is, in effect, incalculable. Think perhaps of an heirloom, or the comfort blanket that your child clutched in infancy. If these were lost, you couldn't simply buy a replacement. Nor would you dream of casually repurposing them, using the comforter to clean the kitchen, say. For they are suffused with memories and meaning, and as such are genuinely sacred to us.

So to reformulate the question, what does "sacred" mean? It derives from the Latin *sacer*, which relates to something being "set apart" in some way—outside the normal realm of experience. In the West, the term gradually became bound up with the idea of God, and with holy places, people, and objects. But not *exclusively*, as intimated above with respect to our own sacred possessions. And that is perhaps the best way to view the sacred, as simply something qualitatively *other* and non-ordinary, as special or distinct in some profound and meaningful way.

Spirituality, then, is the realm of experience that revolves around the sacred, whatever this term means to us. And what a realm it is, populated with profoundly important phenomena, majestic in its glory. But within this richness are common threads. Some words here depict the sacred as an overarching power that exists outside us, embodied in a divine being perhaps. Other items identify a sacred dimension within people themselves, as alluded to in English by "soul" and "spirit." Then there are words for practices that help people *engage* with the sacred. Finally, some concepts pertain to the redemptive experiences of self-transcendence that such engagement can facilitate. Across all these, a world of mystery awaits.

Vættir

Vættir
Old Norse / n.
vɛt.teə / veh-teear

Nature spirits, wights, sprites.

Animistic entities in Norse mythology.

Natural phenomena as divine beings.

Vættir

RAGNARÖK

Ragnarök
Icelandic / n.
ˈɹæg.nə.ɹɒk / *rag*-nuh-rok

Twilight of the Gods.

The final and epochal judgment of the gods
in Norse mythology, involving the fall of many.

Followed by existential renewal of life, the earth, and select gods.

Qì

Qì (氣)
Chinese / n.
tɕʰiː / chee

The breath of life.

An animating spirit or energy.

A suprapersonal divine force that flows in and around people.

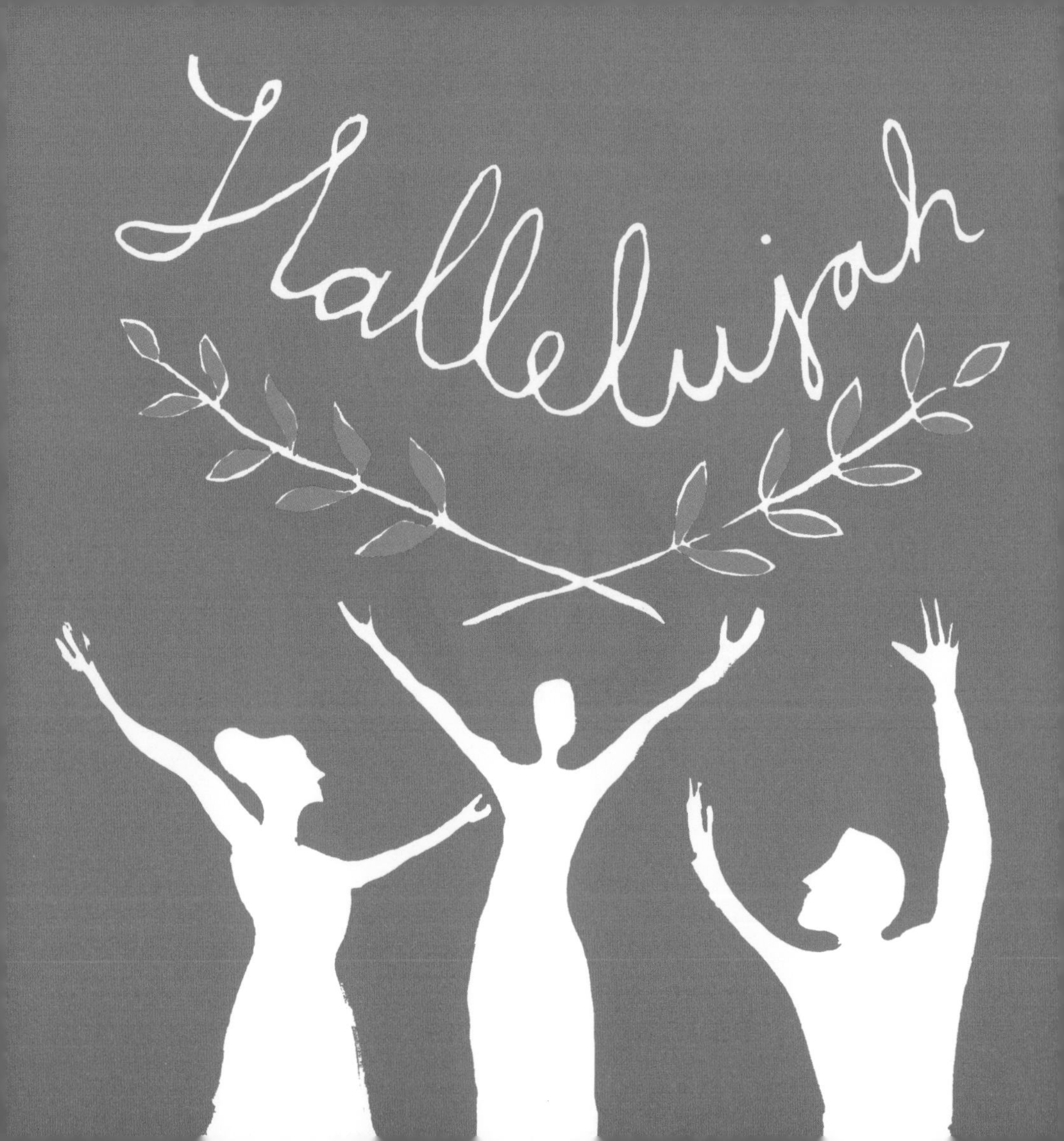
Hallelujah

HALLELUJAH

Hallelujah (הַלְלוּיָה)
Hebrew / n., exclamation
ˌhæ.lɪˈluːjə / ha-leh-*loo*-yuh

God be praised.

An expression of worship and rejoicing in Judaism and Christianity.

Gratitude toward life and the divine.

QANGLAAGIX

Qanglaagix
Aleut / pron.
kæn.glɑːgʰɪx / kan-glah-ghikh

The Raven—a mythological figure of the Inuit, Aleut,
and Yup'ik peoples (also known as Tulukaruq by the Yup'ik).

Not a creator deity, but a figure who guides people
and shapes the world.

Also features in myths as a divine "trickster,"
bringing elements of chaos.

Ren

Ren

Ren (rn)
Egyptian / n.
rən / rn

A key constituent of the soul
in ancient Egyptian religion and culture.

A person's unique name, possessing magical properties.

Assures the person's continued existence for as long as it is spoken.

Mana

Mana
Polynesian languages / n.
ˈmɑ.nə / *ma*-nuh

Spiritual energy or power.

A sacred, impersonal force that may nevertheless
be harnessed or channeled by human beings.

A divine principle of Polynesian cultures.

Nirvāṇa

Nirvāṇa (निर्वाण)
Sanskrit / n.
nɪəˈwaːnə / nir-*vwah*-nuh

To extinguish or blow out (as per a flame).

Release from *saṃsāra*, the cycle of birth, death,
and rebirth that characterizes existence in Buddhist
and other Indian religious teachings.

Ultimate happiness and a total liberation from suffering.

Nirvāṇa

Tonglen

Tonglen (གཏོང་ལེན)
Tibetan / n.
tɒŋ.lɛn / tong-len

Giving and taking, sending and receiving.

An other-focused meditation practice of compassion.

Involves "breathing in" the suffering of others, transmuting it in one's heart, and then "breathing out" love and joy to them.

Chapter 11

FLOURISHING

Well, what an adventure! Our journey through the wonders of our experiential world is all but complete. It just remains to glance back, to survey the terrain we've covered in these past ten chapters. For we have indeed traveled through a great land, spanning three major regions, each themselves composed of many parts.

We began by exploring the feeling of happiness itself, a rich and beautiful landscape featuring the tranquil glades of contentment (chapter 1), the soaring peaks of pleasure (chapter 2), and the mysterious woodlands of ambivalent feelings (chapter 3). The second great region covered relationships—perhaps our main source of happiness—including the intimacies of love (chapter 4) and social bonds more broadly (chapter 5), as well as links to the world around us, involving aesthetic appreciation (chapter 6) and connection to place (chapter 7). Finally, the third region was the awe-inspiring mountain of personal development, composed of three main faces around which our path might ideally wend, namely character (chapter 8), wisdom (chapter 9), and spirituality (chapter 10).

Stepping back, how might we view this great vista as a whole? Is there a concept that enfolds all these great realms? There may indeed be: flourishing. This is a central term in positive psychology, used by scholars when invoking a grand vision of what it means to live well. For instance, a founding metaphor of the field was a continuum stretching from minus 10 to plus 10. Suffering with a mental illness or affliction might place one in negative territory, which hopefully could be ameliorated. But even if one were mercifully free of such burdens, this would not necessarily mean one was *excelling*. Thus, truly being well, and living up to one's potential, was conceptualized as the positive half of the spectrum, which is often described, in a word, as "flourishing."

Okay, the metaphor isn't perfect. People are far more complex and multifaceted than a single continuum implies. Perhaps all of us are struggling in some ways (battling away below zero), while doing well in other ways (gliding in positive territory). So it may be better to conceive of us as simultaneously situated on *multiple* spectra. Indeed, picture separate continua for all ten themes in this book—from contentment to spirituality—as well as others not featured here, such as physical health. In fact, health is as important to flourishing as the themes included here, probably even more so. It only lacks its own chapter as there are fewer untranslatable words pertaining to it, perhaps because experiences of health are less culturally specific.

But to return to the main point: We exist upon many different spectra, doing well on some, less so on others.

But in each case, if we are in positive territory on a given spectrum, we are flourishing in that respect. And overall, the more spectra upon which we are succeeding, the more fully we are flourishing as total human beings. This, then, is what we might aim for. It includes enjoying those warm, bright emotions that are so prototypical of happiness, from contentment to pleasure. But it also includes the more complex ambivalent feelings that, too, are part of living fully and deeply. And it involves loving and being loved, and connecting with our social networks more broadly, and furthermore with the world around us. Then beyond that, it means working on our self-development, cultivating our character, wisdom, and spirituality.

So *that* is the goal, or at least as much of it as we can manage. None of us are perfect, but we do the best we can. And this is the theme of this final chapter, which covers our journey as a whole, our quest to flourish. All the words here relate to this overall task and vision, and pertain to all ten themes collectively. I hope these final few items—and indeed all the terms you've encountered in the book—are helpful in reflecting on your journey to this point and in illuminating the path ahead. Wherever you've come from, and wherever you're going, may you travel in peace and hope.

Bytie

Bytie (бытие)
Russian / n.
bɨtʲɪˈje / bweet-ee-*yeeh*

True being.

Authentic or spiritual existence.

The counterpart to mundane, regular, daily life.

joie de vivre

Joie de vivre
French / n.
ˌʒwɑː də ˈviːvrə / *jwa* de *vee*-vruh

Joy of living.

Exuberant zest for life.

The knack of knowing how to live well.

Meraki

Meraki (μεράκι)
Greek / n.
mɛˈræ.ki: / meh-*rrack*-ee

Ardor, especially for one's own actions and creations.

Love for what one does.

Passion and enthusiasm for certain experiences and behaviors.

Mitzvah

Mitzvah (מִצְוָה)
Hebrew / n.
ˈmɪts.və / *mitz*-vuh

An ethical precept.

A good, noble act or deed.

Commanded observance in fulfillment of religious duty.

Aufheben

Aufheben
German / v.
ˈaʊ̯fˌheːbən / *orf*-hee-bn

Self-transcendence.

To negate and yet preserve.

The sublimation of the self, which is both negated
("seen through" and dismissed) and yet preserved
(set within a larger experiential context).

AUFHEBEN

EUDAIMONIA

EUDAIMONIA

Eudaimonia (εὐδαιμονία)
Greek / n.
juːdɪˈmoʊ.niə / yoo-de-moe-nee-uh

Being infused with a benevolent and divine spirit.

Thriving and living life to the fullest.

Cultivating and experiencing deep forms of well-being.

KANSO

Kanso (簡素)
Japanese / n.
ˈkæn.sɒ / *kan*-soh

Elegant simplicity in art and in life.

The philosophy and practice of minimizing
attachments and possessions.

A pleasing and aesthetic absence of clutter.

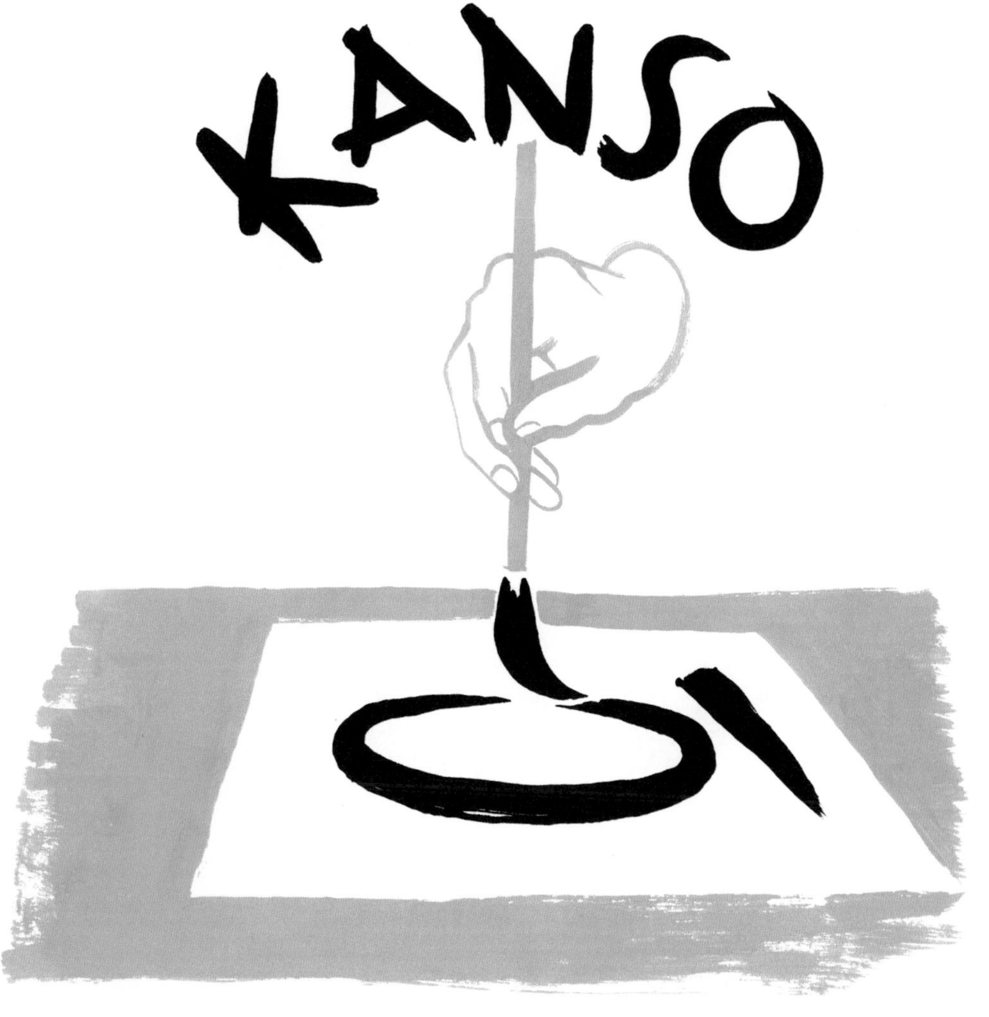
KANSO

Karma

Karma (कर्म)
Sanskrit / n.
ˈkɑːmə / *kar*-muh

Action and its fruits.

A theory and principle of ethical causality.

Positive and negative outcomes resulting respectively
from good and bad behaviors.

tempus fugit

Tempus fugit
Latin / phrase
ˈtɛm.pəs ˈfuːdʒɪt / tem-puss foo-jit

Time flies, flees, escapes.

The recognition that time passes quickly and is running out.

An existential injunction to seize the day.

Acknowledgments

I would like to thank some very special people without whom this book would not have been possible. First, my beautiful wife, Kate, my soul mate and best friend, who brings such love, laughter, and light to my life. Our cheeky dog, Daisy, who keeps us on our toes but certainly helps make our house a home. My kind, wise, and loving parents, who have always supported me, even on my wayward tangents, and built the foundation for my life; special thanks here to my mum, who not only helped spark the idea for the lexicography, but thought of the title for this book itself. My brother and sister who, are the sweetest, kindest, and most fun and inspiring people you could hope to meet. All my wonderful circle of family and friends, whom I don't deserve but am ever grateful for. My stellar agent, Esmond, who took a chance on me and ever since has helped make my ideas a reality. The fantastic Sara and all her team at Tarcher, who have been so passionate about this project and have done such a great job in realizing its potential. Annika, whose amazing illustrations have truly brought this book to life in ways I couldn't have foreseen. All the people who've contributed to my project over the past few years with their generous suggestions and enthusiastic support. And finally, you, dear reader, for taking an interest in all of this—I hope the book helps bring you the happiness you deserve.

About the Author

Tim Lomas was born and raised in West London. At nineteen he went to China to teach English for six months, where he became interested in meditation and Buddhism, before returning to study psychology at Edinburgh University. After graduating, he spent six years as a musician—songwriting, touring, and recording with a ska band called Big Hand—while also working part-time as a psychiatric nursing assistant. He then undertook a PhD at the University of Westminster, studying the impact of meditation on men's mental health. For the past six years he has been a lecturer in positive psychology at the University of East London, during which time he has published numerous books and papers. His present research interests include creating a lexicography of untranslatable words relating to well-being, which is the basis for this book. His Positive Lexicography Project has been featured in *The New Yorker*, *Scientific American*, *Time*, *The Sunday Times*, and *The Daily Mail*, as well as on radio programs such as BBC Radio 4's "All in the Mind." He currently lives in Oxford with his wife, Kate, and dog, Daisy.